"Real beauty lies in
killing-strength, I always say."

"An idiosyncratic attitude," Tuf commented. "Proceed, sir."

"Yes," said Harald Norn. "Well, the Twelve Great Houses of Lyronica compete in the gaming pits. It began—oh, centuries ago. Before that, the houses warred. This way is much better. Family honor is upheld, fortunes are made, and no one is injured. You see, each house controls great tracts, scattered widely over the planet, and since the land is very thinly settled, animal life teems. The Lords of the Great Houses, many years ago during a time of peace, started to have animal fights. It was a pleasant diversion, rooted deep in history."

"So," said Tuf. "You require from me a monster."

GEORGE R. R. MARTIN

TUF VOYAGING

BAEN BOOKS

TUF VOYAGING

A Baen Book

Baen Publishing Enterprises
260 Fifth Avenue
New York, N.Y. 10001

First paperback edition, March 1987

ISBN: 0-671-65624-4

Library of Congress Catalog Card Number: 85-18655

Cover art by David Willson

Printed in the United States of America

Distributed by
SIMON & SCHUSTER
1230 Avenue of the Americas
New York, N.Y. 10020

for Roger & Judy Zelazny,

who helped make Santa Fe feel like home.

ACKNOWLEDGMENTS

"The Plague Star" copyright © 1985 by Davis Publications, Inc. From *Analog*, January & February 1985.

"Loaves and Fishes" copyright © 1985 by Davis Publications, Inc. From *Analog*, October 1985.

"Guardians" copyright © 1981 by Davis Publications, Inc. From *Analog*, October 12, 1981.

"Second Helpings" copyright © 1985 by Davis Publications, Inc. From *Analog*, November 1985.

"A Beast for Norn" copyright © 1986 by George R.R. Martin. A shorter and substantially different version of this story appeared in *Andromeda* (Orbit, UK, 1976), copyright © 1976 by Futura Publications, Ltd.

"Call Him Moses" copyright © 1978 by The Condé Nast Publications, Inc. From *Analog*, February 1978.

"Manna from Heaven" copyright © 1985 by Davis Publications, Inc. From *Analog*, Mid-December 1985.

PROLOGUE

**CATALOG SIX
ITEM NUMBER 37433-800912-5442894
SHANDELLOR CENTER FOR THE ADVANCEMENT
OF CULTURE AND KNOWLEDGE
XENOANTHROPOLOGY DIVISION**

item description: crystal voice coding
item found: H'ro Brana (co/ords SQ19, V7715, I21)
tentative dating: recorded approx. 276 standard years
ago
classify under:
    slave races, Hrangan
    legends & myths, Hruun
    medical,
    —disease, unidentified
    trade bases, abandoned

Hello? Hello?

Yes, I see it works. Good.

I am Rarik Hortvenzy, apprentice factor, speaking a warning to whomever finds my words.

Dusk comes now, for me the last. The sun has sunk beneath the western cliffs, staining the land with blood, and now the twilight eats its way toward me inexorably. The stars come out, one by one, but the only star that matters burns night and day, day and night. It is always with me, the brightest thing in the sky but for the sun. It is the plague star.

This day I buried Janeel. With my own hands I buried her, digging in the hard rocky ground from dawn through late afternoon, until my arms were afire

1

with pain. When my ordeal was done, when the last
spadeful of this wretched alien dirt had been thrown
upon her head, when the last stone had been placed
atop her cairn, then I stood over her and spat upon her
grave.

It is all her fault. I told her so, not once but many
times as she lay dying, and when the end was near she
finally admitted her guilt. Her fault that we came here.
Her fault that we did not leave when we might have.
Her fault that she is dead—yes, no doubt of it—and her
fault that I shall rot unburied when my own time comes,
my flesh a feast for the beasts of the dark, and the flyers
and night-hunters we once hoped to trade with.

The plague star twinkles but little, shines down upon
the land with a clear bright light. This is wrong, I told
Janeel once; a plague star ought to be red. It ought to
glower, to drape itself with scarlet radiance, to whisper
into the night hints of fire and of blood. This clear white
purity, what has that to do with plague? That was in the
first days, when our charter ship had just set us down to
open our proud little trade complex, set us down and
then moved on. In that time the plague star was but
one of fifty first-magnitude stars in these alien skies,
hard even to pick out. In that time we smiled at it, at
the superstitions of these primitives, these backward
brutes who thought sickness came from the sky.

Yet then the plague star began to wax. Night after
night it burned more brightly, until it became visible
even by day. Long before that time the pestilence had
begun.

The flyers wheel against the darkening sky. Gliders,
they are, and from afar they have a beauty. They call to
my mind the shadowgulls of my homeplace, Budakhar
upon the living sea, on the world Razyar. Yet here is no
sea, only mountains and hills and dry desolation, and I
know too that these flyers have small beauty when close
at hand. Lean and terrible creatures they are, half as
tall as a man, with skin like tanned leather pulled tight
across their strange hollow bones. Their wings are dry
and hard as a drumskin, their talons sharp like daggers,
and beneath the great bony crest that sweeps back like

a hooked blade from their narrow skulls, their eyes are a hideous red.

Janeel said to me they were sentient. They have a tongue, she said. I have heard their voices, thin keening screeching voices that scrape raw the nerves. I have never learned to speak this tongue, nor did Janeel. Sentient, she said. We would trade with them. Ho, they wanted no part of us or our trade. They knew enough to steal, yes, and that is where their sentience ended. Yet we and they have this much in common: death.

The flyers die. The night-hunters, with their massive twisted limbs and gnarly two-thumbed hands, with their eyes that burn in their bulging skulls like embers from a dying fire, ho, they die, too. They have a frightening strength, and those strange great eyes can see in the black when stormclouds cover even the plague star. In their caverns the hunters whisper of the great Minds, the masters they served once, the ones who will someday return and call on them to go forth to war once again. Yet the Minds do not come, and the night-hunters die—even as the flyers, even as those of the more furtive races whose bodies we find in the flint hills, even as the mindless beasts, even as the crops and trees, even as Janeel and I.

Janeel told me this would be a world of gold and gems for us; it is a world of death. H'ro Brana was the name in her ancient charts; I will not call it by that. She knew the names for all its peoples. I recall but one—*Hruun*. That is the true name of the night-hunters. A slave race, she said, of the Hrangans, the great enemy, gone now, defeated a thousand years past, their slaves abandoned in that long fall. It was a lost colony, she said, a handful of sentients eager for trade. She knew so much and I so little, but now I have buried her and spat upon her grave and I know the truth of it. If slaves they were, then bad slaves surely, for their masters set them upon a hell, beneath the cruel light of the plague star.

Our last supply ship came through half a year past. We might have gone. Already the plagues had begun.

The flyers crawled upon the mountain summits, tumbled from the cliffs. I found them there, their skin inflamed and oozing fluid, great cracks in the leather of their wings. Night-hunters came to us covered with livid boils, and from us they bought umbrellas in great number, to keep them safe from the rays of the plague star. When the ship landed, we might have gone. Yet Janeel said stay. She had names for these sicknesses that killed the flyers and night-hunters. She had names for the drugs that would cure these ills. To name a thing is to understand, she thought. We might be healers, gain their brutal trust, and our fortunes would be made. She bought all the medicines that ship carried, and sent for others, and we began to treat these plagues that she had named.

When the next plague came, she named it, too. And the next, and the next, and the next. Yet there were plagues beyond counting. First she ran out of drugs, and soon out of names as well, and this dawn I dug her grave. She had been a slender, active female, but in dying she grew very stiff and her limbs puffed up to twice their size. I had to dig a large grave to fit her rigid, swollen corpse. I have named the thing that killed her: Janeel's Plague, I call it. I have no skill at names. My own plague is different from hers, and has no name. When I move, a living flame runs through my bones, and my skin has gone gray and brittle. Each dawn when I wake I find the bedclothes covered with bits of my flesh that have fallen away from my bones, and stained with blood from the wet raw places beneath.

The plague star is huge and bright above me, and now I understand why it is white. White is the color of purity, ho, and the plague star purifies this land. Yet its touch corrupts and decays. There is a fine irony in that, is there not?

We brought many weapons, sold few. The night-hunters and the flyers can use no weapons against this thing that slays them, and from the first have put more faith in umbrellas than in lasers. I have armed myself with a flamer from our storeroom, and poured myself a glass of dark wine.

I will sit here in the coolness and talk my thoughts to this crystal and I will drink my wine and watch the flyers, the few who still live, as they dance and soar against the night. Far off, they look so like shadowgulls above my living sea. I will drink my wine and remember how that sea sounded when I was but a Budakhar boy who dreamed of stars, and when the wine is gone I will use the flamer.

(long silence)

I can think of no more words to say. Janeel knew many words and many names, but I buried her this morning.

(long silence)

If my voice is ever found . . .

(short pause)

If this is found after the plague star has waned, as the night-hunters say it will, do not be deceived. This is no fair world, no world for life. Here is death, and plagues beyond numbering. The plague star will shine again.

(long silence)

My wine is gone.

(end of recording)

1
THE PLAGUE STAR

"**No**," Kaj Nevis told the others firmly. "That's out. We'd be damned stupid to involve any of the big transcorps."

"Oh, stuff and nonsense," Celise Waan snapped back at him. "We have to get there, don't we? So we need a ship. I've chartered ships from Starslip before, and they're perfectly comfortable. The crews are polite and the cuisine is more than adequate."

Nevis gave her a withering look. He had a face made for it—sharp and angular, with hair swept back hard and a great scimitar of a nose, his small dark eyes half-hidden by heavy black eyebrows. "For what purpose did you charter these ships?"

"Why, for field trips, of course," Celise Waan replied. She plucked another cream ball from the plate in front of her, lifting it delicately between thumb and forefinger and popping it into her mouth. "I've supervised many important researches. The Center provided the funding."

"Let me point out the nose on your damn face," Nevis said. "This is not a field trip. We are not poking into the mating habits of primitives. We are not digging around for obscure knowledge that no sane person could possibly give a damn about, as you're accustomed to doing. This little conspiracy of ours is about to go after a treasure of almost unimaginable value. If we find it, we don't intend to turn it over to the proper authorities, either. You need me to see to its disposition through less-than-licit channels. And you trust me so little that you won't tell where the damn thing is until we're underway, and Lion here has hired a bodyguard. Fine, I don't give a damn. But understand this—I am not the only untrustworthy man on ShanDellor. Vast profit is involved here, and vast power. If you're going to continue to yammer at me about *cuisine*, then I'm leaving. I have better things to do than sit here counting your chins."

Celise Waan snorted disdainfully. She was a big, round, red-faced woman, with a loud, wet snort. "Starslip is a reputable firm," she said. "Besides, the salvage laws—"

"—are meaningless," said Nevis. "We have one set of laws here on ShanDellor, another on Kleronomas, a third on Maya, and none of them mean a damn thing. And if ShanDi law did apply, we'd get only one-quarter the value of the find—if we got anything at all. Assuming this plague star of yours is really what Lion thinks it is, and assuming that it's still in working order, whoever controls it will enjoy an overwhelming military superiority in this sector. Starslip and the other big transcorps are as greedy and ruthless as I am, I promise you. Furthermore, they are big enough and powerful enough so that the planetary governments watch them closely. In case it has escaped your notice, let me point out that there are only four of us. Five, if you count the hireling," he said, nodding toward Rica Dawnstar, who favored him with an icy grin. "A big liner has more than five pastry chefs. Even on a small courier, we'd be outnumbered by the crew. Once they saw what we had, do you imagine for even a second that we'd be allowed to keep it?"

"If they cheat us, we'll sue them," the fat anthropologist said, with a hint of petulance in her voice. She plucked up the last cream ball.

Kaj Nevis laughed at her. "In what courts? On what world? That's assuming we're allowed to live, which is unlikely on the face of it. You are a remarkably stupid and ugly woman."

Jefri Lion had been listening to the squabble with an uncomfortable expression on his face. "Here, here," he interrupted at last. "Let's have no name-calling, Nevis. No call for it. We're all in this together, after all." A short, square block of a man, Lion wore a chameleon cloth jacket of military cut, decorated with rows of ribbons from some forgotten campaign. The fabric had turned a dusty gray in the dimness of the small restaurant, a gray that matched the color of Lion's bristling spade-shaped beard. There was a thin sheen of sweat on his broad, balding forehead. Kaj Nevis made him nervous; the man had a reputation, after all. Lion looked around to the others for support.

Celise Waan pouted and stared at the empty plate in front of her, as if her gaze could fill it with cream balls again. Rica Dawnstar—"the hireling," as Nevis called her—leaned back in her seat with a look of sardonic amusement in her bright green eyes. Beneath her drab jumpsuit and silvery mesh-steel vest, the long, hard body looked relaxed, almost indolent. No concern of hers if her employers wanted to argue all night and all day.

"Insults are useless," Anittas said. It was hard to tell what the cybertech was thinking; his face was as much polished metal and translucent plastic as flesh, and only minimally expressive. The shiny bluesteel fingers of his right hand interlocked with the mocha-colored fleshy digits of his left; he studied Nevis with two shining silver-metal eyes that moved smoothly in black plastic sockets. "Kaj Nevis has made some valid points. He is experienced in these areas, where we are not. What is the use of having brought him into this affair if we are unwilling to listen to his counsel?"

"Yes, that's so," Jefri Lion agreed. "What do you suggest then, Nevis? If we must avoid the transcorps, how will we reach the plague star?"

"We need a ship," Celise Waan said, loudly stating the obvious.

Kaj Nevis smiled. "The transcorps have no monopoly

on ships. That's why I suggested we meet here today, rather than at Lion's office. This dump is close to the port. The man we want will be here, I'm sure."

Jefri Lion looked hesitant. "An independent? Some of them have rather, uh, unsavory reputations, don't they?"

"Like me," Nevis reminded him.

"Still. I've heard rumors of smuggling, even piracy. Do we want to take that kind of a chance, Nevis?"

"We don't want to take any chances at all," Kaj Nevis said. "And we won't. It's a matter of knowing the right people. I know lots of people. The right people. The wrong people." He made a small gesture with his head. "Now, way in the back there, that dark woman with all the black jewelry. That's Jessamyn Caige, mistress of the *Free Venture*. She'd hire out to us, no doubt. At a very reasonable rate."

Celise Waan craned around to look. "Is she the one, then? I hope this ship of hers has a gravity grid. Weightlessness makes me nauseous."

"When are you going to approach her?" Jefri Lion asked.

"I'm not," Kaj Nevis told them. "Oh, I've used Jessamyn to move a cargo or two for me, but I won't take the risk of actually riding with her, and I'd never dream of involving her in anything this big. The *Free Venture* has a crew of nine—more than enough to handle me and the hireling. No offense, Lion, but the rest of you don't count."

"I'll have you know I'm a soldier," Jefri Lion said, in a wounded tone. "I've seen combat."

"A hundred years ago," Nevis said. "As I said, the rest of you don't count. And Jessamyn would as soon kill all of us as spit." The small, dark eyes regarded each of them in turn. "That's why you need me. Without me, you are just naive enough to engage Jessamyn, or one of the transcorps."

"My niece serves with a very successful independent trader," Celise Waan said.

"And who might that be?" Kaj Nevis inquired.

"Noah Wackerfuss," she said, "of the *World of Bargains.*"

Nevis nodded. "Fat Noah," he said. "That would be a lot of fun, I'm damn sure. I might mention that *his* ship is kept constantly in weightlessness. Gravity would kill the old degenerate—not that it matters. Wackerfuss isn't especially blood-thirsty, that's so. Fifty-fifty chance he wouldn't kill us. He is, however, as greedy and as shrewd as they come. At the very least, he'd find a way to get a full share. At worst, he'd get it all. And his ship has a crew of twenty—all women. Have you ever asked your niece about the precise nature of her duties?"

Celise Waan flushed. "Do I have to listen to this man's innuendoes?" she asked Lion. "This was my discovery. I won't be insulted by this third-rate hoodlum, Jefri."

Lion frowned unhappily. "Really now, enough of this squabbling. Nevis, there's no need to flaunt your expertise. We brought you into this for good cause, I'm sure we all agree. You must have some idea of who we can engage to take us to the plague star, don't you?"

"Of course," Nevis agreed.

"Who?" prompted Anittas.

"The man is an independent trader, of sorts. Not a very successful one. And he's been stuck on ShanDellor, for want of a cargo, for half of a standard year now. He must be getting desperate—desperate enough, I'd think, so that he'll jump at this opportunity. He has a small, battered ship with a long, ridiculous name. It's not luxurious, but it will take us there, which is all that matters. There's no crew to worry about, only the man himself. And he—well, he's a little ridiculous, too. He'll give us no trouble. He's big, but soft, inside and out. He keeps cats, I hear. Doesn't much like people. Drinks a lot of beer, eats too much. I doubt that he even carries a weapon. Reports are that he barely scrapes by, flitting from world to world and selling absurd trinkets and useless little geegaws from this beat-up old ship of his. Wackerfuss thinks the man's a joke. But even if he's wrong, what can one man alone do? If he so much as threatens to report us, the hireling and I can dispose of him and feed him to his cats."

"Nevis, I'll have no talk like that!" Jefri Lion objected. "I won't have any killing on this venture."

"No?" Nevis said. He nodded toward Rica Dawnstar. "Then why did you hire her?" His smile was very nasty, somehow; her returning grin was pure mocking malice. "Just so," Nevis said, "I knew this was the place. Here's our man now."

None of them except Rica Dawnstar was much versed in the art of subtle conspiracy; the other three all turned to stare at the door, and the man who had just entered. He stood very tall, almost two-and-a-half meters, and his great soft gut swelled out above his thin metal belt. He had big hands, a long, curiously blank face, and a stiff, awkward posture; everywhere his skin was as white as bleached bone, and it appeared that he had not a hair on him anywhere. He wore shiny blue trousers and a deep maroon shirt whose balloon sleeves were frayed at the ends.

He must have felt their scrutiny, for he turned his head and stared back, his pale face expressionless. He kept on staring. Celise Waan looked away first, and then Jefri Lion, and finally Anittas. "Who is he?" the cyborg demanded of Kaj Nevis.

"Wackerfuss calls him Tuffy," Nevis said. "His real name, I'm told, is Haviland Tuf."

Haviland Tuf picked up the last of the green star-forts with a delicacy that belied his great size, then straightened to regard the gaming board with satisfaction. The entire cluster was red; cruisers and dreadnaughts and star-forts and all the colonies, red everywhere. "I must claim the victory," he said.

"Again," said Rica Dawnstar. She stretched, to untie the knots that hours bent over the game had put in her limbs. She had the deadly grace of a lioness, and beneath her silver mesh-steel vest her needler was snug in its shoulder holster.

"Perhaps I might be so bold as to suggest another contest," said Haviland Tuf.

Dawnstar laughed. "No thanks," she said. "You're too good at this. I was born a gambler, but with you it's no gamble. I'm tired of coming in second."

"I have been most fortunate in the games we have played thus far," Haviland Tuf said. "Undoubtedly, my luck will have run its course by now, and you will obliterate my poor forces on your next attempt."

"Oh, undoubtedly," Rica Dawnstar replied, grinning, "but forgive me if I postpone the attempt until the boredom becomes terminal. At least I'm better than Lion. Right, Jefri?"

Jefri Lion was seated in a corner of the ship's control room, perusing a stack of old military texts. His chameleon cloth jacket had turned the same brown as the synthawood panelling of the bulkhead behind him. "The game does not conform to authentic military principles," he said, with a hint of annoyance in his voice. "I employed the same tactics that Stephen Cobalt Northstar used when the 13th Human Fleet enveloped Hrakkean. Tuf's counterthrust was completely wrong under the circumstances. If the rules had been written properly, it ought to have been routed."

"Indeed," said Haviland Tuf. "You have the advantage of me, sir. You, after all, have the good fortune to be a military historian, and I am merely a humble trader. I lack your familiarity with the great campaigns of history. How fortunate for me that thus far, the deficiencies of the game itself, and my extraordinary fortune, have conspired to make up for my ignorance. Still, I would welcome the opportunity to strengthen my grasp of military principles. If you would care to assay the game once again, I will carefully study your subtle strategies so that I might in future incorporate a sounder, more authentic approach into my own poor play."

Jefri Lion, whose silver fleet had been the first eliminated in every game they had played during the past week, cleared his throat and looked uncomfortable. "Yes, uh, you see, Tuf," he began.

He was saved from embarrassment by a sudden shriek and stream of profanity that issued from the adjoining compartment. Haviland Tuf was on his feet at once; Rica Dawnstar was right behind him.

They emerged into the passageway just as Celise Waan staggered out of the living quarters, in pursuit of a small, fleet black-and-white form that went hurtling past them into the control room. "Catch it!" Celise Waan screamed at them. Her face was red and puffy and swollen, and she looked furious.

The door was small, Haviland Tuf large. "For what purpose, might I inquire?" he asked, blocking the way.

The anthropologist held out her left hand. There were three short, deep scratches across her palm, welling blood. "Look what it did to me!" she said.

"Indeed," said Haviland Tuf. "And what did you do to her?"

Kaj Nevis emerged from the living quarters with a thin, hard smile on his face. "She picked it up to toss it across the room," he said.

"It was on my bed!" said Celise Waan. "I wanted to take a little nap, and the damned creature was asleep on my bed!" She whirled to face Nevis. "And you, wipe that smirk off your face. It's bad enough we all have to be cooped up together in this shabby little ship. I simply refuse to share what little space there is with this impossible man's filthy little *animals*. And it's *your* fault, Nevis. You got us into this! Now do something. I demand that you make Tuf get rid of those vicious pests, do you hear me, I demand it!"

"Excuse me," Rica Dawnstar said from behind Tuf. He glanced back at her and moved aside. "Is this one of the vicious pests you had in mind?" Dawnstar asked, with a grin, as she stepped into the passageway. She was cradling a cat against her chest with her left hand, and petting it with her right. It was a huge tom with long, soft, gray hair and arrogant yellow eyes; it must have weighed twenty pounds, but Rica held it as easily as if it had been a kitten. "What do you propose Tuf do with old Mushroom here?" she asked as the cat began to purr.

"It was the other one that hurt me, the black-and-white one," Celise Waan said, "but that one's just as bad. Look at my face! Look at what they've done to me! I can scarcely breathe, and I'm breaking out all over, and whenever I try to get a little sleep I wake up with one of them on my chest. Yesterday I was having a little snack, and I put it down just for a moment, and when I came back the black-and-white one had knocked over my plate and was rolling my spice-puffs around in the dirt as if they were toys! Nothing is safe around these animals. I've lost two light pencils and my best pinky ring. And now *this*, this *attack*! Really, this is just intolerable. I must insist that these damned animals be put down in the cargo hold at once. *At once*, do you hear?"

"My hearing is quite adequate, thank you," said Haviland Tuf. "If your missing property has not turned up by the end of our voyage, I will be most pleased to reimburse you for its value. Your request in regard to Mushroom and Havoc, however, I must regretfully deny."

"I'm a passenger on this joke of a starship!" Celise Waan screamed at him.

"Must you insult my intelligence as well as my hearing?" Tuf replied. "Your status as a passenger here is obvious, madam; it is not necessary for you to point it out. Permit me to point out, however, that this small ship which you feel so free to insult is my home and my livelihood, such that it is. Furthermore, while you are undeniably a passenger here and therefore enjoy certain rights and prerequisites, Mushroom and Havoc must logically have substantially greater rights, since this is their permanent abode, so to speak. It is not my custom to take passengers aboard my *Cornucopia of Excellent Goods at Low Prices*. As you have observed, the space available is scarcely adequate to my own needs. Regretfully, I have suffered various professional vicissitudes of late, and there is no gainsaying the fact that my supply of standards was veering toward inadequacy when Kaj Nevis approached me. I have bent all my efforts to accommodate you aboard this craft which you so malign, to the extent that I have given over my ship's living quarters to your collective needs and made

my own poor bed in the control room. Despite my
undeniable need, I am now coming to deeply regret the
foolish and altruistic impulse that bid me take this
charter, especially as the payment I have received was
barely sufficient to refuel and provision for this voyage
and pay the ShanDi landing tax. You have taken grievous advantage of my gullibility, I fear. Nonetheless, I
am a man of my word and will do my best to convey
you to this mysterious destination of yours. For the
duration of the voyage, however, I must require you to
tolerate Mushroom and Havoc, even as I tolerate you."

"Well, I never!" Celise Waan declared.

"I have no doubt," said Haviland Tuf.

"I'm not going to put up with this any longer," the
anthropologist said. "There's no reason we all have to
be crammed up inside one room like soldiers in a
barracks. This ship was not nearly this small from outside." She pointed a pudgy arm. "Where does that door
go?" she demanded.

"To the hold and cargo compartments," Haviland Tuf
said evenly. "There are sixteen of them. Even the
smallest, admittedly, has twice the space of my meager
living quarters."

"Aha!" said Waan. "And are we carrying any cargo?"

"Compartment sixteen is packed with plastic reproductions of Cooglish orgy-masks, which I was unfortunately unable to sell on ShanDellor, a situation I lay
entirely at the door of Noah Wackerfuss, who undercut
my price and deprived me of my small hope of profit.
In compartment twelve I store certain personal effects,
miscellaneous equipment, collectibles, and bric-a-brac.
The rest of the ship is quite empty, madam."

"Excellent!" said Celise Waan. "In that case, we will
convert the smaller compartments into private rooms
for each of us. It should be a simple matter to move our
bedding."

"Quite simple," said Haviland Tuf.

"Then do it!" snapped Celise Waan.

"As you wish," said Tuf. "Will you be wanting to rent
a pressure suit?"

"What?"

Rica Dawnstar was grinning. "The holds aren't part of the life-support system," she said. "No air. No heat. No pressure. No gravity, even."

"Ought to suit you just fine," Kaj Nevis put in.

"Indeed," said Haviland Tuf.

Day and night are meaningless aboard a starship, but the ancient rhythms of the human body still made their demands, and technology had to conform. Therefore the *Cornucopia*, like all but the huge triple-shift warships and transcorp liners, had its sleep cycle—a time of darkness and silence.

Rica Dawnstar rose from her cot and checked her needler, from long force of habit. Celise Waan was snoring loudly; Jefri Lion tossed and turned, winning battles in his head; Kaj Nevis was lost in dreams of wealth and power. The cybertech was sleeping too, though it was a deeper sort of sleep. To escape the boredom of the voyage, Anittas had parked on a cot, plugged into the ship's computer, and turned himself off. His cyberhalf monitored his biohalf. His breath was slow as a glacier and very regular, his body temperature down, his energy consumption cut to almost nothing, but the lidless silver-metal sensors that served him as eyes sometimes seemed to shift slightly, tracking some unseen vision.

Rica Dawnstar moved quietly from the room. Up in the control chamber, Haviland Tuf sat alone. His lap was full of gray tomcat; his huge pale hands moved over the computer keys. Havoc, the smaller black-and-white cat, was playing around his feet. She had gotten hold of a light pencil and was batting it to and fro on the floor. Tuf never heard Rica enter; no one heard Rica Dawnstar move unless she wanted them to hear.

"You're still up," she said from the door, leaning back against the jamb.

Tuf's seat swiveled around and he regarded her impassively. "A most remarkable deduction," he said. "Here I sit before you, active, busy, driven by the demands of my ship. From the scant evidence of your eyes and ears, you leap to the conclusion that I am not yet asleep. Your powers of reasoning are awesome."

Rica Dawnstar sauntered into the room and stretched out on Tuf's cot, still neatly made up from the previous sleep cycle. "I'm awake too," she said, smiling.

"I can scarcely believe it," said Haviland Tuf.

"Believe it," Rica said. "I don't sleep much, Tuf. Two or three hours a night. It's an asset in my profession."

"No doubt," said Tuf.

"On board ship, though, it's a bit of a liability. I'm bored, Tuf."

"A game, perhaps?"

She smiled. "Perhaps of a different sort."

"I am always eager to learn new games."

"Good. Let's play the conspiracy game."

"I am unfamiliar with its rules."

"Oh, they're simple enough."

"Indeed. Perhaps you would be good enough to elaborate." Tuf's long face was still and noncommittal.

"You would never have won that last game if Waan had thrown in with me when I asked her to," Rica said conversationally. "Alliances, Tuf, can be profitable to all parties concerned. You and I are the odd ones out here. We're the hirelings. If Lion is right about the plague star, the rest of them will divide wealth so vast it's incomprehensible, and you and I will receive our fees. Doesn't seem quite fair to me."

"Equity is often difficult to judge, and still more difficult to achieve," said Haviland Tuf. "I might wish my compensation were more generous, but no doubt many could make the same complaint. It is nonetheless the fee that I negotiated and accepted."

"Negotiations can be reopened," suggested Rica Dawnstar. "They need us. Both of us. It occurred to me that if we worked together, we might be able to . . . ah . . . insist upon better terms. Full shares. A six-way split. What do you think?"

"An intriguing notion, with much to recommend it," said Tuf. "Some might venture to suggest that it was unethical, true, but the true sophisticate retains a certain moral flexibility."

Rica Dawnstar studied the long, white, expressionless face for a moment, and grinned. "You don't buy it, do you, Tuf? Down deep, you're a stickler for rules."

"Rules are the essence of games, the very heart of them, if you will. They give structure and meaning to our small contests."

"Sometimes it's more fun just to kick over the board," Rica Dawnstar said. "More effective, too."

Tuf steepled his hands in front of his face. "Though I am not content with my niggardly fee, nonetheless I must fulfill my contract with Kaj Nevis. I would not have him speak poorly of me or the *Cornucopia of Excellent Goods at Low Prices*."

Rica laughed. "Oh, I doubt that he'll speak poorly of you, Tuf. I doubt that he'll speak of you at all, once you've served your purpose and he's discarded you." She was pleased to see that her statement startled Tuf into blinking.

"Indeed," he said.

"Aren't you curious about all this? About where we're going, and why Waan and Lion kept the destination secret until we were aboard? About why Lion hired a bodyguard?"

Haviland Tuf stroked Mushroom's long gray fur, but his eyes never left Rica Dawnstar's face. "Curiosity is my great vice. I fear you have seen through to the heart of me, and now you seek to exploit my weakness."

"Curiosity killed the cat," said Rica Dawnstar.

"An unpleasant suggestion, but unlikely on the face of it," Tuf commented.

"But satisfaction brought him back," Rica finished. "Lion knows this is something huge. And hugely dangerous. To get what they want out of this, they needed Nevis, or somebody like Nevis. They have a nice four-way split set up, but Kaj has the kind of reputation that makes you wonder if he'll settle for a fourth. I'm here to see that he does." She shrugged, and patted her needler in its shoulder holster. "Besides, I'm insurance against any other complications that might arise."

"Might I point out that you yourself constitute an additional complication?"

She smiled icily. "Just don't point it out to Lion," she said, rising and stretching. "You think about it, Tuf. The way I see it, Nevis has underestimated you. Don't you go underestimating him. Or me. Never, never, *never* underestimate me. The time may come when you'll wish you had an ally. And it may come sooner than you'd like."

Three days shy of arrival, Celise Waan was complaining again over dinner. Tuf had served a spiced vegetable brouhaha in the manner of Halagreen; a piquant dish, but for the fact that this was the sixth such serving on the voyage. The anthropologist shoved the vegetables around on her plate, made a face, and said, "Why can't we have some real food?"

Tuf paused, speared a fat mushroom deftly with his fork, lifted it in front of his face. He regarded it in silence for a moment, shifted the angle of his head and regarded it from another angle, turned it around and regarded that aspect of it, and finally prodded it lightly with his finger. "I fail to grasp the nature of your complaint, madam," he said at last. "This mushroom, at least, seems real enough to my own poor senses. True, it is but a small sample of the whole. Perhaps the rest of the brouhaha is illusory. Yet I think not."

"You know what I meant," Celise Waan said in a shrill tone. "I want meat."

"Indeed," said Haviland Tuf. "I myself want wealth beyond measure. Such fantasies are easily dreamed, and less easily made real."

"I'm tired of all these puling vegetables!" Celise Waan screeched. "Are you telling me that there is not a bit of meat to be had on this entire puling ship?"

Tuf made a steeple of his fingers. "It was not my intent to convey such misinformation, certainly," he said. "I am not an eater of flesh myself, but there is some small poor quantity of meat aboard the *Cornucopia of Excellent Goods at Low Prices*, this I freely admit."

A look of furious satisfaction crossed Celise Waan's face. She glanced at each of the other diners in turn.

Rica Dawnstar was trying to suppress a grin; Kaj Nevis was not even trying; Jefri Lion was looking fretful. "You see," she told them, "I told you he was keeping the good food for himself." With all deliberation, she picked up her plate and spun it across the room. It rang off a metal bulkhead and dumped its load of spiced brouhaha on Rica Dawnstar's unmade bed. Rica smiled sweetly. "We just swapped bunks, Waan," she said.

"I don't care," Celise Waan said. "I'm going to get a decent meal for once. I suppose the rest of you will be wanting to share now."

Rica smiled. "Oh no, dear. It's all yours." She finished up her brouhaha, cleaned her plate with a crust of onion bread. Lion looked uncomfortable, and Kaj Nevis said, "If you can get this meat out of Tuf, it's all yours."

"Excellent!" she proclaimed. "Tuf, bring me this meat!"

Haviland Tuf regarded her impassively. "True, the contract I made with Kaj Nevis requires me to feed you through the duration of this voyage. Nothing was said about the nature of the provender, however. Always I am put upon. Now I must cater to your culinary whims, it seems. Very well, such is my poor lot in life. And yet, now I find myself taken by a sudden whim of my own. If I must indulge your whim, would it not be equitable that you should similarly bend to mine?"

Waan frowned suspiciously. "What do you mean?"

Tuf spread his hands. "It is nothing, really. In return for the meat you crave, I ask only a moment's indulgence. I have grown most curious of late, and I would have that curiosity satisfied. Rica Dawnstar has warned me that, unsatisfied, curiosity will surely kill my cats."

"I'm for that," said the fat anthropologist.

"Indeed," said Tuf. "Nonetheless, I must insist. I offer you a trade—food, of the type you have requested so melodramatically, for a poor useless nugget of information, the surrender of which costs you nothing. We are shortly to arrive in the system of Hro B'rana, your chartered destination. I would know why we travel there, and the nature of what you expect to find on this plague star of which I have heard you speak."

Celise Waan turned to the others again. "We paid

good standards for food," she said. "This is extortion. Jefri, put your foot down!"

"Um," said Jefri Lion. "There's really no harm, Celise. He'll find out anyway, when we arrive. Perhaps it is time he knew."

"Nevis," she said, "aren't you going to do anything?"

"Why?" he demanded. "It doesn't make a damn bit of difference. Tell him and get your meat. Or not. I don't care."

Waan glared at Kaj Nevis, and then even more fiercely at the cool pale face of Haviland Tuf, crossed her arms, and said, "All right, if that's the way it has to be, I'll sing for my supper."

"A normal speaking voice will be quite acceptable," said Tuf.

Celise Waan ignored him. "I'll make this short and sweet. The discovery of the plague star is my greatest triumph, the capstone of my career, but none of you have the wit or the courtesy to appreciate the work that went into it. I am an anthropologist with the ShanDellor Center for the Advancement of Culture and Knowledge. My academic specialty is the study of primitive cultures of a particular sort—cultures of colony worlds left to isolation and technological devolution in the wake of the Great War. Of course, many human worlds were so affected, and a number of these have been studied extensively. I worked in less well-known fields—the investigation of nonhuman cultures, especially those of former Hrangan slave worlds. One of the worlds I studied was Hro B'rana. Once it was a flourishing colony, a breeding ground for Hruun and dactyloids and lesser Hrangan slave races, but today it's a devastation. Such sentients that still live there live short, ugly, brutal lives, although like most such decayed cultures, they also have tales of a vanished golden age. But the most interesting thing about Hro B'rana is a legend, a legend unique to them—the plague star.

"Let me stress that the devastation on Hro B'rana is extreme, and the underpopulation severe, despite the fact that the environment is not especially harsh. Why? Well, the degenerate descendants of both Hruun and dactyloid colonists, whose cultures are otherwise utterly different and very hostile to each other, have a common answer to that: the plague star. Every third generation, just as they are climbing out of their misery, as populations are swelling once again, the plague star waxes larger and larger in their nighttime skies. And when this star becomes the brightest in the heavens, then the season of plagues begins. Pestilences sweep across Hro B'rana, each more terrible than the last. The healers are helpless. Crops wither, animals perish, and three-quarters of the sentient population dies. Those who survive are thrown back into the most brutal sort of existence. Then the plague star wanes, and with its waning the plagues pass from Hro B'rana for another three generations. That is the legend."

Haviland Tuf's face had been expressionless as he listened to Celise Waan relate the tale. "Interesting," he said now. "I must surmise, however, that our present expedition has not been mounted simply to further your career by investigating this arresting folk tale."

"No," Celise Waan admitted. "That was once my intent, yes. The legend seemed an excellent topic for a monograph. I was trying to get funding from the Center for a field investigation, but they turned down my request. I was annoyed, and justly so. Those short-sighted fools. I mentioned my annoyance, and the cause, to my colleague, Jefri Lion."

Lion cleared his throat. "Yes," he said. "And my field, as you know, is military history. I was intrigued, of course. I buried myself in the Center databanks. Our files are not nearly as complete as those at Avalon and Newholme, but there wasn't time for a more thorough investigation. We had to act quickly. You see, my theory—well, it's more than theory, really—I believe, in fact I'm all but certain, that I know what this plague star is. It's no legend, Tuf! It's real. It must be a derelict, yes, abandoned but still operational, still carrying out its programs more than a millennium after the Collapse. Don't you see? Can't you guess?"

"I admit to failure," said Tuf, "lacking your familiarity with the subject at hand."

"It's a warship, Tuf, a warship in a long elliptical orbit around Hro B'rana. It's one of the most devastating weapons Old Earth ever put into the void against the Hrangans, in its own way as terrible as that mythical hellfleet they talk about from those last days before the Collapse. But it has vast potential for good as well as ill! It's the repository of the most advanced biogenetic science of the Federal Empire, a functioning artifact packed full of secrets lost to the rest of humanity."

"Indeed," said Tuf.

"It's a seedship," Jefri Lion finished, "a biowar seedship of the Ecological Engineering Corps."

"And it's *ours*," said Kaj Nevis, with a small grim smile.

Haviland Tuf studied Nevis briefly, nodded to himself, and rose. "My curiosity is satisfied," he announced. "Now I must fulfill my portion of the trade."

"Ahhh," said Celise Waan. "My meat."

"The supply is copious, though the variety is admittedly small," said Haviland Tuf. "I shall leave you the task of preparing the meat in a manner most pleasant to your palate." He went to a storage locker, punched in a code, and removed a small carton, which he carried back to the table under his arm. "This is the only meat aboard my vessel. I cannot vouch for its taste or quality. Yet I have not yet received a complaint on either count."

Rica Dawnstar burst into laughter and Kaj Nevis snickered. Haviland Tuf, neatly and methodically, removed a dozen cans of catfood from their carton, and stacked them in front of Celise Waan. Havoc leapt onto the table and began to purr.

"It's not as big as I expected," Celise Waan said, her tone as petulant as ever.

"Madam," said Haviland Tuf, "the eyes can often deceive. My main viewscreen is admittedly modest, a bare meter in diameter, and this must of course diminish the size of any object displayed thereon. The ship itself is of sizable dimensions."

Kaj Nevis came forward. "How sizable?"

Tuf folded his hands together atop the bulge of his

stomach. "I cannot say with any precision. The *Cornucopia of Excellent Goods at Low Prices* is but a modest trading vessel, and its sensory instrumentation is not all that it might be."

"Approximately, then," Kaj Nevis snapped.

"Approximately," Tuf repeated. "Regarded at the angle at which my viewscreen is now displaying it, with the longest axis taken as 'length,' the ship we are approaching would seem to be, approximately, some thirty standard kilometers long, approximately some five kilometers in width, approximately some three kilometers in height, but for the domed section amidships, which rises slightly higher, and the forward tower which ascends, approximately, one additional kilometer above the deck from which it rises."

They had all gathered in the control room, even Anittas, who had been awakened from his computer-regulated sleep when they emerged from drive. A hush fell over them; even Celise Waan seemed briefly at a loss for something to say. All of them stared at the viewscreen, at the long black twisted shape that floated against the stars, here and there shining with faint lights and pulsing with unseen energies.

"I was right," Jefri Lion muttered at last, to break the silence. "A seedship—an EEC seedship! Nothing else could possibly be so large!"

Kaj Nevis smiled. "Damn," he said.

"The system must be vast," Anittas said speculatively. "The Earth Imperials had a sophistication far beyond ours. It's probably an Artificial Intelligence."

"We're rich," burbled Celise Waan, her many and varied grievances forgotten for the moment. She grabbed hold of Jefri Lion's hands and waltzed him around in a circle, fairly bouncing. "We're rich, rich, we're rich and *famous*, we're all rich!"

"This is not entirely correct," said Haviland Tuf. "I do not doubt that you may indeed become wealthy in the near future; for the moment, however, your pockets contain no more standards than they did a moment ago. Nor do Rica Dawnstar and I share your prospects of economic advancement."

Nevis stared at him hard. "Are you complaining, Tuf?"

"Far be it from me to object," Tuf said in a flat voice. "I was merely correcting Celise Waan's misstatement."

Kaj Nevis nodded. "Good," he said. "Now, before any of us get any richer, we have to get aboard that thing and see what kind of shape it's in. Even a derelict ought to net us a nice salvage fee, but if that ship's in working order, there's no limit, no limit at all."

"It is obviously functional," Jefri Lion said. "It has been raining plagues on Hro B'rana every third generation for a thousand standard years."

"Yeah," said Nevis, "well, that's true, but it's not the whole story. It's dead in orbit now. What about the drive engines? The cell library? The computers? We've got a lot to check. How do we get aboard, Lion?"

"A docking might be possible," Jefri Lion replied. "Tuf, that dome, do you **see it**?" He pointed.

"My vision is unimpaired."

"Yes, well, I believe that's the landing deck under there. It's as big as a spacefield. If we can get the dome to open, you can take your ship right in."

"If," said Haviland Tuf. "A most difficult word. So short, and so often fraught with disappointment and frustration." As if to underline his words, a small red light came on beneath the main viewscreen. Tuf held up a long pale finger. "Take note!" he said.

"What is it?" asked Nevis.

"A communication," Tuf proclaimed. He leaned forward and touched a much worn button on his lasercom.

The plague star vanished from the screen. In its place appeared a weary-looking face—that of a man of middle years, sitting in a communications room. He had deep lines in his forehead and graven down his cheeks, a full head of thick black hair, and tired blue-gray eyes. He was wearing a uniform out of a history tape, and on his head was a green billed cap emblazoned with a golden theta. "This is *Ark*," he announced. "You have entered our defense sphere. Identify yourself or be fired upon. This is your first warning."

Haviland Tuf held down his SEND button. "This is

the *Cornucopia of Excellent Goods at Low Prices*," he annunciated clearly, "Haviland Tuf commanding. We are harmless unarmed traders out of ShanDellor, *Ark.* Might we request permission to approach for docking?"

Celise Waan gaped. "It's manned," she said. "The crew is still alive!"

"A fascinating development," Jefri Lion said, tugging at his beard. "Perhaps this is a descendant of the original EEC crew. Or perhaps the chronowarp was employed! To warp the very weave of the fabric of time, to hurry it or hold it still, yes, they could do even that. The chronowarp! Think of it!"

Kaj Nevis made a snarling sound. "A thousand damn years and you tell me they're still alive? How the hell are we supposed to deal with that?"

The image on the viewscreen flickered briefly. Then the same tired man in the uniform of the Earth Imperials said, "This is *Ark.* Your ID is improperly coded. You are moving through our defense sphere. Identify yourself or be fired upon. This is your second warning."

"Sir," said Haviland Tuf, "I must protest! We are unarmed and unprotected. We mean you no harm. We are peaceful traders, scholars, fellow humans. Our intentions are not hostile, and moreover, we lack any means of doing harm to a ship as formidable as your *Ark.* Must we be met with belligerence?"

The screen flickered. "This is *Ark.* You have penetrated our defense sphere. Identify yourself immediately or be destroyed. This is your third and final warning."

"Recordings," said Kaj Nevis, with some enthusiasm. "That's it! No cold storage, no damned stasis field. There's no one there. Some computer is playing recordings at us."

"I fear you are correct," said Haviland Tuf. "The question must be asked: if the computer is programmed to play recorded messages at incoming ships, what else might it be programmed to do?"

Jefri Lion broke in. "The codes!" he said. "I have a whole set of Federal Empire codes and ID sequences on crystal chips in my files! I'll go get them."

"An excellent plan," said Haviland Tuf, "with but a single obvious deficiency, that being the time it will require to locate and utilize these encoded chips. Had we the leisure to accomplish this, I might applaud your suggestion. I fear we do not, alas. The *Ark* has just fired upon us."

Haviland Tuf reached forward. "I am taking us into drive," he announced. But as his long pale fingers brushed the keys, suddenly the *Cornucopia* shook violently. Celise Waan shrieked and went down; Jefri Lion stumbled into Anittas; even Rica Dawnstar had to grab the back of Tuf's chair to retain her footing. Then all the lights went out. Haviland Tuf's voice came out of the dark. "I fear I spoke too soon," he said, "or perhaps, more accurately, acted too tardily."

For a long moment, they were lost in silence and darkness and dread, waiting for the second hit that would spell an end to them.

And then the blackness ebbed a little; dim lights appeared on all the consoles around them, as the *Cornucopia*'s instrumentation woke to a flickering half-life. "We are not entirely disabled," Haviland Tuf proclaimed from the command chair where he sat stiffly. His big hands stretched out over the computer keys. "I will get a damage report. Perhaps we shall be able to retreat after all."

Celise Waan began to make a noise; a high, thin, hysterical wailing that went on and on. She was still sprawled on the deck. Kaj Nevis turned on her. "Shut up, you damned cow!" he snapped, and he kicked her. Her wail turned into blubbering. "We're dead meat sitting here like this," Nevis said loudly. "The next shot will blow us to pieces. Damn it, Tuf, move this thing!"

"Our motion is undiminished," Tuf replied. "The hit we took did not terminate our velocity, yet it did deflect us somewhat from our previous trajectory toward the *Ark*. Perhaps that is why we are not being fired upon now." He was studying wan green figures that uncoiled across one of the smaller telescreens. "I fear my ship has suffered some incapacitation. Shifting into

drive now would be inadvisable; the stress would undoubtedly rend us to pieces. Our life support systems
have also taken damage. The projections indicate that
we will run out of oxygen in approximately nine standard hours."

Kaj Nevis cursed; Celise Waan began to beat her fists
on the deck. "I can conserve oxygen by shutting down
once more," Anittas offered. Everyone ignored him.

"We can kill the cats," Celise Waan suggested.

"Can we move?" Rica Dawnstar asked.

"The maneuvering engines are still operable," Tuf
said, "but without the ability to shunt into stardrive, it
will take us approximately two ShanDish years to reach
even Hro B'rana. Four of us can take refuge in pressure
suits. The viral airpacs will recycle oxygen indefinitely."

"I refuse to live in a pressure suit for two years,"
Celise Waan said forcefully.

"Excellent," said Tuf. "As I have only four suits, and
we are six in number, this will be of help. Your noble
self-sacrifice will be long remembered, madam. Before
we put this plan into motion, however, I believe we
might consider one other option."

"And what's that?" Nevis asked.

Tuf swiveled about in his command chair and looked
at each of them in the dimness of the darkened control
room. "We must hope that Jefri Lion's crystalline chip
does indeed contain the proper approach code, so that
we might effect a docking with the *Ark,* without being
made the target of ancient weaponry."

"The chip!" Lion said. It was hard to see him. In the
darkness, his chameleon cloth jacket had turned a deep
black. "I'll go get it!" He went rushing back toward
their living quarters.

Mushroom padded quietly across the room, and leapt
up into Tuf's lap. Tuf settled a hand on him, and the big
tom began to purr loudly. It was somehow a reassuring
sound. Perhaps they would be all right after all.

But Jefri Lion was gone for too long a time.

When they finally heard him return, his footsteps
were leaden, defeated.

"Well?" Nevis said. "Where is it?"

"Gone," Lion said. "I looked everywhere. It's gone. I could have sworn I had it with me. My files—Kaj, truly, I meant to bring it along. I couldn't bring everything, of course, but I duplicated most of the important records, the things I thought might prove useful—material on the war, on the EEC, some histories of this sector. My gray case, you know. It had my little computer, and more than thirty crystal chips. I was going over some of them last night, remember, in bed? I was reviewing the material about the seedships, what little we know, and you told me that I was keeping you awake. I had a chip full of old codes, I know I did, and I really meant to bring it along. But it's not there." He came closer. They saw he was carrying the hand computer, holding it out almost as an offering. "I went through the box four times, and searched all the chips I had out on my bed, on the table, everywhere. It's not here. I'm sorry. Unless one of you took it?" Jefri Lion glanced about the room. No one spoke. "I must have left the codes back on ShanDellor," he said. "We were in such haste to leave, I . . ."

"You senile old fool," said Kaj Nevis. "I ought to kill you right now, and save a little air for the rest of us."

"We're dead," wailed Celise Waan, "we're dead, dead, dead."

"Madam," said Haviland Tuf, petting Mushroom, "you continue to be premature. You are no more deceased now than you were wealthy a short time ago."

Nevis turned to face him. "Oh? You have an idea, Tuf?"

"Indeed," said Haviland Tuf.

"Well?" prompted Nevis.

"The *Ark* is our only salvation," Tuf said. "We must board her. Without Jefri Lion's code crystal, we cannot move the *Cornucopia of Excellent Goods at Low Prices* closer for a docking, for fear of being fired upon once again. This much is obvious. Yet an interesting concept has occurred to me." He raised a finger. "Perhaps the *Ark* might display less hostility toward a smaller target—a man in a pressure suit, say, propelled by air jets!"

Kaj Nevis looked thoughtful. "And when this man

reaches the *Ark*, what then? Is he supposed to knock on the hull?"

"Impractical," admitted Haviland Tuf, "and yet I believe I have a method of dealing with this problem as well."

They waited. Tuf stroked Mushroom. "Go on," Kaj Nevis said impatiently.

Tuf blinked. "Go on? Indeed. I fear I must beg your indulgence. My mind is most distracted. My poor ship has suffered grievous harm. My modest livelihood lies ruined and devastated, and who will pay for the necessary repairs? Will Kaj Nevis, soon to enjoy such wealth, shower me with largesse? I fear not. Will Jefri Lion and Anittas buy for me a new ship? Unlikely. Will the esteemed Celise Waan grant me a bonus above and beyond my fee to compensate for my great loss? She has already promised to seek legal redress against me, to have my poor vessel confiscated and my landing license revoked. How then am I to cope? Who will succor me?"

"Never mind about that!" Kaj Nevis said. "How do we get inside the *Ark*? You said you had a way!"

"Did I?" said Haviland Tuf. "I believe you are correct, sir. Yet I fear the weight of my woes has driven the concept from my poor, distracted mind. I have forgotten it. I can think of nothing but my sorry economic plight."

Rica Dawnstar laughed, and clapped Tuf soundly across his broad back.

He looked up at her. "And now I am roughly pummeled and beaten as well, by the fierce Rica Dawnstar. Please do not touch me, madam."

"This is blackmail," screeched Celise Waan. "We'll have you put in prison for this!"

"And now my integrity is impugned, and I am showered with threats. Is it any wonder I cannot think, Mushroom?"

Kaj Nevis snarled. "All right, Tuf. You win." He looked around. "Do I hear any objections to making Tuffy here a full partner? A five-way split?"

Jefri Lion cleared his throat. "He deserves at least that, if his plan works."

Nevis nodded. "You're in, Tuf."

Haviland Tuf rose with immense, ponderous dignity, brushing Mushroom from his lap. "My memory returns to me!" he announced. "There are four pressure suits in the locker, yonder. If one of you would be so kind as to don one and render me your aid, together we shall go to procure a most useful piece of equipment from storage compartment twelve."

"What the hell," Rica Dawnstar exclaimed when they came back, carrying their booty between them. She laughed.

"What is it?" demanded Celise Waan.

Haviland Tuf, who loomed large in his silver-blue pressure suit, lowered the legs to the ground and helped Kaj Nevis get it upright. Then he removed his helmet and inspected their prize with satisfaction. "It is a spacesuit, madam," he said. "I would think that obvious."

It *was* a spacesuit, of sorts, but it was like no suit any of them had ever seen before, and clearly, whoever had constructed it had not had humans in mind. It towered over all of them, even Tuf; the ornate crest on the great beetling helmet was a good three meters off the deck, and almost brushed the top of the bulkhead. There were four thick double-jointed arms, the bottom two ending in gleaming, serrated pincers; the legs were broad enough to contain the trunks of small trees, and the footpads were great circular saucers. On the broad, hunched back were mounted four huge tanks; a radar antenna sprang from the right shoulder; and everywhere the rigid black metal of which it was constructed was filigreed in strange swirling patterns of red and gold. It stood among them like an armored giant of old.

Kaj Nevis jerked a thumb at the armor. "It's here," he said. "So what? How will this monstrosity help us?" He shook his head. "It looks like a piece of junk to me."

"Please," said Tuf. "This mechanism, which you so disparage, is an antique rich with history. I acquired this fascinating alien artifact, at no small cost to myself, on Unqi when I passed through that sector. This is a genuine Unquin battlesuit, sir, represented to be of the

Harneriin dynasty, which fell some fifteen hundred years
ago, long before humanity reached the Unquish stars.
It has been fully restored."

"What does it *do*, Tuf?" asked Rica Dawnstar, always
quick to come to the point.

Tuf blinked. "Its capabilities are many and varied.
Two strike closest to home in regard to our present
quandary. It has an augmented exoskeleton, and when
fully charged will magnify the inherent strength of its
occupant by a power of ten, approximately. Furthermore, its equipment includes a most excellent cutting
laser, engineered to slice through duralloy of a thickness of one-half meter, or of plate steel of significantly
greater thickness, when directly applied at zero range.
In brief, this ancient battlesuit will be our means of
entry into the ancient warship that looms as our only
salvation."

"Splendid!" said Jefri Lion, clapping his hands together in approval.

"It might work at that," Kaj Nevis commented. "What's
the drill?"

"I must admit to some deficiency of equipment for
deep space maneuvering," Tuf replied. "Our resources
include four standard pressure suits, but only two jetpacs.
The Unquin battlesuit, I am pleased to report, has its
own propulsion vents. I propose the following plan. I
will don the battlesuit and make egress from the *Cornucopia of Excellent Goods at Low Prices*, accompanied
by Rica Dawnstar and Anittas in pressure suits and
jetpacs. We will proceed to the *Ark* with all due speed.
If we make the journey safely, we will use the battlesuit's
most excellent capabilities to gain entrance through an
airlock. I am told that Anittas is expert in ancient cybernetic systems and obsolete computers. Very well, then.
Once inside, he will no doubt have little trouble gain-
ing control of the *Ark* and will supersede the hostile
programming now in place. At that point, Kaj Nevis
will be able to pilot my crippled ship in for a docking,
and all of us will have attained safety."

Celise Waan turned a vivid shade of red. "You're
leaving us to die!" she screeched. "Nevis, Lion, we

must stop them! Once they're on the *Ark*, they'll blow us up! We can't trust them."

Haviland Tuf blinked. "Why must my morality be constantly assaulted by these accusations?" he asked. "I am a man of honor. The course of action you have suggested had never crossed my mind."

"It's a good plan," said Kaj Nevis. He smiled, and began to unseal his pressure suit. "Anittas, hireling, suit up."

"Are you going to let them abandon us here?" Celise Waan demanded of Jefri Lion.

"I'm sure they mean us no harm," Lion said, tugging on his beard, "and if they did, Celise, how do you propose I stop them?"

"Let us move the battlesuit down to the main airlock," Haviland Tuf said to Kaj Nevis while Dawnstar and the cybertech were suiting up. Nevis nodded, kicked his way free of his own pressure suit, and moved to help Tuf.

With some difficulty, they wrestled the huge Unquish suit down to the *Cornucopia*'s main lock. Tuf shed his pressure suit and unbolted the armored entry port, then pulled over a stepstool and began to climb laboriously inside. "Just a moment, Tuffy," Kaj Nevis said, grabbing him by the shoulder.

"Sir," said Haviland Tuf, "I do not like to be touched. Unhand me." He turned back and blinked in surprise. Kaj Nevis had produced a vibroknife. The slender, humming blade, which could slice through solid steel, was a blur of motion less than a centimeter from Tuf's nose.

"A good plan," Kaj Nevis said, "but let's make one little change. I'll wear the supersuit, and go with Anittas and little Rica. You stay here and die."

"I do not approve of this substitution," said Haviland Tuf. "I am chagrined that you too would truckle to unfounded suspicion of my motives. I assure you, as I have assured Celise Waan, that thought of treachery has never crossed my mind."

"Funny," said Kaj Nevis. "It crossed *my* mind. Seemed like a damn fine idea, too."

Haviland Tuf assumed a look of wounded dignity. "Your base plans are undone, sir," he announced. "Anittas and Rica Dawnstar have come up behind you. It is well known that Rica Dawnstar was hired to forestall just such behavior from you. I advise you to surrender now. It will go easier on you."

Kaj Nevis grinned.

Rica had her helmet cradled under her arm. She observed the tableau, shook her pretty head slightly, and sighed. "You should have taken my offer, Tuf. I told you the time would come when you'd be sorry you didn't have an ally." She donned the helmet, sealed it, scooped up an airjet. "Let's go, Nevis."

Comprehension finally dawned on the broad face of Celise Waan. To her credit, this time she did not succumb to hysteria. She looked about for a weapon, found nothing obvious, and finally grabbed Mushroom, who was standing nearby and watching events with curiosity. "You, you, YOU!" she shouted, heaving the cat across the room. Kaj Nevis ducked. Mushroom yowled mightily and bounced off Anittas.

"Kindly cease flinging about my cats," Haviland Tuf said.

Nevis, recovering quickly, brandished the vibroknife at Tuf in a most unpleasant fashion, and Tuf backed slowly away. Nevis paused long enough to scoop up Tuf's discarded pressure suit and slice it deftly into a dozen long silver-blue ribbons. Then, carefully, he climbed into the Unquin battlesuit. Rica Dawnstar sealed it up after him. It took Nevis some time to figure out the alien control systems, but after about five minutes, the bulging faceplate began to glow a baleful blood red, and the heavy upper limbs moved ponderously. He switched to the lower, pincered arms experimentally while Anittas opened the inner door of the lock. Kaj Nevis lumbered in, clacking his pincers, followed by the cybertech and, lastly, Rica Dawnstar. "Sorry, folks," she announced as the door was sliding shut. "It's nothing personal. Just arithmetic."

"Indeed," said Haviland Tuf. "Subtraction."

*   *   *

Haviland Tuf sat in his command chair, enthroned in darkness, watching the flickering instrumentation before him. Mushroom, his dignity much offended, had settled in Tuf's lap, and was graciously allowing himself to be soothed. "The *Ark* is not firing on our erstwhile compatriots," he told Jefri Lion and Celise Waan.

"This is all my fault," Jefri Lion was saying.

"No," said Celise Waan. "It's *his* fault." She jerked a fat thumb toward Tuf.

"You are not the most appreciative of women," Haviland Tuf observed.

"Appreciative? What am I supposed to appreciate?" she said angrily.

Tuf made a steeple of his hands. "We are not without resources. To begin with, Kaj Nevis left us one functioning pressure suit," he pointed out.

"And no propulsion systems."

"Our air will last twice as long with our numbers diminished," Tuf said.

"But will still run out," snapped Celise Waan.

"Kaj Nevis and his cohorts did not use the Unquin battlesuit to destroy the *Cornucopia of Excellent Goods at Low Prices* after their exit, as well they might have."

"Nevis preferred to see us die a lingering death," the anthropologist replied.

"I think not. More likely, in point of fact, he wished to preserve this vessel as a last refuge should his plan to board the *Ark* somehow miscarry," Tuf mused. "In the nonce, we have shelter, provisions, and the possibility of maneuver, however limited."

"What we have is a crippled ship that is rapidly running out of air," said Celise Waan. She started to say something else, but just then Havoc came bounding into the control room, all energy and bounce, in hot pursuit of a bit of jewelry she'd sent rolling in before her. It landed by Celise Waan's feet; Havoc pounced on it, and sent it spinning with a tentative swipe. Celise Waan yelped. "My glowstone ring! I've been looking for that! Damn you, you filthy thief." She bent and snatched for the ring. Havoc closed with her, and she gave the cat a lusty blow with her fist. She missed. Havoc's claws were more accurate. Celise Waan shrieked.

Haviland Tuf was on his feet. He snatched up the cat and the ring, tucked Havoc safely under his arm, and handed the ring stiffly to its bleeding owner. "Your property," he said.

"Before I die, I swear I'm going to grab that creature by the tail and smash its brains on a bulkhead—if it has any brains."

"You do not sufficiently appreciate the virtues of the feline," said Tuf, retreating to his chair. He soothed Havoc's feelings as he had earlier soothed Mushroom. "Cats are most intelligent animals. In fact, it is well known that all cats have a touch of psi. The primitives of Old Earth were known to worship them."

"I've studied primitives who worship fecal matter," the anthropologist said testily. "That animal is a filthy beast!"

"The feline is fastidiously clean," Tuf said calmly. "Havoc herself is scarcely more than a kitten, and her playfulness and chaotic temperament remain undiminished," he said. "She is a most willful creature, and yet, that is but part of her charm. Curiously, she is also a creature of habit. Who could fail to be warmed by the joy she takes in play with small objects left lying about? Who could fail to be amused by the foolish frequency with which she loses her playthings beneath the consoles in this very room? Who indeed. Only the most sour and stony-hearted." Tuf blinked rapidly—once, twice, three times. On his long, still face, it was a thunderstorm of emotion. "Off, Havoc," he said, gently swatting the cat from his lap. He rose, then sank to his knees with a stiff dignity. On hands and knees, Haviland Tuf began to crawl about the room and feel beneath the control consoles.

"What are you doing?" demanded Celise Waan.

"I am searching for Havoc's lost toys," said Haviland Tuf.

"I'm bleeding and we're running out of air and you're looking for *cat toys*!" she said in exasperation.

"I believe I have just stated as much," Tuf said. He

pulled a handful of small objects out from under the console, and then a second handful. After thrusting his arm all the way back and patting about systematically, he finally gave up, gathered his cache, dusted himself off, and began to sort the prizes from the dust. "Interesting," he said.

"What?" she demanded.

"These are yours," he said to Celise Waan. He handed her another ring and two light pencils. "These are mine," he said, shoving aside two more light pencils, three red cruisers, a yellow dreadnaught, and a silver star-fort. "And this, I believe, is yours." He held it out to Jefri Lion: a shaped crystal the size of a thumbnail.

Lion all but bounded to his feet. "The chip!"

"Indeed," said Haviland Tuf.

There was a moment of endless suspense after Tuf had lasered the docking request. A thin crack appeared in the middle of the great black dome, and then another, at cross angles to the first. Then a third, a fourth, more and still more. The dome split into a hundred narrow pie-shaped wedges, which receded into the hull of the *Ark*.

Jefri Lion let go of his breath. "It works," he said, in a voice full of awe and gratitude.

"I reached that conclusion some time ago," Tuf said, "when we successfully penetrated the defense sphere without being fired upon. This is merely a confirmation."

They watched the proceedings on the viewscreen. Beneath the dome appeared a landing deck fully as large as the ports of many a lesser planet. The deck was pockmarked with circular landing pads, several of which were occupied. As they waited, a ring of blue-white light flicked on around one vacant pad.

"Far be it from me to dictate your behavior," said Haviland Tuf, his eyes on his instruments, his hands in careful, methodical motion. "I would, however, advise that each of you strap in securely. I am extending the landing legs and programming us for a landing on the indicated pad, but I am uncertain how much damage the legs have sustained, uncertain even as to whether all three legs remain in place. Therefore I counsel caution."

The landing deck yawned blackly beneath them. They began a stately descent into its cavernous depths. The illuminated ring of the landing pad loomed larger and larger on one viewscreen; a second showed the wan blue light of the *Cornucopia*'s gravity engines flickering off distant metal walls and the silhouettes of other ships. In a third, they saw the dome reassembling itself, a dozen sharp teeth grinding together once more, as if they had just been swallowed by some vast spacefaring animal.

The impact was surprisingly gentle. They settled into place with a sigh and a whisper and only the smallest of bumps. Haviland Tuf killed their engines, and spent a moment studying the instruments and the scenes on his telescreens. Then he turned to face the others. "We are docked," he announced, "and the time has come to make our plans."

Celise Waan was busily unstrapping herself. "I want to get out of here," she said, "find Nevis and that bitch Rica, and give them both a good piece of my mind."

"A good piece of your mind might be considered an oxymoron," said Haviland Tuf. "I think your proposed course of action unwise in the extreme. Our former colleagues must now be considered our rivals. Having just abandoned us to death, they shall undoubtedly be nonplussed to discover us still alive, and might very well take steps to rectify this contradiction."

"Tuf is right," Jefri Lion said. He was moving from one screen to another, peering at them with fascination. The ancient seedship had rekindled his spirit and his imagination, and he was bristling with energy. "It's us against them, Celise. This is war. They'll kill us if they can, have no doubt of it. We must be similarly ruthless! This is a time for clever tactics."

"I bow to your martial expertise," Tuf said. "What strategies do you suggest?"

Jefri Lion tugged on his beard. "Well," he said, "well, let me think. What's the situation here? They have Anittas. The man's half-computer himself. Once he interfaces with the shipboard systems, he should be able to determine how much of the *Ark* is functional, yes, and perhaps to exercise some control over its functioning, too. That could be dangerous. He might be trying it right now. We know they got aboard first. They may or may not know we're aboard. We have the advantage of surprise, perhaps!"

"They have the advantage of having all the weaponry," said Haviland Tuf.

"No problem!" said Jefri Lion. He rubbed his hands together eagerly. "This is a warship, after all. The EEC specialized in biowar, true, but this was a military vessel and I'm sure the crew had personal sidearms, that sort of thing. There's got to be an armory. All we have to do is find it."

"Indeed," said Haviland Tuf.

Lion was rolling now. "Our advantage, well, not to be immodest about it, but our advantage is me. Aside from what Anittas can discover from the computers, they'll be blundering about in the dark. But I've studied the old Federal Empire ships. I know everything about them." He frowned. "Well, everything that wasn't lost or classified, anyway. At least I know a few things about the general plans of these seedships. We'll have to find the armory first, and it should be close. It was standard procedure to store weaponry near the landing deck, for ground parties and such. After we're armed, we ought to look for—hmmmm, let me think—well, yes, the cell library, that's crucial. The seedships had vast cell libraries, cloning material from literally thousands of worlds preserved in a stasis field. We must discover if the cells are still viable! If the stasis field has failed and the samples have decayed, all we have gained is a very large ship. But if the systems are still operational, the *Ark* is literally priceless!"

"While I appreciate the importance of the cell library," Tuf said, "it strikes me that a more immediate priority might be the location of the bridge. Making the perhaps unwarranted but nonetheless attractive assumption that none of the original crew of the *Ark* is alive after the passage of a millennium, we are then alone on this vessel with our enemies, and whichever party gains control of shipboard functions first will enjoy a rather formidable advantage."

"A good point, Tuf!" Lion exclaimed. "Well then, let's get to it."

"Right," said Celise Waan. "I want out of this cat trap."

Haviland Tuf raised a finger. "A moment, please. A problem presents itself. We are three in number, and possess only a single pressure suit among us."

"We're inside a *ship*," Celise Waan said in a voice that dripped sarcasm. "What do we need with suits?"

"Perhaps nothing," Tuf admitted. "It is true, as you imply, that the landing field seems to function as a very large airlock; my instruments indicate that we are now surrounded by an entirely breathable oxygen-nitrogen atmosphere, pumped in when the closure of the dome was complete."

"So what's the problem, Tuf?"

"No doubt I am being overcautious," Haviland Tuf said. "I admit to some disquiet, however. This *Ark*, though perhaps abandoned and derelict, is nonetheless dutiful. Witness the plagues it still regularly visits on Hro B'rana. Witness the efficiency with which it defended itself against our approach. We cannot know, as yet, why this ship was abandoned, nor how the last of the crew met their end, but it seems clear that it was their intent that the *Ark* live on. Perhaps the external defense sphere was only the first of several lines of automatic defense."

"An intriguing notion," said Jefri Lion. "Traps?"

"Of a particular kind. The atmosphere that awaits us may seethe with pestilence, plague, and biogenetic contagion. Dare we risk it? I would be more comfortable in a pressure suit, myself, though each of you is free to decide otherwise."

Celise Waan looked uncomfortable. "I should get the suit," she said. "We only have one, and you owe it to me, after the beastly way I've been treated."

"We need not enter into that discussion again,

madam," said Tuf. "We are on a landing deck. Around
us, I observe nine other spacecraft of varying design.
One is a Hruun fighter, one a Rhiannese merchant; two
are of designs unfamiliar to me. And five are plainly
shuttlecraft of some sort, identical to each other, larger
than my own poor vessel here, undoubtedly part of the
Ark's own original equipment. It is my experience that
spacecraft invariably are equipped with pressure suits.
It is my intention, therefore, to don our single remaining suit, exit, and search these neighboring ships until I
have found suits for each of you."

"I don't like it," Celise Waan snapped. "You get out,
and we're still stuck here."

"Such are the vicissitudes of life," Tuf said, "that
each of us must sometimes accept that which he does
not like."

The airlock gave them a bit of trouble. It was a small
emergency lock, with manual controls. They had no
difficulty opening the outer door, entering, and sealing
it behind them. The inner door was another and more
difficult proposition.

Atmosphere came flooding back into the large chamber as soon as the outer door was closed, but the inner
door was jammed somehow. Rica Dawnstar tried it
first; the huge metal wheel refused to turn, the lever
would not depress. "OUT OF MY WAY," Kaj Nevis
said, his voice twisted into a rasping croak by the alien
comm circuits built into the Unquin battlesuit, and
boosted to deafening levels by external speakers. He
trundled past her, the huge saucer feet ringing loudly
on the deck, and the battlesuit's great upper arms seized
the wheel and turned. The wheel resisted for a moment, then twisted and buckled, and finally came loose
of the door entirely.

"Good work," Rica said over her suit speaker. She
laughed.

Kaj Nevis growled something thunderously unintelli-
gible. He seized the lever and tried to move it, and
succeeded only in breaking it off.

Anittas moved closer to the stubborn inner lock mechanism. "A set of code buttons," he said, pointing. "The proper code sequence, if we knew it, would no doubt gain us entry automatically. There's a computer outlet, too. If I could interface, perhaps I could pull the correct code out of the system."

"WHAT'S STOPPING YOU?" Kaj Nevis demanded. His faceplate glowed balefully.

Anittas lifted his arms, turned his hands over helplessly. With the more obviously organic portions of his body covered by the silver-blue of his pressure suit, and his silver metallic eyes peering out through the plastic, he looked more like a robot than ever. Kaj Nevis, standing huge above him, looked like a much larger robot. "This suit," Anittas said, "is improperly designed. I cannot interface directly without removing it."

"REMOVE IT, THEN," Nevis said.

"Will that be safe?" asked Anittas. "I am unsure."

"There's air in here," Rica Dawnstar put in. She gestured toward the appropriate bank of indicators.

"Neither of you has removed your suit," Anittas pointed out. "Were I to make a mistake, and open the outer door instead of the inner one, I might die before I could seal up again."

"DON'T MAKE A MISTAKE," Kaj Nevis boomed.

Anittas crossed his arms. "The air might be unhealthy. This ship has been derelict for a thousand standard years, Kaj Nevis. Even the most sophisticated system goes down from time to time, experiences failures and glitches. I am unwilling to risk my person."

"OH?" Nevis thundered. There was a grinding sound. One of the lower arms came up slowly; the serrated metal pincer opened, seized Anittas about the middle, and pinned him against the nearest wall. The cybertech squawked protest. An upper arm came across, and a huge metal-gloved hand dug in under the collar of the pressure suit. It pulled. The helmet and the entire top of the suit came ripping off Anittas. His head almost came off, as well.

"I LIKE THIS SUIT," Kaj Nevis announced. He gave the cybertech a little squeeze with the pincer.

Metal fabric tore and blood began oozing through. "YOU'RE BREATHING, AREN'T YOU?"

Anittas was almost hyperventilating, in fact. He nodded.

The battlesuit flung him to the floor. "THEN GET TO WORK," Nevis told him.

That was when Rica Dawnstar began to feel nervous. She backed away casually, leaned against the outer door as far from Nevis as she could get, and considered the situation while Anittas removed his gloves and the shards of his ruined suit and slid the bluesteel fingers of his right hand into the waiting computer plugs. She had strapped her shoulder holster on over her pressure suit, so her needler would be accessible, but suddenly its presence didn't seem entirely as reassuring as it usually did. She studied the thickness of the Unquin armor, and wondered if maybe she had been unwise in her choice of ally. A three-way split was much better than Jefri Lion's small fee, to be sure. But what if Nevis decided he didn't like a three-way split?

They heard a sharp, sudden *pop* and the inner door began to slide open. Beyond was a narrow corridor leading down into blackness. Kaj Nevis moved to the doorway and peered into the dark, his glowing red faceplate throwing scarlet reflections on the walls. Then he turned ponderously. "YOU, HIRELING!" he boomed at Rica Dawnstar, "GO SCOUT IT OUT."

She came to a decision. "Aye, aye, bossman," she said. She drew her needler, moved quickly to the door and down the corridor, followed it about ten meters to a cross-corridor. From there she looked back. Nevis, hugely armored, filled the airlock door. Anittas stood beside him. The cybertech, normally so silent, still, and efficient, was shaking. "Stay right there," Rica called back to them. "It's not safe!" Then she turned and picked a direction at random and began to run like hell.

It took Haviland Tuf much longer than he had antici-pated to locate the suits. The nearest of the other spacecraft was the Hruun fighter, a chunky green ma-chine bristling with weaponry. It was sealed up securely, however, and although Tuf circled it several times and studied the various instruments that seemed designed to command access, none of his tugging, prodding, pushing, or fiddling produced the desired result, and he was forced to give it up finally and proceed onward.

The second ship, one of the strange ones, was wide open, and he wandered through it with a certain amount of intellectual fascination. Its interior was a maze of narrow corridors whose walls were as irregular and pebbly as a cave, and soft to the touch. Its instruments were incomprehensible. Its pressure suits, when he located what looked to be pressure suits, might have been functional, but could never have been worn by anyone over a meter tall or bilaterally symmetrical.

The Rhiannese merchant, his third try, had been gutted; Tuf could locate nothing useful.

Finally, there was nothing to be done for it but to hike all the way to one of the five distant shuttlecraft that stood side by side, snug in custom launching berths. They were big ships, larger than the *Cornucopia of Excellent Goods at Low Prices*, with black pitted hulls and rakish wings, but they were clearly of human design and seemingly in good repair. Tuf finally puzzled his way into one of them, whose berth bore a metal plate with an engraved silhouette of some fanciful animal and a legend proclaiming it to be named *Griffin*. Pressure suits were located where they should have been located. They were in excellent shape, considering that they were a thousand years old, and quite striking as well: a deep green in color, with golden helmet, gloves, and boots, and a golden theta emblazoned upon the breast of each. Tuf selected two of them and carried them back across the echoing twilit plain of the landing deck, to where the scarred, crippled teardrop that was his *Cornucopia* squatted on its three splayed legs.

When he got to the base of the ramp that led up to the main lock, he almost stumbled over Mushroom.

The big tom was sitting on the deck. He got up and

made a plaintive noise, rubbing himself against Tuf's booted leg.

Haviland Tuf stopped for an instant and stared down at the old gray tom. He bent awkwardly, gathered up the cat, and stroked him for a time. When he climbed the ramp to the airlock, Mushroom followed, and Tuf found it necessary to shoo him away. He cycled through with a pressure suit under each arm.

"It's about time," Celise Waan said when Tuf entered.

"I told you Tuf hadn't abandoned us," Jefri Lion said.

Haviland Tuf let the pressure suits fall to the deck, where they lay like a puddle of green and gold. "Mushroom is outside," Tuf said in a flat, passionless voice.

"Well, yes," Celise Waan said. She grabbed a suit and began squeezing into the green metallic fabric. It bound her tightly about the middle; the members of the Ecological Engineering Corps had seemingly been less fleshy than she. "Couldn't you have gotten me a larger size?" she complained. "Are you sure these suits still work?"

"The construction seems sound," Tuf said. "It will be necessary to infuse the airpacs with whatever living bacteria remain from the ship's cultures. How did Mushroom come to be outside?"

Jefri Lion cleared his throat uncomfortably. "Uh, yes," he said. "Celise was afraid you weren't coming back, Tuf. You were gone so long. She thought you'd left us here."

"A base and foundless suspicion," said Tuf.

"Uh, yes," said Lion. He looked away, reached for his own suit.

Celise Waan pulled on a golden boot, sealed it. "It's your fault," she said to Tuf. "If you hadn't been gone so long, I wouldn't have gotten restless."

"Indeed," said Tuf. "What, might I venture to ask, has your restlessness to do with Mushroom?"

"Well, I thought you weren't coming back, and we had to get out of here," the anthropologist said. She sealed up her second boot. "But you made me nervous, you know, with all your talk of plagues. So I cycled the cat through the airlock. I tried to get that damned

black-and-white one, but it kept running away and hissing at me. The gray one just let me pick it up. I
dumped it out and we've been watching it through the
screens. I figured we could see whether or not it got
sick. If it didn't show any symptoms, well, then probably it would be safe for us to risk coming out."

"I grasp the principle," said Haviland Tuf.

Havoc came bounding in the room, playing with
something. She saw Tuf and headed toward him, walking with a pronounced kittenish swagger.

"Jefri Lion," said Tuf, "if you would, please appre-
hend Havoc, take her back to the living quarters, and
confine her there."

"Uh, certainly," Lion said. He caught up Havoc as
she went by him. "Why?"

"I would prefer henceforth to keep Havoc secure and
separated from Celise Waan," Tuf said.

Celise Waan, helmet cradled under her arm, made a
noise of derision. "Oh, stuff and nonsense. The gray
one is fine."

"Permit me to mention a concept with which you are
perhaps unfamiliar," said Haviland Tuf. "It is referred
to as an incubation period."

"I'm going to kill that bitch," Kaj Nevis threatened as
he and Anittas made their way down a dark hallway.
*"Damn her. You can't get a decent mercenary any-
more."* The battlesuit's huge head turned to search for
the cybertech, the faceplate glowing. *"Hurry up."*

"I cannot match your strides," Anittas said as he
hurried up. His sides ached from the effort of keeping
up with Nevis's pace; his cyberhalf was strong as metal
and quick as electronic circuitry, but his biohalf was
poor tired wounded flesh, and blood still oozed from
the cuts Nevis had opened around his midsection. He
was feeling dizzy and hot, as well. "It's not far now," he
said. "Down this corridor and to the left, third door. It
is a substantial substation. I felt it when I was plugged
in. I will be able to meld with the main system." And
rest, he thought. He was incredibly weary, and his
biohalf ached and throbbed.

"I WANT THE DAMN LIGHTS ON," Nevis commanded. "AND THEN I WANT YOU TO FIND HER
FOR ME. DO YOU UNDERSTAND?"

Anittas nodded, and pushed himself harder. Two small
hot pinpoints of red burned on his cheeks, unseen by
his silver-metal eyes, and for an instant his vision blurred
and wavered, and he heard a loud buzzing in his ears.
He stopped.

"WHAT'S WRONG NOW?" Nevis demanded.

"I am experiencing some loss of function," Anittas
said. "I must reach the computer room and run a check
on my systems." He started forward again, and staggered. Then his balance deserted him totally, and he
fell.

Rica Dawnstar was positive that she had lost them.
Kaj Nevis was pretty formidable in his giant metal
monkey suit, no doubt of that, but he was anything but
silent. Rica had eyes like one of Tuf's cats, another
advantage in her profession. Where she could see, she
ran; in the corridors that were totally black, she felt her
way along, as quickly and quietly as she could. Down
here the *Ark* was a maze of rooms and hallways. She
threaded her way through the labyrinth, turning and
twisting and turning once again, doubling back on herself, and listening carefully as Nevis's clanging tread
grew steadily fainter and finally faded altogether.

Only then, when she knew she was safe, did Rica
Dawnstar begin to explore the warren in which she
found herself. There were light plates set in the walls.
Some responded to the touch of her hand, others did
not. She lit her way wherever she could. The first
section she passed through was residential—small sleeping rooms off narrow corridors, each with a bed, desk,
computer console, and telescreen. Some rooms were
empty and sterile; in others she found beds unmade
and clothing strewn across the floor. Everything was
neat and clean. Either the residents had just moved out
the night before, or the *Ark* had kept this whole portion
of the ship sealed and inviolate and in repair, until their
approach had somehow activated it.

The next section had not been so fortunate. Here the rooms were full of dust and debris, and in one she found an ancient skeleton, a woman, still asleep in a bed that had collapsed into shapeless decay centuries before. What a difference a little air can make, Rica thought.

The corridors led into other corridors, wider ones. She peered into storage rooms, into chambers full of equipment and others packed with empty cages, into spotless white laboratories in endless succession that lined the sides of a corridor as wide as the boulevards of Shandicity. That led her, eventually, to a junction with an even grander corridor. She hesitated, unsure for a moment, and drew her needler. This way to the control room, she thought to herself—or to something important, at any rate. She stepped out onto the main way, spotted something in the corner; dim shapes, hunched down into little niches in the wall. Cautiously, Rica moved toward them.

When she got close, she laughed and holstered her weapon. The dark shapes were a row of scooters of some kind—small three-wheeled vehicles, each with two seats and big soft balloon tires. They were set into charging-slots in the walls.

Rica pulled one out, swung herself lithely into the driver's seat, flicked on the power. The gauges registered a full charge. It even had a headlight, which cut through the dark and the shadows ahead quite nicely, thank you. Grinning, she rolled off down the broad corridor. She wasn't going very fast, but what the hell, at least she was getting there.

Jefri Lion led them to an armory. It was there that Haviland Tuf killed Mushroom.

Lion was flashing a hand torch over the room in swift, excited arcs, exclaiming at the stockpile of laser rifles, projectile weapons, screechguns, and light-grenades. Celise Waan was complaining that she had no familiarity with weapons, and didn't think she could kill anybody anyway. She was a scientist and not a soldier, after all, and she thought all this was barbaric.

Haviland Tuf held Mushroom cradled in his arms. The big tomcat had purred loudly when Tuf had re-emerged from the *Cornucopia* and scooped him up, but no longer. Now he was making a pitiful sound, half mewing, half choking. When Tuf tried to stroke him, the long, soft gray fur came out in clumps. Mushroom screeched. Something was growing inside his mouth, Tuf saw; a web of fine black hairs crept from a black fungoid mass. Mushroom howled again, more loudly, and struggled to get free, wielding his claws uselessly against the metal of Tuf's suit. His big yellow eyes were covered with film.

The others had not noticed; their minds were on larger concerns than the cat that Tuf had voyaged with all his life. Jefri Lion and Celise Waan were arguing with each other. Tuf held Mushroom very still, despite the tom's struggles. He stroked him one last time and spoke soothingly to him. Then, in a single swift clean motion, he snapped the cat's neck.

"Nevis has already tried to kill us," Jefri Lion was saying to Celise Waan. "I don't care what your qualms are, really, you must do your part. You can't expect Tuf and me to carry the whole burden of our defense." Behind the thick plastic faceplate of his pressure suit, Lion frowned. "I wish I knew more about that battlesuit that Nevis is wearing," Lion said. "Tuf, will laser fire cut through that Unquin armor? Or would some kind of explosive projectile be more effective? A laser, I would think. Tuf?" He turned around, swinging the hand torch back and forth so shadows danced wildly against the chamber walls. "Tuf, where are you? Tuf?"

But Haviland Tuf was gone.

The door to the computer room refused to open. Kaj Nevis kicked it. The metal buckled inward in the center and the top of the door popped free of the frame. Nevis kicked it again, and again, his massive armored foot slamming with awful force against the thinner metal of the door. Then he shoved the crumpled remains of the barrier out of his way and entered, with Anittas cradled in his stiff lower arms. "I LIKE THIS DAMNED SUIT," he said. Anittas groaned.

The substation was filled with a thin subsonic humming, a buzz of anxiety. Tiny colored lights blinked on and off like fireflies.

"In the circuit," Anittas said. His hand flailed about weakly in what could have been either a gesture or a spasm. "Get me in the circuit," he repeated. The parts of him that were still organic looked terrible. His skin was covered with beads of black sweat; tiny drops of moisture as shiny as liquid ebony oozed from every fleshy pore. Mucus ran freely from his nose, and he was bleeding from his single organic ear. He couldn't stand or walk and his speech seemed to be deteriorating as well. The dull red glow from the battlesuit's helmet gave him a deep crimson caul that made him look even worse. "Hurry," he told Nevis. "The circuit, please, get me in the circuit."

"SHUT UP OR I'LL DUMP YOU HERE," Nevis answered. Anittas shuddered, as if the magnified volume of Nevis's voice was a physical assault. Nevis scanned the room until he found the interface station. He lugged the cybertech over there, and dropped him down in a white plastic chair that seemed to flow out of the console and deck. Anittas screamed. "SHUT UP!" Nevis repeated. He picked up the cybertech's arm clumsily, almost ripping it out of its socket. It was hard to gauge his strength in this damned suit, and fine manipulation was even harder, but he wasn't about to take it off—he *liked* this suit, yes he did. Anittas screamed again. Nevis ignored him, spread the tech's bluesteel fingers, jammed them into the interface. "THERE!" he said. He stepped back.

Anittas slumped forward, his head slamming against the metal and plastic of the console. His mouth gaped open. Blood dripped out, mingled with some thick black fluid, almost like oil. Nevis scowled. Had he gotten him there too late? Had the goddamned cybertech gone and croaked on him?

Then the lights blinked on, and the thin wild humming rose in pitch, and all the tiny little colored lights flashed on and off, on and off, on and off. Anittas was in the circuit.

* * *

Rica Dawnstar was rolling down the main way, feeling almost jaunty despite everything, when the blackness ahead of her became a blaze of light. Overhead, the ceiling panels stirred from long slumber, one after another, racing down the kilometers, turning the night into a day so bright it hurt her eyes for a moment.

Startled, she braked to a halt, and watched the wave of light recede into infinity. She glanced behind her. Back from where she'd come, the corridor was still filled with darkness.

She noticed something that hadn't been obvious before, in the dark. Set into the corridor floor were six thin parallel lines, translucent plastic guide-strips in red, blue, yellow, green, silver, purple. Each no doubt leading somewhere. Pity she didn't know which led where.

But as she watched, the silver tracery began to glow with an inner light. It stretched out in front of her, a thin, scintillating silvery ribbon. Simultaneously, the overhead panel just above her darkened. Rica frowned, and edged her scooter forward a couple of meters, out of the shadows and back into the light. But when she paused, that light went out as well. The silver ribbon in the floor throbbed insistently. "All right," Rica said, "we'll do it your way." She gunned her scooter and moved down the corridor, as the lights winked out behind her.

"He's come!" Celise Waan screeched when the corridor lit up. She seemed to jump a good meter in the air.

Jefri Lion stood his ground and scowled. He was holding a laser rifle in his hands. A high-explosive dart-pistol rode in a holster on one hip and a screechgun on the other. A huge two-man plasma cannon was strapped securely to his back. He wore a bandolier of mindbombs over his right shoulder, a bandolier of light-grenades over his left, and a large vibroknife sheathed on his thigh. Inside his golden helmet, Lion was smiling, his blood pounding. He was ready for anything. He hadn't felt this good in over a century, since the last time he

saw action with Skaeglay's Volunteers against the Black
Angels. To hell with all that dusty academic stuff. Jefri
Lion was a man of action, and now he felt young again.

"Be quiet, Celise," he said. "No one's come. It's just
us. The lights came on, that's all."

Celise Waan seemed unconvinced. She was armed,
too, but she kept dragging the laser rifle along the deck
because she said it was too heavy, and Jefri Lion was
half afraid of what would happen if she tried to arm and
throw one of her light-grenades. "Look," she pointed,
"what's that?"

The floor had two bands of colored plastic inset into
it, Jefri Lion saw. One was black, one orange. Now the
orange one lit up. "It's some sort of computerized
guideway," he pronounced. "Let's follow it."

"No," Celise Waan said.

Jefri Lion scowled. "Listen here, I'm the commander
and you'll do what I say. We can handle anything we
might meet. Now move along."

"No!" Celise Waan said stubbornly. "I'm tired. It's
not safe. I'm staying right here."

"I'm giving you a direct order," said Jefri Lion
impatiently.

"Oh, stuff and nonsense. You can't give me orders.
I'm a full Wisdom and you're only an Associate Scholar."

"This isn't the Center," Lion said with irritation.
"Are you coming?"

"No." She sat down in the middle of the corridor and
crossed her arms.

"Very well, then. Good luck to you." Jefri Lion turned
his back on her and began to follow the orange guide-
light alone. Behind him, immobile, his army stubbornly
and sullenly watched him depart.

Haviland Tuf had come to a strange place.

He had wandered down endless dark, narrow corridors, carrying Mushroom's limp body, hardly thinking,
without plan or destination. Finally, he had emerged
from one such corridor into what seemed to be a large
cavern. The walls fell away on all sides of him. He was
swallowed by empty darkness, and his bootsteps sent

echoes ringing off distant walls. There were sounds in
the dark—a low humming, at the threshold of hearing,
and a louder sound, a liquid sound, like the ebb and
flow of some endless underground ocean. But he was
not underground, Haviland Tuf reminded himself. He
was lost aboard an ancient starship called *Ark*, and
surrounded by villains, and Mushroom was dead by his
own hand.

He walked on. How long he could not say. His
footsteps rang. The floor was level and bare and seemed
to go on forever. Finally he walked right into something
in the dark. He was moving slowly, so he was not hurt,
but he dropped Mushroom in the collision. He groped
ahead, tried to determine what sort of object had stopped
him, but it was hard to tell through the fabric of his
gloves. It was large and curved.

That was when the lights came on.

For Haviland Tuf, there was no explosion of light;
what illumination existed in this place was dim, murky,
subdued. As it shone down from above, it cast ominous
black shadows everywhere, and gave the lighted areas a
curious greenish cast, as if they were covered with
some radiant moss.

Tuf gazed about. It was more a tunnel than a cavern,
perhaps. He had walked all the way across it, a distance
of at least a kilometer, he judged. But its breadth was
nothing to its length; it must run the full length of the
ship, along its major axis, for it seemed to vanish into
dimness in both directions. The ceiling above was a
shroud of green shadows; high, high overhead, echoes
rang off its dimly seen curves. There were machines, a
good many machines—computer substations built into
the walls, strange devices the like of which Haviland
Tuf had never seen, flat worktables with waldoes and
microhands built into them. Yet the main feature of this
huge, echoing shaft was the vats.

Everywhere there were vats. They lined both walls
as far as the eye could see in either direction, and a few
even bulged down from the ceiling. Some of the vats
were immense, their swollen translucent walls large
enough to contain the *Cornucopia*. Elsewhere they were

cells the size of a man's hand, thousands of them, ascending from floor to ceiling like plastic honeycombs. The computers and work-stations dwindled into insignificance beside them, small details easily overlooked. And now Haviland Tuf discerned the source of the liquid sound he had heard. Most of the vats were empty, he saw through the greenish gloom, but a few— one here, one there, two farther on—seemed to be full of colored fluids, bubbling, or stirred by the feeble motions of half-seen shapes within.

Haviland Tuf regarded the vista before him for a long time, its scale making him feel very small. Yet finally he turned away, and bent to pick up Mushroom once again. As he knelt, he saw what he had walked into in the dark: a vat, a medium-large one, its transparent walls curving away from him. This vat was full of a thick, murky yellowish liquid, shot through with moving swirls of red. Tuf heard a faint gurgling, and felt a slight vibration, as if something were stirring inside. He leaned closer, peered in, and then craned his head up.

Within, floating, unborn and yet alive, the tyrannosaur stared down at him.

In the circuit there was no pain. In the circuit he had no body. In the circuit he was mind, pure sweet white mind, and he was part of something vast and powerful and infinitely greater than himself, greater than any of them. In the circuit he was more than human, more than cyborg, more than mere machine. In the circuit he was something like a god. Time was nothing in the circuit; he was as swift as thought, as swift as silicon circuitry opening and closing, as swift as the messages that raced along superconductive tendons, as swift as the flash of microlasers weaving their invisible webs in the central matrix. In the circuit, he had a thousand ears and a thousand eyes and a thousand hands to ball into fists and strike with; in the circuit he could be everywhere at once.

He was Anittas. He was *Ark*. He was cybertech. He was more than five hundred satellite stations and monitors, he was twenty Imperial 7400s ruling the twenty sectors of the ship from twenty scattered substations, he was Battlemaster, Codebreaker, Astrogator, Drive Doctor, Medcenter, Ship's Log, Librarian, Bio-Librarian, Microsurgeon, Clonetender, Maintenance and Repair, Communications, and Defense. He was all the hardware and all the software and all the back-up systems and all secondary and tertiary back-ups. He was twelve hundred years old and thirty kilometers long and the heart of him was the central matrix, barely two meters square and all but infinite in size. He touched here and there and everywhere and moved on, his consciousness racing down the circuits, branching, dancing, riding on the lasers. Knowledge raced through him in a torrent, like a great river running wild, with all the cool steady sweet white power of a high voltage cable. He was *Ark*. He was Anittas. And he was dying.

Down deep in his bowels, down in the ship's intestines, down at substation seventeen by airlock nine, Anittas let his silver-metal eyes track and focus on Kaj Nevis. He smiled. On his half-human face, it was a grotesque expression. His teeth were chrome steel. "You fool," he said to Nevis.

The battlesuit took one threatening step closer. A pincer raised itself with a grinding, metallic sound, opened and closed. "WATCH YOUR MOUTH."

"Fool I said and fool it is," Anittas told him. His laughter was a horrible sound; it was full of pain and metallic echoes, and his lips were bleeding freely, leaving wet red smears on those shining silver teeth. "You killed me, Nevis, and for nothing—for impatience. I could have given it all to you. It's empty, Nevis. The ship is empty, they're all dead. And the system is empty, too. I'm alone in here. No other mind in the circuit. It's an idiot, Kaj Nevis. The *Ark* is an idiot giant. They were afraid, those Earth Imperials. They'd achieved true Artificial Intelligence. Oh yes, they had their great AI warships, their robot fleets, but the AIs had minds of their own, and there were incidents. It's in the histories—there was Kandabaer and the action off Lear and the revolt of *Alecto* and *Golem*. The seedships were too powerful, they knew that as they

built them. The *Ark* had duties for two hundred—
strategists and scientists and eco-engineers and crew
and officers—and she could carry more than a thousand
soldiers, too, and feed all of them, and operate at full
capacity, and lay waste to *worlds*, oh yes. And everything worked through the system, Nevis, but it's a safe
system, a big system, a sophisticated system, a system
that can repair itself and defend itself and do a thousand
things at once—if you tell it to. The two hundred
crewmen made it efficient, but you could run it with
only one, Nevis. Not efficiently, no, not at anything
near full capacity, but you could do it. It can't run
itself—it's got no mind, no AI, it waits for orders—but
one man can tell it what to do. One man! I could have
done it easily. But Kaj Nevis got impatient and killed
me."

Nevis moved still closer. "YOU DON'T SOUND
DEAD TO ME," he said, opening and closing his pincer
with a sudden menacing snap.

"But I am," said Anittas. "I am sucking power from
the system, boosting my cyberhalf, giving myself back a
speech capacity. But I'm dying all the while. Plagues,
Nevis. The ship was horribly undermanned in its last
days, only thirty-two left, and there was an attack, a
Hruun attack. They broke the code, opened the dome,
and landed. They stormed up the halls, more than a
hundred of them. They were winning, threatening to
take the ship. The defenders fought them every step of
the way. They sealed off whole sectors of the *Ark*,
evacuated all the air, turned off all the power. They got
a few that way. They set up ambushes, fought them
meter for meter. There are still places that are battle-
scarred, dysfunctional, beyond the *Ark*'s repair capacities. They let loose plague and pestilence and parasite,
and from their vats they summoned their pet nightmares, and they fought, and died, and won. In the end
all the Hruun were dead. And you know what, Kaj
Nevis? All but four of the defenders were dead as well.
One of those was grievously wounded, two others sick,
and the last was dead inside. Would you like to know
their names? No, I thought not. You have no curiosity,

Kaj Nevis. It is no matter. Tuf will want to know, as will the ancient Lion."

"TUF? LION? WHAT ARE YOU TALKING ABOUT? THEY'RE DEAD, BOTH OF THEM."

"Incorrect," Anittas said. "They are both aboard even now. Lion has found the armory. He's a walking arsenal, and he's coming for you. Tuf has found something even more important. Rica Dawnstar is following the silver trace to the main control room, the captain's chair. You see, Kaj Nevis, the gang's all here. I have awakened every part of the *Ark* that remains functional, and I am leading them all by the hand."

"STOP IT, THEN," Nevis commanded. He did not hesitate. The great metal pincer reached out and embraced Anittas about his biometal throat. Black sweat oozed down onto the pincer's serrated blade. "STOP THEM RIGHT NOW."

"I have not completed my story, Kaj Nevis," the cybertech said. His mouth was a smear of blood. "The last Imperials knew they could not go on. They shut down the ship, gave it up to vacuum and silence and the void. They made it go derelict. Yet not entirely, you see. They feared another attack, by the Hruun or perhaps, in time, others yet unknown. So they told the *Ark* to defend itself. They armed the plasma cannon and external lasers and kept the defense sphere functional, as we learned to our sorrow. And they programmed the ship to take a terrible vengeance for them, to return again and again and again to Hro B'rana, whence the Hruun had come, and to deliver its gift of plague and pestilence and death. To guard against the Hruun building up immunity, they subjected their plague tanks to constant radiation, to encourage endless mutation, and they established a program for automatic genetic manipulation to fashion ever newer and more deadly viruses."

"I DON'T GIVE A DAMN," Kaj Nevis said. "HAVE YOU STOPPED THE OTHERS? CAN YOU KILL THEM? I WARN YOU, DO IT NOW OR YOU'RE DEAD."

"I am dead anyway, Kaj Nevis," Anittas said, "I've

told you that. The plagues. They left a secondary defense in place. Should the ship be breached once again, the *Ark* was programmed to wake itself, to fill the corridors with atmosphere, oh yes, but an atmosphere tainted by a dozen different disease vectors. The plague tanks have been churning and boiling for a thousand standard years, Kaj Nevis, mutating again and again. There is no name for what I have contracted. Some kind of spore, I think. There are antigens, medicines, vaccines—the *Ark* has been manufacturing those, as well—but it's too late for me, too late by far. I breathed it in, and it's eating my biohalf alive. My cyberhalf is inedible. I could have given us this ship, Kaj Nevis. Together we might have had the power of a god. Instead we die."

"*YOU* DIE," Nevis corrected. "AND THE SHIP IS MINE."

"I think not. I have kicked the idiot giant soundly, Kaj Nevis, and it is awake again. Still an idiot, oh yes, but awake, and ready for orders you have neither the knowledge nor the capacity to give. I am leading Jefri Lion straight here, and Rica Dawnstar is ascending toward central control even now. And more—"

"NO MORE," Nevis said curtly. The pincer crunched through metal and bone and took the cybertech's head clean off with a single swift snap. The head bounced off Anittas's chest, hit the floor, and rolled. Blood jetted from the neck, and a thick protruding cable gave a final futile hiss and threw off a blue-white spark before the body sagged against the computer console. Kaj Nevis drew back his arm and swung, smashing the console again and again, until it was a ruin and hundreds of shards of plastic and metal were scattered over the floor.

There was a high, thin whirring sound.

Kaj Nevis turned, faceplate glowing a bright bloody red, searching for the source.

On the floor, the head was looking at him. The eyes, the shiny silver eyes, tracked and focused. The mouth split into a wet grin. "And more, Kaj Nevis," the head said to him. "I have activated the final line of defense programmed by those last Imperials. The stasis field is down. The nightmares are waking up now. The guardians are about to come forth and destroy you."

"DAMN YOU!" Nevis shouted. He set a huge, flat foot atop the cybertech's head, and brought down all his weight. Steel and bone alike crunched under the impact, and Nevis worked his foot back and forth, back and forth, grinding away until there was nothing beneath his heel but a red-gray paste spotted by flakes of white and silver.

And then, at last, he had silence.

For a long ways, two kilometers or more, the six traces in the floor ran parallel, although only the silver was alive and glowing. The red broke away first, veering off to the right at a junction. The purple terminated a kilometer farther on, at a wide door that proved to be the entrance to a spotless automated kitchen-mess hall complex. Rica Dawnstar was tempted to pause and explore a bit more, but the silver trace was throbbing and the overhead lights were going out one by one, urging her onward, down the main way.

Finally she came to the end. The broad corridor she was following curved gradually to the left and met another corridor just as grand. Their terminus was a huge wheel from which a half dozen lesser hallways branched off like spokes. The ceiling was high above her. Looking up, Rica spotted at least three other levels, connected with catwalks, bridges, and great circling balconies. At the hub of the wheel was a single large shaft that ascended from floor to ceiling—an elevator, clearly.

The blue trace followed one spoke, the yellow a second, the green a third. The shining silver guideway led straight to the elevator doors. The doors opened at her approach. Rica drove her scooter right to the base of the shaft, stopped, dismounted, hesitated. The elevator beckoned. But it looked awfully enclosed in there.

She hesitated too long.

All the lights went out.

There was only the silver trace, a single thin line like

a finger, pointing straight ahead. And the elevator itself, its lights still blazing.

Rica Dawnstar frowned, drew her needler, and stepped
inside. "Up, please," she announced. The doors closed
and the elevator began to ascend.

Jefri Lion walked with a spring in his step, despite
the weight of the weapons he was carrying. He felt
even better since leaving Celise Waan behind; that
woman was nothing but a nuisance anyway, and he
doubted that she'd be of much use in a skirmish. He
had considered the possibility of stealth, and rejected
it. He was not afraid of Kaj Nevis and his battlesuit.
Oh, it was formidably armored, he had no doubt of
that, but after all, it was of alien manufacture, and Lion
was armed with the deadliest weaponry of the Earth
Imperials, the height of the technological and military
prowess of the Federal Empire of Old Earth as it had
been before the Collapse. He'd never even heard of the
Unquish, so what kind of armigers could they be? No
doubt some obscure Hrangan slave race. He would deal
with Nevis in short order if he found him, and with that
treacherous Rica Dawnstar, too—her and that stupid
needler. He'd like to see how a needler could possibly
stand up against a plasma cannon. Yes, he'd like to see
that.

Lion wondered what plans Nevis and his cohorts
were making for the *Ark*. Something illegal and immoral, no doubt. Well, it made no matter, because he
was going to take this ship—he, Jefri Lion, Associate
Scholar in Military History at the ShanDellor Center,
and one-time Second Tactical Analyst of the Third Wing
of Skaeglay's Volunteers. He was going to capture an
EEC seedship, perhaps with Tuf's help if he could find
him, but he would do it in any event. Afterwards, there
would be no selling of this treasure for crass personal
gain. No, he would take the ship all the way to Avalon,
to the great Academy of Human Knowledge, and turn it
over to them with the proviso that he remain in charge
of its study. It was a project that would last him the rest
of his life, and when it ended Jefri Lion, scholar and

warrior, would be spoken of in the same breath as Kleronomas himself, who had made the Academy what it was.

Lion strode down the center of the corridor with his head thrown back, following the orange trace, and as he walked he began to whistle a jaunty marching tune that he had learned in Skaeglay's Volunteers a good forty years ago. He whistled and walked, walked and whistled.

Until the trace died out.

Celise Waan sat on the deck for a long time, her arms crossed tightly against her breasts, her face set in a petulant frown. She sat until the sound of Lion's foot-steps had faded away entirely. She sat and brooded on all the insults and wrongs she had been forced to en-dure. They were all impossible, every one of them. She should have known better than to throw in her lot with such an unpromising and disrespectful crew. Anittas was more machine than man, Rica Dawnstar was an insolent little wretch, Kaj Nevis was no better than a common criminal, and Haviland Tuf was just unspeak-able. Even Jefri Lion, her colleague, had proved unreli-able in the end. The plague star was *her* discovery, and she had let them in on it, and what had it gotten her? Discomfort, rudeness, and finally abandonment. Well, Celise Waan didn't intend to stand for it anymore. She had decided not to share the ship with any of them. It was her find, and she would go back to Shandicity and claim it under the salvage laws of ShanDellor, as was her right, and if any of her wretched companions had any complaints, they would have to take her to litiga-tion. Meanwhile, she didn't intend to talk to any of them, not ever again.

Her rear was getting sore and her legs had begun to fall asleep. She had been sitting in one position for a long time. Her back ached, too, and she was hungry. She wondered if there was any place she could get a decent meal aboard this derelict. Perhaps there was. The computers seemed to be working, and the defense systems, and even the lights, so perhaps the commissary was functioning as well. She got up and decided to go see.

                          *   *   *

It was obvious to Haviland Tuf that something was happening.

The noise level in the great shaft was rising, slowly but appreciably. He could make out a low humming sound quite distinctly, and those gurgling sounds were more noticeable as well. And in the tyrannosaur vat, the suspension fluid seemed to be thinning and changing colors. The red swirls had faded or been sucked away, and the yellow liquid grew more transparent with every passing moment. Tuf watched a waldo unfold from one side of the vat. It appeared as though it was giving the reptile an injection, though Tuf had difficulty observing the details, since the lighting was poor.

Haviland Tuf decided on a strategic retreat. He backed away from the dinosaur vat, and began to walk down the shaft. After he had come only a short way, he came upon one of the computer stations and work areas he had observed. Tuf paused.

He had experienced little difficulty discerning the nature and purpose of this chamber he had chanced upon. The *Ark* had at its heart a vast cell library, containing tissue samples from literally millions of different kinds of plant and animal and viral lifeforms from an uncounted number of worlds, or so Jefri Lion had informed him. These samples were cloned, as the ship's tacticians and eco-engineers deemed appropriate, and so the *Ark* and its lost sister ships could send forth disease to decimate a world's population, insects to devastate its crops, fast-breeding armies of small animals to wreak havoc on the ecology and food chain, or even terrible alien predators to strike fear into the heart of the enemy. Yet everything began with the cloning.

Tuf had found the cloning room. The work areas included equipment obviously intended for complex microsurgery, and the vats were undoubtedly where the cell samples were tended and grown to maturity. Lion had told him about the chronowarp as well, that vanished secret of the Earth Imperials, a field that could literally warp the fabric of time itself, albeit only in a small area, and at vast cost in energy. That way the clones could be brought to maturity in hours, or held, unchanging and alive, for millennia.

Haviland Tuf considered the work area, the computer station, and Mushroom, whose small body he still carried.

Cloning began with a single cell.

The techniques were no doubt stored in the computer. Perhaps there was even an instruction program. "Indeed," Haviland Tuf announced to himself. It seemed quite logical. He was no cybertech, to be sure, but he was an intelligent man who had operated various types of computer systems for virtually his entire lifespan.

Haviland Tuf stepped up to the work station, deposited Mushroom gently beneath the hood of the microscreen, and turned on the computer console. He could make no sense of the commands at first, yet he persisted.

After a few minutes he was intent on his labors—so intent that he did not notice the loud gurgling sound behind him when the thin yellow fluid in the dinosaur vat began to drain away.

Kaj Nevis smashed his way out of the system substation looking for something to kill.

He was angry—angry at himself for being impatient and unthinking. Anittas could have been useful; Nevis just hadn't considered the possibility of contagion in the ship's air. The damn cybertech would have had to have been killed eventually, of course, but that would not have been difficult. And now everything was falling apart. Nevis felt secure in the battlesuit, but still uneasy. He didn't like hearing that Tuf and the others had somehow gotten aboard. Tuf knew more about this damn suit than he did, after all; maybe he knew its weaknesses.

Kaj Nevis had already pinpointed one of those weaknesses himself—his air supply was running low. A modern pressure suit, like the one Tuf was wearing, included an airpac. The bacteria infused in its filters turned carbon dioxide into oxygen as fast as a human being could turn oxygen into carbon dioxide, so there was never any danger of running out of air, unless the damn bugs went and died on you. But this battlesuit was primitive; it carried a large but finite supply of air in those four huge tanks on its back. And the gauge in his helmet, if he was reading it correctly, indicated that one of those tanks was nearly empty. That still left three, which ought to give him more than enough time to get rid of the rest of them, if only he could find them. Still, it made Nevis uneasy. He was surrounded by perfectly breathable air, to be sure, but he was damned if he was going to crack his helmet after what had happened to the cybertech. The organic part of Anittas's body had decayed faster than Nevis would have believed, and the black goop that had eaten up the cybertech inside was as loathsome a sight as Kaj had ever seen, in a life that had featured lots of loathsome sights. He'd sooner suffocate, Kaj Nevis had decided.

But there was no danger of that. If the damned *Ark* could be contaminated, it could be cleansed, too. He'd find the control room and figure out how to do it. Even one clean sector would be enough. Of course, Anittas had said that Rica Dawnstar was already at the control room, but that did not faze him. In fact, he was kind of looking forward to that reunion.

He chose a direction at random and set off, his armored steps pounding against the deck. So let them hear him—what did he care. He *liked* this suit.

Rica Dawnstar sprawled in the captain's chair and surveyed the readouts she had projected on the main telescreen. Well-padded, large, covered with comfortable old plastic, the chair felt like a throne. It made a good place to rest. The trouble was, you really couldn't do anything *but* rest from there. The bridge had obviously been designed so that the captain sat in his throne and gave orders, and the other officers—there were nine other work stations on the upper bridge, twelve more in the lower-level control pit—did all the actual programming and punching of buttons. Lacking the foresight to have come aboard with nine flunkies, Rica was forced to move back and forth across the bridge, from one station to another, to try and get the *Ark* up and running again.

It took her a while—it was tedious work—and when she entered commands from the wrong substation, nothing happened. But slowly, step by step, she was figuring it all out. At least she felt as though she was making progress.

And she was secure. That had been her first objective, locking that elevator so that nobody else could come up and surprise her. As long as she was here and they were down there, Rica Dawnstar held the trump card. Every sector of the ship had its own substation, and every specialized function, from defense to cloning to propulsion to data storage, had its own sub-nexus and command post, but from up here she could oversee all of them, and countermand any command that anybody else might try and enter. If she noticed. And if she could figure out how. That was the problem. She could only man one station at a time, and she could only get things done when she figured out the proper sequence of commands. She was doing it, yes, by trial and error, but that was a lengthy and cumbersome progress.

She slumped back in her padded throne and watched the readouts, feeling proud of herself on several counts. She had managed to elicit a shipwide status check, it seemed. The *Ark* had already given her a full damage report on those sectors and systems that had been inoperative for a thousand years, waiting for repairs beyond the ship's capacities. Now it was telling her what programming was presently engaged.

The bio-defense listing was especially impressive, in a frightening sort of way. It went on and on. Rica had never heard of three-quarters of the diseases that had been unleashed to greet them, but they sounded unpleasant in the extreme. Anittas was no doubt one with the great program beyond the universe by now. Obviously, her next objective should be to try and seal off the bridge from the rest of the ship, irradiate and disinfect and try to see if she could get some uncontaminated air in here. Otherwise her suit was going to start getting pretty gamey in a day or two.

Up on the telescreen, it read:

BIO-DEFENSE PHASE ONE(MICRO)
REPORT COMPLETE
BIO-DEFENSE PHASE TWO (MACRO)
REPORT COMMENCING

Rica frowned. Macro? What the hell did that mean? Big plagues?

STAND-BY BIO-WEAPONS AT READY: 47

the screen told her, and it followed that cryptic bit of information with a lengthy list of species numbers. It was a boring list. Rica slumped back in the captain's throne again. When the list ended, more messages rolled across the screen.

ALL CLONING PROCEDURES COMPLETE
MALFUNCTIONS IN VATS: 671, 3312, 3379
MALFUNCTIONS ABORTED
STASIS FIELDS TERMINATED
RELEASE CYCLE COMMENCING

Rica Dawnstar wasn't sure she liked the sound of that. Release cycle, she thought. What was it releasing? On the one hand, Kaj Nevis was still out there; if this second-phase defense could discomfort, distract, or dispose of him, that was all to her benefit. On the other hand, she already faced the task of getting rid of all these plagues. She didn't need any more problems. The reports began to flash by more quickly.

SPECIES # 22-743-88639-04090
HOMEWORLD: VILKAKIS
COMMON NAME: HOODED DRACULA

it said. Rica sat up straight. She'd heard of Vilkakis and its hooded draculas. Nasty things. Some kind of flying nocturnal bloodsucker, she seemed to recall. Dim-witted, but incredibly sensitive to sound, and insanely aggressive. The message flicked out. In its place appeared a single line.

INITIATING RELEASE

the screen told her. It held a moment and was replaced by a shorter line, a single word that flashed once, twice, three times, and then was gone:

RELEASED

Now, could a hooded dracula possibly have Kaj Nevis for lunch? Unlikely, Rica thought—not so long as he wore that stupid armored suit. "Great," she said aloud. She didn't have a battlesuit, which meant that the *Ark* was creating problems for her, not for Nevis.

SPECIES # 13-612-71425-88812
HOMEWORLD: ABBATOIR
COMMON NAME: HELLKITTENS

Rica had no idea what a hellkitten was, but she didn't especially want to find out. She had heard of Abbatoir, of course—a quaint little world that had eaten three different colonizing parties; its lifeforms were supposed to be uniformly unpleasant. Unpleasant enough to chew through Nevis's battlesuit, though? That seemed doubtful.

INITIATING RELEASE

How many things was the ship going to belch forth? Forty-some-odd, she recalled. "Terrific," she said dourly. Fill up the ship with forty-plus hungry monsters, any one of them sufficient to lunch on her mother's favorite daughter. No, this wouldn't do, not at all. Rica stood up and surveyed the bridge. So where did she have to go to put an end to this nonsense?

RELEASED

Rica vaulted over the captain's chair, strode briskly back to the area she'd pegged as the defense command station, and told it to cancel its current programming.

SPECIES # 76-102-95994-12965
HOMEWORLD: JAYDEN TWO
COMMON NAME: WALKING-WEB

Lights flashed in front of her, and the small telescreen on the console told her that the *Ark*'s external defense sphere was down. But up on the main screen, the parade went on.

INITIATING RELEASE

Rica uncorked a string of curses. Her fingers moved swiftly over the console, trying to tell the system that it wasn't the external defenses she wanted dropped, it was bio-defense phase two. The machine didn't seem to understand her.

RELEASED

Finally she got a response from the board. It told her she was at the wrong console. She scowled and glanced around. Of course. This was external defense, weapons systems. There had to be some kind of bio-control station, too.

SPECIES # 54-749-37377-84921
HOMEWORLD: PSC92, TSC749, UNNAMED
COMMON NAME: ROLLERAM

Rica moved to the next station.

INITIATING RELEASE

The system responded to her cancel demand with a baffled query. No active program on this subsystem.

RELEASED

Four, Rica thought sourly. "That's enough," she said loudly. She stepped over to the next station, punched in a cancel, moved on without waiting to see if there was an effect, paused at another console to enter another cancel, moved on.

SPECIES # 67-001-00342-10078
HOMEWORLD: EARTH (EXTINCT)
COMMON NAME: TYRANNOSAURUS REX

She ran now. Run, cancel, run, cancel, run, cancel.

INITIATING RELEASE

She made a circuit of the entire bridge, as quickly as she could. By the time she was done, she wasn't even certain which command, at which station, had done the trick. But up on the screen, the message read:

RELEASE CYCLE TERMINATED
BIO-WEAPONS ABORTED: 3
BIO-WEAPONS RELEASED: 5
STAND-BY BIO-WEAPONS AT READY: 39

BIO-DEFENSE PHASE TWO (MACRO)
REPORT COMPLETE

Rica Dawnstar stood with her hands on her hips, frowning. Five loose. That wasn't too bad. She thought she'd managed to catch it after four, but she must have been a split-second too late. Oh, well. What the hell was a tyrannosaurus rex, anyway?

At least there was no one out there but Nevis.

Without the trace to guide him, Jefri Lion had wasted no time getting lost in the maze of interconnected corridors. Finally, he had adopted a simple policy; choose the wider corridors over the narrower, turn right where the passages were of the same size, go down whenever possible. It seemed to work. In no time at all, he heard a noise.

He flattened himself against a wall, although the attempt at concealment was somewhat compromised by the ungainly bulk of the plasma cannon on his back. He listened. Yes, definitely, a noise. Up ahead of him. Footsteps. *Loud* footsteps, though at some distance, but coming his way—Kaj Nevis in his battlesuit.

Smiling to himself with satisfaction, Jefri Lion unslung the plasma cannon and began to erect its tripod.

The tyrannosaur roared.

It was, thought Haviland Tuf, a thoroughly frightening sound. He pressed his lips firmly together in annoyance and squirmed back another half-meter into his niche. He was decidedly uncomfortable. Tuf was a big man, and there was very little room down here. He sat with his legs jammed under each other awkwardly, his back bent over in a painful manner, and his head bumping against the work station above. Yet he was not ungrateful. It was a small niche, true, but it had given him a place to seek shelter. Fortunately, he had been deft enough to attain that shelter. He was fortunate, also, in that the work station, with its waldos and microscanner and computer terminal, rested upon a heavy, thick, metal table that extruded itself from floor and wall, and not simply a flimsy item of furniture to be easily brushed aside.

Nonetheless, Haviland Tuf was not entirely pleased with himself. He felt foolish; his dignity had been decisively compromised. No doubt his ability to concentrate on the task at hand was, in its own way, commendable. Still, that degree of concentration might be considered a liability when it allowed a seven-meter-tall carnivorous reptile to sneak up on one.

The tyrannosaur roared again. Tuf could feel the work station vibrate overhead. The dinosaur's massive head appeared about two meters in front of his face, as the beast leaned over, counterbalanced by its great tail, and tried to get in at him. Fortunately, its head was too large and the niche too small. The reptile pulled out and screamed its frustration; echoes rebounded all up and down the central cloning chamber. Its tail lashed around and smashed into the work station; the sheltering table shook to the impact, something shattered up above, and Tuf winced.

"Go away," he said as firmly as he could. He rested his hands atop his paunch and attempted to look stern.

The tyrannosaur paid him no heed.

"These vigorous efforts will avail you naught," Tuf pointed out. "You are too large and the table too sturdily built, as would be readily apparent to you had you a brain larger than a mushroom. Moreover, you are undoubtedly a clone produced from the genetic record contained within a fossil. Therefore, it might be argued that I have a superior claim to life, on the grounds that you are extinct and ought properly to remain so. Begone!"

The tyrannosaur's reply was a furious squirming lunge and a wet bellow that sprayed Tuf with fine droplets of dinosaur saliva. The tail came down once more.

When she first caught a flicker of movement out of the corner of her eye, Celise Waan squeaked in panic.

She backpedaled and whirled to face—to face what? There was nothing there. But she had been certain that she'd seen something, up near that open door. What, though? Nervously, she unholstered her dart-pistol. She'd abandoned the laser rifle quite a distance back. It was cumbersome and heavy, and the effort of lugging it around had tired her out. Besides, she doubted that she'd be able to hit anything with it. The pistol was much preferable, in her view. As Jefri Lion had explained it, it threw explosive plastic darts, so she would not actually have to score a *hit*, just come close.

Warily, she moved toward the open door. She paused to one side of it, raised her pistol high, thumbed off the safety, and then peered quickly into the room.

Nothing.

It was some kind of storage room, she saw, full of plastisealed equipment piled high on floater skids. She glanced around uneasily. Had she imagined it, then? No. As she was about to turn away, she saw it once more, a tiny darting shape that appeared on the periphery of her vision and vanished before she could quite get a clear look at it.

But this time she had seen where it had gone. She

hurried after it, feeling bolder now; it had, after all, been quite small.

She had it cornered, she saw when she rounded the looming equipment skid. But what was it? Celise Waan moved closer, gun at the ready.

It was a cat.

It stared at her steadily, its tail flicking back and forth. It was kind of a funny cat. Very small—a kitten, really. It was pale white, with vivid scarlet stripes, an oversized head, and astonishing lambent crimson eyes.

Another cat, thought Celise Waan. That was all she needed: another cat.

It hissed at her.

She drew back, a little startled. Tuf's cats hissed at her from time to time, especially the nasty black-and-white one, but not like *that*. That hiss was almost, well, reptilian. Chilling, somehow. And its tongue . . . it seemed to have a very long, very peculiar tongue.

It hissed again.

"Here, kitty," she called. "Here, kitty."

It stared at her, unblinking, cold, haughty. Then it drew itself back and spat at her. The spittle struck her square in the center of her faceplate. It was thick greenish stuff, and it obscured her vision for a moment until she wiped it away with the back of her arm.

Celise Waan decided that she'd had enough of cats. "Nice kitty," she said, "come here, kitty. I've got a present for you."

It hissed again, drew back to spit.

Celise Waan grunted and blew it to hell.

The plasma cannon would dispose of Kaj Nevis handsomely; on that score Jefri Lion had no doubt. The strength of the armor on that alien battlesuit was an unknown factor. If it was at all comparable to the armored suits worn by the Federal Empire's own assault squads during the Thousand Years War, it might be able to deflect laser fire, to withstand small explosions, to ignore sonic attacks, but a plasma cannon could melt through five meters of solid duralloy plate. One good plasma ball would instantly turn any kind of personal armor into slag, and Nevis would be incinerated before he even understood what had hit him.

The difficulty was the size of the plasma cannon. It was unfortunately cumbersome, and the so-called portable version, with its small energy-pac, took almost a full standard minute after each shot to generate another plasma ball in its force chamber. Jefri Lion was acutely and uncomfortably aware that, were he to miss Kaj Nevis, he would be unlikely to get a second shot. Moreover, even on its tripod, the plasma cannon was unwieldy, and it had been many years since he had been in the field, and even then, his strong suits had been his mind and his tactical sense, not his reflexes. After so many decades at the ShanDellor Center, he had no great confidence in his eye-hand coordination.

So Jefri Lion concocted a plan.

Fortunately, plasma cannons had often been employed for automated perimeter defense, and this one had the standard minimind and autofire sequence. Jefri Lion erected the tripod in the middle of a broad corridor, approximately twenty meters down from a major intersection. He programmed in an extremely narrow field of fire, and calibrated the targetting cube with the utmost precision. Then he initiated the autofire sequence and stepped back with satisfaction. Inside the energy-pac he saw the plasma ball forming, burning brighter and brighter, and after a minute the ready light flashed on. Now the cannon was set, and its minimind was vastly quicker and more deadly accurate than Lion could ever hope to be firing manually. It was targeted on the center of the corridor intersection ahead, but it would fire only at objects whose dimensions exceeded certain preprogrammed limits.

So Jefri Lion could dash right through the cannon's target cube without fear, but Kaj Nevis, following in his absurdly huge battlesuit, would meet with a hot surprise. Now it only remained to lure Nevis into the appropriate position.

It was a stroke of tactical genius worthy of Napoleon or Chin Wu or Stephan Cobalt Northstar. Jefri Lion was infinitely pleased with himself.

The heavy footsteps had grown louder as Lion had worked with the plasma cannon, but in the last minute or so they had begun to fade; Nevis had obviously taken a wrong turn and would not be coming to the right position of his own accord. Very well then, Jefri Lion thought; he would bring him there.

He walked to the precise center of the fire zone with complete confidence in his own abilities, paused there briefly, smiled, and set off down the cross-corridor to attract the attention of his unwary prey.

Up on the great curved telescreen, the *Ark* revolved in three-dimensional cross-section.

Rica Dawnstar, having abandoned the captain's throne for a less comfortable but more efficient post at one of the bridge work stations, studied the display, and the data flashing by underneath it, with some annoyance. It seemed she had a lot more company than she had thought.

The system displayed intruding lifeforms as vivid red pinpoints of light. There were six pinpoints. One of them was on the bridge. Since Rica was quite alone, obviously that was her. But five others? Even if Anittas was still alive, there should have been only two additional dots. It didn't add up.

Maybe the *Ark* hadn't been derelict after all—maybe there was still someone aboard. Except the system claimed to depict authorized *Ark* personnel as green dots, and there was no green to be seen.

Other scavengers? Highly unlikely.

It had to mean that Tuf, Lion, and Waan had somehow docked after all. That made the most sense. And, indeed, the system claimed there was an intruding lifeform in a ship up on the landing deck.

All right. That added up. Six red dots equalled her and Nevis and Anittas (how had he lived through the damned plagues? the system insisted it was showing only *living* organisms) plus Tuf and Waan and Lion. One of the others was still up in the *Cornucopia*, and the rest . . .

It was simple to pick out Kaj Nevis. The system

showed power sources as well, as tiny yellow starbursts, and only one of the red pinpoints was surrounded by a tiny yellow starburst. That had to be Nevis in his battlesuit.

But what was that second yellow dot flashing so brightly by itself in an empty corridor on deck six? A hellacious power source, but what? Rica didn't understand. There had been a second red dot quite near to it, but it had moved away, and now seemed to be trailing Nevis, edging steadily closer.

Meanwhile, there were the black dots: the *Ark's* bio-weapons. The huge central axis that cored the asymmetric, tapered cylinder of the ship was positively livid with black pinpricks, but at least those were stationary. Other black dots, which had to be the beasties that had been released, were moving through the corridors. Only there were more than five. There was one clump of them—thirty or more discrete organisms, moving en masse like a shapeless black blotch upon the screen, throwing off strays from time to time. One of the strays had come up near a red light and had suddenly been extinguished.

There was a red dot in that central core area, too.

Rica asked for a display of that sector, and the screen gave her a much tighter cross-section. The red light was very close to a moving black dot down there—some sort of confrontation. She studied the readouts below the graphic. That particular black dot was species #67-001-00342-10078, the tyrannosaurus rex. It was massive, no doubt of that.

She noticed, with some interest, that a red light and one of the wandering blacks were both closing in on Kaj Nevis. That ought to be interesting. It looked like she was missing the party; all hell was breaking loose down there.

And she was up here, safe and secure and in control. Rica Dawnstar smiled.

Kaj Nevis was lumbering down a corridor, growing angrier and angrier, when a sudden explosive blow took him squarely in the back of his head. Inside his helmet, the sound was horrible. The force of the explosion knocked him forward and toppled him. He went smashing to the floor face first, too slow to break his fall with his arms.

But the suit absorbed most of the impact, and Nevis was unharmed. Lying there he made a quick check of his gauges, and smiled wolfishly; the battlesuit was undamaged, unbreached. He rolled over and rose ponderously to his feet.

Twenty meters away, at a corridor intersection, stood a man in a green-and-gold pressure suit, armed as if he had just looted a military museum, and holding a pistol in one gloved hand. "We meet again, blackguard!" the figure called out over external speakers.

"SO WE DO, LION," Nevis replied. "HOW GOOD TO SEE YOU. COME HERE AND SHAKE HANDS." He snapped his pincers. The right one was still stained with the cybertech's blood; he hoped Jefri Lion had noticed. A pity his cutting laser was so short-range, but no matter. He would simply catch Lion, take away his toys, and then play with him a while—pull off his legs, perhaps, and breach his suit, and let the damned air do the rest.

Kaj Nevis lumbered forward.

Jefri Lion stood his ground, raised his dart pistol, aimed it carefully with both hands, fired.

The dart struck Nevis in the chest. There was a loud explosion, but this time he had braced for it. His ears hurt, but he hardly even staggered. Some of the intricate filigree on the armor was blackened, but that was the extent of the damage. "YOU LOSE, OLD MAN," Nevis said. "I LIKE THIS SUIT."

Jefri Lion was silent and methodical. He holstered his dart pistol, unslung a laser rifle and raised it to his shoulder, took aim, fired.

The beam glanced off Nevis's shoulder, struck a wall, and burned a small black hole.

"Reflective microcoating," Jefri Lion said. He put away the laser rifle.

Nevis had eaten up more than three-quarters of the distance between them with his long, powered strides.

Finally Jefri Lion seemed to realize his danger. He threw down the laser rifle, turned, and darted around a corner, out of sight.

Kaj Nevis lengthened his strides and followed.

Haviland Tuf was nothing if not patient.

He sat calmly, with his hands folded atop his bulging stomach and his head aching from the repeated blows the tyrannosaur had inflicted on the sheltering table. He did his best to ignore the hammering that dented the metal above and made him even more uncomfortable, the blood-curdling bestial roars, the excessive and melodramatic displays of carnivore appetite that occasionally prompted the tyrannosaur to bend over and snap its numerous large teeth futilely at Tuf in his shelter. Instead Tuf thought about sweet Rodelyian popberries in honey-butter, tried to recall which particular planet had the strongest and most pungent variety of ale, and devised an excellent new strategy with which to overwhelm Jefri Lion should they ever game again.

Ultimately, his plan bore fruit.

The raging reptile, bored and frustrated, went away.

Haviland Tuf waited until it grew quite still and silent outside. He twisted himself around awkwardly, and lay for a moment on his stomach while the pins and needles in his legs flared and faded and vanished. Then he squirmed forward and cautiously stuck his head out.

Dim green light. Low humming, and distant gurgling sounds. No motion anywhere.

He emerged carefully.

The dinosaur had struck what remained of Mushroom's poor body numerous times with its massive tail. The sight filled Haviland Tuf with a vast and bitter sorrow. The equipment at this particular work station was in a shambles.

Yet there were other work stations, and he needed but a single cell.

Haviland Tuf gathered up a tissue sample and walked ponderously down to the next work station. This time he made it a point to listen for the sound of dinosaur footsteps behind him.

Celise Waan was pleased. She had handled herself quite adroitly, no doubt of it. That nasty little cat-thing wouldn't be bothering her again. Her faceplate was a bit smeared where the cat-spit had struck, but otherwise she had come off splendidly from the encounter. She holstered her pistol deftly, and stalked back out into the corridor.

The smear on her faceplate bothered her a little. It was up near her eyes, and it obscured her vision. She wiped at it with the back of her hand, but that only seemed to spread the smeariness around. Water, that was what she needed. Very well then. She had been looking for food anyway, and where you found food you always found water.

She walked briskly down the corridor, turned a corner, and stopped dead.

Not a meter away, another of those damned cat-things stood staring at her insolently.

This time Celise Waan acted decisively. She went for her pistol. She had some trouble getting it out, however, and her first shot missed the disgusting creature entirely and blew the door off a nearby room. The explosion was loud and startling. The cat hissed, drew back, spit just like the first one had, and then ran.

Celise Waan caught the spittle up near her left shoulder this time. She tried to get off a second shot, but the smeary condition of her helmet's faceplate made it difficult to see where she was aiming.

"Stuff and nonsense," she said loudly in exasperation. It was getting harder and harder to see. The plastic in front of her eyes seemed to be getting cloudy. The edges of the faceplate were still clear, but when she looked straight ahead everything was vague and distorted. She really had to get the helmet cleaned off.

She moved in the direction she thought the cat-thing had taken, going slowly so as not to trip. She tried to listen. She heard a soft scrabbling sound, as if the creature was nearby, but she couldn't be sure.

The faceplate was getting worse and worse. It was like looking through milk-glass. Everything was white and cloudy. This wouldn't do, Celise Waan thought. This wouldn't do at all. How could she hunt down that hideous cat-creature if she was half-blind? For that matter, how could she find where she was going? There was no help for it; she would have to take off this stupid helmet.

But the thought gave her pause; she remembered Tuf and his dire warnings about sickness in the ship's air. Well, yes, but Tuf was such a ridiculous man! Had she seen any proof of what he said? No, none at all. She'd put out that big gray cat of his, and it certainly hadn't seemed to suffer any for the experience. Tuf had been carrying it around the last time she'd seen him. Of course, he had done that big song and dance about incubation periods, but he was probably just trying to frighten her. He seemed to enjoy outraging her sensibilities, the way he had with his revolting catfood trick. No doubt he would find it perversely amusing if he frightened her into remaining in this tight, uncomfortable, smelly suit for weeks.

It occurred to her suddenly that Tuf was probably responsible for these cat-things that were harassing her. The very idea made Celise Waan furious. The man was a barbarous wretch!

She could hardly see a thing now. The milky center of her faceplate had grown almost opaque.

Resolute and angry, Celise Waan unsealed her helmet, took it off, and threw it down the corridor as far as she could.

She took a deep breath. The ship's air was slightly cold, with a faint astringency to it, but it was less musty than the recycled air from the suit's airpac. Why, it tasted good! She smiled. Nothing wrong with this air. She looked forward to finding Tuf and giving him a tongue-lashing.

Then she happened to glance down. She gasped.

Her glove . . . the back of her left hand, the hand she'd used to wipe away the cat-spit, why, a big hole had appeared in the center of the gold fabric, and even the metal weave beneath looked, well, *corroded*.

That cat! That damned cat! Why, if that spit had

actually struck her bare skin, it would have . . . it could have . . . she remembered all of a sudden that she was no longer wearing a helmet.

Down the corridor, the cat-thing suddenly popped out of an open room.

Celise Waan shrieked at it, whipped up her pistol, and fired three times in rapid succession. But it was too fast. It ran away and vanished down around a corner.

She wouldn't feel safe until the pestilential thing was disposed of for good, she decided. If she let it get away, it might pounce on her at any unguarded moment, the way Tuf's obnoxious black-and-white pet was so wont to do. Celise Waan opened her pistol, fed in a fresh clip of explosive darts, and moved off warily in pursuit.

Jefri Lion's heart was pounding as it had not pounded in years; his legs ached and his breath was coming in hard, short little gasps. Adrenalin surged through his system. He pushed himself harder and harder. Just a little farther now, down this corridor and around the corner, and then maybe twenty meters on to the next intersection.

The deck underfoot shook every time Kaj Nevis landed on one of his heavy, armored saucer-feet, and once or twice Jefri Lion almost lost his footing, but the danger only seemed to add spice. He was running like he'd run as a youth, and even Nevis's huge augmented strides were not enough to catch him, though he could feel the other closing on him.

He had pulled out a light-grenade as he ran. When he heard one of Nevis's damnable pincers snap within a meter of the back of his head, Jefri Lion armed it and flipped it over his shoulder and pushed himself even harder, darting around the last corner.

He whirled as he made the turn, just in time to see a sudden soundless flash of blue-white brilliance blossom in the corridor he had evacuated. Even the reflected light that blazed off the walls left Jefri Lion momentarily dazzled. He backpedaled, watching the intersection. Seen directly, the light-grenade ought to have burned out Nevis's retinas, and the radiation ought to be enough to kill him within seconds.

The only sign of Nevis was a huge, utterly black shadow that loomed across the intersection.

Jefri Lion retreated, running backwards now, panting.

Kaj Nevis stepped out slowly into the intersection. His faceplate was so dark it looked almost black, but as Lion watched, the red glow returned, burning brighter and brighter. "DAMN YOU AND ALL YOUR STUPID TOYS," Nevis boomed.

Well, it didn't matter, thought Jefri Lion. The plasma cannon would do the job, there was no doubt of that, and he was only ten meters or so from the fire zone. "Are you giving up, Nevis?" he taunted, trotting backwards easily. "Is the old soldier too fast for you?"

But Kaj Nevis didn't move.

For a moment, Jefri Lion was baffled. Had the radiation gotten to him after all, even through the suit? No, that couldn't be it. Surely Nevis wouldn't give up the chase now, not after Lion had lured him so heartbreakingly close to the fire zone and his plasma-ball surprise.

Nevis laughed.

He was looking up over Lion's head.

Jefri Lion looked up, too, just in time to see something detach itself from the ceiling and come flapping down at him. It was all a sooty black, and it rode on wide dark batwings, and he had a brief vision of slitted yellow eyes with thin red pupils. Then the darkness folded over him like a cape, and leathery, wet flesh closed about him to muffle his sudden, startled scream.

It was all very interesting, Rica Dawnstar thought.

Once you mastered the system, once you got the commands down, you could find out all sorts of things. Like, for example, the approximate mass and body configuration of each of those little lights moving up on the screen. The computer would even work up a three-dimensional simulation for you, if you asked it nicely. Rica asked it nicely.

Now everything was falling into place.

Anittas was gone after all. The sixth intruder, back on the *Cornucopia*, was only one of Tuf's cats.

Kaj Nevis and his supersuit were chasing Jefri Lion

around the ship. Except one of the black dots, the hooded dracula, had just gotten hold of Lion.

The red dot that was Celise Waan had stopped moving, although it hadn't winked out. The creeping black mass was coming toward her.

Haviland Tuf was alone in the central axis, putting something in a cloning vat and trying to ask the system to activate the chronowarp. Rica let the command go through.

All of the other bio-weapons were out in the corridors.

Rica decided to let things sort themselves out a little more down there before she took a hand.

Meanwhile, she'd rummaged up the program to cleanse the interior of the ship of plague. First she'd have to close all the emergency locks, seal off each sector individually. Then the process could begin. Atmosphere evacuation, filtration, irradiation, with massive redundancy built in for safety, and when the replacement atmosphere flowed back, it was infused with all the proper antigens. Complex and time-consuming—but effective.

And Rica was in no special hurry.

Her legs had collapsed first.

Celise Waan lay in the center of the corridor where she had fallen, her throat constricted with terror. It had all happened so suddenly. One moment she was rushing headlong down the hall in pursuit of the cat-thing. And then a wave of dizziness had swept over her, and suddenly she felt too weak to go on. She had decided to rest for a moment, had squatted down to catch her breath. But it didn't help. She only felt worse and worse, and when she tried to get up, her legs had buckled under her and she'd pitched forward onto her face.

After that her legs refused to move. Now she couldn't even feel them. She couldn't feel anything below her waist, in fact, and the paralysis was creeping up her body slowly. She could still move her arms, but it hurt when she did, and her motions were leaden and clumsy.

Her cheek was pressed against the hardness of the

deck. She tried to raise her head, and failed. Her whole upper body shook with a sudden stabbing pain.

Two meters away, a cat-thing peered out from around a corner. It stood staring at her, its eyes huge and scary. Its mouth opened in a hiss.

Celise Waan tried to stifle a scream.

Her pistol was still in her hand. Slowly, jerkily, she dragged it forward to her face. Every motion was agony. She lined it up as best she could, squinting along the top of it, and fired.

The dart actually hit.

She was showered with pieces of cat-thing. One piece, raw and wet and disgusting, landed on her bare cheek.

It made her feel a little better. At least she'd killed the creature that had tormented her. At least she was safe from that. She was still sick and helpless, though. Maybe she should rest. A little nap, yes, she'd feel better after a little nap.

Another cat-thing bounded out into the corridor.

Celise Waan groaned, tried to move, gave up the effort. Her arms were growing heavier and heavier.

A second cat followed the first. Celise pushed her dart-gun to her cheek again, tried to aim. She was distracted when a third cat appeared. The dart went wide, exploded harmlessly way off down the corridor.

One of the cats spit at her. It struck her between the eyes.

The agony was unbelievable. If she could have moved, she would have torn her eyes from their sockets, rolled on the ground, pulled at her skin. But she couldn't move. She screamed.

Her vision distorted into a hideous blur of color and then was gone.

She heard . . . feet. Small, light, padding footsteps. Cat steps.

How many were there?

Celise felt a weight on her back. And then another, and another. Something nudged against her useless right leg; she could dimly sense it shifting.

There was a spitting sound, and agony flared on her cheek.

They were all around her, on top of her, crawling over her. She could feel the stiffness of their fur brushing against her hand. Something bit into the flesh of her neck. She screamed. The biting continued. It took hold, pulling, worrying at her with small sharp teeth.

Another one nipped at a finger. Somehow the pain gave her strength. She flailed at it, pulled back her hand. When she moved, there was a cacophony of hissing all around her as the cat-things protested. She felt them biting her face, her throat, her eyes. Something was trying to squirm down into her suit.

Her hand moved slowly, awkwardly. She brushed aside cat-things, was bitten, persisted. She fumbled at her belt, and at last she felt it, round and hard within her grip. She pulled it loose, brought it up toward her face, held it oh so tight.

Where was the stud that armed it? Her thumb searched. *There.* She twisted it a half-turn, pressed it in as Lion had told her to.

Five, she recited silently, four three two one.

In her last moment, Celise Waan saw the light.

Kaj Nevis had himself a good loud laugh as he watched the show.

He didn't know what the hell the damned thing was, but it was more than enough for Jefri Lion. Its wings folded over him when it hit, and for a few minutes he screamed and struggled, rolling around on the floor with the thing enveloping his head and shoulders. He looked like a man fighting an umbrella. It was downright comic.

After a while, Lion lay still, his legs kicking feebly. The screaming stopped. A sucking sound filled the corridor.

Nevis was amused and pleased, but he figured it was best not to leave any loose ends. The thing was intent on its feeding. Nevis walked up as quietly as he could manage, which wasn't very quietly, and grabbed it. It made a liquid popping sound when he pulled it off of what was left of Jefri Lion.

Damn, Nevis thought, it did one hell of a job. The

whole front of Lion's helmet was staved in. The thing had a kind of bony sucker-beak, and it had punched right through Lion's faceplate and sucked off most of his face. Ugly. The flesh looked almost liquefied, and there was bone showing through.

The monster was flapping madly in his grip, and making a high, hideous noise, half shriek and half whine. Kaj Nevis held it at arm's length and let it flap while he studied it. It struck at his arm, again and again, to no effect. He liked those eyes; real mean, scary eyes. This thing could be handy, he thought. He pictured what it would be like to dump a couple hundred of these down into Shandicity some night. Oh, they'd meet his price. They'd give him any damn thing he asked for—money, women, power, the whole damn world if that was what he wanted. It was going to be fun owning this ship.

In the meantime, though, this particular creature might be a nuisance.

Kaj Nevis took hold of a wing with each hand, and ripped it in half. Then, smiling, he went back the way he had come.

Haviland Tuf checked the instrumentation again, adjusted the fluid flow slightly. Satisfied, he folded his hands atop his stomach and took up his position by the vat. Within, opaque red-black liquid swirled and churned. Tuf felt a certain sense of vertigo watching it; that was a side-effect of the chronowarp, he knew. In that tiny tank, so small he could almost encompass it with his two large hands, vast primal energies were at play, and time itself was hurrying at his command. It filled him with a singular sense of awe and reverence.

The nutrient bath was thinning gradually, becoming almost translucent. Within, Tuf fancied that he could almost see a dark shape taking form, growing, growing visibly, ontogeny taking place before his eyes. Four paws, yes, he could see them. And a tail. That was most definitely a tail, Tuf decided.

He moved back to the instrumentation. It would not do for his creation to be vulnerable to the contagions that had killed Mushroom. He recalled the inoculation the tyrannosaur had received shortly before its unexpected and inconvenient release. No doubt there was a way to administer the appropriate antigens and prophylactics before completing the birth process. Haviland Tuf commenced to do just that.

The *Ark* was almost clean. Rica had sealed the barriers throughout three-quarters of the ship, and the sterilization program was proceeding with its own inexorable, automated logic. The landing deck, engineering, drive room, control tower, bridge, and nine other sectors showed a clean pale blue now on the telescreen status display. Only the great central axis and the main corridors and laboratory areas in close proximity to it were still shaded with that corrosive reddish hue that signified an atmosphere laced through with disease and death in all those myriad forms.

That was the way Rica Dawnstar wanted it. In those interconnected central sectors, another kind of process was working itself out with similar remorseless logic. And the final equation, she had no doubt, would leave her in sole and complete control of the seedship and all its knowledge, power, and wealth.

Now that her environment was clean and safe, Rica had gratefully removed her helmet. She had ordered up some food as well—a thick white slab of protein from some creature called a meatbeast that *Ark* had held in a succulent stasis for a millennium, which she washed down with a tall chilled glass of sweetwater that tasted slightly of Milidian honey. She enjoyed the snack as she watched the reports flow by.

Things had simplified themselves considerably down there. Jefri Lion was gone. A pity, in a way; he'd been harmless enough, although unbelievably naive. Celise Waan was out of it too, and, surprisingly, she'd managed to take the hellkittens out with her. Kaj Nevis had disposed of the hooded dracula.

Nobody left but Nevis and Tuf . . . and her.

Rica grinned.

Tuf was no problem. He was busy making a cat. He could be taken care of easily, one way or the other. No, the only real obstacle now standing between Rica and the prize was Kaj Nevis and the Unquin battlesuit. Kaj was probably feeling real confident by this point. Good. Let him, she thought.

Rica Dawnstar finished her meal and licked the ends of her fingers. It was time for her zoology lesson, she figured. She called up reports on the three bio-weapons still out roaming the ship. If none of them would do, what the hey, she still had thirty-nine more in stasis just waiting for release. She could pick and choose her executioner.

A battlesuit? What she had was better than a hundred battlesuits.

When she had finished reading the zoological profiles, Rica Dawnstar was smiling broadly.

Forget the reserves. The only problem was making the right introductions. She checked out the geography up on the telescreen, and tried to consider just how devious a mind old Kaj Nevis had.

Not nearly devious enough, Rica suspected.

The damned corridors went on and on and never seemed to lead anywhere but to other corridors. His gauges showed that he had already begun drawing air from his third tank. Kaj Nevis knew he had to find the others quickly and get them out of the way so he could settle down to the problem of figuring out how this damned ship worked.

He was striding down one especially long, wide corridor when suddenly a kind of plastic stripe inset into the deck lit up under his feet.

Nevis paused, frowning.

The trace gleamed suggestively. It led straight ahead, and turned to the right at the next intersection.

Nevis took a single step. The section of the trace behind him winked out.

He was being pointed somewhere. Anittas had muttered something about leading people around the ship just before he'd had his little haircut. This was how he did it, then. Could the cybertech still be alive somehow, haunting the *Ark*'s computer? Nevis doubted it.

Anittas had seemed pretty damned dead to him, and he had a lot of experience with making people dead. Who was this then? Dawnstar, of course. Had to be. The cybertech said he'd led her to the control room.

So where was she trying to lead him?

Kaj Nevis thought about it for an instant. In his suit, he felt nigh-on invulnerable. But why take chances? Besides, Dawnstar was a treacherous little bitch. She might very well just lead him around and around forever, until his air ran out.

He turned resolutely and stalked off, moving in the opposite direction from the seductive silver guideline.

At the next turn, a green trace blazed to life, pointing to his left.

Kaj Nevis turned right.

The passage dead-ended in twin spiral escalators. When Nevis paused, one of them began to corkscrew up. He grimaced and walked down the unmoving one.

He descended three decks. At the bottom, the passageway was narrow and dark, and led off in two directions. Before Nevis could make a choice, there was a metallic scraping sound, and a sliding panel came out of a wall and closed off the right-hand corridor.

The bitch was still at it, he thought furiously. He looked down to the left. The corridor seemed to widen somewhat as it went, but it also got darker, and here and there it was broken by the hulks of old machinery. Nevis didn't like the looks of it.

If Dawnstar thought she could herd him along into a trap by closing a few doors, she had another thought coming. Nevis turned back to the sealed right-hand passage, drew back his foot, and kicked. The noise was deafening. He kicked again, and again, and then began to use his armored fists. He brought all the augmented exoskeletal strength of the battlesuit to bear.

Grinning, he stepped over what remained of the sliding panel into the dim, narrow passage that Dawnstar had tried to forbid to him. Underneath his feet was bare metal; the walls almost brushed his shoulders. It was an accessway of some sort, Nevis figured, but maybe it led to someplace important. Hell, it had to lead to someplace important. Why else had Dawnstar tried to keep him out of it?

His saucer-feet rang on the floorplates. He walked. It grew darker, but Kaj Nevis was determined. At one point, the passage made a sharp right-hand bend, almost too narrow for him to get through in the battlesuit. He had to squeeze past that point with his arms retracted and his legs half-bent.

Around the turn, a small square of light appeared up ahead. Nevis moved toward it. Then, abruptly, he stopped. What was that?

There was a black blob of some sort, floating in the air ahead of him.

Kaj Nevis advanced cautiously.

The dark blob was small and round, barely the size of a man's fist. Nevis kept about a meter's distance from it, and studied it. Another creature—as damned ugly as the one that had dined on Jefri Lion, too, but weirder. It was brown and lumpy, and its hide looked like it was made of rocks. It looked almost like it *was* a rock, in fact; Nevis only knew it was alive because it had a mouth—a wet black hole in the rocky skin. Inside, the mouth was all moist and green and moving, and he could make out teeth, or what looked like teeth, except they looked metallic. He thought he saw a triple set of them, half-concealed by rubbery green flesh that pulsed slowly, steadily.

The weirdest thing was how incredibly still it was. At first, Nevis thought it was hovering in the air somehow. But then he came a little closer and saw that he'd been wrong. It was suspended in the center of an incredibly fine web, the strands so very thin they were all but invisible. In fact, the ends of them *were* invisible. Nevis could make out the thickest parts near the nexus where the creature sat pulsing, but the webbing seemed to get thinner and thinner as it spread, and you couldn't see where it attached to wall or floor or ceiling at all, no matter how hard you looked.

A spider, then. A weird one. The rocky appearance made him think it was some kind of silicon-based life. He'd heard of that, here and there. It was real goddamned rare. So he had some kind of silicon-spider here. Big deal.

Kaj Nevis moved closer. Damn, he thought. The web, or what he thought was the web . . . hell, the damned thing wasn't sitting on the web, it was *part* of the web. Those fine, thin, shiny web strands grew out of its body, he saw. He could barely make out the joinings. And there were more than he thought— *hundreds* of them, maybe thousands, most of them too thin to be seen from any kind of distance at all, but when you looked at them from the right angle, you could see the light gleaming off them, all silvery-faint.

Nevis edged back a step, uneasy despite the security of his armored suit, for no good reason that he could name. Behind the silicon-spider, light shone from the end of the accessway. There had to be something important there; that had to be why Rica Dawnstar had tried so hard to keep him away.

That was it, he thought to himself with grim satisfaction. That was probably the damned *control room* back there, and Rica was inside cowering, and this stupid spider was her last line of defense. It gave him the creeps, but what the hell else could it do to him?

Kaj Nevis shifted to his pincer arms and brought up the right pincer to snip the web.

The gleaming, bloodstained, serrated metal blades closed on the nearest visible strand, smoothly and easily. Gleaming, bloodstained, serrated shards of Unquish metal clattered down onto the floor plates.

The whole web began to vibrate.

Kaj Nevis stared at his lower right arm. Half of the pincer had been sheared off. Bile rose in his throat. He took a step backwards, another, a third, putting distance between him and the *thing* back there.

A thousand web strands, thinner than threads, became a thousand legs. They left a thousand holes in the metal walls when they moved, and they scored the floor with their lightest touch.

Nevis ran. He stayed ahead until he came to the narrow place where the passage turned.

He was still lowering the suit's massive arms and

attempting to wedge himself through when the walking-web caught him. It bobbed as it moved toward him, suspended on countless invisible legs, its mouth pulsing. Nevis made terrified choking sounds. A thousand monomolecular silicon arms enveloped him.

Nevis brought up a huge powered hand to grab the head of the thing, to crush it to a pulp, but the arms were everywhere, waving, closing about him languidly. He pushed against them, and they cut through metal, flesh, bone. Blood came spurting from the stump of his wrist. He screamed, briefly.

Then the walking-web tightened its embrace.

A hairline crack appeared in the plastic of the empty vat. The kitten batted at it. The crack widened. Haviland Tuf reached in and caught up the kitten in one large hand, brought it close to his face. It was tiny, and a bit feeble yet: perhaps he had initiated birth too soon. He would be more careful on his next attempt, but this time the insecurity of his position and the need for constant vigilance lest wandering tyrannosaurs interrupt his work had resulted in a certain unseemly haste.

Nonetheless, he judged the trial a success. The kitten mewed. Haviland Tuf determined that it would be necessary to hand-feed it milk from a dropper, yet he had no doubt that he was equal to the task. The kitten's eyes were barely open, and its long gray fur was still wet from the fluids in which it had been so recently immersed. Had Mushroom ever truly been this small?

"I cannot name you Mushroom," he told his new companion solemnly. "Genetically you are one, it is true, yet Mushroom was Mushroom and you are you and I would not have you confused. I shall name you Chaos, a fitting companion to Havoc." The kitten moved in his palm and opened and closed one eye, as if it understood; but then, as Tuf knew, all cats have a touch of psi.

He looked about him. Nothing more remained to be done here. Perhaps it was time to search out his erstwhile and unworthy companions, and attempt to arrive at some sort of mutually beneficial accommodation. Cradling Chaos in his arm, he set off in search of them.

*   *   *

It was all over but the shouting, Rica Dawnstar decided when Nevis's red light vanished from the screen. Now it was down to her and Tuf, which meant that for all practical purposes, she was mistress of the *Ark*.

What the hell would she do with it, she wondered? Hard to say. Sell it to some arms consortium or the highest-bidding world? Doubtful. She didn't trust anyone with quite that much power. Power corrupts, after all. Maybe she should keep it, run it. She was corrupt enough already, she ought to be immune. But it would get awfully lonely living in this morgue alone. She could hire a crew, of course—bring aboard friends, lovers, flunkies. Only how could she trust them? Rica frowned. Well, it was a knotty problem, but she had a long, long time to get a handle on it. She'd think about it later.

Right now, she had a more immediate problem to consider. Tuf had just left the central cloning chamber and was wandering out into the corridors. What was she going to do about him?

She studied the display. The walking-web was still in its lair, snug and warm, probably still feeding. The rolleram, all four metric tons of it, was down in the main corridor of deck six, rolling back and forth like some kind of berserk living cannonball of enormous size, caroming off walls and searching in vain for something organic to roll over, crush, and digest.

The tyrannosaur was on the right level. What was it up to? Rica punched for more detail, and smiled. If her readouts could be believed, it was eating. Eating *what*? For a moment she drew a blank. Then it dawned on her. It had to be gulping down what remained of old Jefri Lion and the hooded dracula. The location seemed about right.

All things considered, it was pretty close to Tuf. Unfortunately, when it began to move again, it headed off in the wrong direction. Maybe she should arrange a meeting.

She couldn't underestimate Tuf, though. He had already escaped the reptile once; he might be able to do it again. And even if she maneuvered him onto the same level as the rolleram, the same problem presented itself. Tuf had a certain native cunning. She'd never be able to lead old Tuffy by the nose the way she had with Nevis. He was too subtle. She recalled the games they'd played aboard the *Cornucopia*. Tuf had won all of them.

Release a few more bio-weapons? Easily done.

Rica Dawnstar hesitated. Ah, hell, she thought, there was an easier way. It was time she took a hand directly.

Hooked over one arm of the captain's throne was a thin coronet of iridescent metal that Rica had earlier removed from a storage cabinet. She picked it up, ran it under a scanner briefly to check the circuitry, and slid it over her head at a rakish angle. Then she donned her helmet, sealed up her suit, and took out her needler. Once more into the breach.

Wandering about in the corridors of the *Ark*, Haviland Tuf found a vehicle of sorts—a small, open, three-wheeled cart. He had been standing for some time, and before that had been hiding underneath a table. He was only too glad to be seated. He drove along at a smooth, steady, comfortable speed, sitting back against the cushion and looking straight ahead. Chaos rode in his lap.

Tuf drove through several kilometers of corridor. He was a cautious and methodical driver. At every intersection he stopped, looked right, looked left, and weighed his choices before proceeding. He turned twice, as dictated partly by stern logic and partly by sheerest whim, but stayed for the most part to the widest corridors. Once he stopped and dismounted to explore a set of doors that seemed interesting. He saw nothing, encountered no one. Now and again, Chaos moved about in his lap.

Then Rica Dawnstar appeared up ahead of him.

Haviland Tuf stopped his cart in the center of a great intersection. He looked right, and blinked several times. He looked left. Then he stared straight ahead, hands folded on top of his stomach, and watched as she came toward him slowly.

She stopped about five meters away, down the corridor. "Out for a drive?" she asked. In her right hand she carried her familiar needler. In her left hand was a tangle of straps that trailed down onto the deck.

"Indeed," said Haviland Tuf. "I have been occupied for some time. Where are the others?"

"Dead," Rica Dawnstar said. "Deceased. Gone. Eliminated from the game. We're the end of it, Tuf."

"A familiar situation," Tuf said flatly.

"This is the last game, Tuf," Rica Dawnstar said. "No rematch. And this time I win."

Tuf stroked Chaos and said nothing.

"Tuf," she said amiably, "you're the innocent in all this. I've got nothing against you. Take your ship and go."

"If you refer to the *Cornucopia of Excellent Goods at Low Prices*," said Haviland Tuf, "might I remind you that it suffered grave damage which has not yet been repaired?"

"Take some other ship, then."

"I think not," Tuf said. "My claim to the *Ark* is perhaps inferior to that of Celise Waan, Jefri Lion, Kaj Nevis, and Anittas, yet you tell me that all of them are deceased, and my claim is surely as good as your own."

"Not quite," said Rica Dawnstar. She raised her needler. "This gives my claim the edge."

Haviland Tuf looked down at the kitten in his lap. "Let this be your first lesson in the hard ways of the universe," he said loudly. "What matters fairness, when one party has a gun and one does not? Brute violence rules everywhere, and intelligence and good intent are trampled upon." He stared back at Rica Dawnstar. "Madam," he said, "I acknowledge your advantage. Yet I must protest. The deceased members of our group admitted me to a full share in this venture before we came aboard the *Ark*. To my knowledge, you were never similarly included. Therefore I enjoy a legal advantage over you." He raised a single finger. "Furthermore, I would advance the proposition that ownership is conferred by use, and the ability to use. The *Ark* should, optimally, be under the command of the person who has demonstrated the talent, intellect, and will to make the most effective use of its myriad capabilities. I submit that I am that person."

Rica Dawnstar laughed. "Oh, really?"

"Indeed," said Haviland Tuf. He cupped Chaos in his hand, and lifted the kitten for Rica Dawnstar to see. "Behold my proof. I have explored this ship, and mastered the cloning secrets of the vanished Earth Imperials. It was an awesome and intoxicating experience, and one I am anxious to replicate. In fact, I have decided to give up the crass calling of the merchant, for the nobler profession of ecological engineer. I would hope you would not attempt to stand in my way. Rest assured, I will furnish you with transport back to ShanDellor and see to it personally that you receive every fraction of the fee promised to you by Jefri Lion and the others."

Rica Dawnstar shook her head in disbelief. "You're priceless, Tuffy," she said. She stepped forward, spinning her needler around her finger. "So you think you ought to get the ship because you can use it, and I can't?"

"You have outlined the very heart of it," Tuf said approvingly.

Rica laughed again. "Here, I don't need this," she said lightly. She tossed her needler at him.

Tuf reached up and snatched it out of the air. "It would seem that my claim has been unexpectedly and decisively strengthened. Now I may threaten to shoot you."

"But you won't," Rica said. "Rules, Tuf. You play the game by the rules. I'm the kid who likes to kick over the board." She slung the tangled straps she had been dragging over her shoulder. "You know what I've been up to while you've been cloning yourself a kitten?"

"Obviously I do not," said Haviland Tuf.

"Obviously," Rica echoed sardonically. "I've been up on the bridge, Tuf, playing the computer and learning just about everything I need to know about the EEC and its *Ark*."

Tuf blinked. "Indeed."

"There's a swell telescreen up there," she said. "Think

of it like a big gaming board, Tuf. I've been watching every move. The red pieces, that was you and the rest of them. Me, too. And the black pieces. The bio-weapons, as the system likes to call them. I like the sound of *monsters* better myself. Shorter. Less formal."

"Fraught with strong connotations, however," Tuf put in.

"Oh, certainly. But to the point. We got through the defense sphere, we even handled the plague defense, but Anittas got himself killed and decided to get a little revenge, so he kicked loose the monster defense. And I sat up on top and watched the red and the black chase each other. But something was missing, Tuf. Know what?"

"I suspect this to be a rhetorical question," Tuf said.

"Indeed," mocked Rica Dawnstar, with laughter. "The *greens* were missing, Tuf! The system was programmed to show intruders in red, its own bio-weapons in black, and authorized *Ark* personnel in green. There were no greens, of course. Only that got me thinking, Tuf. The monster defense was obviously a last resort fallback position, sure. But was it intended for use *only* when the ship was derelict, abandoned?"

Tuf folded his hands. "I think not. The existence of the telescreen display capacity implies the existence of someone to watch said display. Moreover, if the system was coded to display ship's personnel, intruders, and monstrous defenders simultaneously and in variant colors, then the possibility of all three groupings being aboard and active at the same time must have been considered."

"Yes," said Rica Dawnstar. "Now, the key question."

In the corridor behind her, Haviland Tuf glimpsed motion. "Excuse me," he began.

Rica waved him quiet. "If they were prepared to turn loose these caged horrors of theirs to repel boarders in an emergency, *how did they prevent their own people from getting killed?*"

"An interesting quandary," Tuf admitted. "I eagerly anticipate learning the answer to this puzzle. I fear I will have to defer that pleasure, however." He cleared his throat. "Far be it from me to interrupt such a fascinating discourse. I feel obliged to point out, however . . ." The deck shook.

"Yes," Rica said, grinning.

"I feel obliged to point out," Tuf repeated, "that a rather large carnivorous dinosaur has appeared in the corridor behind you, and is presently attempting to sneak up on us. He is not doing a very good job of it."

The tyrannosaur roared.

Rica Dawnstar was undisturbed. "Really?" she said laughing. "Surely you don't expect me to fall for the old there's-a-dinosaur-behind-you gambit. I expected better of you, Tuf."

"I protest! I am completely sincere." Tuf turned on the motor of his cart. "Witness the speed with which I have activated my vehicle, in order to flee the creature's approach. How can you doubt me, Rica Dawnstar? Surely you hear the beast's thunderous approach, the sound of its roaring?"

"What roaring is that?" Rica asked. "No, seriously, Tuf, I was telling you something. The answer. We forgot one little piece of the puzzle."

"Indeed," said Tuf. The tyrannosaur was moving toward them at an alarming velocity. It was in a foul temper, and its roaring made it difficult to hear Rica Dawnstar.

"The Ecological Engineering Corps were more than cloners, Tuf. They were military scientists. They were *genetic engineers* of the first order. They could recreate the lifeforms of hundreds of worlds and bring them alive in their vats, but that was not *all* they could do. They could also tinker with the DNA itself, *change* those lifeforms, redesign them to suit their own purposes!"

"Of course," Tuf said. "Pardon me, but now I fear I must run away from the dinosaur." The tyrannosaur was ten meters behind Rica. It paused. Its lashing tail struck the wall, and Tuf's cart shook to the impact. Slaver was dripping from its fangs, and its stunted forelegs clawed the air with unseemly eagerness.

"That would be very rude," Rica said. "You see, Tuf, that's the answer. These bio-weapons, these monsters— they were held in stasis for a thousand years, likely for longer than that. But they weren't ordinary monsters. They were cloned for a special purpose, to defend the ship against intruders, and they had been genetically manipulated to just that end." The tyrannosaur took one step, two, three, and now it was directly behind her, its shadow casting her in darkness.

"How manipulated?" asked Haviland Tuf.

"I thought you'd never ask," said Rica Dawnstar. The tyrannosaur leaned forward, roared, opened its massive jaws, engulfed her head. "Psionics," she said from between its teeth.

"Indeed," said Haviland Tuf.

"A simple psionic capacity," Rica announced from inside the tyrannosaur's jaws. She reached up and picked something from between its teeth, with a *tsk*ing sound. "Some of the monsters were close to mindless, all instinct. They got a basic instinctual aversion. The more complex monsters were made psionically submissive. The instruments of control were psi-boosters. Pretty little things, like crowns. I'm wearing one now. It doesn't confer psi powers or anything dramatic like that. It just makes some of the monsters avoid me, and other ones obey me." She ducked out of the dinosaur's mouth, and slapped the side of his jaw soundly. "Down, boy," she said.

The tyrannosaur roared, and lowered its head. Rica Dawnstar untangled her harness and saddle and began to strap it into place. "I've been controlling him all the time we've been talking," she said conversationally. "I called him here. He's *hungry*. He ate Lion, but Lion was small, and dead, too, and he hasn't had anything else for a thousand years."

Haviland Tuf looked at the needler in his hand. It seemed worse than useless. He was a poor shot in any case. "I would be most glad to clone him a stegosaurus."

"No thanks," Rica said as she tightened the harness, "you can't get out of the game now. You wanted to play, Tuffy, and I'm afraid you lose all around. You should have gone away when I offered you the chance. Let's review your claim, shall we? Lion and Nevis and the others offered you a full share, yes, but of what? I'm afraid now you get a full share, whether you want one or not—a share of everything they got. So much for your legal argument. As for your moral claim on the basis of superior utility," she slapped the dinosaur again, and grinned, "I think I've demonstrated that I can put the *Ark* to more effective use than you can. Down a little more." The beast leaned over still further, and Rica Dawnstar vaulted into the saddle on its neck. "Up!" she barked. It stood.

"Therefore we put legality and morality aside, and again return to violence," Tuf said.

"I'm afraid so," Rica said from on top of her tyrant lizard. It came forward slowly, as if she were feeling her way. "Don't say I didn't play fair, Tuf. I've got the dinosaur, but you've got my needler. Maybe you'll get a lucky hit. So we're both armed." She laughed. "Only I'm armed to the teeth."

Haviland Tuf stood and tossed back her needler, overhand. It was a good throw. Rica leaned out to one side, caught it. "What's this?" she said. "Giving up?"

"Your scruples about fairness have impressed me," said Tuf. "I would take no advantage. You have a claim, I have a claim. You have an animal." He stroked his kitten. "I have an animal, too. Now you have a gun." He activated his cart and backed away from the intersection, rolling quickly down the corridor behind him, or at least as quickly as he could go in reverse.

"Have it your way," Rica Dawnstar said. She was done playing. She felt a little sad. Tuf was turning his cart about to flee headlong instead of backwards. The tyrannosaur opened its mouth wide, and slaver ran from half-meter-long teeth. It screamed a scream that was pure red primal hunger a million years old, and came roaring down on him.

It roared down the corridor and into the intersection.

Twenty meters away along the cross-corridor, the minimind of the plasma cannon took cognizance of the fact that something exceeding the programmed target dimensions had entered the fire zone. There was the faintest of clicks.

Haviland Tuf was turned away from the glare; he put his body between Chaos and the heat and awful noise. It lasted only an instant, fortunately, although the smell of burnt reptile would linger in that spot for years, and sections of the deck and walls would need to be replaced.

"I had a gun, too," said Haviland Tuf to his kitten.

Later, much later, when the *Ark* was clean and he and Havoc and Chaos were settled comfortably into the captain's suite, and he had moved all his personal effects and taken care of all the bodies and done what repairs he could and figured out how to placate the incredibly noisy creature that lived down on deck six, Haviland Tuf began to search the ship methodically. On the second day, he found a store of clothing, but the men and women of the EEC had been shorter than he, and more slender, so none of the uniforms fit.

He did, however, find a hat he took rather a liking to. It was a green duckbilled cap, and it fit snugly atop his bald, milk-white head. On the front of it, in gold, was the theta that had been the sigil of the corps.

"Haviland Tuf," he said to himself in the mirror, "ecological engineer."

It had a certain ring to it, he thought.

2
LOAVES AND FISHES

Her name was Tolly Mune, but they called her all sorts of things.

Those entering her domain for the first time used her title with a certain amount of deference. She had been Portmaster for more than forty standard years, and Deputy Portmaster before that, a colorful fixture in the great orbital community that was officially known as the Port of S'uthlam. Downstairs, planetside, the office was only another box on the bureaucratic flowcharts, but up in orbit the Portmaster was foreman, chief executive, judge, mayor, arbiter, legislator, mastermech, and head cop all in one. So they called her the P.M.

The Port had started small and grown over the centuries, as S'uthlam's swelling population made the world an increasingly important market and a key link in the network of interstellar trade for the sector. At port center was the station itself, a hollow asteroid some sixteen kilometers in diameter, with its parks and shops and dormitories and warehouses and labs. Six predecessor stations, each larger than the last and each now outdated, the oldest built three centuries back and no bigger than a good-sized starship, clung to the Spiderhome like fat metal buds on a stone potato.

Spiderhome was what they called it now, because it sat at the center of the web, an intricate silver-metal net cast across the dark of space. Radiating from the station in all directions were sixteen great spurs. The newest was four kilometers long, and building; seven of the originals (the eighth had been destroyed in an explosion) stabbed twelve kays out into space. Inside the great tubes were the port's industrial zones—warehouses, factories, shipyards, customs gates, and embarkation centers, plus docking facilities and repair bays for every class of starship known in the sector. Long pneumatic tubetrains ran through the center of the spurs, moving cargo and passengers from gate to gate and to the crowded, noisy, bustling nexus in Spiderhome, and the elevator downstairs.

Other, lesser tubes branched from the spurs, and still lesser passages from them, crossing and recrossing the void, binding everything together in a pattern that grew in intricacy each year, as more and more additions were made.

And between the web strands were the flies—shuttles going up and down from the surface of S'uthlam with consignments too big or too volatile for the elevator, mining ships coming in with ore and ice from the Frags, food freighters from the terraformed farming asteroids inward they called the Larder, and all manner of interstellar traffic: luxurious Transcorp liners, traders from worlds as close as Vandeen or as distant as Caissa and Newholme, merchant fleets from Kimdiss, warships from Bastion and Citadel, even alien starcraft, Free Hruun and Raheemai and gethsoids and other, stranger species. They all came to the Port of S'uthlam and were welcome.

The ones who lived in Spiderhome, who worked in the bars and mess halls, moved the cargos, bought and sold, repaired and fueled the ships, they called themselves spinnerets as a badge of honor. To them, and to the flies who came calling often enough to be regulars, Tolly Mune was Ma Spider—irascible, foul-mouthed, rough-humored, frighteningly competent, omnipresent, indestructible, as big as a force of nature and twice as mean. Some of them, those who had crossed her or earned her displeasure, had no love for the Portmaster; to them she was the Steel Widow.

She was a big-boned, well-muscled, homely woman, as gaunt as any honest S'uthlamese but so tall (almost two meters) and so broad (those shoulders) that she had been considered something of a freak downstairs. Her face was as creased and comfortable as old leather. Her age was forty-three local, nearing ninety standard, but she didn't look an hour over sixty; she attributed that to a life in orbit. "Gravity's the thing that ages you," she would say. Except for a few starclass spas and hospitals and tourist hotels in the Spiderhome, and the big liners with their gravity grids, the Port turned in endless weightlessness, and free fall was Tolly Mune's natural element.

Her hair was silver and iron, bound up tightly when she worked, but off-duty it flowed behind her like a comet's tail, following her every motion. And she did move. That big, gaunt, raw-boned body of hers was firm and graceful; she swam through the spokes of the web and the corridors, halls, and parks of Spiderhome as fluidly as a fish through water, her long arms and thin, muscular legs pushing, touching, propelling her along. She never wore shoes; her feet were almost as clever as her hands.

Even out in naked space, where veteran spinnerets wore cumbersome suits and moved awkwardly along tether lines, Tolly Mune chose mobility and form-fitting skinthins. Skinthins gave only minimal protection against the hard radiation of S'ulstar, but Tolly took a perverse pride in the deep blue-black cast of her skin, and swallowed anti-carcinoma pills by the handful each morning rather than opt for slow, clumsy safety. Out in the bright hard black between the web strands, she was the master. She wore airjets at wrist and ankle, and no one was more expert in their use. She zipped freely from fly to fly, checking here, visiting there, attending all the meetings, supervising the work, welcoming important flies, hiring, firing, solving any problem that might arise.

Up in her web, Portmaster Tolly Mune, Ma Spider, the Steel Widow, was everything she had ever wanted to be, equal to every task, and more than satisfied with the cards she'd drawn.

Then came a night-cycle when she was buzzed from a sound sleep by her Deputy Portmaster. "It better be goddamned important," she said when she stared at him over her vidscreen.

"You better access Control," he said.

"Why?"

"Fly coming in," he said. "Big fly."

Tolly Mune scowled. "You wouldn't dare wake me up for nothing. Let's have it."

"A *real* big fly," he stressed. "You have to see this. It's the biggest damn fly I've ever laid eyes on. Ma, no fooling, this thing is thirty kays long."

"Puling hell," she said, in the last uncomplicated moment of her life, before she made the acquaintance of Haviland Tuf.

She swallowed a handful of bright blue anti-carcinogens, washed them down with a healthy squeeze from a bulb of beer, and studied the holo apparition that stood before her. "Large ship you've got there," she said casually. "What the hell is it?"

"The *Ark* is a biowar seedship of the Ecological Engineering Corps," replied Haviland Tuf.

"The EEC?" she said. "You don't say."

"Must I repeat myself, Portmaster Mune?"

"This is the Ecological Engineering Corps of the old Federal Empire, now?" she asked. "Based on Prometheus? Specialists in cloning, biowar—the ones who custom-tailored all kinds of ecological catastrophe?" She watched Tuf's face as she spoke. He dominated the center of her small, cramped, disorderly, and too-seldom-visited office in Spiderhome, his holographic projection standing among the drifting, weightless clutter like some huge white ghost. From time to time a balled up sheet of paper floated through him.

Tuf was big. Tolly Mune had met flies who liked to magnify themselves in holo, so they came across as bigger than they were. Maybe that was what this Haviland Tuf was doing. Somehow she thought not, though; he didn't seem the sort. Which meant he really did stand some two-and-a-half meters tall, a good half-meter above the tallest spinneret she'd ever met. And that one had been as much a freak as Tolly herself; S'uthlamese were a small people—a matter of nutrition and genetics.

Tuf's face gave absolutely nothing away. He interlocked his long fingers calmly on top of the swollen bulge of his stomach. "The very same," he replied. "Your historical erudition is to be commended."

"Why, thank you," she said amiably. "Correct me if I'm wrong, though, but being historically erudite and all, I seem to recall that the Federal Empire collapsed, oh, a thousand years ago. And the EEC vanished too—disbanded, recalled to Prometheus or Old Earth, destroyed in combat, gone from human space, whatever. Of course, the Prometheans still have a lot of the old biotech, it's said. We don't get many Prometheans way out here, so I couldn't say for sure. But they're a bit jealous about sharing any of their knowledge, I've heard. So, let me see if I've got this straight. You've got a thousand-year-old EEC seedship there, still functional, which you just happened to find one day, and you're the only person on board and the ship is yours?"

"Correct," said Haviland Tuf.

She grinned. "And I'm the Empress of the Crab Nebula."

Tuf's face remained expressionless. "I fear I have been connected to the wrong person then. I wished to speak to the Portmaster of S'uthlam."

She took another squeeze of beer. "I'm the puling Portmaster," she snapped. "Enough of this goddamned nonsense, Tuf. You're sitting out there in a thing that looks suspiciously like a warship and happens to be about thirty times the size of the largest so-called dreadnaught in our so-called Planetary Defense Flotilla, and you're making one hell of a lot of people extremely nervous. Half of the groundworms in the big hotels think you're an alien come to steal our air and eat our children, and the other half are certain that you're a special effect we've thoughtfully provided for their amusement. Hundreds of them are renting suits and vacuum sleds right now, and in a couple of hours they'll be crawling all over your hull. And my people don't know what the hell to make of you either. So come to the goddamned point, Tuf. What do you want?"

"I am disappointed," said Tuf. "I have hied myself here at great difficulty to consult the spinnerets and cybertechs of Port S'uthlam, whose expertise is far famed and whose reputation for honest, ethical dealing is second to none. I did not think to encounter unexpected truculence and unfounded suspicions. I require certain alterations and repairs, nothing more."

Tolly Mune was only half listening. She stared at the feet of the holographic projection, where a small, hairy, black-and-white thing had suddenly appeared. "Tuf," she said, her throat a little dry, "excuse me, but some kind of goddamned vermin is rubbing up against your leg." She sucked at her beer.

Haviland Tuf bent and scooped up the animal. "Cats may not properly be referred to as vermin, Portmaster Mune," he said. "Indeed, the feline is an implacable foe of most pests and parasites, and this is but one of the many fascinating and beneficial attributes of this admirable species. Are you aware that humanity once worshipped cats as gods? This is Havoc."

The cat began to make a deep rumbly noise as Tuf cradled it in the crook of one massive arm and began to apply long, regular strokes to its black-and-white hair.

"Oh," she said. "A . . . pet, is that the term? The only animals on S'uthlam are food stock, but we do get visitors who keep pets. Don't let your . . . cat, was it?"

"Indeed," said Tuf.

"Well, don't let it out of your ship. I remember once when I was Deputy P.M., we had the damnedest mess . . . some brain-damaged fly lost his puling pet at the same time this alien envoy was visiting, and our security crews mistook one for the other. You wouldn't believe how upset everyone got."

"People are often overexcitable," said Haviland Tuf.

"What kind of alterations and repairs were you talking about?"

Tuf responded with a ponderous shrug. "Some small things, no doubt most easily accomplished by experts as proficient as your own. As you have pointed out, the *Ark* is indeed a most ancient vessel, and the vicissitudes of war and centuries of neglect have left their marks. Entire decks and sectors are dark and dysfunctional, damaged beyond the ship's admittedly admirable capacities for self-repair. I wish to have these portions of the craft repaired and restored to full function.

"Additionally, the *Ark*, as you might know from your study of history, once carried a crew of two hundred. It is sufficiently automated so that I have been able to operate it by myself, but not without certain inconveniences, it must be admitted. The central command center, located on the tower bridge, is a wearisome daily commute from my living quarters, and I have found the bridge itself to be inefficiently designed for my purposes, requiring me to walk constantly from one work station to the next in order to perform the multitude of complex duties required to run the ship. Certain other functions require me to leave the bridge entirely and journey hither and yon about the immensity of the vessel. Still other tasks I have found impossible to accomplish, since they would seem to require my simultaneous presence in two or more locations kilometers apart on different decks. Near to my living quarters is a small, yet comfortable auxiliary communications room that appears to be fully functional. I would like your cybertechs to reprogram and redesign the command systems so that in future I will be able to accomplish anything that might need accomplishing from there, without the need of making the exhausting daily trek to the bridge—indeed, without the need of leaving my seat.

"Beyond these major tasks, I have in mind only a few further alterations. Some minor modernizations, perhaps. The addition of a kitchen with a full array of spices and flavorings, and a large recipe library, in order that I might dine on food somewhat more varied and interesting to the palate than the grimly nutritious military fare the *Ark* is now programmed to provide. A large stock of beers and wines and the mechanisms necessary to ferment my own in future, during lengthy deep-space voyagings. The augmentation of my existing entertainment facilities through the acquisition of some books, holoplays, and music chips dating from this last millennium. A few new security programs. Other trifling minor changes. I will provide you with a list."

Tolly Mune listened to him with astonishment. "Goddamn," she said when he had finished. "You really do have a derelict EEC seedship, don't you?"

"Indeed," said Haviland Tuf. A little stiffly, she thought.

She grinned. "My apologies. I'll scramble a crew of spinnerets and cybertechs, scream 'em right over to have a look, and we'll get you an estimate. Don't hold your goddamned breath, though. That big a ship, it'll take quite a while before they begin to sort things out. I'd better post some security, too, or you'll have all kinds of curiosity seekers tramping through your halls and stealing souvenirs." She looked his hologram up and down thoughtfully. "I'll need you to give my crew a briefing and point them in the right direction. After that, it'd be better if you got out from underfoot and let them run amuck. You can't bring that damned monstrosity into the web, it's too puling big. You got any way of getting out of there?"

"The *Ark* is equipped with a full complement of shuttlecraft, all operational," said Haviland Tuf, "but I have scant desire to leave the comforts of my quarters. Certainly my ship is large enough so that my presence will not seriously inconvenience your crews."

"Hell, you know that and I know that, but they work better if they don't think someone's looking over their shoulders," said Tolly Mune. "Besides, I'd think you'd want to get out of that can a bit. You've been shut up alone for how long?"

"Several standard months," Tuf admitted, "although I am not strictly alone. I have enjoyed the company of my cats, and have pleasantly occupied myself learning the capabilities of the *Ark* and expanding my knowledge of ecological engineering. Still, I will concede your point that perhaps a bit of recreation is in order. The opportunity to sample a new cuisine is always to be relished."

"Wait'll you try S'uthlamese beer! And the port has other diversions as well—exercise facilities, hotels, sports, drug dens, sensoria, sex parlors, live theater, gaming halls."

"I have some small skill at certain games," Tuf said.

"And then there's tourism," Tolly Mune said. "You can just take the tubetrain down the elevator to the surface, and all the districts of S'uthlam are yours to explore."

"Indeed," said Tuf. "You have intrigued me, Portmaster Mune. I fear I am of a curious temperament. It is my great weakness. Unfortunately, my funds preclude a lengthy stay."

"Don't worry about that," she replied, smiling. "We'll just put it on your repair bill, settle up afterwards. Now, just hop in your goddamned shuttle and bring yourself to, let's see . . . dock nine-eleven is vacant. See the Spiderhome first, then take the train downstairs. You ought to be a goddamned sensation. You're on the newsfeeds already, you know. The groundworms and flies will be crawling all over you."

"A decaying piece of meat might find this prospect appealing," said Haviland Tuf. "I do not."

"Well then," the Portmaster said, "go incognito."

The steward on the tubetrain wheeled out a tray of beverages shortly after Haviland Tuf had strapped himself in for the trip downstairs. Tuf had sampled S'uthlamese beer in the restaurants of Spiderhome, and found it thin, watery, and notably devoid of taste. "Perhaps your offerings include some malt products brewed offworld," he said. "If so, I would gladly purchase one."

"Certainly," the steward said. He reached into the cart and produced a squeeze bulb full of dark brown liquid, bearing a cursive logo Tuf recognized as Shan-Dellor script. A card plate was offered, and Tuf punched in his code number. The S'uthlamese currency was the calorie; the charge for the bulb amounted to almost four-and-a-half times the actual caloric content of the beer, however. "Import costs," the steward explained.

Tuf sucked his bulb with ponderous dignity as the

tubetrain fell down the elevator toward the surface of the planet below. It was not a comfortable ride. Haviland Tuf had found the cost of starclass accommodations prohibitively high, and had therefore settled for premiere class, the next best available, only to discover himself crammed into a seat seemingly designed for a S'uthlamese child, and a small S'uthlamese child at that, in a row of eight similar seats divided by a narrow central aisle.

Sheer chance had given him the aisle seat, fortunately; without such placement, Tuf entertained grave doubts about whether he could have made the voyage at all. But even here, it was impossible to move without brushing against the bare thin arm of the woman to his left, a contact that Tuf found distasteful in the extreme. When he sat in his accustomed manner, the crown of his head bumped against the ceiling, so he was forced to hunker down, and tolerate a most annoying tightness in his neck as a result. Farther back on the tubetrain, Tuf understood, were the first-, second-, and third-class accommodations. He resolved to avoid experiencing their dubious comforts at all costs.

When the descent commenced, the majority of the passengers pulled privacy hoods down over their heads, and punched up the personal diversion of their choice. The offerings, Haviland Tuf noted, included three different musical programs, a historical drama, two erotic fantasy loops, a business interface, something listed as a "geometric pavane," and direct stimulation to the pleasure center of the brain. Tuf considered investigating the geometric pavane, until discovering that the privacy hood was too small for his head, his skull being unduly large and long by S'uthlamese standards.

"You the big fly?" asked a voice from across the aisle.

Tuf looked over. The S'uthlamese were sitting in silent isolation, their heads enveloped by their dark eyeless helmets. Aside from the cluster of stewards far at the rear of the car, the only passenger still in the world of reality was the man in the aisle seat across from him one row back. Long, braided hair, copper-colored skin, and plump, fleshy cheeks branded the man as much an offworlder as Tuf himself. "The big fly, right?"

"I am Haviland Tuf, an ecological engineer."

"I knew you were a fly," the man said. "Me, too. I'm Ratch Norren, from Vandeen." He held out a hand.

Haviland Tuf looked at it. "I am familiar with the ancient ritual of shaking hands, sir. I have noted that you are carrying no weapons. It is my understanding that the custom was originally intended to establish this fact. I am unarmed as well. You may now withdraw your hand, if you please."

Ratch Norren grinned and pulled back his arm. "You're a funny duck," he said.

"Sir," said Haviland Tuf, "I am neither a funny duck nor a large fly. I would think this much obvious to any person of normal human intelligence. Perhaps standards are different on Vandeen."

Ratch Norren reached up and pinched his own cheek. It was a round, full, fleshy cheek, covered with red powder, and he gave it a good strong pinch. Tuf decided this was either a particularly perverse tic or a Vandeeni gesture the significance of which escaped him. "The fly stuff," the man said, "that's just spinneret talk. An idiom. They call all us offworlders flies."

"Indeed," said Tuf.

"You are the one who arrived in that giant warship, right? The one who was on all the newsfeeds?" Norren did not wait for an answer. "Why are you wearing the wig?"

"I am traveling incognito," said Haviland Tuf, "though it appears that you have penetrated my disguise, sir."

Norren pinched his cheek again. "Call me Ratch," he said. He looked Tuf up and down. "Pretty feeb disguise, though. Wig or no wig, you're still a big fat giant with a complexion like a mushroom."

"In future, I shall employ makeup," said Tuf. "Fortunately, none of the native S'uthlamese have displayed your perspicacity."

"They're just too polite to mention it. That's how it is on S'uthlam. There's so many of them, you know? Most of them can't afford any kind of real privacy, so they go in for a lot of pretend privacy. They won't take any notice of you in public unless you want to be noticed."

Haviland Tuf said, "The inhabitants of Port S'uthlam that I encountered did not seem unduly reticent, nor overburdened with elaborate etiquette."

"The spinnerets are different," Ratch Norren replied offhandedly. "Things are looser up there. Say, let me give you a little advice. Don't sell that ship of yours here, Tuf. Take it to Vandeen. We'll give you a lot better price for it."

"It is not my intention to sell the *Ark*," Tuf replied.

"No need to dickerdaddle with me," Norren said. "I don't have the authority to buy it anyhow. Or the standards. Wish I did." He laughed. "You just go to Vandeen and get in touch with our Board of Coordinators. You won't regret it." He glanced about, as if he were checking to see that the stewards were far away and the other passengers still dreaming behind their privacy helmets, and then dropped his voice to a conspiratorial whisper. "Besides, even if the price wasn't a factor, I hear that warship of yours has got nightmare-class power, right? You don't want to give the S'uthlamese power like that. No lying, I love 'em, I really do, come here regularly on business, and they're good people, when you get one or two of them alone, but there are so *many* of them, Tuffer, and they just breed and breed and breed, like goddamned rodents. You'll see. A couple centuries back, there was a big local war just on account of that. The suthies were planting colonies all over the damned place, grabbing every piece of real estate they could, and if anybody else happened to be living there, the suthies would just outbreed 'em. We finally put an end to it."

"We?" said Haviland Tuf.

"Vandeen, Skrymir, Henry's World, and Jazbo, officially, but we had help from a lot of neutrals, right? The peace treaty restricted the S'uthlamese to their own solar system. But you give them that hellship of yours, Tuf, and maybe they break free again."

"I had understood the S'uthlamese to be a singularly honorable and ethical people."

Ratch Norren pinched his cheek again. "Honorable, ethical, sure, sure. Great folks to cut deals with, and the swirls know some blistery erotic tricks. I tell you, I got a hundred suthie friends, and I love every one of 'em. But between them, my hundred friends must have maybe a thousand children. These people breed, that's the problem, Tuf, you listen to Ratch. They're all liferoos, right?"

"Indeed," said Haviland Tuf. "And what, might I inquire, is a liferoo?"

"Liferoos," Norren repeated impatiently. "Anti-entropists, kiddie-culters, helix-humpers, genepool puddlers. Religious fanatics, Tuffer, religious crazies." He might have said more, but the steward was wheeling the beverage cart back down the aisle just then. Norren sat back in his seat.

Haviland Tuf raised a long pale finger to check the steward's progress. "I will have another bulb, if you please," he said. He hunched over in silence for the remainder of the trip, sucking thoughtfully on his beer.

Tolly Mune floated in her cluttered apartment, drinking and thinking. One wall of the room was a huge vidscreen, six meters long and three meters high. Customarily, Tolly keyed it to display scenic panoramas; she liked the effect of having a window overlooking the high, cool mountains of Skrymir, or the dry canyons of Vandeen with their swift whitewater rivers, or the endless city lights of S'uthlam itself spreading across the night, with the shining silver tower that was the base of the elevator ascending up and up and up into the dark, moonless sky, soaring high above even starclass tower-homes four kays tall.

But tonight she had a starscape spread across her wall, and against it was outlined the grim metallic majesty of the immense starship called *Ark*. Even a screen as large as hers—one of the perks of her status as Portmaster—could not really convey the ship's sheer size.

And the things it represented—the hope, the threat—were immeasurably bigger than the *Ark* itself, Tolly Mune knew.

Off to her side, she heard the buzzing of her comm unit. The computer would not have disturbed her unless it was the call she had been waiting for. "I'll take it," she said. The stars blurred, the *Ark* dissolved, and the vidscreen ran with liquid colors for an instant before resolving itself into the face of First Councillor Josen Rael, majority leader of the Planetary High Council.

"Portmaster Mune," he said. At this merciless magnification, she could see all the tension in his long neck, the tightness around the thin lips, the hard glitter in his dark brown eyes. The top of his head, domed and balding, had been powdered, but was beginning to sweat nonetheless.

"Councillor Rael," she replied. "Good of you to call. You've gone over the reports?"

"Yes. Is this call shielded?"

"Certainly," she said. "Speak freely."

He sighed. Josen Rael had been a fixture in planetary politics for a decade now. He had first made the newsfeeds as councillor for war, later had climbed to councillor for agriculture, and for four standard years he had been the leader of the council's majority faction, the technocrats, and therefore the single most powerful man on S'uthlam. The power had made him look old and hard and tired, and this was the worst Tolly Mune had ever seen him. "You're certain of the data, then?" he said. "Your crews have made no mistake? This is too crucial for error, I don't have to tell you that. This is truly an EEC seedship?"

"Damn right," said Tolly Mune. "Damaged and in disrepair, yes, but the puling thing is still functional, more or less, and the cell library is intact. We've verified it."

Rael ran long, blunt fingers through his thinning white hair. "I should be jubilant, I suppose. When this is over, I will have to pretend to be jubilant for the newsfeeds. But right now, all I can think of are the dangers. We've had a council meeting. Closed. We can't risk too much getting out until the affair is settled. The council was largely in accord—technocrats, expan-

sionists, zeros, the church party, the fringe factions."
He laughed. "I've never seen such unanimity in all the
years I've served. Portmaster Mune, we must have that
ship."

Tolly Mune had known it was coming. She had not
been Portmaster this long without understanding the
politics of the society downstairs. S'uthlam had been
locked into endless crisis all her life. "I'll try to buy it
for you," she said. "This Haviland Tuf was a freelance
trader originally, before he stumbled on the *Ark*. My
crews found his old ship on the landing deck, in terrible
shape. Traders are greedy abortions, every one of them.
That should work for us."

"Offer him whatever it takes," said Josen Rael. "Do
you understand, Portmaster? You have unlimited budgetary authority."

"Understood," said Tolly Mune. But there was another question to be asked. "And if he won't sell?"

Josen Rael hesitated. "Difficult," he muttered. "He
must sell. A refusal would be tragic. Not for the man
himself, but for us, perhaps."

"If he won't sell?" Tolly Mune repeated. "I need to
know the alternatives."

"We must have the ship," Rael told her. "If this Tuf
proves unreasonable, he gives us no choice. The High
Council will exercise its right of eminent domain and
confiscate. The man will be compensated, of course."

"Damn. You're talking about seizing the ship by force."

"No," said Josen Rael. "Everything would be proper—
I've checked. In an emergency, for the good of the
greatest number, the rights of private property must be
set aside."

"Oh, hell and damn, that's puling rationalization,
Josen," said Mune. "You had more common sense when
you were up here. What have they done to you
downstairs?"

He grimaced, and for an instant, he looked a little
like the young man who had worked at her side for a
year, when she had been Deputy Portmaster and he
third assistant administrator for interstellar trade. Then
he shook his head, and the old, tired politician was

back. "I don't feel good about this, Ma," he said, "but what choice do we have? I've seen projections. Mass famine within twenty-seven years unless we have a breakthrough, and there's no breakthrough in sight. Before it comes to that, the expansionists will regain power and we'll have another war, perhaps. Either way, millions will die—billions, perhaps. Against that, what are the rights of this one man?"

"I won't argue that point, Josen, though there are those who would, you know that. But never mind. You want to be practical, I'll give you some goddamned practical things to think over. Even if we *buy* this ship from Tuf legally, there's going to be hell to pay with Vandeen and Skrymir and the rest of the allies, but I doubt that they'd try anything. If we grab it by force, though, that's a set of coordinates to a whole different place—a hard place, too. They can say piracy, maybe. They can define the *Ark* as a military craft—which it was, by the way, and a puling world-buster, too—and say we're in violation of the treaty and come after us again."

"I'll speak to their envoys personally," said Josen Rael wearily. "Assure them that as long as the technocrats are in power, the colonization program will not be resumed."

"And they'll take your puling word? Like goddamned horny hell they will. And will you assure them that the technocrats are *never* going to lose power, that they'll never have the expansionists to deal with again? How will you do that? Are you planning to use the *Ark* to establish a benevolent dictatorship?"

The councillor pressed his lips together tightly, and a flush crept up the back of his long, dark neck. "You know me better than that. Agreed, there are dangers. The ship is a formidable military resource, however. Let us not forget that. If the allies mobilize against us, we will hold the trump card."

"Nonsense," said Tolly Mune. "It has to be repaired and we have to master it. The technology involved has been lost for a thousand years. We'll be studying it for months, maybe years, before we can really use the goddamned thing. Only we won't get the chance. The Vandeeni armada will arrive within weeks to take it away from us, and the others won't be far behind them."

"None of this is your concern, Portmaster," said Josen Rael coldly. "The High Council has discussed the issue thoroughly."

"Don't try and pull rank on *me*, Josen. Remember the time you got drunk on narco-blasters and decided you'd go outside and see how fast urine crystallized in space? I was the one who talked you out of freezing off your hose, esteemed First Councillor. Clean out your puling ears and listen to me. Maybe war isn't my concern, but trade is. The port is our lifeline. We import thirty percent of our raw calories now—"

"Thirty-four percent," Rael corrected.

"Thirty-four percent," Tolly Mune agreed. "And that is going to go nowhere but up, we both know it. We pay for that food with our technological expertise—both manufactured goods and port profits. We service, repair, and build more starships than any other four worlds in the sector, and you know why? Because I've busted my puling buns to make sure we're the *best*. Tuf himself said it. He came here for repairs because we had a reputation—a reputation for being ethical, honest, and fair, as well as technically competent. What's going to happen to that reputation if we confiscate his puling ship? How many other traders are going to bring in *their* ships for repairs if we feel free to help ourselves to any we like? *What's going to happen to my goddamned port?*"

"It would certainly have an adverse effect," Josen Rael admitted.

Tolly Mune made a loud crude noise at him. "Our economy will be destroyed," she said bluntly.

Rael was sweating heavily now, trickles of moisture running down the broad, domed forehead. He mopped at the moisture with a pocket cloth. "Then you must see that it doesn't happen, Portmaster Mune. You must see that it doesn't come to that."

"How?"

"Buy the *Ark*," he said. "I delegate full authority to

you, since you seem to understand the situation so well. Make this Tuf person see reason. The responsibility is yours." He nodded, and the screen went black.

On S'uthlam, Haviland Tuf played the tourist.

It could not be denied that the world was impressive, in its way. During his years as a trader, hopping from star to star in the *Cornucopia of Excellent Goods at Low Prices*, Haviland Tuf had visited more worlds than he could easily remember, but he would be unlikely to forget S'uthlam any time soon.

He had seen a goodly number of breathtaking sights: the crystal towers of Avalon, the skywebs of Arachne, the churning seas of Old Poseidon and the black basalt mountains of Clegg. The city that was S'uthlam—the old names were only districts and neighborhoods now, the ancient cities having grown into one swollen megalopolis centuries ago—rivaled any of them.

Tuf had a certain fondness for tall buildings, and he gazed out upon the cityscape by both day and night, from observation platforms at one kilometer, two, five, nine. No matter how high he ascended, the lights went on and on, sprawling across the land endlessly in all directions, with nowhere a break to be seen. Square and featureless forty- and fifty-story buildings stood cheek-to-jowl in endless rows, crowding each other, living in the perpetual shadow of mirrored towers that rose around them to drink the sun. Levels were built upon other levels that had been built upon still others. The moving sidewalks crossed and crisscrossed in patterns of labyrinthine intricacy. Beneath the surface ran a network of vast subterranean roads where tubetrains and delivery capsules hurtled through the darkness at hundreds of kays per hour, and beneath the roads were basements and sub-basements and tunnels and underways and malls and sub-housing, a whole second city that burrowed as far below the ground as its mirrored sibling ascended above it.

Tuf had seen the lights of the metropolis from the *Ark*; from orbit, the city swallowed half a continent. From the surface, it seemed large enough to swallow galaxies. There were other continents; they, too, blazed by night with the lights of civilization. The sea of light had no islands of darkness within it; the S'uthlamese had no room to spare for luxuries like parks. Tuf did not disapprove; he had always thought parks to be a perverse institution, designed principally to remind civilized humanity how raw and crude and uncomfortable life had been when they had been forced to live it in nature.

Haviland Tuf had sampled a great variety of cultures in his wanderings, and he judged the culture of the S'uthlamese to be inferior to none. It was a world of variety, of dizzying possibilities, of a richness that partook both of vitality and decadence. It was a cosmopolitan world, plugged into the network that linked the stars, freely plundering the music, drama, and sensoria imported from other worlds, and using those unceasing stimuli to endlessly transform and mutate its own cultural matrix. The city offered more modes of recreation and more entertainment of more varied sorts than Tuf had ever seen in any one place before—sufficient choices to occupy a tourist for several standard years, if one desired to taste it all.

During his years of travel, Haviland Tuf had seen the advanced science and technological wizardry of Avalon and Newholme, Tober-in-the-Veil, Old Poseidon, Baldur, Arachne, and a dozen other worlds out on the sharpened leading edge of human progress. The technology demonstrated on S'uthlam was equal to the most advanced of them. The orbital elevator itself was an impressive feat—Old Earth was supposed to have built such constructs in the ancient days before the Collapse, and Newholme had raised one once, only to have it fall during the war, but nowhere else had Tuf ever observed such a colossal artifact, not even on Avalon itself, where such elevators had been studied and rejected on the grounds of economy. And the slidewalks, the tubetrains, the manufactories, all were advanced and efficient. Even the government seemed to work.

S'uthlam was a wonder world.

Haviland Tuf observed it, traveled through it, and

sampled its marvels for three days before he returned to his small, cramped, premiere-class sleeping quarters on the seventy-ninth floor of a tower hotel, and summoned the host. "I wish to make arrangements for an immediate return to my ship," he said, seated on the edge of the narrow bed he had summoned from a wall, the chairs being uncomfortably small. He folded large white hands neatly atop his stomach.

The host, a tiny man barely half Tuf's height, seemed nonplussed. "It was my understanding that you were to stay for another ten days," he said.

"That is correct," said Tuf. "Nonetheless, it is the nature of plans to be changed. I wish to return to orbit as soon as is conveniently possible. I would be most grateful if you would see to the arrangements, sir."

"There's so much you haven't seen yet!"

"Indeed. Yet I find that what I have seen, however small a sample of the whole it may be, has been more than sufficient."

"You don't like S'uthlam?"

"It suffers from an excess of S'uthlamese," Haviland Tuf replied. "Several other flaws might also be mentioned." He held up a single long finger. "The food is abysmal, for the most part chemically reformulated, largely without taste, of a distinctly unpleasant texture, full of unusual and disquieting colors. Moreover, the portions are inadequate. I might also be so bold as to mention the constant intrusive presence of a large number of newsfeed reporters. I have learned to recognize them by the multifocus cameras they wear in the center of their foreheads as a third eye. Perhaps you have observed them lurking about your lobby, sensorium, and restaurant. By my rough estimate, there seem to be about twenty of them."

"You're a celebrity," the host said, "a public figure. All of S'uthlam is interested in learning about you. Surely, if you don't wish to grant interviews, the peeps haven't dared intrude on your privacy? The ethics of the profession . . ."

"Have no doubt been observed to the letter," Haviland Tuf finished, "as I must concede that they have kept their distance. Nonetheless, each night when I have returned to this insufficiently large room and accessed the newsfeeds, I have been welcomed by scenes of myself looking over the city, eating tasteless rubbery food, visiting various scenic tourist attractions, and entering sanitary facilities. Vanity is one of my great faults, I must confess, but nonetheless, the charm of this notoriety has quickly palled. Moreover, most of their camera angles have been unflattering in the extreme, and the humor of the newsfeed commentators has bordered on being offensive."

"Easily solved," the host said. "You might have come to me earlier. We can rent you a privacy shield. It clips on the belt, and if any peep approaches within twenty meters, it will jam his third eye and give him a splitting headache."

"Less easily solved," said Tuf impassively, "is the total lack of animal life I have observed."

"Vermin?" the host said, with a horrified look. "You're upset because we have no *vermin*?"

"Not all animals are vermin," said Haviland Tuf. "On many worlds, birds, canines, and other species are kept and cherished. I myself am fond of cats. A truly civilized world preserves a place for felines, but on S'uthlam it appears the populace would find them indistinguishable from lice and bloodworms. When I made the arrangements for my visit here, Portmaster Tolly Mune assured me that her crew would take care of my cats, and I accepted said assurances, but if indeed no S'uthlamese has ever before encountered an animal of a species other than human, I believe I have just cause to wonder as to the quality of the care they are presently receiving."

"We have animals," the host protested. "Out in the agrifactory zones. Plenty of animals—I've seen tapes."

"No doubt you have," said Tuf. "A tape of a cat and a cat, however, are somewhat different things, and require different treatment. Tapes can be stored on a shelf. Cats cannot." He pointed at the host. "These are in the nature of quibbles, however. The crux of the matter, as I have previously mentioned, lies more in the number of S'uthlamese than in their manner. There are too many people, sir. I have been jostled repeatedly on every occasion. In eating establishments, the tables are too close to other tables, the chairs are insufficient to my size, and strangers sometimes seat themselves beside me and pummel me with rude elbows. The seats in theaters and sensoriums are cramped and narrow. The sidewalks are crowded, the lobbies are crowded, the tubes are crowded—there are people everywhere who touch me without my leave or consent."

The host slipped into a polished professional smile. "Ah, humanity!" he said, waxing eloquent. "The glory of S'uthlam! The teeming masses, the sea of faces, the endless pageant, the drama of life! Is there anything quite as invigorating as rubbing shoulders with our fellow man?"

"Perhaps not," said Haviland Tuf flatly. "Yet I find I am now sufficiently invigorated. Furthermore, permit me to point out that the average S'uthlamese is too short to rub against my shoulders, and has therefore been forced to content him- or herself with rubbing up against my arms, legs, and stomach."

The host's smile faded. "You are taking the wrong attitude, sir. To fully appreciate our world, you must learn to see it through S'uthlamese eyes."

"I am unwilling to go about on my knees," said Haviland Tuf.

"You're not anti-life, are you?"

"Indeed not," said Haviland Tuf. "Life is infinitely preferable to its alternative. However, in my experience, all good things can be carried to extremes. This would seem to be the case on S'uthlam." He raised a hand for silence before the host could respond. "More particularly," Tuf continued, "I have developed something of an antipathy, no doubt overhasty and unjustified, to some of the individual specimens of life I have come upon during chance encounters in my travels. A few have even expressed open hostility to me, directing at me epithets clearly derogatory of my size and mass."

"Well," said the host, flushing, "I'm sorry, but you

are, uh, ample, and on S'uthlam it is, uh, socially unacceptable to be, uh, overweight."

"Weight, sir, is entirely a function of gravity, and is therefore most malleable. Moreover, I am unwilling to concede you the authority to judge my weight over, under, or just right, these being subjective criteria. Aesthetics vary from world to world, as do genotypes and hereditary predisposition. I am quite satisfied with my present mass, sir. To return to the matter at hand, I wish to terminate my stay immediately."

"Very well," said the host. "I will book passage for you on the first tubetrain tomorrow morning."

"This is unsatisfactory. I would prefer to leave at once. I have examined the schedules and discovered a listing for a train in three standard hours."

"Full," snapped the host. "Nothing left on that one but second- and third-class seating."

"I shall endure as best I can," said Haviland Tuf. "No doubt the close press of so much humanity will leave me much invigorated and improved when I depart my train."

Tolly Mune floated in the middle of her office in a lotus position, looking down on Haviland Tuf.

She kept a special chair for flies and groundworms who were unaccustomed to weightlessness. It was a rather uncomfortable chair, all things considered, but it was bolted securely to the deck and equipped with a web-harness to keep its occupant in place. Tuf had pushed over to it with awkward dignity and strapped himself down tightly, and she had settled in comfortably in front of him, at about the level of his head. A man the size of Tuf could not possibly be accustomed to having to look up at anyone during conversation; Tolly Mune figured it gave her a certain psychological edge.

"Portmaster Mune," Tuf said, appearing remarkably unfazed by his inferior position, "I must protest. I comprehend that these repeated references to my own person as a fly are merely an instance of colorful local slang with no opprobrium attached. Still, I cannot but take a certain umbrage at this obvious attempt to, shall we say, pull my wings off."

Tolly Mune grinned down at him. "Sorry, Tuf," she said. "Our price is firm."

"Indeed," said Haviland Tuf. "Firm. An interesting word. Were I not awed to be in the mere presence of such an esteemed personage as yourself, and uneasy about giving offense, I might go so far as to suggest that this firmness approaches rigidity. Politeness forebears me from mouthing any statements about greed, avarice, and deep-space piracy in order to further my end of these thorny negotiations. I will point out however, that the sum of fifty million standards is several times greater than the gross planetary product of a good number of worlds."

"Small worlds," said Tolly Mune, "and this is a large job. You've got one hell of a big ship there."

Tuf remained impassive. "I concede that the *Ark* is indeed a large ship, but fear this has little bearing on matters, unless it is customary for you to charge by the square meter rather than by the hour."

Tolly Mune laughed. "This isn't like fitting some old freighter with a few new pulse-rings or reprogramming your drive navigator. You're talking thousands of hours even with three full crews of spinnerets on triple-shift, you're talking massive systems work by the best cyber-techs we've got, you're talking manufacture of custom parts that haven't been used in hundreds of years, and that's just for starts. We'll have to research this damn museum piece of yours before we start ripping it apart, or we'll never be able to get her back together. We'll have to lure some planetside specialists up the elevator, maybe even go out of system. Think of the time, the energy, the calories. The docking fees alone— That thing is *thirty kilometers long*, Tuf. You can't get her into the web. We'll have to build a special dock around her, and even then she'll take up the berths we could have used for three hundred ordinary ships. You don't want to know what it would cost, Tuf." She did some quick figuring on her wrist computer, and shook her head. "If you're here one local month, a real optimistic projection, that's nearly a million cals in docking fees alone. More than three hundred thousand standards in your money."

"Indeed," said Haviland Tuf.

Tolly Mune spread her hands helplessly. "If you don't like our price, you could, of course, take your business elsewhere."

"This suggestion is impractical," said Haviland Tuf. "Unfortunately, as simple as my requests are, it appears that only a handful of worlds possess the expertise to fulfill my requirements—a sad commentary on the present state of human technological prowess."

"Only a handful?" Tolly Mune raised a corner of her mouth. "Perhaps we have priced our services too low."

"Madam," said Haviland Tuf. "Surely you would not be so crass as to take advantage of my naive frankness."

"No," she said. "As I said, our price is firm."

"It appears we have reached an embarrassing and knotty impasse. You have your price. I, unfortunately, do not."

"I never would have guessed. A ship like yours, I would have figured you to have calories to burn."

"No doubt I shall soon pursue a lucrative career in the field of ecological engineering," said Haviland Tuf. "Unfortunately, I have not yet commenced my practice, and in my previous trade I had recently suffered some unaccountable financial reverses. Perhaps you would be interested in some excellent plastic reproductions of Cooglish orgy-masks? They make unusual and stimulating wall decorations, and are also said to have certain mystic aphrodisiac properties."

"I'm afraid not," Tolly Mune replied, "but you know what, Tuf? Today is your lucky day."

"I fear you are making light with me," said Haviland Tuf. "Even if you are about to inform me of a half-price sale or two-for-one service special, I am not optimally positioned to take advantage of it. I will be bitterly and brutally candid with you, Portmaster Mune, and admit that I am presently suffering from a temporary inadequacy of funds."

"I have a solution," said Tolly Mune.

"Indeed," said Tuf.

"You're a trader, Tuf. You don't really need a ship as large as the *Ark*, do you? And you know nothing about ecological engineering. This derelict is of no possible good to you. But it does have considerable salvage value." She smiled warmly. "I've talked to the folks downstairs on S'uthlam. The High Council felt it might be in your best interest to sell us your find instead."

"Their concern is touching," said Haviland Tuf.

"We'll pay you a generous salvage fee," she said. "Thirty percent of the ship's estimated value."

"The estimate to be made by you," said Tuf flatly.

"Yes, but that's not all. We'll toss in a million standards cash, over and above the salvage fee, and we'll give you a new ship. A brand-new Longhaul Nine, the biggest freighter we make, with fully automated kitchen, passenger quarters for six, gravity grid, two shuttles, cargo bays big enough to hold the largest Avalonian and Kimdissi traders side-by-side, triple redundancy, the latest Smartalec-series computer, voice-activated, and even a weapons capability if you want one. You'll be the best-equipped independent trader in this whole sector."

"Far be it from me to deprecate such generosity," said Tuf. "The very thought of your offer makes me want to swoon. And yet, though I would no doubt be far more comfortable aboard the handsome new ship you offer me, I have come to have a certain foolish sentimental attachment to the *Ark*. Ruined and useless as it is, it is nonetheless the last remaining seedship of the vanished Ecological Engineering Corps, a living piece of history as it were, a monument to their valor and genius, and yet still not without its small uses. Some time ago, as I made my lonely way across space as best I could, the whim struck me to give up the uncertain life of a trader and take up, instead, the profession of ecological engineer. As illogical and no doubt ignorant as this decison was, it still has a certain appeal to me, and I fear that my stubborn nature is a great vice. Therefore, Portmaster Mune, it is with the deepest regret that I must decline your offer. I shall keep the *Ark*."

Tolly Mune gave herself a little twist, spun upside down, and pushed off lightly from the ceiling, so as to come right up into Tuf's face. She pointed a finger at him. "Damn it to hell," she said, "I have no patience with this haggling over every puling calorie, Tuf. I'm a busy woman and I don't have the time or the energy for your trader's games. You're going to sell—I know it and you know it—so let's get this over with. Name your price." She poked his nose lightly with the point of her finger. "Name," poke, "your," poke, "price," poke.

Haviland Tuf unstrapped his harness and kicked off from the floor. He was so huge he made her feel petite—*her*, who'd been called a giant half her life. "Kindly cease your assault upon my person," he said. "It can have no positive benefit upon my decision. I fear you grossly misapprehend me, Portmaster Mune. I have been a trader, true, but a poor one—perhaps because I have never mastered the skill as a haggler which you wrongly impute to me. I have stated my position concisely. The *Ark* is not for sale."

"I have a certain amount of affection for you, from my years upstairs," Josen Rael said crisply over a shielded comm-link, "and there's no denying that your record as Portmaster has been exemplary. Otherwise, I'd remove you right now. You let him get back to his ship? How *could* you? I thought you had better sense than that."

"I thought you were a politician," Tolly Mune said with a certain amount of scorn in her voice. "Josen, think of the goddamned ramifications if I had security grab him in the middle of Spiderhome! Tuf isn't exactly inconspicuous, even when he slips into his silly wig and tries to go incognito. This place is lousy with Vandeeni, Jazbots, Henrys, you name it, all of them watching Tuf and watching the *Ark*, waiting to see what we do. He's already been approached by a goddamned Vandeeni agent. They were observed deep in conversation on the tubetrain."

"I know," the Councillor said unhappily. "Still, something should have . . . you could have had him taken surreptitiously."

"And then what do I do with him?" Tolly Mune said. "Kill him and shove him out an airlock? I won't do that, Josen, and don't even think of having it done for me. If you try it, I'll expose you to the newsfeeds and bring down the whole puling house."

Josen Rael mopped at his sweat. "You're not the only one with principles," he said defensively. "I would not suggest any such thing. Still, we must have that ship, and now that Tuf is back inside it, our task has been made more difficult. The *Ark* still has formidable defenses. I've had scenarios done, and the odds are good that it might be able to withstand a full-scale assault by our entire Planetary Defense Flotilla."

"Oh, puling hell, he's parked a bare five kays beyond the terminus of tube nine, Josen. A goddamned full-scale assault by *anybody* would probably destroy the port and bring down the elevator on top of your puling head! Just hold your bladder, and let me work on this. I'll get him to sell, and I'll do it legally."

"Very well," the Councillor replied. "I'll give you a little more time. But I warn you, the High Council is following the affair closely, and they're impatient. You have three days. If Tuf hasn't thumbed a transfer slip by then, I'm sending up some assault squads."

"Don't worry," said Tolly Mune, "I have a plan."

The communications room of the *Ark* was long and narrow, its walls covered with arrays of blank, dark telescreens. Haviland Tuf had settled in comfortably with his cats. Havoc, the boisterous black-and-white female, was curled up on his legs asleep, while long-haired gray Chaos, scarcely out of his kittenhood, rambled back and forth across Tuf's ample shoulders, rubbing against his neck and purring loudly. Tuf had folded his hands atop his paunch patiently as various computers took his request and reviewed it, relayed it, checked it, transferred it, and cross-indexed it. He had been waiting for some time. When the geometric pavane on the screen finally cleared, he was looking at the typically sharp features of an elderly S'uthlamese woman. "Curator," she announced. "Council databanks."

"I am Haviland Tuf, of the starship *Ark*," he announced.

She smiled. "I recognized you from the newsfeeds.

How may I be of help?" She blinked, "Ack, there's something on your neck."

"A kitten, madam," he said. "Quite friendly." He reached up and scratched Chaos under the chin. "I require your assistance in a small matter. As I am but a hopeless slave to my own curiosity, and always eager to improve my meager store of knowledge, I have recently been occupying myself in the study of your world—its history, customs, folklore, politics, social patterns, and the like. I have of course availed myself of all the standard texts and popular data services, but there is one particular bit of information that I have been hitherto unable to secure. A small thing, truly, no doubt laughably easy to find had I only the wisdom to know where to look, but nonetheless unaccountably absent from all the sources I have checked. In pursuit of this crumb of data, I have contacted the S'uthlam Educational Processing Center and your major planetary library, both of which referred me to you. Thus, here I am."

The Curator's face had grown guarded. "I see. The council databanks are not generally open to the public, but perhaps I can make an exception. What are you looking for?"

Tuf raised his finger. "A single small nubbin of information, as I have said, but I would be in your debt if you would be so kind as to answer my query and salve my burning curiosity. Precisely what is the current population of S'uthlam?"

The woman's face grew cold and clouded. "That information is restricted," she said flatly. The screen went black.

Haviland Tuf paused for a moment before plugging back into the data service he had been employing. "I am interested in a general survey of S'uthlamese religion," he told the search program, "and in particular in a description of the beliefs and ethical systems of the Church of Life Evolving."

Some hours later, Tuf was deeply immersed in his text and playing absently with Havoc, who had woken up feisty and hungry, when Tolly Mune's call came through. He stored the information he had been reviewing and summoned her face on another of the room's screens. "Portmaster," he said.

"I hear you're trying to pry into planetary secrets, Tuf," she said, grinning at him.

"I assure you that I had no such intent," Tuf replied, "but in any case, I am a most ineffectual spy, as my attempt was a dismal failure."

"Let's have dinner together," Tolly Mune said, "and maybe I can answer your little question for you."

"Indeed," said Haviland Tuf. "In that case, Portmaster, permit me to invite you to dine aboard the *Ark*. My cuisine, while unexceptional, is nonetheless more flavorful and considerably more bountiful than the fare available in your port."

"Afraid not," said Tolly Mune. "Too goddamned many duties, Tuf, I can't leave my station. Don't get your guts in an uproar, though. A big freighter just arrived from the Larder—our farming asteroids, a little in from here, terraformed and fertile as hell. The P.M. gets first grab at the calories. Fresh neograss salads, tunnel-hog ham steaks in brown sugar sauce, spicepods, mushroom bread, jellyfruit in real squirter cream, and beer." She smiled. "*Imported* beer."

"Mushroom bread?" said Haviland Tuf. "I do not eat of animal flesh, but the remainder of your menu sounds most attractive. I shall gladly accept your kind invitation. If you will prepare a dock for my arrival, I will shuttle over in the *Manticore*."

"Use dock four," she said. "Very close to Spiderhome. Is that one Havoc or Chaos?"

"Havoc," Tuf replied. "Chaos has departed on mysterious errands of his own, as cats are wont to do."

"I've never actually seen a live animal," said Tolly Mune cheerfully.

"I shall bring Havoc with me for your elucidation."

"See you soon," Tolly Mune closed.

They dined at one-quarter gee.

The Crystal Room clung to the underside of Spiderhome, its exterior a dome of transparent crystalline plasteel. Beyond the all-but-invisible walls of the dome, they were surrounded by the black clarity of space, fields of cool clean stars, and the intricate traceries of the web. Below was the rocky exterior of the station, transport tubes tangled thickly across its surface, the swollen silvery blisters of habitats clinging to nexus points, the sculpted minarets and shining arrow-towers of starclass hotels rising into the cold darkness. Directly overhead hung the immense globe of S'uthlam itself, pale blue and brown, aswirl with cloud patterns, the elevator hurtling up toward it, higher and higher, until the huge shaft became a thin bright thread and then was lost to the eye entirely. The perspectives were dizzying, and more than a little unsettling.

The room was customarily used only on major state occasions; it had last been opened three years ago, when Josen Rael had come upstairs to entertain a visiting dignitary. But Tolly Mune was pulling out all the stops. The food was prepared by a chef she borrowed for the night from a Transcorp liner, the beer was commandeered from a trader in transit to Henry's World; the service was a rare antique from the Museum of Planetary History; the great ebonfire table, made of gleaming black wood shot through with long scarlet veins, had room enough for twelve; and everything was served by a silent, discreet phalanx of waiters in gold and black livery.

Tuf entered cradling his cat, considered the splendor of the table, and gazed up at the stars and the web.

"You can see the *Ark*," Tolly Mune told him. "There, that bright dot, beyond the web to the upper left."

Tuf glanced at it. "Is this effect achieved through three-dimensional projection?" he asked, stroking the cat.

"Hell no. This is the real thing, Tuf." She grinned. "Don't worry, you're safe. That's triple-thick plasteel. Neither the world nor the elevator is likely to fall on us, and the chances of the dome being struck by a meteor are astronomically low."

"I perceive a substantial amount of traffic," said Haviland Tuf. "What are the chances of the dome being struck by a tourist piloting a rented vacuum sled, a lost circuit-tracer, or a burned-out pulse-ring?"

"Higher," admitted Tolly Mune. "But the instant it happens, the airlocks will seal, claxons will sound, and an emergency cache will spring open. They're required in any structure that fronts on vacuum. Port regs. So in the unlikely event that anything happens, we'll have skinthins, breather pacs, even a laser torch if we want to try and repair the damage before the spinnerets get here. But it's only happened two, three times in all the years there's been a port, so just enjoy the view and don't get too nervous."

"Madam," said Haviland Tuf with ponderous dignity, "I was not nervous, merely curious."

"Right," she agreed. She gestured him to his seat. He folded himself stiffly into it and sat quietly stroking Havoc's black-and-white fur while the waiters brought out appetizer plates and baskets of hot mushroom bread. The savories were of two sorts—tiny pastries stuffed with deviled cheese and mushroom pate, and what appeared to be small snakes, or perhaps large worms, cooked in an aromatic orange sauce. Tuf fed two of the latter to his cat, who devoured them eagerly, before lifting one of the pastries, sniffing at it, and biting into it delicately. He swallowed and nodded. "Excellent," he pronounced.

"So that's a cat," said Tolly Mune.

"Indeed," replied Tuf, tearing off some mushroom bread—a wisp of steam rose from the interior of the loaf when he broke it open—and methodically slathering it with a thick coating of butter.

Tolly Mune reached for her own bread, burning her fingers on the hot crust. But she persisted; it would not do to show any weakness in front of Tuf. "Good," she said, around the first mouthful. She swallowed. "You know Tuf, this meal we're about to have—most S'uth-lamese don't eat this well."

"This fact had not escaped my notice," said Tuf, lifting another snake between thumb and forefinger and holding it out for Havoc, who climbed halfway up his arm to get at it.

"In fact," said Tolly Mune, "the actual caloric content of this meal approximates what the average citizen consumes in a week."

"On the strength of the savories and bread alone, I would venture to suggest that we have already enjoyed more gustatory pleasure than the average S'uthlamese does in a lifetime," Tuf said impassively.

The salad was set before them; Tuf tasted it and pronounced it good. Tolly Mune pushed her own food around on her plate and waited until the waiters had retreated to their stations by the walls. "Tuf," she said, "you had a question, I believe."

Haviland Tuf raised his eyes from his plate and stared at her, his long white face blank and still and expressionless. "Correct," he said. Havoc was looking at her, too, from slitted eyes as green as the neograss in their salads.

"Thirty-nine billion," said Tolly Mune in a crisp, quiet voice.

Tuf blinked. "Indeed," he said.

She smiled. "Is that your only comment?"

Tuf glanced up at the swollen globe of S'uthlam overhead. "Since you solicit my opinion, Portmaster I shall venture to say that while the world above us seems formidably large, I cannot but wonder if it is indeed large enough. Without intending any censure of your mores, culture, and civilization, the thought does occur to me that a population of thirty-nine billion persons might be considered, on the whole, a trifle excessive."

Tolly Mune grinned. "You don't say?" She sat back, summoned a waiter, called for drinks. The beer was thick and brown, with a heavy fragrant head; they served it in huge double-handled mugs of etched glass. She lifted hers a bit awkwardly, watching the liquid slosh about. "The one thing I'll never get used to about gravity," she said. "Liquids ought to be in squeeze bulbs, goddamnit. These seem so damned . . . messy— like an accident waiting to happen." She sipped, and came away with a foam mustache. "Good, though," she said, wiping her mouth with the back of her hand. "Time to quit this damned fencing, Tuf," she continued as she lowered the mug back to the table with the excessive care of one unaccustomed to even this trace gravity. "You obviously had some suspicion of our population problem, or you would never have inquired after it. And you've been soaking up all kinds of other information. To what end?"

"Curiosity is my sad affliction, madam," Tuf said, "and I sought merely to solve the puzzle that was S'uthlam, with perhaps the vaguest hope that in study I might come across some means of resolving our present impasse."

"And?" Tolly Mune said.

"You have confirmed the assumption I was forced to make about your excessive population. With that datum in place, all becomes clear. Your sprawling cities climb ever higher because you must accommodate this swelling population even as you struggle futilely to preserve your agricultural areas from encroachment. Your proud port is impressively busy, and your great elevator moves constantly, because you lack the capacity to feed your own population and must import food from other worlds. You are feared and perhaps even hated by your neighbors because centuries ago you attempted to export your population problem through emigration and annexation, until stopped violently by war. Your people keep no pets because S'uthlam has no room for any nonhuman species that is not a direct, efficient, and necessary link in the food chain. You are on the average distinctly smaller than the human norm due to the rigors of centuries of nutritional deprivation and rationing in all but name, economically enforced. Therefore generation succeeds generation, each smaller and thinner than the last, struggling to subsist on ever-diminishing provender. All these woes are directly attributable to your surfeit of population."

"You don't sound very approving, Tuf," Tolly Mune said.

"I intend no criticism. You are not without your virtues. In the main, you are an industrious, cooperative, ethical, civilized, and ingenious folk, and your society, your technology and especially your rate of intellectual advance, is much to be admired."

"Our technology," said Tolly Mune drily, "is the only thing that has saved our goddamned asses. We import thirty-four percent of our raw calories. We grow perhaps another twenty percent on what agricultural land remains to us. The rest of our food comes out of the food factories, processed from petrochemicals. That percentage goes up every year. Has to. Only the food factories can gear up fast enough to keep pace with the population curve. One goddamned problem, though."

"You are running out of petroleum," ventured Haviland Tuf.

"Damned right we are," said Tolly Mune. "A nonrenewable resource and all that, Tuf."

"Undoubtedly your governing bodies know approximately when the famine will come upon you."

"Twenty-seven standard years," she said. "More or less. The date changes constantly, as various factors are altered. We may get a war before we get famine. That's what some of our experts believe. Or maybe we'll get war *and* famine. Either way we get a lot of dead people. We're a civilized people, Tuf, you said it yourself. So goddamned civilized you wouldn't believe it. Cooperative, ethical, life-affirming, all that bladder-bloat. Even that's breaking down, though. Conditions in the undercities are growing worse, have been for generations, and some of our leaders go so far as to say they're devolving down there, turning into some kind of puling *vermin*. Murder, rape, all the violent crimes, the rates go up each year. Within the past eighteen months, two reports of cannibalism. All that will get a lot worse in years to come. Rising with the puling population curve. You receiving my transmission, Tuf?"

"Indeed," he said impassively.

The waiters returned, bearing the entrees. Slices of meat were piled high on the platter, still steaming from the oven, and four different types of vegetables were available. Haviland Tuf allowed his plate to be filled to overflowing with spicepods, mashed smackles, sweetroot, and butterknots, and bid the waiter cut several thin slivers of ham for Havoc. Tolly Mune took a thick ham slice herself, and drowned it in brown sauce, but after the first taste she found herself without appetite; she watched Tuf eat. "Well?" she prompted.

"Perhaps I can be of some small service to you in this quandary," Tuf said, deftly spearing a forkful of spicepods.

"You can be a big service to us," Tolly Mune said. "Sell us the *Ark*. It's the only way out, Tuf. You know it. I know it. Name your own price. I appeal to your goddamned sense of morality. Sell, and you'll save millions of lives—maybe billions. Not only will you be wealthy, you'll be a hero. Say the word and we'll name the goddamned planet after you."

"An interesting notion," said Tuf. "Yet, my vanity notwithstanding, I fear you greatly overestimate the prowess of even the lost Ecological Engineering Corps. In any case the *Ark* is not for sale, as I have already informed you. Perhaps I might venture to suggest an obvious solution to your difficulties? If it proves efficacious, I would be pleased to allow you to name a city or a small asteroid after me."

Tolly Mune laughed and took a healthy swallow of beer. She needed it. "Go on, Tuf. Say it. Tell me this easy, obvious solution."

"A plethora of terms come to mind," said Tuf. "Population control is the heart of the concept, to be achieved through biochemical or mechanical birth control, sexual abstinence, cultural conditioning, legal prohibitions. The mechanisms may vary, but the end result must be the same. The S'uthlamese must breed at a somewhat diminished rate."

"Impossible," said Tolly Mune.

"That is scarcely so," said Tuf. "Other worlds, vastly older than S'uthlam, have accomplished the same."

"Makes no damned difference," Tolly Mune said. She made a sharp gesture with her mug, and beer sloshed on the table. She ignored it. "You don't win any prizes for original thinking, Tuf. This is anything but a new idea. In fact, we've got a political faction that has been advocating this for, hell, hundreds of years. The zeros, we call 'em. They want to zero out the population curve. I'd say maybe seven, eight percent of the citizenry supports them."

"Mass famine will undoubtedly increase the number of adherents to their cause," Tuf observed, lifting a heavily laden forkful of mashed smackles. Havoc yowled in approval.

"By then it will be too puling late, and you damn well know it. Problem is, the teeming masses down there really don't believe any such thing is coming, no matter what the politicians say, no matter how many dire predictions they hear over the newsfeeds. We've heard *that* before, they say, and damned if they haven't. Grandmother and great-grandfather heard similar predictions about famine just around the corner. But S'uthlam has always been able to avoid the catastrophe before. The technocrats have stayed on top for centuries by perpetually managing to keep the day of collapse a generation away. They always find a solution. Most citizens are confident they always *will* find a solution."

"Such solutions as you imply are by their very nature only stopgaps," commented Haviland Tuf. "Surely this must be obvious. The only true solution is population control."

"You don't understand us, Tuf. Restrictions against birth are anathema to the vast majority of S'uthlamese. You'll never get any meaningful number of people to accept them—certainly not just to avoid some damned unreal catastrophe that none of them believe in anyway. A few exceptionally stupid and exceptionally idealistic politicians have tried, and they've been dragged down overnight, denounced as immoral, as anti-life."

"I see," said Haviland Tuf. "Are you a woman of strong religious conviction, Portmaster Mune?"

She made a face and drank some more beer. "Hell no. I suppose I'm an agnostic. I don't know, I don't think about it much. But I'm also a zero, though I'd never admit it downstairs. A lot of spinnerets are zeros. In a small closed system like the port, the effects of unrestrained breeding soon become damned apparent, and damned scary. Downstairs, it's not so puling clear. And the church . . . are you familiar with the Church of Life Evolving?"

"I have a certain cursory familiarity with its precepts," Tuf said, "of admittedly recent acquisition."

"S'uthlam was *settled* by the elders of the Church of Life Evolving," Tolly Mune said. "They were escaping from religious persecution on Tara, and they were persecuted because they bred so damned fast they were threatening to take over the planet, which the rest of the Tarans didn't much like."

"An understandable sentiment," said Tuf.

"Same damned thing killed the colonization program the expansionists launched a few centuries back. The church—well, its fundamental belief is that the destiny of sentient life is to fill up the universe, that life is the ultimate good. Anti-life—entropy—is the ultimate evil. The church believes that life and anti-life are in a kind of race. We must evolve, the church says, evolve through higher and higher states of sentience and genius into eventual godhood, and we must achieve that godhood in time to avert the heat-death of the universe. Since evolution operates through the biological mechanism of breeding, we must therefore breed, must ever expand and enrich the gene-pool, must spread our seed to the stars. To restrict birth . . . we might be interfering with the next step in human evolution, might be aborting a genius, a proto-god, the carrier of the one mutant chromosome that would pull the race up to the next, transcendent rung on the ladder."

"I believe I grasp the essentials of the credo," Tuf said.

"We're a free people, Tuf," Tolly Mune said. "Religious diversity, freedom of choice, all that. We've got Erikaners, Old Christers, Children of the Dreamer. We've got Steel Angel bastions and we've got Melder communes, anything you want. But more than eighty percent of the population still belongs to the Church of Life Evolving, and if anything, their beliefs are stronger now than they've ever been. They look around, and they see all the obvious fruits of the church's teachings. When you've got billions of people, you've got millions at genius level, and you've got the stimulus of virulent cross-fertilization, of savage competition for advance-

ment, of incredible need. So, puling hell, it's only
logical, S'uthlam has achieved miraculous technological
breakthroughs. They see our cities, our elevator, they
see the visitors coming from a hundred worlds to study
here, they see us eclipsing all the neighboring worlds.
They *don't* see a catastrophe, and the church leaders
say everything will be fine, so why the bloody hell
should anybody stop breeding!" She slapped the table
hard, turned to a waiter. "You!" she snapped. "More
beer. And quick." She turned back to face Tuf. "So
don't give me these naive suggestions. Birth restrictions
are utterly infeasible given our situation. Impossible.
You understand that, Tuf?"

"There is no need to impugn my intelligence," said
Haviland Tuf. He stroked Havoc, who had settled into
his lap, surfeit with ham. "The plight of S'uthlam has
touched my heart. I shall endeavor to do what I can to
relieve your world's distress."

"You'll sell us the *Ark*, then?" she said sharply.

"This is an unwarranted assumption," Tuf replied.
"Yet I shall certainly do what I can in my capacity as an
ecological engineer, before moving on to other worlds."

The waiters were bringing out the dessert—fat blue-
green jellyfruit swimming in bowls of thickened, clotted
cream. Havoc sniffed the cream and leapt up on to the
table for a closer investigation as Haviland Tuf lifted the
long silver spoon they had provided him.

Tolly Mune shook her head. "Take it away," she
snapped, "too damn rich. Just beer for me."

Tuf looked up and raised a finger. "A moment! No
use in letting your portion of this delightful confection
go to waste. Havoc will surely enjoy it."

The Portmaster sipped a fresh mug of brown beer,
and scowled. "I've run out of things to say, Tuf. We
have a crisis here. We must have that ship. This is your
last chance. Will you sell?"

Tuf looked at her. Havoc moved in quickly on the
dessert. "My position is unchanged."

"I'm sorry, then," Tolly Mune said. "I didn't want to
do this." She snapped her fingers. In the quiet of that
moment, when the only sound was Havoc lapping at

the clotted cream, the noise was like a gunshot. All around the clear crystalline walls, the tall, attentive waiters reached beneath their snug gold-and-black jackets and produced nerveguns.

Tuf blinked, and moved his head first right, then left, studying each man in turn while Havoc plundered his jellyfruit. "Treachery," he said flatly. "I am gravely disappointed. My trust and good nature have been ill used."

"You forced my hand. Tuf, you damned fool—"

"Such rank abuse exacerbates this betrayal rather than justifying it," said Tuf, with spoon in hand. "Am I now to be secretly and villainously slain?"

"We're civilized people," Tolly Mune said angrily, furious at Tuf, at Josen Rael, at the goddamned Church of Life Evolving, and mostly at herself for letting it come to this. "No, you won't be killed. We won't even steal that goddamned derelict of a ship you care so damned much about. This is all legal, Tuf. You're under arrest."

"Indeed," said Tuf. "Please accept my surrender. I am always anxious to comply with all pertinent local laws. On what charge am I to be tried?"

Tolly Mune smiled thinly, without joy, knowing full well they'd be calling her the Steel Widow in Spiderhome tonight. She pointed down to the far end of the table, where Havoc sat licking cream off her whiskers. "Bringing illegal vermin into the Port of S'uthlam," she said.

Tuf laid down his spoon carefully and folded his hands atop his paunch. "It is my recollection that I brought Havoc here with me on your specific invitation."

Tolly Mune shook her head. "Won't wash, Tuf. I've got our talk recorded. True, I observed that I'd never seen a live animal before, but that's a simple factual declaration, and no court could possibly construe it as an incitement for you to commit a criminal violation of our health statutes. No court of ours, anyway." Her smile was almost apologetic.

"I see," said Tuf. "In that case, let us dispense with time-consuming legal machinations. I will plead guilty and pay the prescribed fine for this minor infraction."

"Good," said Tolly Mune. "The fine is fifty standards." She gestured, and one of her men strode forward and gathered up Havoc from the table. "Of course," she finished, "the vermin in question must be destroyed."

"I hate gravity," Tolly Mune said to Josen Rael's smiling, magnified face after she'd finished her report on the dinner. "It exhausts me, and I hate to think what all that goddamned *drag* does to my muscles, my internal organs. How can you worms live that way? And all that puling food! It was obscene the way he put it away, and the *smells* . . ."

"Portmaster, we have more important things to discuss," Rael said. "It's done, then? We have him?"

"We have his cat," she said glumly. "More precisely, *I* have his goddamned cat." As if on cue, Havoc yowled and pressed her face against the meshwork plasteel cage that the security men had rigged up in a corner of her apartment. The cat yowled a lot; it was distinctly uncomfortable in weightlessness, and kept spinning out of control when it tried to move. Every time it caromed off the side of the cage, Tolly Mune winced with guilt. "I was sure he'd thumb the transfer to save the puling cat."

Josen Rael looked upset. "I can't say I think much of your plan, Portmaster. Why in the name of life would anyone surrender a treasure the magnitude of this *Ark* to preserve an animal specimen? Especially since you tell me he has other samples of the same type of vermin back aboard his craft?"

"Because he's got an emotional attachment to this particular vermin," Tolly Mune said, with a sigh. "Except that Tuf is even cagier than I thought. He called my bluff."

"Destroy the vermin, then. Show him we mean what we say."

"Oh, be sane, Josen!" she replied impatiently. "Where does that leave us? If I go ahead and kill the damned cat, then I've got nothing. Tuf knows that, and he knows that I know that, and he knows that I know that he knows. At least this way, we've got something he wants. We're stalemated."

"We'll change the law," Josen Rael suggested. "Let me . . . yes, the penalty for smuggling vermin into port should include confiscation of the ship used for the smuggling!"

"A goddamned masterstroke," said Tolly Mune. "Too bad the charter prohibits retroactive laws."

"I have yet to hear a better plan from you."

"That's because I don't have one yet, Josen. But I will. I'll argue him out of it. I'll swindle him out of it. We know he's got weaknesses. Food, his cats. Maybe there's something else, something we can use. A conscience, a libido, a weakness for drink, for gambling." She paused, thoughtful. "Gambling," she repeated. "Right. He likes to play games." She pointed a finger at the screen. "Stay out of it. You gave me three days, and my time's not up yet. So hold your bladder." She wiped his features off the huge vidscreen, and replaced them with the darkness of space, with the *Ark* floating against a field of unwinking stars.

The cat somehow seemed to recognize the image up on the screen, and made a thin, plaintive mewing sound. Tolly Mune looked over, frowned, and asked to be put through to her security monitor. "Tuf," she barked, "where is he now?"

"In the Worldview Hotel starclass gaming salon, Ma," the woman on duty responded.

"The Worldview?" she groaned. "He would pick a goddamned worm palace, wouldn't he? What's that under, full gee? Oh, puling hell, never mind. Just see that he stays there. I'm coming down."

She found him playing five-sided quandary against a couple of elderly groundworms, a cybertech she had had suspended for systems-looting a few weeks back, and a moon-faced, fleshy trade negotiator from Jazbo. Judging from the mountain of counters stacked in front of him, Tuf was winning handily. She snapped her fingers, and the salon hostess came gliding over with a chair. Tolly Mune sat herself next to Tuf and touched him lightly on the arm. "Tuf," she said.

He turned his head and pulled away from her. "Kindly

refrain from laying hands upon my person. Portmaster Mune."

She pulled her hand back. "What are you doing, Tuf?"

"At the moment, I am assaying an interesting new strategem of my own devising against Negotiator Dez. I fear it will be proved unsound, but we shall see. In a larger sense, I strive to earn a few meager standards through the application of statistical analysis and applied psychology. S'uthlam is by no means inexpensive, Portmaster Mune."

The Jazbot, his long hair gleaming with iridescent oils, his fat face covered with rank-scars, laughed roughly and displayed a mouth of polished black teeth inset with tiny crimson jewels. "I challenge, Tuf," he said, touching a button underneath his station to flash his array upon the lighted surface of the table.

Tuf leaned forward briefly. "Indeed," he said. A long pale finger moved appropriately, and his own formation lit up within the gaming circle. "I fear you are lost, sir. My experiment has been proven successful, though no doubt by mere fluke."

"Blast you and your damnable luck!" the Jazbot said, lurching unsteadily to his feet. More counters changed hands.

"So you game well," Tolly Mune said to him. "It won't do you a damned bit of good, Tuf. The odds in these places favor the house. You'll never gamble your way to the money you need."

"I am not unaware of this," Tuf replied.

"Let's talk."

"We are engaged in talking at this very moment."

"Let's talk *privately*," she stressed.

"During our last private discussion, I was set upon by men with nerveguns, verbally pummeled, cruelly deceived, deprived of a beloved companion, and denied the opportunity to enjoy dessert. I am not favorably predisposed to accept further invitations."

"I'll buy you a drink," said Tolly Mune.

"Very well," said Tuf. He rose ponderously, scooped up his counters, and bid farewell to the other players.

The two of them walked to a privacy booth on the far side of the gaming room, Tolly Mune puffing a bit from the strain of fighting gravity. Once inside, she slumped into the cushions, ordered iced narcoblasts for two and opaqued the curtain.

"The ingestion of narcotic beverages will have scant effect on my decision-making capacities, Portmaster Mune," said Haviland Tuf, "and while I am willing to accept your largesse as a token of redress for your earlier perversion of civilized hospitality, my position is nonetheless unchanged."

"What do you want, Tuf?" she said wearily, after the drinks had come. The tall glasses were rimed with frost, the liquor cobalt blue and icy.

"Like all of humanity, I have many desires. At the moment I most urgently wish the safe return of Havoc to my custody."

"I told you, I'll swap the cat for the ship."

"We have discussed this proposal, and I have rejected it as inequitable. Must we go over the same ground again?"

"I have a new argument," she said.

"Indeed." Tuf sipped at his drink.

"Consider the question of ownership, Tuf. By what right do you own the *Ark*? Did you build it? Did you have any role in its creation? Hell no."

"I found it," said Tuf. "True, this discovery was made in the company of five others, and it cannot be denied that their claims to ownership were, in some cases, superior to my own. They, however, are dead, and I am alive. This strengthens my claim considerably. Moreover, I presently possess the artifact in question. In many ethical systems, possession is the key, indeed ofttimes the overriding determinant of ownership."

"There are worlds where the state owns everything of value, where your goddamned ship would have been seized out of hand."

"I am mindful of this and purposely avoided such worlds when choosing my destination," said Haviland Tuf.

"We could take your damned ship by force if we

wanted, Tuf. Maybe it's power that conveys ownership, eh?"

"It is true that you command the fierce loyalty of numerous lackey armed with nerveguns and lasers, while I am alone, a humble trader and neophyte ecological engineer, companioned only by his harmless cats. Nonetheless, I am not without certain small resources of my own. It is theoretically possible for me to have programmed defenses into the *Ark* that would make such a seizure perhaps less easily accomplished than you imagine. Of course this supposition is entirely hypothetical, but you might do well to give it due consideration. In any case, brutal military action would be illegal under the laws of S'uthlam."

Tolly Mune sighed. "Some cultures hold that utility confers ownership. Others opt for need."

"I am not unfamiliar with these doctrines."

"Good. S'uthlam needs the *Ark* more than you do, Tuf."

"Incorrect. I have need of the *Ark* to pursue my chosen profession and earn a livelihood. Your world has no need of the ship itself, but rather of ecological engineering. Therefore I have offered you my services, only to find my generous offer spurned and dubbed insufficient."

"Utility," Tolly Mune interrupted. "We have a whole goddamned world of brilliant scientists. You're nothing but a trader, by your own admission. We can make better use of the *Ark*."

"Your brilliant scientists are largely specialists in physics, chemistry, cybernetics, and other like fields. S'uthlam is not especially advanced in the areas of biology, genetics, or ecology. This is doubly obvious. If you possessed such expertise as you imply, firstly, your need for the *Ark* would not be urgent, and secondly, your ecological problem would never have been allowed to reach its present ominous proportions. Therefore I question your assertion that your people would put the ship to more efficient use. Since coming upon the *Ark* and commencing my voyage here, I have dutifully immersed myself in study, and I would be so bold as to suggest that I am now the single most qualified ecological engineer in human space, possibly excluding Prometheus."

Haviland Tuf's long white face was without expression; he shaped each pronouncement carefully and fired them at her in cool salvos. Yet, unflappable as he was, Tolly Mune sensed that behind Tuf's calm facade was a weakness—pride, ego, a vanity she could twist to her own ends. She jabbed a finger at his face. "Words, Tuf. Nothing but puling empty words. You can call yourself an ecological engineer, but that doesn't mean a damned thing. You can call yourself a jellyfruit, but you'd still look damned silly squatting in a bowl of clotted cream!"

"Indeed," Tug said.

"I'll make you a wager," she said, going for the kill, "that you don't know what the hell you're doing with that damned ship."

Haviland Tuf blinked, and made a steeple of his hands on the table. "This is an interesting proposition," he said. "Continue."

Tolly Mune smiled. "Your cat against your ship," she said. "I've described our problem. Solve it, and you get back Havoc, safe and sound. Fail, and we get the *Ark*."

Tuf raised a finger. "This scheme is flawed. Although you set me a formidable task, I am not loath to accept such a challenge, were the suggested stakes not so imbalanced. The *Ark* and Havoc are both mine, though you have unscrupulously, albeit legally, seized custody of the latter. Therefore it appears that by winning, I simply get back that which is rightfully mine to begin with, whereas you stand to gain a great prize. This is inequitable. I have a counteroffer. I came to S'uthlam for certain repairs and alterations. In the event of my success, let this work be performed without cost to me."

Tolly Mune lifted her drink to her mouth to give herself a moment to consider. The ice had turned slushy, but the narcoblaster still had a nice sting to it. "Fifty million standards of free repairs? That's too damn much."

"Such was my opinion," said Tuf.

She grinned. "The cat," she said, "may have been yours to start with, but now she's ours. But I'll go this far on the repairs, Tuf—I'll give you credit."

"On what terms and at what interest rate?" Tuf asked.

"We'll do the refitting," she said, smiling. "We'll start immediately. If you win—which you won't—you get the cat back, and we'll give you an interest-free loan for the cost of the repair bill. You can pay us off from the money you make out there"—she waved vaguely toward the rest of the universe—"doing your damned eco-engineering. But we get a lien on the *Ark*. If you haven't paid half the money back in five standard years, or all of it in ten, the ship is ours."

"The original estimate of fifty million standards was excessive," Tuf said, "obviously an inflated figure intended solely to force me to sell you my ship. I suggest we settle on a sum of twenty million standards as the basis for this agreement."

"Ridiculous," she snapped. "My spinnerets couldn't even *paint* your goddamned ship for twenty million standards. But I'll go down to forty-five."

"Twenty-five million," Tuf suggested. "As I am alone aboard the *Ark*, it is not strictly necessary that all decks and systems be restored to full optimal function. A few distant, dysfunctional decks are of no ultimate importance. I will trim my work order to include only the repairs that must be made for my safety, comfort, and convenience."

"Fair enough," she said. "I'll go to forty million."

"Thirty," Tuf insisted, "would seem more than enough."

"Let's not quibble over a few million standards," said Tolly Mune. "You're going to lose, so it doesn't matter one hot damn."

"I have a somewhat different viewpoint. Thirty million."

"Thirty-seven," she said.

"Thirty-two," Tuf replied.

"Obviously, we're going to settle on thirty-five, right? Done!" She stuck out her hand.

Tuf looked at it. "Thirty-four," he said calmly.

Tolly Mune laughed, withdrew her hand, and said, "What does it matter? Thirty-four."

Haviland Tuf stood up.

"Have another drink," she said, gesturing. "To our little wager."

"I fear I must decline," Tuf said. "I will celebrate after I have won. For the nonce, there is work to do."

"I cannot believe you've done this," Josen Rael said, very loudly. Tolly Mune had turned the volume up high on her comm unit, to drown out the constant irritating protests of her captive cat.

"Give me a little sanity, Josen," she said querulously. "This is goddamned brilliant."

"You've *bet* the future of our world! Billions and billions of lives! Do you seriously expect me to honor this little pact of yours?"

Tolly Mune sucked on her beer bulb and sighed. Then, in the same voice she would have used to explain things to an especially slow child, she said, "We *can't lose,* Josen. Think about it, if that wormy thing in your skull isn't too atrophied by gravity to be capable of thought. Why the hell did we want the *Ark?* To feed ourselves, of course. To avoid the famine, to solve the problem, to work a puling biological miracle. To multiply the loaves and fishes."

"Loaves and fishes?" the First Councillor said, baffled.

"Times infinity. It's a classical allusion, Josen. Christian, I think. Tuf is going to take a try at making fish sandwiches for thirty billion. I think he'll just get flour on his face and choke on a fish bone, but that doesn't matter. If he fails, we get the goddamned seedship, all nice and legal. If he succeeds, we don't *need* the *Ark* any more. We win either way. And the way I got things rigged, even if Tuf does win, he'll still owe us thirty-four million standards. If by some miracle he pulls it off, odds are we'll get the ship anyway, when he comes up short on his damned note." She drank some more beer and grinned at him. "Josen, you're damned lucky I don't want your job. Has it ever dawned on you that I'm a lot smarter than you?"

"You're a lot less politic too, Ma," he said, "and I doubt you'd last a day in my job. I can't deny that you do yours well, however. I suppose your plan is viable."

"You *suppose?*" she said.

"There are political realities to consider. The expansionists want the ship itself, you must realize, against the day they regain power. Fortunately, they are a minority. We'll outvote them in council once again."

"See that you do, Josen," Tolly Mune said. She broke the connection and sat floating in the dimness of her home. On her vidscreen, the *Ark* came into view again. Her work crews were all over it now, jury-rigging a temporary dock. Permanence would come later. She expected the *Ark* to be around for a good few centuries, so they needed a place to keep the damned thing, and even if Tuf did make off with it by some freakish chance, a major expansion of the web was long overdue and would provide new docking facilities for hundreds of ships. With Tuf paying the bill, she saw no sense in postponing the construction any longer. A long translucent plasteel tube was being assembled, section by section, to link the huge seedship to the end of the nearest major spur, so shipments of materials and teams of spinnerets could reach it more easily. Cybertechs were already inside, linked to the ship's computer system, reprogramming to suit Tuf's requirements and, incidentally, dismantling any internal defenses he might have coded in. Secret orders from the Steel Widow herself; Tuf didn't know. It was just a little extra precaution, in case he was a poor loser. She didn't want any monsters or plagues popping out of her prize box when she opened it.

As for Tuf, her sources said he had been in his own computer room almost continuously since leaving the Worldview's gaming salon. On her authority as Portmaster, the council databanks had been authorized to give him whatever information he required, and he certainly required a great deal, from the reports she was getting. He had the *Ark's* own computers datastorming extensive series of projections and simulations. Tolly Mune had to give him credit; he was giving it his best.

The cage in the corner thumped as Havoc crashed against its side and gave out a small, hurt mew. She felt sorry for the cat. She felt sorry for Tuf, too. Maybe, when he failed, she'd see if she couldn't get him that Longhaul Nine anyway.

Forty-seven days passed.

Forty-seven days passed with the work crews working triple-shift, so the activity around the *Ark* was constant, unrelenting, and frenetic. The web crawled out to the seedship and covered it; cables snaked around it like vines; a network of pneumatic tubes plunged in and out of its airlocks as if it were a dying man in a downstairs medcenter; plasteel bubbles swelled out on its hull like fat silver pimples; tendrils of steel and duralloy crisscrossed it like veins; vacuum sleds buzzed about its immensity like stinging insects trailing fire; and everywhere, inside and out, walked platoons of spinnerets. Forty-seven days passed and the *Ark* was repaired, refinished, modernized, restocked.

Forty-seven days passed without Haviland Tuf leaving his ship for so much as a minute. At first he lived in his computer room, the spinnerets reported, with the simulations running day and night and the data crashing in all around him. These past few weeks he had most often been seen riding in a small three-wheeled cart down the thirty-kilometer length of the seedship's huge central shaft, a green duck-billed cap perched atop his head, a small long-haired gray cat in his lap. He took only scant and perfunctory notice of the S'uthlamese workers, but at intervals he would pull over to recalibrate instrumentation at scattered random work stations or check the endless series of vats, large and small, that lined those towering walls. The cybertechs noticed that certain cloning programs were up and running, and that the chronowarp had been engaged, drawing off enormous amounts of energy. Forty-seven days passed with Tuf in near seclusion, companioned only by Chaos, working.

Forty-seven days passed during which Tolly Mune talked neither to Tuf nor to First Councillor Josen Rael. Her duties as Portmaster, neglected during the onset of the *Ark* crisis, were more than sufficient to keep her occupied. She had disputes to hear and adjudicate, promotions to review, construction to supervise, beribboned fly diplomats to entertain before flushing them down the elevator, budgets to draw up, payrolls to thumb. And she had a cat to deal with, too.

At first, Tolly Mune feared the worst. Havoc refused to eat, seemed unable to reconcile herself to weightlessless, fouled the air in the Portmaster's apartment with her waste products, and insisted on making some of the most pitiful noises the Portmaster had ever had the misfortune to hear. She got worried enough to bring in her chief verminologist, who assured her that the cage was spacious enough and the portions of protein paste were more than adequate. The she-cat did not agree, and continued to sicken, mewing and hissing until Tolly Mune was certain that insanity, either feline or human, was just around the corner.

Finally she took steps. She discarded the nutritious protein paste and began to feed the creature with the meat-sticks Tuf had sent over from the *Ark*. The ferocity with which Havoc attacked them when she thrust the ends through the bars was reassuring. Once she licked at Tolly Mune's fingers after consuming a stick in record time; it was a strange sensation, but not entirely unpleasant. The cat took to rubbing up against the cage, too, as if she wanted contact; Tolly touched her tentatively, and was repaid with a far more pleasant sound than the cat had uttered previously. The touch of the creature's black-and-white fur was almost sensuous.

After eight days, she let it out of its cage. The larger confines of the office would be a sufficient prison, she thought. No sooner did Tolly Mune slide back the cage door than Havoc bounded through, but when the bound took her sailing clear across the room, she began hissing wildly in distress. Tolly kicked off after her and snatched her as she tumbled, but the cat struggled wildly, clawing long gashes down the backs of her hands. After the medtech had come and gone, Tolly Mune called through to security. "Requisition a room in the Worldview," she said, "a tower room with gravity control. Tell them to set the grid for one-quarter gee."

"Who's the guest?" they asked her.

"A port prisoner," she snapped, "armed and dangerous."

After the move, she visited the hotel daily at the end
of her work-shift, at first strictly to feed her hostage and
check on its welfare. By the fifteenth day, she was
lingering long enough to soak up a few calories and give
the cat the contact it craved. The beast's personality
had changed dramatically. It made sounds of pleasure
when she opened the door for her daily inspection
(although it still tried constantly to escape), rubbed up
against her leg without provocation, kept its claws
sheathed, and even seemed to be growing fat. Whenever Tolly Mune permitted herself to sit, Havoc was in
her lap instantly. On the twentieth day she slept over.
On the twenty-sixth she moved in temporarily.

Forty-seven days passed, and by the end of them
Havoc had grown accustomed to sleeping next to her,
curled up on her pillow, her soft black-and-white fur
brushing against the Portmaster's cheek.

On the forty-eighth day, Haviland Tuf called. If he
was shocked to see his cat nestled in her lap, he gave
no sign. "Portmaster Mune," he said.

"Give up yet?" she asked him.

"Scarcely," Tuf replied. "In point of fact, I stand
ready to claim my victory."

It was too important a meeting for a tele-link, even a
shielded tele-link, Josen Rael had ruled. The Vandeeni
might have ways of penetrating the shields. And yet,
because Tolly Mune had dealt with Tuf firsthand and
might understand him in a way the council could not,
her presence was imperative, and her aversion to gravity was considered unimportant. She took the elevator
down to the surface, for the first time in more years
than she cared to contemplate, and was whisked by
aircab to the highest chamber atop the council tower.

The huge drafty room had a certain spartan dignity.
It was dominated by a long, wide conference table with
a mirror-bright monitor-top. Josen Rael sat in the position of authority, in a high-backed black chair with the

globe of S'uthlam worked in three-dimensional relief above his head. "Portmaster Mune," he said, nodding to her as she struggled to an unoccupied seat near the foot of the table.

The room was crowded with the powerful—the inner council, the elite of the technocratic faction, key bureaucrats. Half her life had passed since the last time she had been summoned downstairs, but Tolly Mune watched the newsfeeds, and recognized many of the people—the young councillor for agriculture, surrounded by under-councillors, his assistants for botanical research, oceanic development, food processing. The councillor for war and his cyborg tactician. The transport administrator. The curator of the databanks and her chief analyst. The councillors for internal security, science and technology, interstellar relations, industry. The commander of the Planetary Defense Flotilla. The senior officer of the world police. They all nodded at her blankly.

To his credit, Josen Rael dispensed with all formality. "You've had a week with Tuf's projections and the seedstock and samples he provided us," he asked his council. "Well?"

"It's difficult to judge with any degree of accuracy," said the data analyst. "His projections may be right on target or they may be completely wrong, based on mistaken assumptions. I can't begin to check for accuracy until, well, I'd say it will take several plantings at least, several years. These things Tuf has cloned for us, these plants and animals and the like, all of them are new to S'uthlam. Until we have some hard experience with them, to determine how they will flourish under S'uthlamese conditions, we can't be certain how much of a difference they'll make."

"If any," said the councillor for internal security, a short square brick of a woman.

"If any," echoed the analyst.

"You're being much too conservative," the councillor for agriculture interrupted. He was the youngest man in the room, brash and outspoken, and at the moment his smile looked as though it might crack his thin face clean in two. "My reports are all positively *glowing*." He had a tall pile of crystal data-chips on the conference table in front of him. He spread them out and shoved one into a port on his station; lines of readout began to scroll down the mirrored table-top, below the polished surface. "This is our analysis of the thing he calls omni-grain," the councillor said. "Incredible, really incredible. A gene-tailored hybrid, completely edible. *Completely edible*, councillors, every part of the plant. The stalks grow waist high, like neograss, very high in carbohydrates, crunchy texture, not at all bad with a little dressing, but primarily useful as fodder for food animals. The heads yield an excellent cereal grain with a better food-to-chaff ratio than nanowheat or s'rice. The yield is easy to transport, stores forever without refrigeration, is impossible to bruise, and is high in protein. And the roots are edible tubers! Not only that, but it grows so damn fast that it will give us twice as many crops per season. Just guesswork, of course, but I estimate that if we plant omni-grain on the kays we've got alloted to nanowheat, neograss, and s'rice, we'll reap three, four times the calories from the same plots."

"It must have some disadvantages," Josen Rael objected. "It sounds too good to be true. If this omni-grain is so perfect, why haven't we heard of it before? Tuf certainly didn't gene-splice it together in these past few months."

"Of course not. It's been around for centuries. I found a reference to it in the databanks, believe it or not. It was developed by the EEC during the war, as military fodder. The stuff grows so quickly that it's ideal when you're not sure whether you'll be reaping the crops you're sowing or fertilizing them, ah, personally. But it was never adapted by civilians. The taste was considered inferior. Not awful or unpleasant, you understand, just inferior to existing grains. Also, it exhausts the soil in a very short time."

"Aha," said the councillor for internal security. "So it's a trap of sorts?"

"By itself, yes. You'd get maybe five years of bountiful crops and then disaster. But Tuf has also sent along some vermin—incredible things, super-worms and other aerators—and a symbiote, a kind of slime-mold that will grow together with the omni-grain without harming it, living off—get this now—living off *air pollution* and certain kinds of useless petrochemical waste, and using that to restore and enrich the soil." He threw up his hands. "It's an incredible breakthrough! If our own research teams had developed this, we'd have already declared a holiday."

"What about the other things?" Josen Rael asked curtly. The First Councillor's face did not reflect any of the enthusiasm of his subordinate.

"Almost as exciting," was the reply. "The oceans— we've *never* been able to get a decent caloric yield from the oceans, relative to their size, and the last administration practically fished them to extinction with their sea-sweepers. Tuf is giving us a dozen new sorts of fast-breeding fish, and a variety of plankton . . ." He fished around in front of him, found another data-chip, plugged it in. "Here, this plankton, it will gum up the sea lanes, certainly, but ninety percent of our commerce is subsurface or airborne, so it doesn't matter. The fish will thrive on it, and under the right conditions, the plankton itself will grow so thick it will cover the water to a depth of three meters, like some vast gray-green carpet."

"An alarming prospect," said the councillor for war. "Is it edible? By humans, I mean."

"No." The agri-councillor grinned. "But when it's dead and decaying, it will serve admirably as a raw material for our food factories, once the petroleum runs out."

All the way down at the far end of the table, Tolly Mune laughed loudly. Heads turned to face her. "I'll be damned," she said. "He gave us loaves and fishes after all."

"The plankton's not really a fish," the councillor said.

"If it lives in the goddamned ocean, it's a puling fish as far as I'm concerned."

"Loaves and fishes?" asked the councillor for industry.

"Go on with your report," Josen Rael said impatiently. "Was there anything else?"

There was. There was a nutritious lichen that would grow on the highest mountains, and another that could survive even in airless conditions under hard radiation. "More Larder asteroids," announced the agricultural councillor, "without having to spend decades and billions of cals terraforming." There were parasitic food-vines that would infest S'uthlam's steamy equatorial swamps and gradually choke out and displace the fragrant and poisonous native forms that now grew there in profusion. There was a grain called snow-oats that would grow on frozen tundra, and tunnel-tubers that could honeycomb even the frozen earth beneath a glacier with huge airy passages walled by buttery brown nut-meat. There were genetically improved cattle, pigs, fowl, and fish; a new bird that Tuf claimed would eliminate the leading S'uthlamese agricultural pest; and seventy-nine new varieties of edible mushroom and fungus that could be raised in the darkness of the undercities and nourished with human waste products.

And when the councillor had finished his report, there was silence.

"He's won," Tolly Mune said, grinning. The rest were all deferring to Josen Rael, but she was damned if she was going to sit and play politics. "I'll be damned, Tuf actually did it."

"We do not know that," said the databanks curator.

"It will be years before we have meaningful statistics," said the analyst.

"There may be a trap," warned the councillor for war. "We must be cautious."

"Oh, to hell with that," said Tolly Mune. "Tuf has proved that—"

"*Portmaster*," interrupted Josen Rael, very sharply.

Tolly Mune closed her mouth; she had never heard him use that tone before. The others all looked at him as well.

Josen Rael took out a cloth and mopped the perspiration from his brow. "What Haviland Tuf has proven, beyond any doubt, is that the *Ark* is far too valuable for us to even consider letting it go. We will now discuss how best to seize it, while minimizing the loss of life and the diplomatic repercussions." He called upon the councillor for internal security.

Portmaster Tolly Mune listened quietly to her report, and sat through an hour of the discussion that followed, while they argued about tactics, the proper diplomatic stance, the most efficient utilization of the seedship, which department ought to take charge of it, and what to say to the newsfeeds. The discussion promised to last half the night, but Josen Rael said firmly that they would not break until the whole affair had been settled to the last jot and tittle. Food was ordered, records were sent for, subordinates and specialists were summoned and dismissed. Josen Rael gave orders that they were not to be interrupted for any reason whatsoever. Tolly Mune listened. Finally, she got unsteadily to her feet. "Sorry," she apologized, "it's . . . it's the puling gravity. Not used to it. Where's the nearest sani . . . sanitary . . . ulp."

"Of course, Portmaster," said Josen Rael. "Outside, the left corridor, fourth door down."

"Thank you," she said. They resumed talking as Tolly Mune staggered outside. She could hear their droning through the door. There was one police guard. She nodded to him, walked off briskly, and turned right.

Once out of his sight, she began to run.

On the roofdeck she commandeered an aircab. "The elevator," she snapped, "and scream it." She showed him her priority band.

A train was just about to leave. It was full. She bumped a starclass passenger. "Emergency in the web," she said. "I have to get back in a hurry." They made a record ascent, since after all she was Ma Spider, and transportation was waiting in Spiderhome to whisk her to her quarters.

She sailed in, sealed the door, turned on her comm, coded it to transmit a recording of her deputy's face, and tried to punch through to Josen Rael. "I'm sorry," the computer said with cybernetic sympathy. "He's in meeting, and cannot be interrupted at this time. Would you care to leave a message?"

"No," she said. She sent her own image when she punched through to her foreman out on the *Ark*. "How are things floating, Frakker?"

He looked tired, but he managed a smile for her. "We're going great, Ma," he said. "I guesstimate ninety-one percent done. Work will be complete in another six, seven days, and then it will be just clean-up."

"The work's done now," Tolly Mune said.

"What?" He looked baffled.

"Tuf has been lying to us," she said glibly. "He's a con man, a puling abortion, and I'm pulling the crews on him."

"I don't understand," the cybertech said.

"Sorry. Details are classified, Frakker. You know how it goes. Just get off the *Ark*. All of you. Spinnerets, cybertechs, security, everybody. I'll give you an hour, then I'm coming over, and if I find anybody on that derelict except Tuf and his goddamned vermin, I'll ship their rectums out to the Larder faster than you can say *Steel Widow*, you got that?"

"Uh, yes."

"I mean *now!*" snapped Tolly Mune. "*Move*, Frakker."

She cleared the screen, keyed in a top-priority shield, and placed her final call. Haviland Tuf, infuriatingly, had instructed the *Ark* to screen his calls while he napped. It took her fifteen priceless minutes to find the right formula of words to convince the idiot machine that this was an emergency.

"Portmaster Mune," Tuf responded when his image finally materialized before her, wearing an absurd fuzzy robe belted around his overample stomach. "To what do I owe the singular delight of your call?"

"The refitting is ninety percent done," Tolly Mune said. "Everything important. You'll have to live with anything we left undone. My spinnerets are scuttling off down the web, fast. They'll all be gone in, uh, now it's down to forty-odd minutes. When that time's up, I want you out of port, Tuf."

"Indeed," said Haviland Tuf.

"You're spaceworthy," she said. "I've seen your specs. You'll rip apart the dock, but there's no time to pull it down and it's a small price to pay for what you've done. Shift to drive and get out of our system and don't look back over your shoulder, unless you want to turn to goddamned salt."

"I fail to understand," said Haviland Tuf.

Tolly Mune sighed. "So do I, Tuf, so do I. Don't argue with me. Prepare for departure."

"Am I to make the assumption that your High Council found my humble offering to be a satisfactory solution to your crisis, so that I have been adjudged winner of our wager?"

She groaned. "Yes, if that's what you want to hear, you give great vermin, they loved the omni-grain, the slime-mold was a real hit, you win, you're brilliant, you're wonderful. Now scream it, Tuf, before someone thinks to ask the sickly old Portmaster a question and they notice that I'm gone."

"Your haste has left me nonplussed," said Haviland Tuf, folding his hands calmly atop his paunch and staring at her.

"*Tuf,*" Tolly Mune said, from between clenched teeth. "You won your goddamned wager, but you'll lose your ship if you don't wake up and learn to dance. Get moving! Do I have to spell it out for you, damn it? Treachery, Tuf. Violence. Betrayal. Right at this very moment, the High Council of S'uthlam is discussing all the fine details of how to grab the *Ark* and dispose of you, and arguing about what kind of perfume will make it smell the best. Now do you understand? As soon as they finish talking, and it won't be long, they'll give the orders, and security will be converging on you with vacuum sleds and nerveguns. The Planetary Defense Flotilla has four protector-class ships and two dreadnaughts in the web right now, and if they go on alert, you might not even be able to run. I don't want any goddamned space battle slagging my port and killing my people."

"An understandable aversion," Tuf said. "I shall initiate immediate implementation of departure programming. One small difficulty remains, however."

"What?" she said, all wire-edged impatience.

"Havoc remains in your custody. I cannot leave S'uthlam until she has been returned safely to me."

"Forget the puling cat!"

"A selective memory is not among my capabilities," Tuf said. "I have fulfilled my portion of our understanding. You must return Havoc or be in breach of contract."

"I *can't*," Tolly Mune said angrily. "Every fly, worm, and spinneret in the station knows that damned cat is our hostage. If I jump on a train with Havoc under my arm, it will be noticed, and someone is going to ask questions. Wait for that cat, and you're risking everything."

"Nonetheless," said Haviland Tuf, "I fear I must insist."

"Goddamn you," swore the Portmaster. She wiped out his image with a single furious snap of her fingers.

When she reached the Worldview's lofty atrium, the host greeted her with a brilliant smile. "Portmaster!" he said happily. "How good to see you. You're being paged, you know. If you'd care to take the call in my private office . . ."

"Sorry," she said, "pressing business. I'll check in from the room." She rushed past him to the elevators.

Outside the door were the guards she had posted. "Portmaster Mune," the left one said. "We were notified to watch for you. You're to call in to the security office at once."

"Certainly," she said. "You two, get down to the atrium, and fast."

"Is there a problem?"

"A big one. A brawl. I don't think the staff can handle it alone."

"We'll take care of it, Ma." They ran off together.

Tolly Mune went inside. The room was a relief; only a quarter gee, compared to the full gravity of the corridors and atrium. It was a tower suite. Beyond a triple-thick window of transparent plasteel was the vast globe of S'uthlam, the rocky surface of Spiderhome, and the brilliance of the web. She could even see the bright

line that was the *Ark*, shining in the yellow light of
S'ulstar.

Havoc was curled up asleep on the floater cushion in
front of the window, but the cat hopped down when
she entered and came bounding across the carpet, purring loudly. "I'm glad to see you, too," Tolly Mune said,
scooping up the creature. "But now I have to get you
out of here." She looked around for something large
enough to hide her hostage.

The comm unit began to scream at her. She ignored
it and continued to search. "Goddamn it," she said
furiously. She had to hide the puling cat, but how? She
tried wrapping her up in a towel, but Havoc didn't like
that idea at all.

The comm unit cleared—a security override. The
head of port security was staring at her. "Portmaster
Mune," he said, deferential for the moment, though
she wondered how long that would last once the situation became clear to him. "There you are. The First
Councillor seems to believe you have some difficulty. Is
there a problem?"

"None at all," she said. "Is there any reason for
intruding on my privacy, Danja?"

He looked abashed. "My apologies, Ma. Orders. We
were instructed to locate you immediately and report
on your whereabouts."

"Do that," she said.

He apologized again and the screen blanked. Obviously, no one had yet informed him that the *Ark* was
being cleared. Good, that bought her a bit more cushion. She moved methodically through the suite one
final time, taking a good ten minutes to search everywhere and anywhere for something to stash Havoc in,
before she finally gave it up as a lost cause. She'd just
have to brazen it out, stride to the docks and requisition vacuum sled, skinthins, and a carrier for the cat.
She moved toward the door, opened it, stepped out
. . .

. . . and saw the guards running toward her.

She darted back inside. Havoc yowled in protest.
Tolly Mune triple-locked the door and rasied the pri-

vacy shield. That didn't stop them from banging. "Portmaster Mune," one of them called through the door, "there was no brawl. Open please, we need to talk."

"Go away," she snapped. "Orders."

"Sorry, Ma," he replied, "they want us to take that cat downstairs. That's right from the council, they say."

Behind her, the comm unit came on once more. This time it was the councillor for internal security herself. "Tolly Mune," the woman said, "you are wanted for questioning. Surrender yourself immediately."

"I'm right here," Tolly Mune snapped back. "Ask your goddamned questions." The guards kept pounding on the door.

"Explain your return to port," the woman said.

"I work here," Tolly Mune said sweetly.

"Your actions are not in accord with policy. They have not been approved by High Council."

"High Council's actions haven't been approved by me," the Portmaster said. Havoc hissed at the screen.

"Place yourself under arrest, if you please."

"I'd rather not." She lifted a small, thick table—it was easy under a quarter gee—and sent it sailing into the vidscreen. The councillor's square features disintegrated in a shower of glass and sparks.

At the door, the guards had coded in a security override. She countermanded it, using Portmaster's priority, and heard one of them swearing. "Ma," the other one said, "that won't do any good. Open up, now. You can't get by us and it won't take them more than ten, twenty minutes to cancel your priority."

He was right, Tolly Mune realized. She was trapped, and once they unsealed the door it was all over. She looked around helplessly, searching for a weapon, a way out, anything. There was nothing.

Far away at the end of the web the *Ark* shone with reflected sunlight. It ought to be clear by now. She hoped Tuf had had the sense to seal up tight when the last spinneret had departed. But would he leave without Havoc? She looked down, stroked the cat's fur. "All this trouble for you," she said. Havoc purred. She looked back at the *Ark*, then at the door.

"We could pump some gas in," one of the guards was saying. "The room's not airtight, after all."

Tolly Mune smiled.

She placed Havoc back on the floater cushion, climbed up on a chair, and pulled the cover off the emergency sensor box. It had been a long time since she'd done any mech work. It took her a few moments to trace the circuits, and a few more moments to puzzle out how to make the sensors think the airseal had been broken.

When she did, an alarm claxon began to shrill hideously in her ear. There was a sudden hissing and foaming around the edges of the door as the airseal was activated. The gravity went out, the air stopped circulating, and on the far side of the room, a panel slid open on the cache of emergency vacuum gear.

Tolly Mune moved to it quickly. Inside were breather pacs, airjets, a half dozen sets of skinthins. She dressed and sealed herself up. "Come here," she said to Havoc. The cat didn't like all the noise. "Careful now, don't claw the fabric." She shoved Havoc inside a bubble helmet, attached it to a limp set of skinthins, clipped on a breather pac and turned it all the way up, way past the recommended pressure. The skinthins inflated like a balloon. The cat tried her claws against the inside of the plasteel helmet and yowled piteously. "I'm sorry," said Tolly Mune. She let Havoc float in mid-room while she removed the laser torch from its brackets.

"Who said it was a puling false alarm?" she said as she kicked herself toward the window, torch in hand.

"Perhaps you would care for some mulled mushroom wine," said Haviland Tuf. Havoc was rubbing up against his leg. Chaos was up his shoulder, long gray tail twitching, peering down at the black-and-white cat as if he were trying to remember just who that was. "You appear to be tired."

"Tired?" Tolly Mune said. She laughed. "I just burned my way out of a starclass hotel and crossed kilometers of open space, flying on nothing but airjets and using my feet to tug along a cat in an overinflated pair of skinthins. I had to outdistance the first security squad they scrambled from the dockside ready-room, and use a laser torch to cripple the sled the second bunch came cruising up on, dodging their snares the whole time, still pulling your damned cat. Then I got to spend a half-hour crawling around on the outside of the *Ark*, knocking on the hull like a brain-damage case, all the time watching my port go insane with activity. I lost the cat twice and had to chase her down again before she floated off to S'uthlam, and whenever I misjudged an airblast, off we went. Then a puling *dreadnaught* came heaving up at me. I got to enjoy the suspense of wondering when the hell you'd raise your defense sphere, and got to relish the exciting pyrotechnics when the flotilla decided to test your screens. I had a nice long time to ponder whether they'd see me, crawling around like so much vermin on the skin of some damned animal, and Havoc and I had this great conversation about what we'd do when it occurred to them to send in a wave of security on sleds. We decided I'd speak sternly to them and she'd scratch their eyes out. And then you *finally* notice us and drag us inside just as the goddamned flotilla is opening up with plasma torpedoes. And you think I might be *tired?*"

"There is no call for sarcasm," said Haviland Tuf.

Tolly Mune snorted. "Do you have a vacuum sled?"

"Your crew abandoned four in their haste to depart."

"Good. I'll take one with me." A glance at the instruments told her that Tuf finally had the seedship under way. "What's happening out there?"

"The flotilla continues to hound me," said Tuf. "The dreadnaughts *Double Helix* and *Charles Darwin* pursue, with their protector escorts close astern, and a cacophony of commanders clamor at me, making rude threats, stern martial pronouncements, and insincere entreaties. Their efforts are to no avail. My defensive screens, now that your spinnerets have so excellently restored them to full function, are more than equal to any weaponry in the S'uthlamese armory."

"Don't test it," Tolly Mune said sourly. "Just get into drive as soon as I'm gone, and get the hell out of here."

"This is sound advice," Haviland Tuf agreed.

Tolly Mune looked at the banks of vidscreens along both walls of the long, narrow communications room that they had refitted as Tuf's control center. Slumped in her chair and crumpled under the gravity, she suddenly looked and felt her age.

"What will become of you?" Tuf asked.

She looked at him. "Oh, that's a choice question. Disgrace. Arrest. Removal from office—maybe trial for high treason. Don't worry, they won't execute me. Execution is anti-life. A penal farm on the Larders, I suppose." She sighed.

"I see," said Haviland Tuf. "Perhaps you might wish to reconsider my offer to furnish you with transportation out of the S'uthlamese system. I would be only too glad to take you to Skrymir or Henry's World. If you wished to remove yourself further from the site of your infamy, I understand that Vagabond is quite pleasant during its Long Springs."

"You'd sentence me to a life under gravity," she said. "No thanks. This is my world, Tuf. Those are my own puling people. I'll go back and take what comes. Besides, you're not getting off the hook that easily." She pointed. "You owe me, Tuf."

"Thirty-four million standards, as I recall," Tuf said. She grinned.

"Madam," said Tuf, "if I might so bold as to ask—"

"I didn't do it for you," she said quickly.

Haviland Tuf blinked. "My pardon if I seem to be prying into your motives. Such is not my intent. I fear curiosity will be my downfall someday, but for the nonce I must inquire—why *did* you do it?"

Portmaster Tolly Mune shrugged. "Believe it or not, I did it for Josen Rael."

"The First Councillor?" Tuf blinked again.

"Him, and the others. I knew Josen when he was just starting out. He's not a bad man, Tuf. He's not evil. None of them are evil. They're decent men and women, doing their best. All they want to do is to feed their children."

"I do not understand your logic," said Haviland Tuf.

"I sat at that meeting, Tuf. I sat there and listened to them talk, and I heard what the *Ark* had done to them. They were honest, honorable, ethical people, and the *Ark* had already turned them into cheats and liars. They believe in peace, and they were talking about the war they might have to fight to keep this puling ship of yours. Their entire creed is based on the holy sanctity of human life, and they were blithely discussing how much killing might be necessary—starting with yours. You ever study history, Tuf?"

"I make no special claims to expertise, but neither am I entirely ignorant of what has gone before."

"There's an ancient saying, Tuf. Came out of Old Earth. Power corrupts, it went, and absolute power corrupts absolutely."

Haviland Tuf said nothing. Havoc bounded onto his knees and settled down. He began to stroke her with a huge pale hand.

"The dream of the *Ark* had already begun to corrupt my world," Tolly Mune told him. "What the hell would the reality of possession have done to us? I didn't want to find out."

"Indeed," said Tuf. "A further question suggests itself."

"What's that?"

"I now control the *Ark*," Tuf said, "and therefore wield near absolute power."

"Oh, yes," Tolly Mune said.

Tuf waited, saying nothing.

She shook her head. "I don't know," she said. "Maybe I didn't think things through. Maybe I was just making it up as I went along. Maybe I'm the biggest damned fool you'll find for light-years."

"You do not seriously believe this," said Tuf.

"Maybe I just figured it was better you got corrupted than my own people. Maybe I think you're naive and harmless. Or maybe it was instinct." She sighed. "I don't know if there is such a thing as an incorruptible man, but if there is, you're the one, Tuf. The last goddamned innocent. You were willing to lose the whole thing for her." She pointed at Havoc. "For a cat. Damned puling vermin." But she smiled as she said it.

"I see," said Haviland Tuf.

The Portmaster pulled herself wearily to her feet. "Now it's time to go back and make that speech to a less appreciative audience," she said. "Point me to the sleds and tell them that I'm coming out."

"Very well," said Tuf. He raised a finger. "One further point remains to be clarified. As your crews did not complete all of the agreed-upon work, I do not think it equitable to charge me the full price of thirty-four million standards. I suggest an adjustment. Would thirty-three million five-hundred thousand standards be acceptable to you?"

She stared at him. "What difference does it make?" she asked. "You're never coming back."

"I beg to differ," said Haviland Tuf.

"We tried to steal your ship," she said.

"True. Perhaps thirty-three million would be fair, the rest being considered a penalty of sorts."

"You're really planning to return?" Tolly Mune said.

"In five years," said Tuf, "the first payment on the loan will be due. By that time, moreover, we will be able to judge what effect, if any, my small contributions have had upon your food crisis. Perhaps more ecological engineering will be necessary."

"I don't believe it," she said, astonished.

Haviland Tuf reached up to his shoulder and scratched Chaos behind the ear. "Why," he asked reproachfully, "are we always doubted?"

The cat did not reply.

3
GUARDIANS

Haviland Tuf thought the Six Worlds Bio-Agricultural Exhibition a great disappointment.

He had spent a long wearying day on Brazelourn, trooping through the cavernous exhibition halls, pausing now and then to give a cursory inspection to a new grain hybrid or a genetically improved insect. Although the *Ark*'s cell library held cloning material for literally millions of plant and animal species from an uncounted number of worlds, Haviland Tuf was nonetheless always alert for any opportunity to expand his stock-in-trade.

But few of the displays on Brazelourn seemed especially promising, and as the hours passed Tuf grew bored and uncomfortable in the jostling, indifferent crowds. People swarmed everywhere—Vagabonder tunnel-farmers in deep maroon furs, plumed and perfumed Areeni landlords, somber nightsiders and brightly garbed evernoons from New Janus, and a plethora of the native Brazeleen. All of them made excessive noise and favored Tuf with curious stares as he passed among them. Some even brushed up against him, bringing a frown to his long face.

Ultimately, seeking escape from the throngs, Tuf decided he was hungry. He pressed his way through the fairgoers with dignified distaste, and emerged from the vaulting five-story Ptolan Exhibit Hall. Outside, hundreds of vendors had set up booths between the great

168

buildings. The man selling pop-onion pies seemed least busy of those nearby, and Tuf determined that a pop-onion pie was the very thing he craved.

"Sir," he said to the vendor, "I would have a pie."

The pieman was round and pink and wore a greasy apron. He opened his hotbox, reached in with a gloved hand, and extracted a hot pie. When he pushed it across the counter at Tuf, he stared. "Oh," he said, "you're a big one."

"Indeed, sir," said Haviland Tuf. He picked up the pie and bit into it impassively.

"You're an offworlder," the pieman observed. "Not from no place nearby, neither."

Tuf finished his pie in three neat bites, and cleaned his greasy fingers on a napkin. "You belabor the obvious, sir," he said. He held up a long, callused finger. "Another," he said.

Rebuffed, the vendor fetched out another pie without further observations, letting Tuf eat in relative peace. As he savored the flaky crust and tartness within, Tuf studied the milling fairgoers, the rows of vendors' booths, and the five great halls that loomed over the landscape. When he had done eating, he turned back to the pieman, his face as blank as ever. "Sir. If you will, a question."

"What's that?" the other said gruffly.

"I see five exhibition halls," said Haviland Tuf. "I have visited each in turn." He pointed. "Brazelourn, Vale Areen, New Janus, Vagabond, and here Ptola." Tuf folded his hands together neatly atop his bulging stomach. "Five, sir. Five halls, five worlds. No doubt, being a stranger as I am, I am unfamiliar with some subtle point of local usage, yet I am perplexed. In those regions where I have heretofore traveled, a gathering calling itself the Six Worlds Bio-Agricultural Exhibition might be expected to include exhibits from six worlds. Plainly that is not the case here. Perhaps you might enlighten me as to why?"

"No one came from Namor."

"Indeed," said Haviland Tuf.

"On account of the troubles," the vendor added.

"All is made clear," said Tuf. "Or, if not all, at least a

portion. Perhaps you would care to serve me another pie, and explain to me the nature of these troubles. I am nothing if not curious, sir. It is my great vice, I fear."

The pieman slipped on his glove again and opened the hotbox. "You know what they say. Curiosity makes you hungry."

"Indeed," said Tuf. "I must admit I have never heard them say that before."

The man frowned. "No, I got it wrong. Hunger makes you curious, that's what it is. Don't matter. My pies will fill you up."

"Ah," said Tuf. He took up the pie. "Please proceed."

So the pie-seller told him, at great rambling length, about the troubles on the world Namor. "So you can see," he finally concluded, "why they didn't come, with all this going on. Not much to exhibit."

"Of course," said Haviland Tuf, dabbing his lips. "Sea monsters can be most vexing."

Namor was a dark green world, moonless and solitary, banded by wispy golden clouds. The *Ark* shuddered out of drive and settled ponderously into orbit around it. In the long, narrow communications room, Haviland Tuf moved from seat to seat, studying the planet on a dozen of the room's hundred viewscreens. Three small grey kittens kept him company, bounding across the consoles, pausing only to slap at each other. Tuf paid them no mind.

A water world, Namor had only one landmass decently large enough to be seen from orbit, and that none too large. But magnification revealed thousands of islands scattered in long, crescent-shaped archipelagoes across the deep green seas, earthen jewels strewn throughout the oceans. Other screens showed the lights of dozens of cities and towns on the nightside, and pulsing dots of energy outlay where settlements sat in sunlight.

Tuf looked at it all, and then seated himself, flicked on another console, and began to play a war game with the computer. A kitten bounded up into his lap and went to sleep. He was careful not to disturb it. Some time later, a second kitten vaulted up and pounced on it, and they began to tussle. Tuf brushed them to the floor.

It took longer than even Tuf had anticipated, but finally the challenge came, as he had known it would. "*Ship in orbit,*" came the demand, "ship in orbit, this is Namor Control. State your name and business. State your name and business, please. Interceptors have been dispatched. State your name and business."

The transmission was coming from the chief landmass. The *Ark* tapped into it. At the same time, it found the ship that was moving toward them—there was only one—and flashed it on another screen.

"I am the *Ark*," Haviland Tuf told Namor Control.

Namor Control was a round-faced woman with close-cropped brown hair, sitting at a console and wearing a deep green uniform with golden piping. She frowned, her eyes flicking to the side, no doubt to a superior or another console. "*Ark*," she said, "state your homeworld. State your homeworld and your business, please."

The other ship had opened communications with the planet, the computer indicated. Two more viewscreens lit up. One showed a slender young woman with a large, crooked nose on a ship's bridge, the other an elderly man before a console. They both wore green uniforms, and they were conversing animatedly in code. It took the computer less than a minute to break it, so Tuf could listen in. ". . . damned if I know what it is," the woman on the ship was saying. "There's never been a ship that big. My God, just look at it. Are you getting all this? Has it answered?"

"*Ark*," the round-faced woman was still saying, "state your homeworld and your business, please. This is Namor Control."

Haviland Tuf cut into the other conversation, to talk to all three of them simultaneously. "This is the *Ark*," he said. "I have no homeworld, sirs. My intentions are purely peaceful—trade and consultation. I learned of your tragic difficulties, and moved by your plight, I have come to offer you my services."

The woman on the ship looked startled. "What are *you* . . ." she started. The man was equally nonplussed, but he said nothing, only gaped open-mouthed at Tuf's blank white visage.

"This is Namor Control, *Ark,*" said the round-faced woman. "We are closed to trade. Repeat, we are closed to trade. We are under martial law here."

By then the slender woman on the ship had composed herself. "*Ark,* this is Guardian Kefira Qay, commanding NGS *Sunrazor.* We are armed, *Ark.* Explain yourself. You are a thousand times larger than any trader I have ever seen, *Ark.* Explain yourself or be fired upon."

"Indeed," said Haviland Tuf. "Threats will avail you little, Guardian. I am most sorely vexed. I have come all this long way from Brazelourn to offer you my aid and solace, and you meet me with threats and hostility." A kitten leapt up into his lap. Tuf scooped it up with a huge white hand, and deposited it on the console in front of him, where the viewer would pick it up. He gazed down at it sorrowfully. "There is no trust left in humanity," he said to the kitten.

"Hold your fire, *Sunrazor,*" said the elderly man. "*Ark,* if your intentions are truly peaceful, explain yourself. What are you? We are hard-pressed here, *Ark,* and Namor is a small, undeveloped world. We have never seen your like before. Explain yourself."

Haviland Tuf stroked the kitten. "Always I must truckle to suspicion," he told it. "They are fortunate that I am so kind-hearted, or else I would simply depart and leave them to their fate." He looked up, straight into the viewer. "Sir," he said. "I am the *Ark.* I am Haviland Tuf, captain and master here, crew entire. You are troubled by great monsters from the depths of your seas, I have been told. Very well. I shall rid you of them."

"*Ark,* this is *Sunrazor.* How do you propose doing that?"

"The *Ark* is a seedship of the Ecological Engineering Corps," said Haviland Tuf with stiff formality. "I am an ecological engineer and a specialist in biological warfare."

"Impossible," said the old man. "The EEC was wiped out a thousand years ago, along with the Federal Empire. None of their seedships remain."

"How distressing," said Haviland Tuf. "Here I sit in an illusion. No doubt, now that you have told me my ship does not exist, I shall sink right through it and plunge into your atmosphere, where I shall burn up as I fall."

"Guardian," said Kefira Qay from the *Sunrazor*, "these seedships may indeed no longer exist, but I am fast closing on something that my scopes tell me is almost thirty kilometers long. It does not appear to be an illusion."

"I am not yet falling," admitted Haviland Tuf.

"Can you truly help us?" asked the round-faced woman at Namor Control.

"Why must I always be doubted?" Tuf asked the small grey kitten.

"Lord Guardian, we must give him the chance to prove what he says," insisted Namor Control.

Tuf looked up. "Threatened, insulted, and doubted as I have been, nonetheless my empathy for your situation bids me to persist. Perhaps I might suggest that *Sunrazor* dock with me, so to speak. Guardian Qay may come aboard and join me for an evening meal, while we converse. Surely your suspicions cannot extend to mere conversation, that most civilized of human pastimes."

The three Guardians conferred hurriedly with each other and with a person or persons offscreen, while Haviland Tuf sat back and toyed with the kitten. "I shall name you Suspicion," he said to it, "to commemorate my reception here. Your siblings shall be Doubt, Hostility, Ingratitude and Foolishness."

"We accept your proposal, Haviland Tuf," said Guardian Kefira Qay from the bridge of the *Sunrazor*. "Prepare to be boarded."

"Indeed," said Tuf. "Do you like mushrooms?"

The shuttle deck of the *Ark* was as large as the landing field of a major starport, and seemed almost a junkyard for derelict spacecraft. The *Ark*'s own shuttles stood trim in their launch berths, five identical black ships with rakish lines and stubby triangular wings angling back, designed for atmospheric flight and still in good repair. Other craft were less impressive. A teardrop-shaped trading vessel from Avalon squatted wearily on three extended landing legs, next to a driveshift courier scored by battle, and a Karaleo lionboat whose ornate trim was largely gone. Elsewhere stood vessels of stranger, more alien design.

Above, the great dome cracked into a hundred pie-wedge segments, and drew back to reveal a small yellow sun surrounded by stars, and a dull green manta-shaped ship of about the same size as one of Tuf's shuttles. The *Sunrazor* settled, and the dome closed behind it. When the stars had been blotted out again, atmosphere came swirling back in to the deck, and Haviland Tuf arrived soon after.

Kefira Qay emerged from her ship with her lips set sternly beneath her big, crooked nose, but no amount of control could quite conceal the awe in her eyes. Two armed men in golden coveralls trimmed with green followed her.

Haviland Tuf drove up to them in an open three-wheeled cart. "I am afraid that my dinner invitation was only for one, Guardian Qay," he said when he saw her escort. "I regret any misunderstanding, yet I must insist."

"Very well," she said. She turned to her guard. "Wait with the others. You have your orders." When she got in next to Tuf she told him, "The *Sunrazor* will tear your ship apart if I am not returned safely within two standard hours."

Haviland Tuf blinked at her. "Dreadful," he said. "Everywhere my warmth and hospitality is met with mistrust and violence." He set the vehicle into motion.

They drove in silence through a maze of interconnected rooms and corridors, and finally entered a huge shadowy shaft that seemed to extend the full length of the ship in both directions. Transparent vats of a hundred different sizes covered walls and ceiling as far as the eye could see, most empty and dusty, a few filled with colored liquids in which half-seen shapes stirred feebly. There was no sound but a wet, viscous dripping somewhere off behind them. Kefira Qay studied everything and said nothing. They went at least three kilometers down the great shaft, until Tuf veered off into a blank wall that dilated before them. Shortly thereafter they parked and dismounted.

A sumptuous meal had been laid out in the small, spartan dining chamber to which Tuf escorted the Guardian Kefira Qay. They began with iced soup, sweet and piquant and black as coal, followed by neograss salads with a gingery topping. The main course was a breaded mushroom top full as large as the plate on which it was served, surrounded by a dozen different sorts of vegetables in individual sauces. The Guardian ate with great relish.

"It would appear you find my hunble fare to your taste," observed Haviland Tuf.

"I haven't had a good meal in longer than I care to admit," replied Kefira Qay. "On Namor, we have always depended on the sea for our sustenance. Normally it is bountiful, but since our troubles began . . ." She lifted a forkful of dark, misshapen vegetables in a yellow-brown sauce. "What am I eating? It's delightful."

"Rhiannese sinners' root, in a mustard sauce," Haviland Tuf said.

Qay swallowed and set down her fork. "But Rhiannon is so far, how do you . . ." She stopped.

"Of course," Tuf said, steepling his fingers beneath his chin as he watched her face. "All this provender derives from the *Ark,* though originally it might be traced back to a dozen different worlds. Would you like more spiced milk?"

"No," she muttered. She gazed at the empty plates. "You weren't lying, then. You are what you claim, and this is a seedship of the . . . what did you call them?"

"The Ecological Engineering Corps, of the long-defunct Federal Empire. Their ships were few in number, and all but one destroyed by the vicissitudes of war. The *Ark* alone survived, derelict for a millennium. The details need not concern you. Suffice it to say that I found it, and made it functional."

"You *found* it?"

"I believe I just said as much, in those very same words. Kindly pay attention. I am not partial to repeating myself. Before finding the *Ark*, I made a humble living from trade. My former ship is still on the landing deck. Perhaps you chanced to see it."

"Then you're really just a trader."

"Please!" said Tuf with indignation. "I am an ecological engineer. The *Ark* can remake whole planets, Guardian. True, I am but one man, alone, when once this ship was crewed by two hundred, and I do lack the extensive formal training such as was given centuries ago to those who wore the golden theta, the sigil of the Ecological Engineers. Yet, in my own small way, I contrive to muddle through. If Namor would care to avail itself of my services, I have no doubt that I can help you."

"Why?" the slender Guardian asked warily. "Why are you so anxious to help us?"

Haviland Tuf spread his big white hands helplessly. "I know, I might appear a fool. I cannot help myself. I am a humanitarian by nature, much moved by hardship and suffering. I could no more abandon your people, beset as they are, than I could harm one of my cats. The Ecological Engineers were made of sterner stuff, I fear, but I am helpless to change my sentimental nature. So here I sit before you, prepared to do my best."

"You want nothing?"

"I shall labor without recompense," said Tuf. "Of course, I will have operating expenses. I must charge a small fee to offset them. Say, three million standards. Do you think that fair?"

"Fair," she said sarcastically. "Fairly high, I'd say. There have been others like you, Tuf—arms merchants and soldiers of fortune who have come to grow rich off our misery."

"Guardian," said Tuf, reproachfully, "you do me grievous wrong. I take little for myself. The *Ark* is so large, so costly. Perhaps two million standards would suffice? I cannot believe you would grudge me this pittance. Is your world worth less?"

Kefira Qay sighed, a tired look etched on her narrow face. "No," she admitted. "Not if you can do all you promise. Of course, we are not a rich world. I will have to consult my superiors. This is not my decision alone." She stood up abruptly. "Your communications facilities?"

"Through the door and left down the blue corridor. The fifth door on the right." Tuf rose with ponderous dignity, and began cleaning up as she left.

When the Guardian returned he had opened a decanter of liquor, vividly scarlet, and was stroking a black-and-white cat who had made herself at home on the table. "You're hired, Tuf," said Kefira Qay, seating herself. "Two million standards. *After* you win this war."

"Agreed," said Tuf. "Let us discuss your situation over glasses of this delightful beverage."

"Alcoholic?"

"Mildly narcotic."

"A Guardian uses no stimulants or depressants. We are a fighting guild. Substances like that pollute the body and slow the reflexes. A Guardian must be vigilant. We guard and protect."

"Laudable," said Haviland Tuf. He filled his own glass.

"*Sunrazor* is wasted here. It has been recalled by Namor Control. We need its combat capabilities below."

"I shall expedite its departure, then. And yourself?"

"I have been detached," she said, wrinkling up her face. "We are standing by with data on the situation below. I am to help brief you, and act as your liaison officer."

The water was calm, a tranquil green mirror from horizon to horizon.

It was a hot day. Bright yellow sunlight poured down through a thin bank of gilded clouds. The ship rested still on the water, its metallic sides flashing silver-blue, its open deck a small island of activity in an ocean of peace. Men and women small as insects worked the dredges and nets, bare-chested in the heat. A great claw full of mud and weeds emerged from the water, dripping, and was sluiced down an open hatchway. Elsewhere bins of huge milky jellyfish baked in the sun.

Suddenly there was agitation. For no apparent reason, people began to run. Others stopped what they were doing and looked around, confused. Still others worked on, oblivious. The great metal claw, open and empty now, swung back out over the water and submerged again, even as another one rose on the far side of the ship. More people were running. Two men collided and went down.

Then the first tentacle came curling up from beneath the ship.

It rose and rose. It was longer than the dredging claws. Where it emerged from the dark green sea, it looked as thick as a big man's torso. It tapered to the size of an arm. The tentacle was white, a soft slimy sort of white. All along its underside were vivid pink circles big as dinner plates, circles that writhed and pulsed as the tentacle curled over and about the huge farming ship. The end of the tentacle split into a rat's nest of smaller tentacles, dark and restless as snakes.

Up and up it went, and then over and down, pinioning the ship. Something moved on the other side, something pale stirring beneath all that green, and the second tentacle emerged. Then a third, and a fourth. One wrestled with a dredging claw. Another had the remains of a net draped all about it, like a veil, which didn't seem to hinder it. Now all the people were running—all but those the tentacles had found. One of them had curled itself around a woman with an axe. She hacked at it wildly, thrashing in the pale embrace, until her back arched and suddenly she fell still. The tentacle dropped her, white fluid pulsing feebly from the gashes she had left, and seized someone else.

Twenty tentacles had attached themselves when the ship abruptly listed to starboard. Survivors slid across the deck and into the sea. The ship tilted more and more. Something was pushing it over, pulling it down. Water sloshed across the side, and into the open hatchways. Then the ship began to break up.

Haviland Tuf stopped the projection, and held the image on the large viewscreen: the green sea and golden sun, the shattered vessel, the pale embracing tentacles. "This was the first attack?" he asked.

"Yes and no," replied Kefira Qay. "Prior to this, one other harvester and two passenger hydrofoils had vanished mysteriously. We were investigating, but we did not know the cause. In this case, a news crew happened to be on the site, making a recording for an educational broadcast. They got more than they bargained for."

"Indeed," said Tuf.

"They were airborne, in a skimmer. The broadcast that night almost caused a panic. But it was not until the next ship went down that things began to get truly serious. That was when the Guardians began to realize the full extent of the problem."

Haviland Tuf stared up at the viewscreen, his heavy face impassive, expressionless, his hands resting on the console. A black-and-white kitten began to bat at his fingers. "Away, Foolishness," he said, depositing the kitten gently on the floor.

"Enlarge a section of one of the tentacles," suggested the Guardian beside him.

Silently, Tuf did as she bid him. A second screen lit up, showing a grainy close-up of a great pale rope of tissue arching over the deck.

"Take a good look at one of the suckers," said Qay. "The pink areas, there, you see?"

"The third one from the end is dark within. And it appears to have teeth."

"Yes," said Kefira Qay. "All of them do. The outer lips of those suckers are a kind of hard, fleshy flange. Slapped down, they spread and create a vacuum seal of sorts, virtually impossible to tear loose. But each of them is a mouth, too. Within the flange is a soft pink flap that falls back, and then the teeth come sliding out—a triple row of them, serrated, and sharper than you'd think. Now move down to the tendrils at the end, if you would."

Tuf touched the console, and put another magnification up on a third screen, bringing the twisting snakes into easy view.

"Eyes," said Kefira Qay. "At the end of every one of those tendrils. Twenty eyes. The tentacles don't need to grope around blindly. They can *see* what they are doing."

"Fascinating," said Haviland Tuf. "What lies beneath the water? The source of these terrible arms?"

"There are cross-sections and photographs of dead specimens later on, as well as some computer simulations. Most of the specimens we took were quite badly mangled. The main body of the thing is sort of an inverted cup, like a half-inflated bladder, surrounded by a great ring of bone and muscle that anchors these tentacles. The bladder fills and empties with water to enable the creature to rise to the surface, or descend far below—the submarine principle. By itself it doesn't weigh much, although it is amazingly strong. What it does, it empties its bladder to rise to the surface, grabs hold, and then begins to fill again. The capacity of the bladder is astounding, and as you can see, the creature is *huge*. If need be, it can even force water *up* those tentacles and out of its mouths, in order to flood the vessel and speed things along. So those tentacles are arms, mouths, eyes, and living hoses all at once."

"And you say that your people had no knowledge of such creatures until this attack?"

"Right. A cousin of this thing, the Namorian man-of-war, was well-known in the early days of colonization. It was sort of a cross between a jellyfish and an octopus, with twenty arms. Many native species are built along the same lines—a central bladder, or body, or shell, or what have you, with twenty legs or tendrils or tentacles in a ring around it. The men-of-war were carnivores, much like this monster, although they had a ring of eyes on the central body instead of at the end of the tentacles. The arms couldn't function as hoses, either. And they were much smaller—about the size of a human. They bobbed about on the surface above the continental shelves, particularly above mud-pot beds, where fish were thick. Fish were their usual prey, although a few unwary swimmers met a bloody awful death in their embrace."

"Might I ask what became of them?" said Tuf.

"They were a nuisance. Their hunting grounds were the same areas we needed—shallows rich with fish and seagrass and waterfruit, over mud-pot beds and scrabbler runs full of chameleon-clams and bobbing freddies. Before we could harvest or farm safely, we had to pretty much clean out the men-of-war. We did. Oh, there are still a few around, but they are rare now."

"I see," said Haviland Tuf. "And this most formidable creature, this living submarine and ship-eater that plagues you so dreadfully, does it have a name?"

"The Namorian dreadnaught," said Kefira Qay. "When it first appeared, we theorized it was an inhabitant of the great deeps that had somehow wandered to the surface. Namor has been inhabited for barely a hundred standard years, after all. We have scarcely begun to explore the deeper regions of the seas, and we have little knowledge of the things that might live down there. But as more and more ships were attacked and sunk, it became obvious that we had an army of dreadnaughts to contend with."

"A navy," corrected Haviland Tuf.

Kefira Qay scowled. "Whatever. A *lot* of them, not one lost specimen. At that point the theory was that some unimaginable catastrophe had taken place deep under the ocean, driving forth this entire species."

"You give no credit to this theory," Tuf said.

"No one does. It's been disproved. The dreadnaughts wouldn't be able to withstand the pressures at those depths. So now we don't know where they came from." She made a face. "Only that they are here."

"Indeed," said Haviland Tuf. "No doubt you fought back."

"Certainly. A game but losing fight. Namor is a young planet, with neither the population nor the resources for the sort of struggle we have been plunged into. Three million Namorians are scattered across our seas, on more than seventeen thousand small islands. Another million huddle on New Atlantis, our single small continent. Most of our people are fisherfolk and sea-farmers. When this all began, the Guardians numbered barely fifty thousand. Our guild is descended from the crews of the ships who brought the colonists from Old Poseidon and Aquarius here to Namor. We have always protected them, but before the coming of the dread-naughts our task was simple. Our world was peaceful, with little real conflict. There was some ethnic rivalry between Poseidonites and Aquarians, but it was good-natured. The Guardians provided planetary defense, with *Sunrazor* and two similar craft, but most of our work was in fire and flood control, disaster relief, police work, that sort of thing. We had about a hundred armed hydrofoil patrol boats, and we used them for escort duty for a while, and inflicted some casualties, but they were really no match for the dreadnaughts. It soon became clear that there were more dreadnaughts than patrol boats, anyway."

"Nor do patrolboats reproduce, as I must assume these dreadnaughts do," Tuf said. Foolishness and Doubt were tussling in his lap.

"Exactly. Still, we tried. We dropped depth charges on them when we detected them below the sea, we torpedoed them when they came to the surface. We killed hundreds. But there were hundreds more, and every boat we lost was irreplaceable. Namor has no technological base to speak of. In better days, we imported what we needed from Brazelourn and Vale Areen. Our people believed in a simple life. The planet couldn't support industry anyway. It is poor in heavy metals and has almost no fossil fuel."

"How many Guardian patrolboats remain to you?" asked Haviland Tuf.

"Perhaps thirty. We dare not use them anymore. Within a year of the first attack, the dreadnaughts were in complete command of our sea lanes. All of the great harvesters were lost, hundreds of sea-farms had been abandoned or destroyed, half of the small fisherfolk were dead, and the other half huddled fearfully in port. Nothing human dared move on the seas of Namor."

"Your islands were isolated from one another?"

"Not quite," Kefira Qay replied. "The Guardians had twenty armed skimmers, and there were another hundred-odd skimmers and aircars in private hands. We commandeered them, armed them. We also had our airships. Skimmers and aircars are difficult and expensive to maintain here. Parts are hard to come by, and we have few trained techs, so most of the air traffic before the troubles was carried by airships—solar-powered, helium-filled, large. There was quite a sizable fleet, as many as a thousand. The airships took over the provisioning of some of the small islands, where starvation was a very real threat. Other airships, as well as the Guardian skimmers, carried on the fight. We dumped chemicals, poisons, explosives and such from the safety of the air and destroyed thousands of dreadnaughts, although the cost was frightful. They clustered thickest about our best fishing grounds and mud-pot beds, so we were forced to blow up and poison the very areas we needed most. Still, we had no choice. For a time, we thought we were winning the fight. A few fishing boats even put out and returned safely, with a Guardian skimmer flying escort."

"Obviously, this was not the ultimate result of the conflict," said Haviland Tuf, "or we would not be sitting here talking." Doubt batted Foolishness soundly across the head, and the smaller kitten fell off Tuf's knee to the floor. Tuf bent and scooped him up. "Here," he said, handing him to Kefira Qay, "hold him, if you please. Their small war is distracting me from your larger one."

"I—why, of course." The Guardian took the small black-and-white kitten in hand gingerly. He fit snugly into her palm. "What is it?" she asked.

"A cat," said Tuf. "He will jump out of your hand if you continue to hold him as if he were a diseased fruit. Kindly put him in your lap. I assure you he is harmless."

Kefira Qay, appearing very uncertain, shook the kitten out of her hand onto her knees. Foolishness yowled, almost tumbling to the floor again before sinking his small claws into the fabric of her uniform. "*Ow*," said Kefira Qay. "It has talons."

"Claws," corrected Tuf. "Tiny and harmless."

"They aren't poisoned, are they?"

"I think not," said Tuf. "Stroke him, front to back. It will make him less agitated."

Kefira Qay touched the kitten's head uncertainly.

"Please," said Tuf. "I said *stroke*, not pat."

The Guardian began to pet the kitten. Instantly, Foolishness began to purr. She stopped and looked up in horror. "It's trembling," she said, "and making a noise."

"Such a response is considered favorable," Tuf assured her. "I beg you to continue your ministrations, and your briefing. If you will."

"Of course," said Qay. She resumed petting Foolishness, who settled down comfortably on her knee. "If you would go on to the next tape," she prompted.

Tuf wiped the stricken ship and the dreadnaught off the main screen. Another scene took their place—a winter's day, windy and chilly by the look of it. The water below was dark and choppy, flecked with white foam as the wind pushed against it. A dreadnaught was afloat the unruly sea, its huge white tentacles extended all around it, giving it the look of some vast swollen flower bobbing on the waves. It reached up as they passed overhead, two arms with their writhing snakes lifting feebly from the water, but they were too far above to be in danger. They appeared to be in the gondola of some long silver airship, looking down through a glass-bottomed viewport, and as Tuf watched, the vantage point shifted and he saw that they were part of a convoy of three immense airships, cruising with stately indifference above the war-torn waters.

"The *Spirit of Aquarius,* the *Lyle D.,* and the *Skyshadow,*" said Kefira Qay, "on a relief mission to a small island grouping in the north where famine had been raging. They were going to evacuate the survivors and take them back to New Atlantis." Her voice was grim. "This record was made by a news crew on the *Skyshadow,* the only airship to survive. Watch."

On and on the airships sailed, invincible and serene. Then, just ahead of the silver-blue *Spirit of Aquarius,* there was motion in the water, something stirring beneath that dark green veil. Something big, but not a dreadnaught. It was dark, not pale. The water grew black and blacker in a great swelling patch, then bulged upward. A great ebony dome heaved into view and grew, like an island emerging from the depths, black and leathery and immense, and surrounded by twenty long black tentacles. Larger and higher it swelled, second by second, until it burst from the sea entirely. Its tentacles hung below it, dripping water, as it rose. Then they began to lift and spread. The thing was fully as large as the airship moving toward it. When they met, it was as if two vast leviathans of the sky had come together to mate. The black immensity settled atop the long silver-blue dirigible, its arms curling about in a deadly embrace. They watched the airship's outer skin tear asunder, and the helium cells rip and crumple. The *Spirit of Aquarius* twisted and buckled like a living thing, and shriveled in the black embrace of its lover. When it was over, the dark creature dropped the remains into the sea.

Tuf froze the image, staring with solemn regard at the small figures leaping from the doomed gondola.

"Another one got the *Lyle D.* on the way home," said Kefira Qay. "The *Skyshadow* survived to tell the story, but it never returned from its next mission. More than a hundred airships and twelve skimmers were lost in the first week the fire-balloons emerged."

"Fire-balloons?" queried Haviland Tuf. He stroked Doubt, who was sitting on his console. "I saw no fire."

"The name was coined the first time we destroyed one of the accursed things. A Guardian skimmer put a round of explosive shot into it, and it went up like a bomb, then sank, burning into the sea. They are extremely inflammable. One laser burst, and they go up spectacularly."

"Hydrogen," said Haviland Tuf.

"Exactly," the Guardian confirmed. "We've never taken one whole, but we've puzzled them out from bits and pieces. The creatures can generate an electric current internally. They take on water, and perform a sort of biological electrolysis. The oxygen is vented into the water or the air, and helps push the things around. Air jets, so to speak. The hydrogen fills the balloon sacs and gives them lift. When they want to retreat to the water, they open a flap on top—see, up there—and all the gas escapes, so the fire-balloon drops back into the sea. The outer skin is leathery, very tough. They're slow, but clever. At times they hide in cloud banks and snatch unwary skimmers flying below. And we soon discovered, to our dismay, that they breed just as fast as the dreadnaughts."

"Most intriguing," said Haviland Tuf. "So, I might venture to suggest, with the emergence of these fire-balloons, you lost the sky as well as the sea."

"More or less," admitted Kefira Qay. "Our airships were simply too slow to risk. We tried to keep things going by sending them out in convoys, escorted by Guardian skimmers and aircars, but even that failed. The morning of the Fire Dawn . . . I was there, commanding a nine-gun skimmer . . . it was terrible . . ."

"Continue," said Tuf.

"The Fire Dawn," she muttered bleakly. "We were . . . we had thirty airships, *thirty*, a great convoy, protected by a dozen armed skimmers. A long trip, from New Atlantis to the Broken Hand, a major island grouping. Near dawn on the second day, just as the east was turning red, the sea beneath us began to . . . seethe. Like a pot of soup that has begun to boil. It was *them*, venting oxygen and water, rising. Thousands of them, Tuf, thousands. The waters churned madly, and they rose, all those vast black shadows coming up at us, as far as the eye could see in all directions. We attacked with lasers, with explosive shells, with everything we had. It was like the sky itself was ablaze. All those things were bulging with hydrogen, and the air was rich and giddy with the oxygen they had vented. The Fire Dawn, we call it. It was terrible. Screaming everywhere, balloons burning, our airships crushed and falling around us, bodies afire. There were dreadnaughts waiting below, too. I saw them snatching swimmers who had fallen from the airships, those pale tentacles coiling around them and yanking them under. Four skimmers escaped from that battle. Four. Every airship was lost, with all hands."

"A grim tale," said Tuf.

Kefira Qay had a haunted look in her eyes. She was petting Foolishness with a blind rhythm, her lips pressed tightly together, her eyes fixed on the screen, where the first fire-balloon floated above the tumbling corpse of the *Spirit of Aquarius*. "Since then," she said at last, "life has been a continuing nightmare. We have lost our seas. On three-fourths of Namor, hunger and even starvation hold sway. Only New Atlantis still has surplus food, since only there is land-farming practiced extensively. The Guardians have continued to fight. The *Sunrazor* and our two other spacecraft have been pressed into service—bombing runs, dumping poison, evacuating some of the smaller islands. With aircars and fast skimmers, we have maintained a loose web of contact with the outer islands. And we have radio, of course. But we are barely hanging on. Within the last year, more than twenty islands have fallen silent. We sent patrols out to investigate in a half-dozen of those cases. Those that returned all reported the same things. Bodies everywhere, rotting in the sun. Buildings crushed and ruined. Scrabblers and crawling maggies feasting on the corpses. And on one island they found something else, something even more frightful. The island was Seastar. Almost forty thousand people lived there, and it was a major spaceport as well, before trade was cut off. It was a terrible shock when Seastar suddenly stopped broadcasting. Go to the next exhibit, Tuf. Go on."

Tuf pressed a series of lights on the console.

A dead thing was lying on a beach, rotting on indigo sands.

It was a still picture, this one, not a tape. Haviland Tuf and Guardian Kefira Qay had a long time to study the dead thing where it sprawled, rich and rotten. Around and about it was a litter of human corpses, lending it scale by their proximity. The dead thing was shaped like an inverted bowl, and it was as big as a house. Its leathery flesh, cracked and oozing pustulence now, was a mottled grey-green. Spread on the sand around it, like spokes from a central wheel, were the thing's appendages—ten twisted green tentacles, puckered with pinkish-white mouths and, alternately, ten limbs that looked stiff and hard and black, and were obviously jointed.

"*Legs*," said Kefira Qay bitterly. "It was a walker, Tuf, before they killed it. We have only found that one specimen, but it was enough. We know why our islands fall silent now. They come from out of the sea, Tuf. Things like that. Larger, smaller, walking on ten legs like spiders and grabbing and eating with the other ten, the tentacles. The carapace is thick and tough. A single explosive shell or laser burst won't kill one of these the way it would a fire-balloon. So now you understand. First the sea, then the air, and now it has begun on the land as well. The *land*. They burst from the water in thousands, striding up onto the sand like some terrible tide. Two islands were overrun last week alone. They mean to wipe us from this planet. No doubt a few of us will survive on New Atlantis, in the high inland mountains, but it will be a cruel life and a short one. Until Namor throws something new at us, some new thing out of nightmare." Her voice had a wild edge of hysteria.

Haviland Tuf turned off his console, and the telescreens all went black. "Calm yourself, Guardian," he said, turning to face her. "Your fears are understandable but unnecessary. I appreciate your plight more fully now. A tragic one indeed, yet not hopeless."

"You still think you can help?" she said. "Alone? You and this ship? Oh, I'm not discouraging you, by any means. We'll grasp at any straw. But . . ."

"But you do not believe," Tuf said. A small sigh escaped his lips. "Doubt," he said to the grey kitten, hoisting him up in a huge white hand, "you are indeed well named." He shifted his gaze back to Kefira Qay. "I am a forgiving man, and you have been through many cruel hardships, so I shall take no notice of the casual way you belittle me and my abilities. Now, if you might excuse me, I have work to do. Your people have sent up a great many more detailed reports on these creatures, and on Namorian ecology in general. It is vital that I peruse these, in order to understand and analyze the situation. Thank you for your briefing."

Kefira Qay frowned, lifted Foolishness from her knee and set him on the ground, and stood up. "Very well," she said. "How soon will you be ready?"

"I cannot ascertain that with any degree of accuracy," Tuf replied, "until I have had a chance to run some simulations. Perhaps a day and we shall begin. Perhaps a month. Perhaps longer."

"If you take too long, you'll find it difficult to collect your two million," she snapped. "We'll all be dead."

"Indeed," said Tuf. "I shall strive to avoid that scenario. Now, if you would let me work. We shall converse again at dinner. I shall serve vegetable stew in the fashion of Arion, with plates of Thorite fire mushrooms to whet our appetites."

Qay sighed loudly. "Mushrooms again?" she complained. "We had stir-fried mushrooms and peppers for lunch, and crisped mushrooms in bitter cream for breakfast."

"I am fond of mushrooms," said Haviland Tuf.

"I am weary of mushrooms," said Kefira Qay. Foolishness rubbed up against her leg, and she frowned down at him. "Might I suggest some meat? Or seafood?" She looked wistful. "It has been years since I've had a mud-pot. I dream of it sometimes. Crack it open and pour butter inside, and spoon out the soft meat . . . you can't imagine how fine it was. Or sabrefin. Ah, I'd kill for a sabrefin on a bed of seagrass!"

Haviland Tuf looked stern. "We do not eat animals here," he said. He set to work, ignoring her, and Kefira Qay took her leave. Foolishness went bounding after her. "Appropriate," muttered Tuf, "indeed."

Four days and many mushrooms later, Kefira Qay began to pressure Haviland Tuf for results. "What are you *doing*?" she demanded over dinner. "When are you going to act? Every day you seclude yourself and every day conditions on Namor worsen. I spoke to Lord

Guardian Harvan an hour ago, while you were off with your computers. Little Aquarius and the Dancing Sisters have been lost while you and I are up here dithering, Tuf."

"Dithering?" said Haviland Tuf. "Guardian, I do not dither. I have never dithered, nor do I intend to begin dithering now. I work. There is a great mass of information to digest."

Kefira Qay snorted. "A great mass of mushrooms to digest, you mean," she said. She stood up, tipping Foolishness from her lap. The kitten and she had become boon companions of late. "Twelve thousand people lived on Little Aquarius," she said, "and almost as many on the Dancing Sisters. Think of that while you're digesting, Tuf." She spun and stalked out of the room.

"Indeed," said Haviland Tuf. He returned his attention to his sweet-flower pie.

A week passed before they clashed again. "Well?" the Guardian demanded one day in the corridor, stepping in front of Tuf as he lumbered with great dignity down to his work room.

"Well," he repeated. "Good day, Guardian Qay."

"It is not a good day," she said querulously. "Namor Control tells me the Sunrise Islands are gone. Overrun. And a dozen skimmers lost defending them, along with all the ships drawn up in those harbors. What do you say to that?"

"Most tragic," replied Tuf. "Regrettable."

"When are you going to be ready?"

He gave a great shrug. "I cannot say. This is no simple task you have set me. A most complex problem. Complex. Yes, indeed, that is the very word. Perhaps I might even say mystifying. I assure you that Namor's sad plight has fully engaged my sympathies, however, and this problem has similarly engaged my intellect."

"That's all it is to you, Tuf, isn't it? A problem?"

Haviland Tuf frowned slightly, and folded his hands before him, resting them atop his bulging stomach. "A problem indeed," he said.

"No. It is not just a problem. This is no game we are playing. Real people are dying down there. Dying because the Guardians are not equal to their trust, and because you do nothing. *Nothing*."

"Calm yourself. You have my assurance that I am laboring ceaselessly on your behalf. You must consider that my task is not so simple as yours. It is all very well and good to drop bombs on a dreadnaught, or fire shells into a fire-balloon and watch it burn. Yet these simple, quaint methods have availed you little, Guardian. Ecological engineering is a far more demanding business. I study the reports of your leaders, your marine biologists, your historians. I reflect and analyze. I devise various approaches, and run simulations on the *Ark's* great computers. Sooner or later I shall find your answer."

"Sooner," said Kefira Qay, in a hard voice. "Namor wants results, and I agree. The Council of Guardians is impatient. Sooner, Tuf. Not later. I warn you." She stepped aside, and let him pass.

Kefira Qay spent the next week and a half avoiding Tuf as much as possible. She skipped dinner and scowled when she saw him in the corridors. Each day she repaired to the communications room, where she had long discussions with her superiors below, and kept up on all the latest news. It was bad. All the news was bad.

Finally, things came to a head. Pale-faced and furious, she stalked into the darkened chamber Tuf called his "war room," where she found him sitting before a bank of computer screens, watching red and blue lines chase each other across a grid. "*Tuf!*" she roared. He turned off the screen and swung to face her, batting away Ingratitude. Shrouded by shadows, he regarded her impassively. "The Council of Guardians has given me an order," she said.

"How fortunate for you," Tuf replied. "I know you have been growing restless of late from inactivity."

"The Council wants immediate action, Tuf. *Immediate*. Today. Do you understand?"

Tuf steepled his hands beneath his chin, almost in an attitude of prayer. "Must I tolerate not only hostility and impatience, but slurs on my intelligence as well? I understand all that needs understanding about your Guardians, I assure you. It is only the peculiar and perverse ecology of Namor that I do not understand. Until I have acquired that understanding, I cannot act."

"You *will* act," said Kefira Qay. Suddenly a laser pistol was in her hand, aimed at Tuf's broad paunch. "You will act now."

Haviland Tuf reacted not at all. "Violence," he said, in a voice of mild reproach. "Perhaps, before you burn a hole in me and thereby doom yourself and your world, you might give me the opportunity to explain?"

"Go on," she said. "I'll listen. For a little while."

"Excellent," said Haviland Tuf. "Guardian, something very odd is happening on Namor."

"You've noticed," she said drily. The laser did not move.

"Indeed. You are being destroyed by an infestation of creatures that we must, for want of a better term, collectively dub *sea monsters*. Three species have appeared, in less than half a dozen standard years. Each of these species is apparently new, or at least unknown. This strikes me as unlikely in the extreme. Your people have been on Namor for one hundred years, yet not until recently have you had any knowledge of these things you call dreadnaughts, fire-balloons, and walkers. It is almost as if some dark analogue of my *Ark* were waging biowar upon you, yet obviously that is not the case. New or old, these sea monsters are native to Namor, a product of local evolution. Their close relatives fill your seas—the mud-pots, the bobbing freddies, the jellydancers and men-of-war. So. Where does that leave us?"

"I don't know," said Kefira Qay.

"Nor do I," Tuf said. "Consider further. These sea monsters breed in vast numbers. The sea teems with them, they fill the air, they overrun populous islands. They kill. Yet they do not kill each other, nor do they seem to have any other natural enemies. The cruel checks of a normal ecosystem do not apply. I have studied the reports of your scientists with great interest. Much about these sea monsters is fascinating, but perhaps most intriguing is the fact that you know nothing about them except in their full adult form. Vast dreadnaughts prowl the seas and sink ships, monstrous fire-balloons swirl across your skies. Where, might I ask, are the little dreadnaughts, the baby balloons? Where indeed."

"Deep under the sea."

"Perhaps, Guardian, perhaps. You cannot say for certain, nor can I. These monsters are most formidable creatures, yet I have seen equally formidable predators on other worlds. They do not number in hundreds or thousands. Why? Ah, because the young, or the eggs, or the hatchlings, they are less formidable than the parents, and most die long before reaching their terrible maturity. This does not appear to happen on Namor. It does not appear to happen at all. What can it all mean? What indeed." Tuf shrugged. "I cannot say, but I work on, I think, I endeavor to solve the riddle of your overabundant sea."

Kefira Qay grimaced. "And meanwhile, we die. We die, and you don't care."

"I protest!" Tuf began.

"Silence!" she said, waving the laser. "I'll talk now, you've given your speech. Today we lost contact with the Broken Hand. Forty-three islands, Tuf. I'm afraid to even think how many people. All gone now, in a single day. A few garbled radio transmissions, hysteria, and silence. And you sit and talk about riddles. No more. You *will* take action now. I insist. Or threaten, if you prefer. Later, we will solve the whys and hows of these things. For the moment, we will kill them, without pausing for questions."

"Once," said Haviland Tuf, "there was a world idyllic but for a single flaw—an insect the size of a dust mote. It was a harmless creature, but it was everywhere. It fed on the microscopic spores of a floating fungus. The folk of this world hated the tiny insect, which sometimes flew about in clouds so thick they obscured the sun. When citizens went outdoors, the insects would land on them by the thousands, covering their bodies with a living shroud. So a would-be ecological engineer proposed to solve their problem. From a distant world, he introduced another insect, larger, to prey on the living dust motes. The scheme worked admirably. The new insects multiplied and multiplied, having no natural enemies in this ecosystem, until they had entirely wiped out the native species. It was a great triumph. Unfortunately, there were unforeseen side effects. The invader, having destroyed one form of life, moved on to other, more beneficial sorts. Many native insects became extinct. The local analogue of bird life, deprived of its customary prey and unable to digest the alien bug, also suffered grievously. Plants were not pollinated as before. Whole forests and jungles changed and withered. And the spores of the fungus that had been the food of the original nuisance were left unchecked. The fungus grew everywhere—on buildings, on food crops, even on living animals. In short, the ecosystem was wrenched entirely askew. Today, should you visit, you would find a planet dead but for a terrible fungus. Such are the fruits of hasty action, with insufficient study. There are grave risks should one move without understanding."

"And certain destruction if one fails to move at all," Kefira Qay said stubbornly. "No, Tuf. You tell frightening tales, but we are a desperate people. The Guardians accept whatever risks there may be. I have my orders. Unless you do as I bid, I will use this." She nodded at her laser.

Haviland Tuf folded his arms. "If you use that," he said, "you will be very foolish. No doubt you could learn to operate the *Ark*. In time. The task would take years, which by your own admission you do not have. I shall work on in your behalf, and forgive you your crude bluster and your threats, but I shall move only when I deem myself ready. I am an ecological engineer. I have my personal and professional integrity. And I must point out that, without my services, you are utterly without hope. Utterly. So, since you know this and I know this, let us dispense with further drama. You will not use that laser."

For a moment, Kefira Qay's face looked stricken. "You . . ." she said in confusion; the laser wavered just a bit. Then her look hardened once again. "You're wrong, Tuf," she said. "I *will* use it."

Haviland Tuf said nothing.

"Not on you," she said. "On your cats. I will kill one of them every day, until you take action." Her wrist moved slightly, so the laser was trained not on Tuf, but on the small form of Ingratitude, who was prowling hither and yon about the room, poking at shadows. "I will start with this one," the Guardian said. "On the count of three."

Tuf's face was utterly without emotion. He stared.

"One," said Kefira Qay.

Tuf sat immobile.

"Two," she said.

Tuf frowned, and there were wrinkles in his chalk-white brow.

"Three," Qay blurted.

"No," Tuf said quickly. "Do not fire. I shall do as you insist. I can begin cloning within the hour."

The Guardian holstered her laser.

So Haviland Tuf went reluctantly to war.

On the first day he sat in his war room before his great console, tight-lipped and quiet, turning dials and pressing glowing buttons and phantom holographic keys. Elsewhere on the *Ark*, murky liquids of many shades and colors spilled and gurgled into the empty vats along the shadowy main shaft, while specimens from the great cell library were shifted and sprayed and manipulated by tiny waldoes as sensitive as the hands of a master surgeon. Tuf saw none of it. He remained at his post, starting one clone after another.

On the second day he did the same.

On the third day he rose and strolled slowly down the kilometers-long shaft where his creations had begun to grow, indistinct forms that stirred feebly or not at all in the tanks of translucent liquid. Some tanks were fully as large as the *Ark*'s shuttle deck, others as small as a fingernail. Haviland Tuf paused by each one, studied the dials and meters and glowing spyscopes with quiet intensity, and sometimes made small adjustments. By the end of the day he had progressed only half the length of the long, echoing row.

On the fourth day he completed his rounds.

On the fifth day he threw in the chronowarp. "Time is its slave," he told Kefira Qay when she asked him. "It can hold it slow, or bid it hurry. We shall make it run, so the warriors I breed can reach maturity more quickly than in nature."

On the sixth day he busied himself on the shuttle deck, modifying two of his shuttles to carry the creatures he was fashioning, adding tanks great and small and filling them with water.

On the morning of the seventh day he joined Kefira Qay for breakfast and said, "Guardian, we are ready to begin."

She was surprised. "So soon?"

"Not all of my beasts have reached full maturity, but that is as it should be. Some are monstrous large, and must be transshipped before they have attained adult growth. The cloning shall continue, of course. We must establish our creatures in sufficient numbers so they will remain viable. Nonetheless, we are now at the stage where it is possible to begin seeding the seas of Namor."

"What is your strategy?" asked Kefira Qay.

Haviland Tuf pushed aside his plate and pursed his lips. "Such strategy as I have is crude and premature, Guardian, and based on insufficient knowledge. I take no responsibility for its success or failure. Your cruel threats have impelled me to unseemly haste."

"Nonetheless," she snapped. "What are you doing?"

Tuf folded his hands atop his stomach. "Biological weaponry, like other sorts of armament, comes in many forms and sizes. The best way to slay a human enemy is a single laser burst planted square in the center of the forehead. In biological terms, the analogue might be a suitable natural enemy or predator, or a species-specific pestilence. Lacking time, I have had no opportunity to devise such an economical solution.

"Other approaches are less satisfactory. I might introduce a disease that would cleanse your world of dreadnaughts, fire-balloons, and walkers, for example. Several likely candidates exist. Yet your sea monsters are close relatives of many other kinds of marine life, and those cousins and uncles would also suffer. My projections indicate that fully three-quarters of Namor's oceangoing life would be vulnerable to such an attack. Alternatively, I have at my disposal fast-breeding fungi and microscopic animals who would literally fill your seas and crowd out all other life. That choice too is unsatisfactory. Ultimately it would make Namor incapable of sustaining human life. To pursue my analogy of a moment ago, these methods are the biological equivilant of killing a single human enemy by exploding a low-yield thermonuclear device in the city in which he happens to reside. So I have ruled them out.

"Instead, I have opted for what might be termed a scattershot strategy, introducing many new species into your Namorian ecology in the hopes that some of them will prove effective natural enemies capable of winnowing the ranks of your sea monsters. Some of my warriors are great deadly beasts, formidable enough to prey even on your terrible dreadnaughts. Others are small and fleet, semi-social pack hunters who breed quickly. Still others are tiny things. I have hope that they will find and feed on your nightmare creatures in their younger, less potent stages, and thereby thin them out. So you see, I pursue many strategies. I toss down the entire deck rather than playing a single card. Given your bitter ultimatum, it is the only way to proceed." Tuf nodded at her. "I trust you will be satisfied, Guardian Qay."

She frowned and said nothing.

"If you are finished with that delightful sweet-mushroom porridge," Tuf said, "we might begin. I would not have you think that I was dragging my feet. You are a trained pilot, of course?"

"Yes," she snapped.

"Excellent!" Tuf exclaimed. "I shall instruct you in the peculiar idiosyncracies of my shuttle craft, then. By this hour, they are already fully stocked for our first run. We shall make long low runs across your seas, and discharge our cargoes into your troubled waters. I shall fly the *Basilisk* above your northern hemisphere. You

shall take the *Manticore* to the south. If this plan is
acceptable, let us go over the routes I have planned for
us." He rose with great dignity.

For the next twenty days, Haviland Tuf and Kefira
Qay crisscrossed the dangerous skies of Namor in a
painstaking grid pattern, seeding the seas. The Guardian flew her runs with elan. It felt good to be in action
again, and she was filled with hope as well. The
dreadnaughts and fire-balloons and walkers would have
their own nightmares to contend with now—nightmares
from half-a-hundred scattered worlds.

From Old Poseidon came vampire eels and nessies
and floating tangles of web-weed, transparent and razor-
sharp and deadly.

From Aquarius Tuf cloned black raveners, the swifter
scarlet raveners, poisonous puff-puppies, and fragrant,
carnivorous lady's bane.

From Jamison's World the vats summoned sand-
dragons and dreerhants and a dozen kinds of brightly
colored water snakes, large and small.

From Old Earth itself the cell library provided great
white sharks, barracuda, giant squid, and clever semi-
sentient orcas.

They seeded Namor with the monstrous grey kraken
of Lissador and the smaller blue kraken of Ance, with
water-jelly colonies from Noborn, Daronnian spinner-
whips, and bloodlace out of Cathaday, with swimmers
as large as the fortress-fish of Dam Tullian, the mock-
whale of Gulliver, and the ghrin'da of Hruun-2, or as
small as the blisterfins of Avalon, the parasitical caesni
from Ananda, and the deadly nest-building, egg-laying
Deirdran waterwasps. To hunt the drifting fire-balloons
they brought forth countless fliers: lashtail mantas, bright
red razorwings, flocks of scorn, semi-aquatic howlers,
and a terrible pale blue thing—half-plant and half-animal
and all but weightless—that drifted with the wind and
lurked inside clouds like a living, hungry spiderweb.
Tuf called it the-weed-that-weeps-and-whispers, and ad-
vised Kefira Qay not to fly through clouds.

Plants and animals and things that were both and

neither, predators and parasites, creatures dark as night or bright and gorgeous or entirely colorless, things strange and beautiful beyond words or too hideous even for thought, from worlds whose names burned bright in human history and from others seldom heard of. And more, and more. Day after day the *Basilisk* and the *Manticore* flashed above the seas of Namor, too swift and deadly for the fire-balloons that drifted up to attack them, dropping their living weapons with impunity.

After each day's run they would repair to the *Ark*, where Haviland Tuf and one or more of his cats would seek solitude, while Kefira Qay habitually took Foolishness with her to the communications room so she could listen to the reports.

"Guardian Smitt reports the sighting of strange creatures in the Orange Strait. No sign of dreadnaughts."

"A dreadnaught has been seen off Batthern, locked in terrible combat with some huge tentacled thing twice its size. A grey kraken, you say? Very well. We shall have to learn these names, Guardian Qay."

"Mullidor Strand reports that a family of lashtail mantas has taken up residence on the offshore rocks. Guardian Horn says they slice through fire-balloons like living knives—that the balloons flail and deflate and fall helplessly. Wonderful!"

"Today we heard from Indigo Beach, Guardian Qay. A strange story. Three walkers came rushing out of the water, but it was no attack. They were crazed, staggering about as if in great pain, and ropes of some pale scummy substance dangled from every joint and gap. What is it?"

"A dead dreadnaught washed up on New Atlantis today. Another corpse was sighted by the *Sunrazor* on its western patrol, rotting atop the water. Various strange fishes were picking it to pieces."

"*Starsword* swung out to Fire Heights yesterday, and sighted less than a half-dozen fire-balloons. The Council of Guardians is thinking of resuming short airship flights to the Mud-Pot Pearls, on a trial basis. What do you think, Guardian Qay? Would you advise that we risk it, or is it premature?"

Each day the reports flooded in, and each day Kefira Qay smiled more broadly as she made her runs in the *Manticore*. But Haviland Tuf remained silent and impassive.

Thirty-four days into the war, Lord Guardian Lysan told her, "Well, another dead dreadnaught was found today. It must have put up quite a battle. Our scientists have been analyzing the contents of its stomachs, and it appears to have fed exclusively on orcas and blue kraken." Kefira Qay frowned slightly, then shrugged it off.

"A grey kraken washed up on Boreen today," Lord Guardian Moen told her a few days later. "The residents are complaining of the stink. It has gigantic round bite-marks, they report. Obviously a dreadnaught, but even larger than the usual kind." Guardian Qay shifted uncomfortably.

"All the sharks seem to have vanished from the Amber Sea. The biologists can't account for it. What do you think? Ask Tuf about it, will you?" She listened, and felt a faint trickle of alarm.

"Here's a strange one for you two. Something has been sighted moving back and forth across the Coherine Deep. We've had reports from both *Sunrazor* and *Skyknife*, and various confirmations from skimmer patrols. A huge thing, they say, a veritable living island, sweeping up everything in its path. Is that one of yours? If it is, you may have miscalculated. They say it is eating barracuda and blisterfins and lander's needles by the thousands." Kefira Qay scowled.

"Fire-balloons sighted again off Mullidor Strand—hundreds of them. I can hardly give credence to these reports, but they say the lashtail mantas just carom off them now. Do you . . ."

"Men-of-war again, can you believe it? We thought they were all nearly gone. So many of them, and they are gobbling up Tuf's smaller fish like nobody's business. You have to . . ."

"Dreadnaughts spraying water to knock howlers from the sky . . ."

"Something new, Kefira, a *flyer*, or a glider rather, swarms of them launch from the tops of these fire-balloons. They've gotten three skimmers already, and the mantas are no match for them . . ."

". . . all over, I tell you, that thing that hides in the clouds . . . the balloons just rip them loose, the acid doesn't bother them anymore, they fling them down . . ."

". . . more dead waterwasps, hundreds of them, thousands, where are they all . . ."

". . . walkers again. Castle Dawn has fallen silent, must be overrun. We can't understand it. The island was ringed by bloodlace and water-jelly colonies. It ought to have been safe, unless . . ."

". . . no word from Indigo Beach in a week . . ."

". . . thirty, forty fire-balloons seen just off Cabben. The Council fears . . ."

". . . nothing from Lobbadoon . . ."

". . . dead fortress-fish, half as big as the island itself . . ."

". . . dreadnaughts came right into the harbor . . ."

". . . walkers . . ."

". . . Guardian Qay, the *Starsword* is lost, gone down over the Polar Sea. The last transmission was garbled, but we think . . ."

Kefira Qay pushed herself up, trembling, and turned to rush out of the communications room, where all the screens were babbling news of death, destruction, defeat. Haviland Tuf was standing behind her, his pale white face impassive, Ingratitude sitting calmly on his broad left shoulder.

"What is *happening*?" the Guardian demanded.

"I should think that would be obvious, Guardian, to any person of normal intelligence. We are losing. Perhaps we have lost already."

Kefira Qay fought to keep from shrieking. "Aren't you going to *do* anything? Fight back? This is all your fault, Tuf. You aren't an ecological engineer—you're a trader who doesn't know what he's doing. That's why this is . . ."

Haviland Tuf raised up a hand for silence. "Please," he said. "You have already caused me considerable vexation. Insult me no further. I am a gentle man, of kindly and benevolent disposition, but even one such as myself can be provoked to anger. You press close to that point now. Guardian, I take no responsibility for this unfortunate course of events. This hasty biowar we have waged was none of my idea. Your uncivilized ultimatum forced me to unwise action in order to placate you. Fortunately, while you have spent your nights gloating over transient and illusory victories, I have continued with my work. I have mapped out your world on my computers and watched the course of your war shudder and flow across it in all its manifold stages. I've duplicated your biosphere in one of my great tanks and seeded it with samples of Namorian life cloned from dead specimens—a bit of tentacle here, a piece of carapace there. I have observed and analyzed and at last I have come to conclusions. Tentative, to be sure, although this late sequence of events on Namor tends to confirm my hypothesis. So defame me no further, Guardian. After a refreshing night's sleep I shall descend to Namor and attempt to end this war of yours."

Kefira Qay stared at him, hardly daring to believe, her dread turning to hope once again. "You have the answer, then?"

"Indeed. Did I not just say as much?"

"What is it?" she demanded. "Some new creatures? That's it—you've cloned something else, haven't you? Some plague? Some monster?"

Haviland Tuf held up his hand. "Patience. First I must be certain. You have mocked me and derided me with such unflagging vigor that I hesitate to open myself to further ridicule by confiding my plans to you. I shall prove them valid first. Now, let us discuss tomorrow. You shall fly no war run with the *Manticore*. Instead, I would have you take it to New Atlantis and convene a full meeting of the Council of Guardians. Fetch those who require fetching from outlying islands, please."

"And you?" Kefira Qay asked.

"I shall meet with the council when it is time. Prior to that, I shall take my plans and my creature to Namor on a mission of our own. We shall descend in the

Phoenix, I believe. Yes. I do think the *Phoenix* most appropriate, to commemorate your world rising from its ashes. Markedly wet ashes, but ashes nonetheless."

Kefira Qay met Haviland Tuf on the shuttle deck just prior to their scheduled departure. *Manticore* and *Phoenix* stood ready in their launch berths amidst the scatter of derelict spacecraft. Haviland Tuf was punching numbers into a mini-computer strapped to the inside of his wrist. He wore a long gray vinyl greatcoat with copious pockets and flaring shoulderboards. A green and brown duck-billed cap decorated with the golden theta of the Ecological Engineers perched rakishly atop his bald head.

"I have notified Namor Control and Guardian Headquarters," Qay said. "The Council is assembling. I will provide transportation for a half-dozen Lords Guardian from outlying districts, so all of them will be on hand. How about you, Tuf? Are you ready? Is your mystery creature on board?"

"Soon," said Haviland Tuf, blinking at her.

But Kefira Qay was not looking at his face. Her gaze had gone lower. "Tuf," she said, "there is something in your pocket. Moving." Incredulous, she watched the ripple creep along beneath the vinyl.

"Ah," said Tuf. "Indeed." And then the head emerged from his pocket, and peered around curiously. It belonged to a kitten, a tiny jet-black kitten with lambent yellow eyes.

"A cat," muttered Kefira Qay sourly.

"Your perception is uncanny," said Haviland Tuf. He lifted the kitten out gently, and held it cupped in one great white hand while scratching behind its ear with a finger from the other. "This is Dax," he said solemnly. Dax was scarcely half the size of the older kittens who frisked about the *Ark*. He looked like nothing but a ball of black fur, curiously limp and indolent.

"Wonderful," the Guardian replied. "Dax, eh? Where did this one come from? No, don't answer that. I can guess. Tuf, don't we have more important things to do than play with cats?"

"I think not," said Haviland Tuf. "You do not appreciate cats sufficiently, Guardian. They are the most civilized of creatures. No world can be considered truly cultured without cats. Are you aware that all cats, from time immemorial, have had a touch of psi? Do you know that some ancient societies of Old Earth worshipped cats as gods? It is true."

"Please," said Kefira Qay irritably. "We don't have time for a discourse on cats. Are you going to bring that poor little thing down to Namor with you?"

Tuf blinked. "Indeed. This poor little thing, as you so contemptuously call him, is the salvation of Namor. Respect might be in order."

She stared at him as if he had gone mad. "What? That? Him? I mean, Dax? Are you serious. What are you talking about? You're joking, aren't you? This is some kind of insane jest. You've got some thing loaded aboard the *Phoenix*, some huge leviathan that will cleanse the sea of those dreadnaughts—something, anything, I don't know. But you can't mean . . . you can't . . . not that."

"Him," said Haviland Tuf. "Guardian, it is so wearisome to have to state the obvious, not once but again and again. I have given you raveners and krakens and lashtail mantas, at your insistence. They have not been efficacious. Accordingly, I have done much hard thinking, and I have cloned Dax."

"A kitten," she said. "You're going to use a *kitten* against the dreadnaughts and the fire-balloons and the walkers. One. Small. *Kitten*."

"Indeed," said Haviland Tuf. He frowned down at her, slid Dax back into the roomy confines of his great pocket, and turned smartly toward the waiting *Phoenix*.

Kefira Qay was growing very nervous. In the council chambers high atop Breakwater Tower on New Atlantis, the twenty-five Lords Guardian who commanded the defense of all Namor were restive. All of them had been waiting for hours. Some had been there all day. The long conference table was littered with personal communicators and computer printouts and empty water glasses. Two meals had already been served and cleared away. By the wide curving window that dominated the far wall, portly Lord Guardian Alis was talking in low urgent tones to Lord Guardian Lysan, thin and stern, and both of them were giving meaningful glances to Kefira Qay from time to time. Behind them the sun was going down, and the great bay was turning a lovely shade of scarlet. It was such a beautiful scene that one scarcely noticed the small bright dots that were Guardian skimmers, flying patrol.

Dusk was almost upon them, the council members were grumbling and stirring impatiently in their big cushioned chairs, and Haviland Tuf had still failed to make an appearance. "When did he say he would be here?" asked Lord Guardian Khem, for the fifth time.

"He wasn't very precise, Lord Guardian," Kefira Qay replied uneasily, for the fifth time.

Khem frowned and cleared his throat.

Then one of the communicators began to beep, and Lord Guardian Lysan strode over briskly and snatched it up. "Yes?" he said. "I see. Quite good. Escort him in." He set down the communicator and rapped its edge on the table for order. The others shuffled to their seats, or broke off their conversations, or straightened. The council chamber grew silent. "That was the patrol. Tuf's shuttle has been sighted. He is on his way, I am pleased to report." Lysan glanced at Kefira Qay. "At last."

The Guardian felt even more uneasy then. It was bad enough that Tuf had kept them waiting, but she was dreading the moment when he came lumbering in, Dax peering out of his pocket. Qay had been unable to find the words to tell her superiors that Tuf proposed to save Namor with a small black kitten. She fidgeted in her seat and plucked at her large, crooked nose. This was going to be bad, she feared.

It was worse than anything she could have dreamed.

All of the Lords Guardian were waiting, stiff and silent and attentive, when the doors opened and Haviland Tuf walked in, escorted by four armed guards in golden coveralls. He was a mess. His boots made a squishing sound as he walked, and his greatcoat was smeared with mud. Dax was visible in his left pocket all right, paws hooked over its edge and large eyes intent. But the Lords Guardian weren't looking at the kitten. Beneath his other arm, Haviland Tuf was carrying a muddy rock the size of a big man's head. A thick coating of green-brown slime covered it, and it was dripping water onto the plush carpet.

Without so much as a word, Tuf went directly to the conference table and set the rock down in the center of it. That was when Kefira Qay saw the fringe of tentacles, pale and fine as threads, and realized that it wasn't a rock after all. "A mud-pot," she said aloud in surprise. No wonder she hadn't recognized it. She had seen many a mud-pot in her time, but not until after they had been washed and boiled and the tendrils trimmed away. Normally they were served with a hammer and chisel to crack the bony carapace, and a dish of melted butter and spices on the side.

The Lords Guardian looked on in astonishment, and then all twenty-five began talking at once, and the council chamber became a blur of overlapping voices.

". . . it *is* a mud-pot, I don't understand . . ."

"What is the meaning of this?"

"He makes us wait all day and then comes to council as filthy as a mudgrubber. The dignity of the council is . . ."

". . . haven't eaten a mud-pot in, oh, two, three . . ."

". . . can't be the man who is supposed to save . . ."

". . . insane, why just look at . . ."

". . . what is that thing in his pocket? Look at it! My God, it *moved!* It's alive, I tell you, I saw it . . ."

"Silence!" Lysan's voice was like a knife cutting through the hubbub. The room quieted as, one by one, the Lords Guardian turned toward him. "We have come together at your beck and call," Lysan said acidly to Tuf. "We expected you to bring us an answer. Instead you appear to have brought us dinner."

Someone snickered.

Haviland Tuf frowned down at his muddy hands, and wiped them primly on his greatcoat. Taking Dax from his pocket, Tuf deposited the lethargic black kitten on the table. Dax yawned and stretched, and ambled toward the nearest of the Lords Guardian, who stared in horror and hurriedly inched her chair back a bit. Shrugging out of his wet, muddy greatcoat, Tuf looked about for a place to put it, and finally hung it from the laser rifle of one of his escort. Only then did he turn back to the Lords Guardian. "Esteemed Lords Guardian," he said, "this is not dinner you see before you. In that very attitude lies the root of all your problems. This is the ambassador of the race that shares Namor with you, whose name, regrettably, is far beyond my small capabilities. His people will take it quite badly if you eat him."

Eventually someone brought Lysan a gavel, and he rapped it long and loud enough to attract everyone's attention, and the furor slowly ebbed away. Haviland Tuf had stood impassively through all of it, his face without expression, his arms folded against his chest. Only when silence was restored did he say, "Perhaps I should explain."

"You are mad," Lord Guardian Harvan said, looking from Tuf to the mud-pot and back again. "Utterly mad."

Haviland Tuf scooped up Dax from the table, cradled him in one arm, and began to pet him. "Even in our moment of victory, we are mocked and insulted," he said to the kitten.

"Tuf," said Lysan from the head of the long table, "what you suggest is impossible. We have explored Namor quite sufficiently in the century we have been here so as to be certain that no sentient races dwell upon it. There are no cities, no roads, no signs of any prior civilization or technology, no ruins or artifacts—*nothing*, neither above nor below the sea."

"Moreover," said another councillor, a beefy woman with a red face, "the mud-pots cannot possibly be sentient. Agreed, they have brains the size of a human brain. But that is about *all* they have. They have no eyes, ears, noses, almost no sensory equipment whatever except for touch. They have only those feeble tendrils as manipulative organs, scarcely strong enough to lift a pebble. And in fact, the tendrils are only used to anchor them to their spot on the seabed. They are hermaphroditic and downright primitive, mobile only in the first month of life, before the shell hardens and grows heavy. Once they root on the bottom and cover themselves with mud, they never move again. They stay there for hundreds of years."

"Thousands," said Haviland Tuf. "They are remarkably long-lived creatures. All that you say is undoubtedly correct. Nonetheless, your conclusions are in error. You have allowed yourself to be blinded by belligerence and fear. If you had removed yourself from the situation and paused long enough to think about it in depth, as I did, no doubt it would become obvious even to the military mind that your plight was no natural catastrophe. Only the machinations of some enemy intelligence could sufficiently explain the tragic course of events on Namor."

"You don't expect us to believe—" someone began.

"Sir," said Haviland Tuf, "I expect you to listen. If you will refrain from interrupting me, I will explain all. Then you may choose to believe or not, as suits your peculiar fancy. I shall take my fee and depart." Tuf looked at Dax. "Idiots, Dax. Everywhere we are beset by idiots." Turning his attention back to the Lords Guardian, he continued, "As I have stated, intelligence was clearly at work here. The difficulty was in finding that intelligence. I perused the work of your Namorian biologists, living and dead, read much about your flora and fauna, recreated many of the native lifeforms aboard the *Ark*. No likely candidate for sentience was immediately forthcoming. The traditional hallmarks of intelligent life include a large brain, sophisticated biological sensors, mobility, and some sort of manipulative organ, such as an opposable thumb. Nowhere on Namor could I find a creature with all of these attributes. My hypothesis, however, was still correct. Therefore I must needs move on to unlikely candidates, as there were no likely ones.

"To this end I studied the history of your plight, and

at once some things suggested themselves. You believed that your sea monsters emerged from the dark oceanic depths, but where did they first appear? In the offshore shallows—the areas where you practiced fishing and sea-farming. What did all these areas have in common? Certainly an abundance of life, that must be admitted. Yet not the *same* life. The fish that habituated the waters off New Atlantis did not frequent those of the Broken Hand. Yet I found two interesting exceptions, two species found virtually everywhere—the mudpots, lying immobile in their great soft beds through the long slow centuries and, originally, the things you called Namorian men-of-war. The ancient native race has another term for those. They call them guardians.

"Once I had come this far, it was only a matter of working out the details and confirming my suspicions. I might have arrived at my conclusion much earlier, but for the rude interruptions of liaison officer Qay, who continually shattered my concentration and finally, most cruelly, forced me to waste much time sending forth grey krakens and razorwings and sundry other such creatures. In the future I shall spare myself such liaisons.

"Yet, in a way, the experiment was useful, since it confirmed my theory as to the true situation on Namor. Accordingly I pressed on. Geographic studies showed that all of the monsters were thickest near mud-pot beds. The heaviest fighting had been in those selfsame areas, my Lords Guardian. Clearly, these mud-pots you find so eminently edible were your mysterious foes. Yet how could that be? These creatures had large brains, to be sure, but lacked all the other traits we have come to associate with sentience, as we know it. And that was the very heart of it! Clearly they were sentient as we do not know it. What sort of intelligent being could live deep under the sea, immobile, blind, deaf, bereft of all input? I pondered that question. The answer, sirs, is obvious. Such an intelligence must interact with the world in ways we cannot, must have its own modes of sensing and communicating. Such an intelligence must be telepathic. Indeed. The more I considered it, the more obvious it became.

"Thereupon it was only a matter of testing my conclusions. To that end, I brought forth Dax. All cats have some small psionic ability, Lords Guardian. Yet long centuries ago, in the days of the Great War, the soldiers of the Federal Empire struggled against enemies with terrible psi powers; Hrangan Minds and *githyanki* soulsucks. To combat such formidable foes, the genetic engineers worked with felines, and vastly heightened and sharpened their psionic abilities, so they could esp in unison with mere humans. Dax is such a special animal."

"You mean that thing is reading our minds?" Lysan said sharply.

"Insofar as you have minds to read," said Haviland Tuf, "yes. But more importantly, through Dax, I was able to reach that ancient people you have so ignominiously dubbed *mud-pots*. For they, you see, are entirely telepathic.

"For millennia beyond counting they have dwelled in tranquility and peace beneath the seas of this world. They are a slow, thoughtful, philosophic race, and they lived side by side in the billions, each linked with all the others, each an individual and each a part of the great racial whole. In a sense they were deathless, for all shared the experiences of each, and the death of one was as nothing. Experiences were few in the unchanging sea, however. For the most part their long lives are given over to abstract thought, to philosophy, to strange green dreams that neither you nor I can truly comprehend. They are silent musicians, one might say. Together they have woven great symphonies of dreams, and those songs go on and on.

"Before humanity came to Namor, they had had no real enemies for millions of years. Yet that had not always been the case. In the primordial beginnings of this wet world, the oceans teemed with creatures who relished the taste of the dreamers as much as you do. Even then, the race understood genetics, understood evolution. With their vast web of interwoven minds, they were able to manipulate the very stuff of life itself, more skillfully than any genetic engineers. And so they evolved their guardians, formidable predators with a biological imperative to protect those you call mud-pots. These were your men-of-war. From that time to this they guarded the beds, while the dreamers went back to their symphony of thought.

"Then you came, from Aquarius and Old Poseidon. Indeed you did. Lost in the reverie, the dreamers hardly noticed for many years, while you farmed and fished and discovered the taste of mud-pots. You must consider the shock you gave them, Lords Guardian. Each time you plunged one of them into boiling water, all of them shared the sensations. To the dreamers, it seemed as though some terrible new predator had evolved upon the landmass, a place of little interest to them. They had no inkling that you might be sentient, since they could no more conceive of a nontelepathic sentience than you could conceive of one blind, deaf, immobile, and edible. To them, things that moved and manipulated and ate flesh were animals, and could be nothing else.

"The rest you know, or can surmise. The dreamers are a slow people lost in their vast songs, and they were slow to respond. First they simply ignored you, in the belief that the ecosystem itself would shortly check your ravages. This did not appear to happen. To them it seemed you had no natural enemies. You bred and expanded constantly, and many thousands of minds fell silent. Finally they returned to the ancient, almost-forgotten ways of their dim past, and woke to protect themselves. They sped up the reproduction of their guardians until the seas above their beds teemed with their protectors, but the creatures that had once suf-ficed admirably against other enemies proved to be no match for you. Finally they were driven to new mea-sures. Their minds broke off the great symphony and ranged out, and they sensed and understood. At last they began to fashion new guardians, guardians formi-dable enough to protect them against this great new nemesis. Thus it went. When I arrived upon the *Ark*, and Kefira Qay forced me to unleash many new threats to their peaceful dominion, the dreamers were initially taken aback. But the struggle had sharpened them and they responded more quickly now, and in only a very short time they were dreaming newer guardians still, and sending them forth to battle to oppose the creatures I had loosed upon them. Even as I speak to you in this most imposing tower of yours, many a terrible new lifeform is stirring beneath the waves, and soon will emerge to trouble your sleep in years to come—unless, of course, you come to a peace. That is entirely your decision. I am only a humble ecological engineer. I would not dream of dictating such matters to the likes of you. Yet I do suggest it, in the strongest possible terms. So here is the ambassador plucked from the sea—at great personal discomfort to myself, I might add. The dreamers are now in much turmoil, for when they felt Dax among them and through him touched me, their world increased a millionfold. They learned of the stars today, and learned moreover that they are not alone in this cosmos. I believe they will be reasonable, as they have no use for the land, nor any taste for fish. Here is Dax as well, and myself. Perhaps we might commence to talk?"

But when Haviland Tuf fell silent at last, no one spoke for quite a long time. The Lords Guardian were all ashen and numb. One by one they looked away from Tuf's impassive features, to the muddy shell on the table.

Finally Kefira Qay found her voice. "What do they *want*?" she asked nervously.

"Chiefly," said Haviland Tuf, "they want you to stop eating them. This strikes me as an eminently sensible proposal. What is your reply?"

"Two million standards is insufficient," Haviland Tuf said some time later, sitting in the communications room of the *Ark*. Dax rested calmly in his lap, having little of the frenetic energy of the other kittens. Elsewhere in the room Suspicion and Hostility were chasing each other hither and yon.

Up on the telescreen, Kefira Qay's features broke into a suspicious scowl. "What do you mean? This was the price we agreed upon, Tuf. If you are trying to cheat us . . ."

"Cheat?" Tuf sighed. "Did you hear her, Dax? After all we have done, such grim accusations are still flung at us willy-nilly. Yes. Willy-nilly indeed. An odd phrase, when one stops to mull on it." He looked back at the telescreen. "Guardian Qay, I am fully aware of the agreed-on price. For two million standards, I solved your difficulties. I analyzed and pondered and provided the insight and the translator you so sorely needed. I have even left you with twenty-five telepathic cats, each linked to one of your Lords Guardian, to facilitate further communications after my departure. That too is included within the terms of our initial agreement, since it was necessary to the solution of your problem. And, being at heart more a philanthropist than a businessman, and deeply sentimental as well, I have even allowed you to retain Foolishness, who took a liking to you for some reason that I am entirely unable to fathom. For that, too, there is no charge."

"Then why are you demanding an additional three million standards?" demanded Kefira Qay.

"For unnecessary work which I was cruelly compelled to do," Tuf replied. "Would you care for an itemized accounting?"

"Yes, I would," she said.

"Very well. For sharks. For barracuda. For giant squid. For orcas. For grey kraken. For blue kraken. For bloodlace. For water jellies. Twenty thousand standards per item. For fortress-fish, fifty thousand standards. For the-weed-that-weeps-and-whispers, eight . . ." He went on for a long, long time.

When he was done, Kefira Qay set her lips sternly. "I will submit your bill to the Council of Guardians," she said. "But I will tell you straight out that your demands are unfair and exorbitant, and our balance of trade is not sufficient to allow for such an outflow of hard standards. You can wait in orbit for a hundred years, Tuf, but you won't get any five million standards."

Haviland Tuf raised his hands in surrender. "Ah," he

said. "So, because of my trusting nature, I must take a loss. I will not be paid, then?"

"Two million standards," said the Guardian. "As we agreed."

"I suppose I might accept this cruel and unethical decision, and take it as one of life's hard lessons. Very well then. So be it." He stroked Dax. "It has been said that those who do not learn from history are doomed to repeat it. I can only blame myself for this wretched turn of events. Why, it was only a few scant months past that I chanced to view a historical drama on this very sort of situation. It was about a seedship such as my own that rid one small world of an annoying pest, only to have the ungrateful planetary government refuse payment. Had I been wiser, that would have taught me to demand my payment in advance." He sighed. "But I was not wise, and now I must suffer." Tuf stroked Dax again, and paused. "Perhaps your Council of Guardians might be interested in viewing this particular tape, purely for recreational purposes. It is holographic, fully dramatized, and well-acted, and moreover, it gives a fascinating insight into the workings and capabilities of a ship such as this one. Highly educational. The title is *Seedship of Hamelin*."

They paid him, of course.

4
SECOND HELPINGS

It was more habit than hobby, and it was certainly not anything acquired deliberately, with malice aforethought; nonetheless, it had undoubtedly been acquired. Haviland Tuf collected spacecraft.

Perhaps it is more accurate to say he accumulated spacecraft. He certainly had the room for them. When Tuf had first set foot upon the *Ark*, he had found there five black, rakish, delta-winged shuttles, the gutted hull of a big-bellied Rhiannese merchant, and three alien starships: a heavily-armed Hruun fighter and two much stranger craft whose histories and builders remained an enigma. To that ragtag fleet was added Tuf's own damaged trading vessel, the *Cornucopia of Excellent Goods at Low Prices*.

That was only the beginning. In his travels, Tuf found other ships gathering on his landing deck much as dust balls gather under a computer console and papers gather on a bureaucrat's desk.

On Freehaven, the negotiator's one-man driveshift courier had been so badly scored by enemy fire while running the blockade that Tuf had been obliged to provide return passage in the shuttle *Manticore*—after a contract had been arrived at, of course. Thus he had acquired one driveshift courier.

On Gonesh, the elephant priests had never actually seen an elephant. Tuf had cloned them a few herds,

215

and for variety had thrown in a brace of mastodon, a wooly mammoth, and a green Trygian trumpet-tusker. The Goneshi, who wished no commerce with the rest of humanity, had paid his fee with the fleet of decrepit starships their colonizing ancestors had arrived in. Tuf had been able to sell two of the ships to museums and the rest of the fleet to a scrapyard, but he had kept one ship on a whim.

On Karaleo, he had bested the Lord of the Burnished Golden Pride in a drinking contest, and had won a luxurious lionboat for his troubles, although the loser had ingraciously removed most of the ornate solid-gold trim before handing it over.

The Artificers of Mhure, who were inordinately proud of their craftmanship, had been so pleased by the clever dragonettes Tuf had provided to check their plague of wing-rats that they had given him an iron-and-silver dragon-shuttle with huge bat-wings.

The knights of St. Christopher, whose resort world had been robbed of much of its charm by the depredations of huge flying saurians they called dragons (partly for effect and partly due to a lack of imagination), had been similarly pleased when Tuf had provided them with georges, tiny hairless simians who loved nothing better than to feast on dragon eggs. So the knights had given him a ship as well. It looked like an egg—an egg built of stone and wood. Inside the yolk were deep padded seats of oiled dragon leather, a hundred fantastical brass levers, and a stained-glass mosaic where a viewscreen ought to be. The wooden walls were hung with rich hand-woven tapestries portraying great feats of chivalry. The ship didn't work, of course—the viewscreen didn't view, the brass levers did nothing, and the life support systems couldn't support life. Tuf accepted it nonetheless.

And so it had gone, a ship here and a ship there, until his landing deck looked like an interstellar junkyard. Thus it was, when Haviland Tuf determined to make his return to S'uthlam, that he had a wide variety of starships at his disposal.

He had long ago reached the conclusion that returning in the *Ark* itself would be unwise. After all, when he had left the S'uthlamese system, the Planetary Defense Flotilla had been in hot pursuit, determined to confiscate the seedship. The S'uthlamese were a highly advanced and technologically sophisticated people who would undoubtedly have made their warships faster and more dangerous in the five standard years since Tuf had last gone among them. Therefore, a scouting sortie was imperative. Fortunately, Haviland Tuf considered himself a master of disguise.

He took the *Ark* out of drive in the cold, empty darkness of interstellar space a light-year from Sulstar, and rode down to his landing deck to inspect his fleet. At length he decided upon the lionboat. It was large and swift, its star-drive and life-support systems were functional, and Karaleo was far enough removed from S'uthlam so that commerce between the two worlds was unlikely. Therefore any flaws in his imposture would most likely go unnoticed. Before he made his departure, Haviland Tuf dyed his milk-white skin a deep bronze color, covered his long hairless features with a wig that gave him a formidable red-gold beard and a wild mane, glued on fierce eyebrows, and draped his massive, paunchy frame in all manner of brightly colored furs (synthetic) and golden chains (quasigilt, actually) until he looked the very part of a Karaleo noble. Most of his cats remained safely behind upon the *Ark*, but Dax, the black telepathic kitten with the lambent golden eyes, rode with him, snug in one cavernous pocket. He gave his ship a likely and appropriate name, stocked it with freeze-dried mushroom stew and two kegs of thick brown St. Christopher Malt, programmed its computer with several of his favorite games, and set out.

When he emerged from drive into normal space near the globe of S'uthlam and its expansive orbital docks, Tuf was hailed at once. Upon the control chamber's huge telescreen—shaped like a large eye, another interesting affectation of the Leonese—appeared the features of a small, spare man with tired eyes. "This is

Spiderhome Control, Port of S'uthlam," he identified himself. "We have you, fly. ID, please."

Haviland Tuf reached out and activated his comm unit. "This is *Ferocious Veldt Roarer*," he said in an even, dispassionate voice. "I wish to secure docking permission."

"What a surprise," the controller said, with bored sarcasm. "Dock four-thirty-seven. Out." His face was replaced by a schematic showing the location of the designated berth relative to the rest of the station. Then the transmission cut off.

A customs team came aboard after docking. One woman inspected his empty holds, ran a swift and cursory safety check to make sure this odd and unlikely craft was not going to explode or melt down or otherwise damage the web, and checked the ship over for vermin. Her companion subjected Tuf to a lengthy inquiry as to his point of origin, destination, business on S'uthlam, and other particulars of his voyage, punching his fictitious answers into a hand computer.

They were almost finished when Dax emerged sleepily from Tuf's pocket and peered at her. "What the . . ." she said, startled. She rose so suddenly she almost dropped her computer.

The kitten—well, he was almost a cat now, but still the youngest of Tuf's pets—had long, silky hair as black as the depths of space, bright golden eyes, and a curiously indolent manner. Tuf plucked him out, cradled him with one arm, stroked him with the other. "This is Dax," he said. The S'uthlamese had a disconcerting habit of regarding all animals as vermin, and he was anxious to forestall any rash actions on the part of the customs official. "He is a pet, madam, and quite harmless."

"I know what he is," the woman said sharply. "Keep him away from me. If he goes for my throat, you're in big trouble, fly."

"Indeed," said Haviland Tuf. "I will do my best to control his ferocity."

She looked relieved. "It's only a little cat, right? What's that called, a catling?"

"Your knowledge of zoology is astute," Tuf replied.

"I don't know doodles about zoology," the customs inspector said, settling herself back into her seat. "But I watch my vidshows from time to time."

"No doubt you chanced to view an educational documentary, then," Tuf said.

"Yawn," the woman said. "Neg on that, fly. I'm more for romance and adventure vids."

"I see," said Haviland Tuf. "And one such drama featured a feline, I assume."

She nodded, and just then her colleague emerged from the hold. "All clean," the other woman said. She spotted Dax, cradled in Tuf's arms, and smiled. "A cat vermin," she said happily. "Sort of cute, isn't it?"

"Don't be fooled," the first inspector warned. "They're soft and cuddly but they can rip your lungs out in the blink of an eye."

"He looks a little small for that," her partner said.

"Ha! Remember the one in *Tuf and Mune*."

"*Tuf and Mune*," Haviland Tuf repeated, his voice without expression.

The second inspector sat down next to the first. "*The Pirate and the Portmaster*," she said.

"He was the ruthless lord of life and death, in a ship as large as the sun. She was the spider queen, torn between love and loyalty. Together they changed the world," the first said.

"You can rent it in Spiderhome if you like that sort of thing," the second told him. "It's got a cat in it."

"Indeed," said Haviland Tuf, blinking. Dax began to purr.

His berth was five kilometers out along the web, so Haviland Tuf caught a pneumatic tubetrain into port center.

He was jostled on every side. On the train there were no seats. He was forced to stand with a stranger's rude elbow thrust into his ribs, the cold plasteel mask of a cybertech mere millimeters from face, and the slick carapace of some alien rubbing up against his back whenever the train slowed. When he disembarked, it was as if the car had decided to vomit out the overabundance of humanity it had ingested. The platform was swarming chaos, noise, and confusion, with passers-by milling all about him. A short young woman with features as sharp as the blade of a stiletto laid an unwelcome hand on his furs and invited him to join her at a sex parlor. No sooner had Tuf disengaged himself than he faced a newsfeed reporter, equipped with third-eye camera and ingratiating smile, who said he was doing a feature on strange flies and wanted an interview.

Tuf pushed past him to a vending booth, purchased a privacy shield, and clipped it on his belt. That provided a certain minimal help. When they saw it, the S'uthlamese politely averted their eyes, in keeping with his wishes, and he was free to proceed through the throngs more or less unmolested.

His first stop was a vidplex. He engaged a private room with couch, ordered up a bulb of watery S'uthlamese beer, and rented a copy of *Tuf and Mune*.

His second stop was the Portmaster's office. "Sir," he said to the man behind the reception console, "a query, if you will. Does Tolly Mune yet serve as Portmaster of S'uthlam?"

The secretary looked him up and down and sighed. "Flies," he said, sighing. "Of course. Who else?"

"Who else indeed," said Haviland Tuf. "It is imperative that I meet with her at once."

"Is it now? You and a thousand others. Name?"

"I am named Weemowet, a traveller out of Karaleo, master of the *Ferocious Veldt Roarer*."

The secretary grimaced and entered that into the console, then slouched back on his floater chair, waiting. Finally he shook his head. "Sorry, Weemowet," he said. "Ma's busy and her computer's never heard of you, your ship, or your planet. I can get you an appointment in about a week, if you'll state your business."

"This is unsatisfactory. My business is of a personal nature, and I would prefer to see the Portmaster immediately."

The secretary shrugged. "Defecate or evacuate the chamber, fly. Best we can do."

Haviland Tuf reflected a moment. Then he reached up, grasped the fringe of his mane, and pulled. It made a ripping sound as it came off his face. "Observe!" he said. "I am not truly Weemowet. I am Haviland Tuf in disguise." He draped his mane and beard over the top of the console.

"Haviland Tuf?" the secretary said.

"Correct."

The man laughed. "I saw that vidshow, fly. If you're Tuf, I'm Stephan Cobalt Northstar."

"Stephan Cobalt Northstar has been dead for more than a millennium. Nonetheless, I am Haviland Tuf."

"You don't look a thing like him," the secretary said.

"I am incognito, disguised as a Leonese noble."

"Oh, right. I forgot."

"Your memory is short. Will you tell Portmaster Mune that Haviland Tuf has returned to S'uthlam and wishes to speak with her at once?"

"No," the man said bluntly, "but I'll be sure to tell all my friends tonight at the orgy."

"I have the sum of sixteen million five hundred thousand standards which I wish to pay over to her," Tuf said.

"Sixteen million five hundred thousand standards?" the secretary said, impressed. "That's a lot of money."

"You have a keen perception of the obvious," Tuf said evenly. "I have found ecological engineering to be quite a lucrative profession."

"Good for you," the man said. He leaned forward. "Well, Tuf or Weemowet or whoever you are, this all has been very droll, but I have work to do. If you don't pick up your hair and scuttle out of my sight in the next few seconds, I'm going to have to call security." He was about to expand on that theme when his console buzzed at him. "Yes?" he said into his headset, frowning. "Ah, yes. Sure, Ma. Well, big, very big, two and a half meters tall, gut on him that's almost obscene. Hmmmm. No, lots of hair, or at least he did before he yanked it off and dumped it on my console. No. Says he's in disguise. Yes. Says he's got millions of standards for you."

"Sixteen million five hundred thousand," Tuf said with some precision.

The secretary swallowed. "Certainly. Right now, Ma." He broke the connection and looked up at Tuf with astonishment. "She wants to see you." He pointed. "Through that door. Careful, her office is zero gee."

"I am aware of the Portmaster's aversion to gravity," said Haviland Tuf. He gathered up his discarded mane, tucked it under one arm, and moved with stiff dignity toward the indicated door, which slid open at his approach.

She was waiting in the inner office, floating in the center of the clutter, her legs crossed, her long silver-and-iron hair moving lazily about her lean, open, homely face like a wreath of smoke. "So you came back," she said when Tuf swam into view.

Haviland Tuf was uncomfortable in zero-gee. He pulled himself to her visitor's chair, securely bolted to what should have been the floor, and strapped himself in. He folded his hands neatly atop the great curve of his stomach. His mane, abandoned, drifted about on the air currents. "Your secretary refused to relay my messages," he said. "How did you come to suspect that it was me?"

She grinned. "Who else would call his ship *Ferocious Veldt Roarer*?" she said. "Besides, it's been five years almost to the day. I had a feeling you'd be the punctual sort, Tuf."

"I see," said Haviland Tuf. With deliberate dignity, he reached inside his synthafurs, broke the sealseam on the inner pocket, and extracted a vinyl wallet lined with crystal datachips in tiny pouches. "Herewith, madam, I am most pleased to tender you the sum of sixteen million five hundred thousand standards, in payment of the first half of my debt to the Port of S'uthlam for the restoration and refitting of the *Ark*. You will find the funds secure in appropriate financial depositories on Osiris, ShanDellor, Old Poseidon, Ptola, Lyss, and New Budapest. These chips will permit access."

"Thanks," she said. She took the wallet, flipped it

open, glanced at it briefly, and let it loose. It floated up toward the mane. "Somehow I knew you'd find the standards, Tuf."

"Your faith in my business acumen is reassuring," said Haviland Tuf. "Now, concerning this vidshow."

"*Tuf and Mune?* You've seen it, then?"

"Indeed," said Tuf.

"Goddamn," Tolly Mune said, grinning crookedly. "So what'd you think, Tuf?"

"I am forced to admit that it evoked a certain perverse fascination in me, for obvious reasons. The idea of such a drama has an undeniable appeal to my vanity, but the execution left much to be desired."

Tolly Mune laughed. "What bothers you the most?"

Tuf raised a single long finger. "In a word, inaccuracy."

She nodded. "Well, the vidshow Tuf masses about half what you do, I'd say, his face is a lot more mobile, his speech wasn't half as stilted, and he had a spinneret's musculature and an acrobat's coordination, but they *did* shave his head in the interests of authenticity."

"He wore a mustache," said Haviland Tuf. "I do not."

"They thought it looked roguish. Then again, look what they did to me. I don't mind that they took fifty years off my age, and I don't mind that they enhanced my face until I looked like a Vandeeni dream-princess, but those goddamned *breasts!*"

"No doubt they wished to emphasize the certainty of your mammalian evolution," said Tuf. "These might be put down as minor alterations in the interests of presenting a more aesthetic entertainment, but I regard the wanton liberties taken with my opinions and philosophies to be a far more serious matter. In particular, I object to my final speech, wherein I opine that the genius of evolving humanity can and will solve all problems, and that eco-engineering has freed the S'uthlamese to multiply without fear or limit, and thus evolve to greatness and ultimate godhood. This is in utter contradiction to the actual views I expressed to you at the time, Portmaster Mune. If you will recall our conversations, I told you distinctly that any solution to your food problem, whether technological or ecological in nature, must of necessity be only a stopgap if your people continued to practice unrestrained reproduction."

"You were the hero," Tolly Mune said. "They couldn't very well have you sound anti-life, could they?"

"Other flaws are also present in the narrative. Those unfortunate enough to view this fiction have received a wildly distorted view of the events of five years ago. Havoc is a harmless though spirited feline whose ancestors have been domesticated since the veritable dawn of human history, and it is my recollection that when you treacherously seized her on a legal technicality in a backhanded scheme to force me to hand over the *Ark*, she and I both tendered our surrender peacefully. At no point did she rip even a single security man apart with her claws, let alone six of them."

"She did claw the back of my hand once," said Tolly Mune. "Anything else?"

"I have nothing but approbation for the policies and conduct of Josen Rael and the High Council of S'uthlam," Tuf said. "It is true that they, and particularly First Councillor Rael, behaved in an unethical and unscrupulous manner. Nonetheless, on their behalf, it must be said that at no point did Josen Rael subject me to torture, nor did he kill any of my cats in an effort to bend me to his will."

"He didn't sweat that much either," said Tolly Mune, "and he *never* drooled. He was actually a decent man." She sighed. "Poor Josen."

"Finally we come to the crux of the matter. Crux indeed—a strange word when one rolls it upon the tongue, but quite appropriate to this discussion. The crux, Portmaster Mune, was and is the nature of our wager. When I brought the newly salvaged *Ark* in for refitting, your High Council resolved to have her. I refused to sell, and as you had no legal pretext for seizing the ship, you confiscated Havoc as vermin, and threatened to destroy her unless I thumbed a transfer. Is this correct in its essentials?"

"Sounds right to me," Tolly Mune said amiably.

"We resolved the impasse with a wager. I would

attempt to forestall S'uthlam's food crisis via eco-engineering, thus averting the great famine that threatened you. If I failed, the *Ark* was yours. If I succeeded, you were to return Havoc and, moreover, perform the refitting and repairs that I required and allow me ten standard years to pay the resulting bill."

"Right," she said.

"To my best recollection, at no point was carnal knowledge of your body included in my terms, Portmaster Mune. I would be the last to diminish the bravura you displayed in adversity, when the High Council shut down the tubes and secured all the docks. You risked your person and career, smashed through a plasteel window, flew across kilometers of stark vacuum clad only in skinthins and propelled by airjets, dodged security squads all the way, and in the end barely avoided destruction by your own Planetary Defense Flotilla as they moved against me. Even one as plain and blunt as myself must admit that these acts possess a certain heroic, even romantic, quality that in ancient days might be the stuff of legends. However, the purpose of this melodramatic albeit daring voyage was to return Havoc to my custody, as per the terms of our agreement, and not to deliver up your body to my," he blinked, "lusts. Furthermore, you made it perfectly clear at that time that your actions were motivated by a sense of honor and fear of the corrupting influence the *Ark* might have upon your leaders. As I recall, neither physical passion nor romantic love played any part in your calculations."

Portmaster Tolly Mune grinned. "Look at us, Tuf. A damned unlikely pair of star-crossed lovers. But you've got to admit, it makes a better story."

Tuf's long face was still and expressionless. "Surely you do not defend this grossly inaccurate vidshow," he said flatly.

The Portmaster laughed again. "Defend it? Puling hell, I *wrote* it!"

Haviland Tuf blinked six times.

Before he could frame a reply, the outer door slid open and the newsfeed peeps came swarming in, a good two dozen of them, yammering and exclaiming and shouting out rude questions. In the center of each forehead, a third eye whirred and blinked.

"This way, Tuffer. Smile."

"Do you have any cats with you?"

"Will you be taking out a marriage contract, Portmaster?"

"Where's the *Ark*?"

"Let's have an embrace, hey!"

"When did you turn brown, trader?"

"Where's the mustache?"

"Any opinion of *Tuf and Mune*, Citizen Tuf?"

"How's Havoc these days?"

Strapped immobile into his chair, Haviland Tuf glanced up, down, and all around with a series of quick, precise head motions. He blinked and said nothing. The torrent of questions continued until Portmaster Tolly Mune came swimming effortlessly through the pack, pushing peeps aside with either hand, and settled down next to Tuf. She slid her arm through his and kissed him lightly on the cheek. "Puling hell," she said, "hold your goddamned bladders, he just got here." She raised a hand. "No questions, sorry. We're invoking privacy. It's been five years, after all. Give us some time to get reacquainted."

"Are you going off to the *Ark* together?" one of the more aggressive reporters asked. She was floating a half-meter in front of Tuf's face, her third eye whirring.

"Of course," said Tolly Mune. "Where else?"

It was not until the *Ferocious Veldt Roarer* was well out of the web, en route back to the *Ark*, that Haviland Tuf deigned to walk back to the cabin he had assigned to Tolly Mune. He was freshly showered, cleansed, and scrubbed, all traces of disguise removed. His long hairless face was as white and unreadable as blank paper. He wore a plain gray coverall that did little to conceal his formidable paunch, and a green duck-billed cap adorned with the golden theta of the Ecological Engineers covered his bald pate. Dax rode upon one broad shoulder.

Tolly Mune had been reclining and sipping on a bulb of St. Christopher Malt, but she grinned when he entered. "This is damn good stuff," she said. "Well now, who's that? Not Havoc."

"Havoc is safely back aboard the *Ark*, with her mate and her kittens, though in truth they can scarcely be said to be kittens any longer. The feline population of my ship has grown somewhat since my last call at S'uthlam, albeit not as precipitously as the human population of S'uthlam is wont to grow." He lowered himself stiffly into a seat. "This is Dax. While every cat is of course special, Dax might accurately be said to be extraordinary. All cats have a touch of psi; this is well known. Due to an unusual set of circumstances I encountered upon the world known as Namor, I initiated a program to enhance and expand upon this innate feline ability. Dax is the end result, madam. We share a certain rapport, and Dax is gifted with a psi ability that is far from rudimentary."

"In short," said Tolly Mune, "you cloned yourself a mindreading cat."

"Your perspicacity remains acute, Portmaster," Tuf replied. He folded his hands. "We have much to discuss. Perhaps you will be so kind as to explain why you have requested that I bring the *Ark* back to S'uthlam, why you have insisted on accompanying me, and most crucially why you have embroiled me in this strange though colorful deception, and even gone so far as to make free with my person?"

Tolly Mune sighed. "Tuf, you remember how things stood when we parted five years ago?"

"My memory is unimpaired," said Haviland Tuf.

"Good. Then you might recall that you left me in a real puling mess."

"You anticipated immediate removal from your post as Portmaster, trial on charges of high treason, and a sentence to a penal farm on the Larder," said Tuf. "Nonetheless, you declined my effort to provide you with free transport to another system of your choice, preferring instead to return to face imprisonment and disgrace."

"Whatever the hell I am, I'm S'uthlamese," she said. "These are my people, Tuf. Big puling fools at times, but still my goddamned people."

"Your loyalty is no doubt commendable. Since you are still Portmaster, I must assume that circumstances changed."

"I changed them," Tolly Mune said.

"Indeed."

"Had to, if I didn't want to spend the rest of my life driving a weeder-wheel through the neograss while gravity pulled me apart." She made a face. "As soon as I got back to port, security grabbed me. I'd defied the High Council, broken laws, damaged property, and helped you escape with a ship they wanted to confiscate. Damned dramatic, wouldn't you say?"

"My opinion has no bearing on the matter."

"So dramatic, in fact, that it had to be either a crime of enormous magnitude or an act of enormous heroism. Josen was sick about it. We went way back, him and me, and he wasn't a bad man really, I told you that. But he was First Councillor, and he knew what he had to do. He had to try me for treason. And I'm no damned fool either, Tuf. I knew what I had to do." She leaned forward. "I wasn't that pleased by my cards either, but I had to play them or fold. To save my bony ass, I had to destroy Josen—discredit him and most of the High Council. I had to make myself a heroine and him a villain, in terms that would be perfectly clear to every goddamned drooling slackjaw in the undercity."

"I see," said Tuf. Dax was purring; the Portmaster was perfectly sincere. "Ergo the overblown melodrama that was called *Tuf and Mune.*"

"I needed cals for legal costs," she said. "That was real enough, puling hell, but I used it as an excuse to sell my version of events to one of the big vidnets. I, let us say, seasoned the story a bit. They were so excited they decided to follow the newsfeed exclusive with a dramatized version. I was more than happy to provide the script. Had a collaborator, of course, but I told him what to write. Josen never understood what was happening. He wasn't as canny a pol as he thought, and his heart was never in it. Besides, I had help."

"From what source?" Tuf inquired.

"A young man named Cregor Blaxon, mostly."

"The name is unknown to me."

"He was on the High Council. Councillor for agriculture. A very crucial post, Tuf, and Blaxon was the youngest man ever to fill it. Youngest man on the Council, too. You'd think he'd be satisfied, right?"

"Please do not presume to tell me my thoughts, unless you have developed psionic abilities in my absence. I would think no such thing, madam. I have found that it is almost always a mistake to assume that any human being is ever satisfied."

"Cregor Blaxon is and was a very ambitious man," Tolly Mune said. "He was part of Josen's administration. Both of them were technocrats, but Blaxon aspired to the First Councillor's seat and that was where Josen Rael had planted his buttocks."

"I grasp his motivation."

"Blaxon became my ally. He was quite impressed with what you'd provided anyway. The omni-grain, the fish and that plankton, the slime-molds, all the damn mushrooms. And he saw what was happening. He used every bit of his power to cut short bio-testing and put your stuff in the field. Screamer priorities all around. Did a smash-run on any puling fool tried to slow things down. Josen Rael was too preoccupied to notice."

"The intelligent and efficient politician is a species virtually unknown in the galaxy," said Haviland Tuf. "Perhaps I might secure a scraping from Cregor Blaxon for the *Ark's* cell library."

"You're getting ahead of me."

"The end of the story is obvious. The appearance of vanity notwithstanding, I will venture a guess that my small effort at eco-engineering was deemed a success, and that Cregor Blaxon's energetic implementation of my solutions rebounded to his credit."

"He called it Tuf's Flowering," Tolly Mune said with a certain cynical twist to the corner of her mouth. "The newsfeeds took up the term. Tuf's Flowering, a new golden age for S'uthlam. Soon we had edible fungus growing along the walls of our sewer systems. We started huge mushroom farms in every undercity. Carpets of neptune's shawl crept across the surface of our seas, and underneath, your fish multiplied at an astounding rate. We planted your omni-grain instead of neograss and nanowheat, and the first crop gave us almost triple the caloric yield. You did one nova-class job of eco-engineering for us, Tuf."

"The compliment is noted with due appreciation," said Tuf.

"Fortunately for me, the Flowering was already in full bud when *Tuf and Mune* hit the nets, long before I went to trial. Creg was extolling your brilliance to the newsfeeds daily and telling billions that our food crisis was done, finished, over." The Portmaster shrugged. "So he made you a hero, for his own reasons. Couldn't help it, if he wanted to replace Josen. And that helped make me a heroine. It all ties together in one big neat puling knot—prettiest goddamned thing you'd ever want to see. I'll spare you the details. The end of it was, Tolly Mune acquitted, restored to office in triumph. Josen Rael in disgrace, denounced by all the opinionaters, forced to resign. Half the High Council resigned with him. Cregor Blaxon became the new technocratic leader and won the elections that followed. Creg's now First Councillor. Josen, poor soul, died two years ago. And you and I have become the stuff of legends, Tuf, the most celebrated lovers since, oh, puling hell, since all those famous romantic couples from ancient times—you know, Romeo and Juliet, Samson and Delilah, Sodom and Gomorrah, Marx and Lenin."

Perched on Tuf's shoulder, Dax began to emit a low, frightened growl. Tiny claws dug through the fabric of Tuf's jumpsuit into his flesh. Haviland Tuf blinked, then reached over and stroked the kitten soothingly. "Portmaster Mune, your smile is broad and your news seems to indicate nothing but the trite yet nonetheless eternally popular happy ending, but Dax has grown alarmed, as if you seethe with turmoil beneath this placid surface. Perhaps you are omitting some crucial part of the tale."

"Just the footnote, Tuf," the Portmaster said.

"Indeed. What might that be?"

"Twenty-seven years, Tuf. Does that trip any claxons in your head?"

"Indeed. Before I embarked upon my program of ecological engineering, your projections indicated S'uthlam to be twenty-seven standard years from mass famine, given the alarming population growth and the declining food resources."

"That was five years ago," said Tolly Mune.

"Indeed."

"Twenty-seven minus five."

"Twenty-two," said Tuf. "I assume there is a point in this exercise in elementary arithmetic."

"Twenty-two years left," Portmaster Tolly Mune said. "Ah, but that was before the *Ark*, before the genius ecologist Tuf and the daring spinneret Mune fixed it all, before the miracle of the loaves and fishes, before courageous young Cregor Blaxon ushered in Tuf's Flowering."

Haviland Tuf turned his head to look at the cat on his shoulder. "I detect a certain note of sarcasm in her voice," he said to Dax.

Tolly Mune sighed, reached into a pocket, and extracted a case of crystalline data-chips. "Here you go, lover," she said. She tossed them through the air.

Tuf reached up, caught the spinning case in a large white hand, said nothing.

"Everything you need is there. Straight from the council databanks. The hard-classified files, of course. All the reports, all the projections, all the analyses, and it's for your eyes only. You understand? That's why I was so puling mysterious and that's why we're heading back to the *Ark*. Creg and the High Council figured our romance made a terrific cover. Let the billions of newsfeed viewers think we're sexing up a storm. As long as their heads are full of visions of the pirate and Portmaster blazing new sexual frontiers, they won't stop to ponder what we're really up to, and everything can be done quietly. We want loaves and fishes, Tuf, but this time on a covered platter, you understand? Those are my instructions."

"What is the most recent projection?" said Haviland Tuf, his voice even and expressionless.

Dax stood up, hissing in alarm, and sudden fear.

Tolly Mune sipped on her beer, and slumped back deep into her chair. She closed her eyes. "Eighteen years," she said. She looked like the hundred-year-old woman she was, instead of a youngster of sixty, and her voice was infinitely weary. "Eighteen years," she repeated, "and counting."

Tolly Mune was far from unsophisticated. Having spent her life on S'uthlam, with its vast continent-wide cities, its teeming billions, its towers rising ten kays into the sky, its deep underways far below the surface, and its great orbital elevator, she was not a woman easily impressed by mere size. But there was something about the *Ark*, she thought.

She felt it from the moment of their arrival, as the great dome of the landing deck cracked open beneath them and Tuf took the *Ferocious Veldt Roarer* down into darkness and settled it among his shuttles and junked starships, upon a circular landing pad that glowed a dim blue in welcome. The dome closed over them and atmosphere was pumped back in; to fill so large a space so quickly it came with gale force, howling and sighing all around them. Finally Tuf opened their locks and preceded her down an ornate stair that slid from the lionboat's mouth like a gilded tongue. Below, a small three-wheeled cart was waiting. Tuf drove past the clutter of dead and abandoned ships, some more alien than any Tolly Mune had ever seen. He drove in silence, looking neither right nor left, Dax a limp, boneless, purring ball of fur stretched across his knees.

Tuf gave her an entire deck to herself. Hundreds of sleeping berths, computer stations, labs, accessways, sanitary stations, recreation halls, kitchens, and no tenants but her. On S'uthlam, a cityspace this large would have housed a thousand people, in apartments smaller than the *Ark*'s storage closets. Tuf turned off the gravity grid on that level, since he knew she preferred zero-gee.

"If you have need of me, you will find my own

quarters on the top deck, under full gravity," he told her. "I intend to address all my energies to the problems of S'uthlam. I will not require your counsel or assistance. No offense is intended, Portmaster, but it has been my bitter experience that such liaisons are more trouble than they are worth and serve only to distract me. If there is an answer to your most vexing quandary, I shall arrive at it soonest by my own efforts, left undisturbed. I shall program a leisurely voyage toward S'uthlam and its web; it is my hope that when we arrive I will be able to solve your difficulty."

"If you can't," she reminded him sharply, "we get the ship. Those were the terms."

"I am fully aware of this," said Haviland Tuf. "In the event you grow restive, the *Ark* offers a full spectrum of diversions, entertainments, and occupations. Feel free to avail yourself to the automated food facilities as well. The fare so provided is not equal to the meals I prepare personally, though it will acquit itself admirably when compared to typical S'uthlamese provender, I have no doubt. Partake of as many meals as you require during the day; I will be pleased to have you join me each evening for dinner at eighteen-hundred ship's time. Kindly be punctual." And so saying, he took his leave.

The computer system that ran the great ship observed cycles of light and darkness, to simulate the passage of day and night. Tolly Mune spent her nights before a holo monitor, viewing dramas several millennia old recorded upon worlds half-legendary. Her days she spent exploring—first the deck that Tuf had ceded her, and then the rest of the ship. The more she saw and learned, the more awed and uneasy Tolly Mune became.

She sat for days in the old captain's chair on the tower ridge that Tuf had bypassed as inconvenient, watching random selections from the ancient log roll down the great vidscreen.

She walked a labyrinth of decks and corridors, found three skeletons in scattered parts of the *Ark* (only two of them human), wondered at one corridor intersection where the thick duralloy bulkheads were blistered and cracked, as if by great heat.

She spent hours in a library she discovered, touching and handling old books, some printed on thin leaves of metal or plastic, others on real paper.

She returned to the landing deck and climbed around a few of the derelict starships Tuf had there. She stood in the armory and gazed on a frightening array of weapons, some of them obsolete, some of them unrecognizable, some of them forbidden.

She wandered down the dim vastness of the central shaft that cored the ship, walked the full thirty kays of its length, her bootsteps echoing overhead, her breath coming hard by the end of her daily treks. Around her were cloning vats, growth tanks, microsurgeries, and computer stations in staggering profusion. Ninety percent of the vats were empty, but here and there the Portmaster found life growing. She peered through dusty glass and thick, translucent fluids at dim, living shapes, shapes as small as her hand, and shapes as large as a tubetrain. It made her feel cold.

In fact, the whole ship seemed chilly and somehow frightening to Tolly Mune.

The only real warmth was to be found on the tiny portion of the top deck where Haviland Tuf spent his nights and days. The long, narrow communications room he had refitted as his central control was cozy and comfortable. His quarters were crowded with worn, overstuffed furniture and an amazing assortment of bric-a-brac accumulated in his voyagings. The smell of food and beer permeated the air here, bootsteps did not echo so, and there was light and noise and life. And cats.

Tuf's cats had free run of most of the ship, but most of them seemed to prefer to stay close to Tuf himself. He had seven now. Chaos, a long-haired gray tom with imperious eyes and an indolent, dominating manner, was the lord of all he surveyed. He could most often be found sitting on top of Tuf's master console in the control chamber, his bushy tail twitching like a metronome. Havoc had lost energy and gained weight in five years. She did not seem to recognize the Portmaster at first, but after a few days the old familiarity returned, and Havoc took up the acquaintance where it had dropped, and sometimes even accompanied Tolly on her wanderings.

Then there were Ingratitude, Doubt, Hostility, and Suspicion. "The kittens," Tuf called them, though they were really young cats now, "born of Choas and Havoc, madam. Originally they comprised a litter of five. I left Foolishness behind on Namor."

"It's always best to leave foolishness behind," she said. "I never figured you to part with a cat, though."

"Foolishness developed an inexplicable fondness for a vexing and unpredictable young woman of Namorian origin," he said. "Since I had many cats and she had none, it seemed the appropriate gesture under the circumstances. Although the feline is a splendid and admirable creature, it remains relatively scarce in this sad modern galaxy. Thus my innate generosity and sense of duty to my fellow humans prompt me to offer cats to worlds such as Namor. A culture with cats is richer and more humane than one deprived of their unique companionship."

"Right," said Tolly Mune, smiling. Hostility was near at hand. She scooped him up carefully, stroked him. His fur was very soft. "Strange names you gave this lot."

"Perhaps more apt to human nature than to the feline," Tuf agreed. "I bestowed them on a whim."

Ingratitude, Doubt, and Suspicion were gray, like their father; Hostility was black and white like Havoc. Doubt was noisy and fat, Hostility was aggressive and rambunctious, Suspicion was shy and liked to hide under Tuf's chair. They liked to play together, a boisterous cat pack, and seemed to find Tolly Mune endlessly fascinating, climbing all over her whenever she paid Tuf a visit. Sometimes they turned up in the least likely places. Hostility landed on her back one day as she ascended an escalator, and the surprise left her breathless and shocked. She grew accustomed to having Doubt in her lap during meals, begging slivers of food.

And then there was the seventh cat: Dax.

Dax, with fur the color of night and eyes like small golden lamps. Dax, the single most lethargic vermin she had ever seen, who preferred being carried to walking. Dax, who peered from Tuf's pocket, or out from beneath his cap, who sat on his knees or rode on his shoulder. Dax, who never played with the older kittens, who seldom made a sound, whose golden glance could somehow displace even huge, lordly Chaos from a chair both of them coveted. The black kitten was with Tuf constantly. "Your familiar," Tolly Mune said to him one mealtime, after she had been aboard for nearly twenty days. She pointed a knife. "That makes you a . . . what was the term?"

"There were several," Tuf said. "Witch, wizard, warlock. The nomenclature derives from Old Earth myth, I believe."

"It fits," said Tolly Mune. "Sometimes I feel this ship is haunted."

"This suggests why it is wiser to rely upon intellect rather than feelings, Portmaster. Accept my assurance that if ghosts or other supernatural entities did in fact exist, they would be represented aboard the *Ark* by cell samples, in order that they might be cloned. I have never encountered such samples. My stock in trade does include species sometimes referred to as hooded draculas, wind-wraiths, lycanthropes, vampires, garghouls, witchweed, and other such terms, but these are not the genuine mythic articles, I fear."

Tolly Mune smiled. "Good thing."

"More wine, perhaps? It is an excellent Rhiannese vintage."

"That's one good idea," she said, splashing some into her glass. She still would have preferred a squeeze bulb; open liquids were sneaky things always waiting to spill. "My throat's dry anyway. You don't need monsters, Tuf. This ship of yours could destroy worlds as it is."

"This is obvious," said Tuf. "Equally obvious, it can save worlds."

"Like ours? You have a second miracle up your sleeve, Tuf?"

"Alas, miracles are as mystic as ghosts and goblins, and there is nothing up my sleeves but my arms. However, the human intellect is still capable of certain less-than-miraculous breakthroughs." He rose slowly to his full height. "If you are quite finished with your pop-onion pie and wine, perhaps you will accompany me to the computer room. I have applied myself diligently to your problems and have arrived at a few conclusions."

Tolly Mune got up quickly. "Lead on," she said.

"Note," said Haviland Tuf. He pressed a command key; a projection flashed upon one of the screens.

"What's this?" asked Molly Tune.

"The projection I made five years ago," he said. Dax hopped into his lap; Tuf reached out and stroked the black kitten. "The parameters used were the then-current S'uthlamese population figures and the projected population growth, as of that time. My analysis indicated that the additional food resources introduced into your society by means of what Cregor Blaxon was so kind as to dub Tuf's Flowering should have given you at minimum ninety-four standard years before the specter of planetary famine again threatened S'uthlam."

"Well, that's one goddamned projection that wasn't worth a pot of vermin," Tolly Mune said bluntly.

Tuf raised a finger. "A more volatile man than myself might take umbrage at the implication that his analysis was defective. Fortunately, I am of a cool and tolerant nature. Nonetheless, you are most incorrect, Portmaster Mune. My projections were as accurate as they could possibly have been."

"Then you're saying that we *don't* have starvation and collapse staring down at us eighteen years in the future? That we've got, what, almost a century?" She shook her head. "I'd like to believe that, but—"

"I said no such thing, Portmaster. Within its prescribed margin of error, the latest S'uthlamese projection also appears to be quite accurate insofar as I have been able to determine."

"Both projections can't be correct," she said. "That's impossible, Tuf."

"You are wrong, madam. During the intervening five

years, the parameters changed. Attend." He reached out and depressed another button. A new line, rising sharply, curved across the screen. "This represents the present curve of population increase on S'uthlam. Note how it climbs, Portmaster. An astonishing rate of ascent. Were I of a poetic turn of mind, I might even say it soars. Fortunately, I am not so afflicted. I am a blunt man who speaks bluntly." He raised a finger. "Before we can hope to rectify your situation, it is necessary to understand that situation and how it came to be. Here all is clarity. Five years ago, I employed the resources of the *Ark,* and, if I may be so bold as to put my accustomed modesty aside, tendered to you extraordinarily efficient service. The S'uthlamese wasted no time in undoing everything I had done. Let me put it succinctly, Portmaster. No sooner had the Flowering taken root, so to speak, than your people rushed back to their private chambers, unleashed their carnal lusts and parental urges, and began reproducing faster than ever. Mean family size is greater now than five years ago, by .0072 persons, and your average citizen becomes a parent sooner by .0102 years. Small changes, you may protest, but when factored into the enormous base population of your world, and modified by all other relevant parameters, they make a dramatic difference. The difference, to be precise, between ninety-four years and eighteen."

Tolly Mune stared at the lines crossing upon the screen. "Puling hell," she muttered. "I should have figured, goddamn it. This sort of information is classified, for obvious reasons, but I should have known." Her hands clenched into fists. "Goddamn it to hell," she said. "Creg made such a newsfeed carnival out of the goddamned Flowering, no wonder this is happening. Why should anyone refrain from birthing—the food problem has been solved, right? The goddamned First Councillor said so. Good times had arrived, right? All the damned zeros had turned out to be puling anti-life alarmists once more, the technocrats had worked another miracle. How could anyone doubt that they'd do it again, and again, and again? Oh, yes. So be a good church member, have more kids, help humanity evolve to godhood and defeat entropy. Hey, why not?" She made a disgusted noise. "Tuf, why are people such puling idiots?"

"This quandary is even more perplexing than the dilemma that is S'uthlam," said Tuf, "and I fear I am not equipped to answer it. So long as you are engaged in the division of blame, you might also assign some to yourself, Portmaster. Whatever misleading impression might have been given by First Councillor Cregor Blaxon was most certainly confirmed in the popular mind by that unfortunate final oration delivered by my impersonator in *Tuf and Mune*."

"All right, damn it. I'm guilty, I helped gnarl it up. That's past now. The question is, what can we do about it?"

"You can do little, I fear," said Haviland Tuf, his face expressionless.

"And you? You worked the loaves and fishes miracle once. Can we get a second helping, Tuf?"

Haviland Tuf blinked. "I am a more experienced ecological engineer now than when I first attempted to deal with the problem of S'uthlam. I am more familiar with the full range of species contained within the *Ark*'s cell library, and the effect of each upon individual ecosystems. I have even increased my stock in trade to a certain extent during the course of my travels hither and yon. Indeed, I can be of service." He cleared the screens and folded his hands atop his stomach. "There will be a price."

"A price? We paid your damn price, remember? My spinnerets fixed your goddamned ship."

"Indeed they did, even as I repaired your ecology. I do not require any further repairs or refitting of the *Ark* at this time. You, however, appear to have damaged your ecology once again so you have further need of my services. It strikes me as only equitable that I be compensated for my efforts. I have many operating expenses, chief among which is my still-formidable debt to the Port of S'uthlam. By dint of exhausting and unremitting labor on numerous scattered worlds, I have raised the first half of the thirty-three million standards you assessed me, but an equal amount remains to be paid, and I have but five additional years to earn it. How can I say if this will be possible? Perhaps the next dozen worlds on which I call will have ecologies without blemish, or will be so impoverished that I will be forced to grant them severe discounts if I am to serve them at all. Day and night the size of my debt preys upon my mind, often interfering with the clarity and precision of my thoughts and thus making me less effective at my profession. Indeed, I have a sudden hunch that when wrestling with a challenge of the vast magnitude of that posed by S'uthlam, my performance might be far superior were my mind to be clear and untroubled."

Tolly Mune had expected something like this. She had told Creg as much, and he'd given her limited budgetary discretion. Still, she managed a frown. "How much do you want, Tuf?"

"The sum of ten million standards leaps to mind," he said. "Being a round number, it might be deducted from my bill easily without posing any knotty problems of arithmetic."

"Too damn much," she said. "Maybe I could get the High Council to agree to lop off, say, two million. No more."

"Let us compromise on nine million," said Tuf. A long finger scratched Dax behind a small black ear; the cat silently turned its golden eyes on Tolly Mune.

"Nine isn't much of a compromise between ten and two," she said drily.

"I am a better ecological engineer than mathematician," said Tuf. "Perhaps eight?"

"Four. No more. Creger will implode on me as it is."

Tuf fixed her with an unblinking stare, and said nothing. His face was cool and still and impassive.

"Four and a half million," she said under the weight of his gaze. She felt Dax staring, too, and suddenly wondered if that damn cat was reading her mind. She pointed. "Damn it," she said, "that little black bastard knows just how high I'm authorized to go, doesn't he?"

"An interesting notion," said Tuf. "Seven million might be acceptable to me. I am in a generous mood."

"Five and one-half," she snapped. What was the use? Dax began to purr loudly.

"Leaving a net principal of eleven million standards to be paid within five years," said Tuf. "Accepted, Portmaster Mune, with one additional proviso."

"What's that?" she said suspiciously.

"I will present my solution to First Councillor Cregor Blaxon and yourself at a public conference, to be attended by newsfeed peeps from all of your vidnets, and broadcast live over the entirety of S'uthlam."

Tolly Mune laughed aloud. "Incredible," she said. "Creg will never agree. You can forget that idea."

Haviland Tuf sat petting Dax, and said nothing.

"Tuf, you don't understand the difficulties. The situation is too damned volatile. You'll have to give on this one."

The silence lingered.

"Puling hell," she swore. "Tell you what, write down what you want to say, and let us look it over. If you avoid anything that might stir up problems, I suppose we can give you access."

"I prefer that my remarks be spontaneous," Tuf said.

"Maybe we can record the conference and broadcast it after editing," she said.

Haviland Tuf kept silent. Dax stared at her, unblinking.

Tolly Mune looked deep into those knowing golden eyes, and sighed. "You win," she said. "Cregor will be furious, but I'm a puling heroine and you're a returning conqueror, I suppose I can cram it down his gullet. But why, Tuf?"

"A whim," said Haviland Tuf. "I am often taken by such fancies. Perhaps I wish to savor a moment in the light of publicity and enjoy my role as savior. Perhaps I wish to show the S'uthlamese billions that I do not wear a mustache."

"I'll believe in goblins and ghouls before I pay one standard for that load of ore," said Tolly Mune. "Tuf, there are reasons why our population size and the gravity of the food crisis are kept secret, you know. Policy reasons. Now, you wouldn't be thinking about, ah, opening that particular box of vermin, would you?"

"An interesting concept," Tuf said, blinking, his face blank and noncommittal.

Dax purred.

"Unaccustomed as I am to public speaking and the unflattering glare of publicity," Haviland Tuf began, "I felt it incumbent upon myself to come before you and explain certain things."

He stood before a four-meter-square telescreen in the largest hall in Spiderhome, with a seating capacity for almost a thousand. The room was packed; newsfeed reporters were jammed in elbow-to-elbow up front, twenty rows of them, a tiny miniaturized camera in the center of each forehead busily recording the scene. Farther back were the curious who had come to watch—spinnerets of all ages, sexes, and professions, from cybertechs and bureaucrats to eroticists and poets, wealthy groundworms who had come up the elevator for the show, flies from distant systems passing through the web. On the platform with Tuf were Portmaster Tolly Mune and First Councillor Cregor Blaxon. Blaxon's smile looked forced; perhaps he was recalling how the newsfeed peeps had all captured the long, awkward moment when Tuf blinked at his proferred hand. For that matter, Tolly Mune looked a bit uneasy.

Haviland Tuf, however, looked impressive. He loomed over every man and woman in the hall, his gray vinyl greatcoat sweeping the floor, the sigil of the EEC upon his green billed cap.

"First," he said, "permit me to point out that I do not wear a mustache." The statement provoked general laughter. "Nor have your esteemed Portmaster and myself ever united in physical congress, vidshows notwithstanding, though I have no reason to doubt that she is a skillful practitioner of the erotic arts whose favors would be held in high esteem by any who enjoy that sort of diversion." The horde of newspeeps, like one clamorous hundred-headed beast, turned and fixed their third eyes upon Tolly Mune. The Portmaster was slumped deep in her seat, with a hand rubbing her temples. Her sigh was audible as far as the fourth row.

"These points of information are minor in nature," said Tuf, "and are advanced solely in the interest of veracity. The major reason that I have insisted upon this gathering is professional rather than personal, however. I have no doubt that each of you listening to this newsfeed is aware of the phenomenon that your High Council called Tuf's Flowering."

Cregor Blaxon smiled and nodded his head.

"I must presume, however, that you are unaware of the imminence of what I will be so bold as to call S'uthlam's Wilting."

The First Councillor's smile wilted, too, and Portmaster Tolly Mune winced. The newspeeps swung back to Tuf en masse.

"You are indeed fortunate that I am a man who honors his debts and obligations, since my timely return to S'uthlam has allowed me to intervene once more in your behalf. Your leaders have been less than frank with you. But for the aid I am about to render you, your world would face starvation within the short span of eighteen standard years."

A moment of stunned silence occurred. Then a small riot began in the rear of the hall. Several people were forcibly ejected. Tuf paid the incident no mind.

"On my last visit, the program of ecological engineering I initiated produced dramatic increases in your food supply, through relatively conventional means, to wit, the introduction of new plant and animal species designed to maximize your agricultural productivity without seriously altering your ecology. Further efforts in this direction are undoubtedly possible, but I fear that the point of diminishing returns has long been passed, and such schemes would avail you little. Accordingly, this time I have accepted as fundamental the need to make radical alterations in your ecosystem and food chain. Some of you will find my suggestions unpleasant. I assure you that the other options you face—to wit, famine, plague, and war—are even more disagreeable.

The choice, of course, remains yours, and I would not dream of making it for you."

The room was as cold as a cryonic storage facility, and deathly silent but for the whirring of the massed third eyes. Haviland Tuf raised a finger. "First," he said. Behind him an image filled the telescreen, broadcast directly from the *Ark*'s computers—the image of a swollen monstrosity as big as a hill, its skin oily and glistening, its bulk shimmering like opaque pink gelatin. "The meatbeast," said Haviland Tuf. "A significant portion of your agricultural land is devoted to the raising of herds of meat animals of various sorts, whose flesh is the delectation of a very small, wealthy minority of S'uth-lamese who can afford such luxury and enjoy eating cooked animal matter. This is extremely inefficient. These beasts consume far more calories than they yield after slaughter, and being themselves the product of natural evolution, much of their body mass is inedible. I therefore suggest you eliminate these species from your world's ecosystem immediately.

"The meatbeasts, as depicted, are among the most notable triumphs of genetic tailoring; except for a small nucleus, these creatures are ever-replicating masses of undifferentiated cells, with no body mass wasted on nonessentials like sensory organs, nerves, or mobility. If one chose to employ metaphor, one might liken them to giant edible cancers. The flesh of the meatbeast contains all essential human nutrients and is high in protein, vitamins, and minerals. One adult meatbeast, growing in the basement of a S'uthlamese apartment tower, will yield as much edible flesh in a standard year as two of your present herds, and the grasslands now employed to raise these herds would be freed for agricultural cultivation."

"How do the damn things taste?" someone shouted out from the back of the room.

Haviland Tuf's head moved slightly, and he looked directly at the speaker. "As I am not myself an eater of animal flesh, I cannot answer that question from personal authority. I imagine, however, that meatbeast would taste very good to any starving man." He raised a hand, palm outward. "Let us proceed," he said, and the picture behind him changed. Now the telescreen showed an endless flat plain under a double sun. The plain was filled from horizon to horizon with plants—ugly looking things as tall as Tuf himself, their stalks and leaves an oily black, their heads drooping beneath the weight of swollen whitish pods that dripped a pale thick fluid.

"These, for reasons unknown to me, are called jersee-pods," said Tuf. "Five years ago, I gave you omni-grain, whose caloric yield per square meter is dramatically higher than that of nanowheat, neograss, and the other grains you had hitherto been planting. I note that you have sowed omni-grain extensively and reaped the benefits thereof. I also note that you have continued to plant nanowheat, neograss, spicepods, smackles, and numerous other types of fruit and vegetables, no doubt for the sake of variety and culinary pleasure. This must cease. Culinary variety is a luxury the S'uthlamese can no longer afford. Caloric efficiency alone must henceforth be your byword. Every square meter of agricultural land on S'uthlam and your so-called Larder asteroids must immediately be turned over to jersee-pods."

"What kind of gunk is that dripping there?" someone called.

"Is that thing a fruit or a vegetable?" a newspeep demanded to know.

"Can you make bread from it?" another asked.

"The jersee-pod," said Tuf, "is inedible."

A sudden clamorous uproar swept over the room, as a hundred people shouted and waved and threw questions and began speeches.

Haviland Tuf waited calmly until there was silence. "Each year," he said, "as your First Councillor can tell you, were he only so inclined, your agricultural lands yield an ever-diminishing percentage of the caloric needs of the swelling S'uthlamese population, the difference being made up by increased production from your food factories, where petrochemicals are processed into nutritious wafers and paste and clever synthetic edibles. Alas, however, petroleum is a nonrenewable resource, and you are running out. This process may be delayed, but ultimately it is inexorable. No doubt you are importing some from other worlds, but that interstellar pipeline can yield you only so much. Five years ago, I introduced into your seas a plankton of a variety called neptune's shawl, colonies of which now creep up your beaches and float upon the waves above your continental shelves. When dead and decayed, neptune's shawl can serve as a substitute for petrochemicals in your food factories.

"Jersee-pods might be looked upon as a nonaquatic analogue to neptune's shawl. The pods produce a fluid with certain biochemical similarities to raw crude oil. It is similar enough so that your food factories, after a minimal retooling easily accomplished by a world of your undoubted technological expertise, can make efficient use of it for processing into foodstuffs. Yet I must stress that you cannot simply plant these pods here and there as a supplement to your present crops. For maximum benefit, they must be planted universally, entirely supplanting the omni-grain, neograss, and other flora on which you have become accustomed to rely for provender."

A slender woman in the back stood up on her chair to be seen above the throng. "Tuf, who are you to tell us that we have to give up real food?" she screamed, anger in her tone.

"I, madam? I am but a humble ecological engineer engaged in the practice of his profession. It is not for me to make your decisions. My task, so obviously thankless, consists of presenting you with the facts and suggesting certain possible remedies which might be efficacious, however unpleasant. Thereafter, the government and people of S'uthlam must make the ultimate determination as to what course to follow." The audience was getting unruly again. Tuf raised a finger. "Quiet, please. I will soon conclude my presentation."

The picture on the telescreen changed once more. "Certain species and ecological strategies that I introduced five years ago, when first employed by S'uthlam, can and should remain in place. The mushroom and fungus farms beneath your undercities should be maintained and expanded. I have several new varieties of fungus to demonstrate to you. More efficient methods of farming the seas are certainly possible, methods which include use of the ocean floor as well as its watery ceiling. The growth of neptune's shawl can be stimulated and encouraged until it covers every square meter of S'uthlam's salt-water surface. The snow-oats and tunnel-tubers you have in place remain optimal food species for your frigid arctic regions. Your deserts have been made to bloom, your swamps have been drained and made productive. All that might be done on land or sea is being attempted. There remains only the air. I therefore propose the introduction of a complete living ecosystem into your upper atmosphere.

"Behind me, upon the screen, you see the final link in this new food chain I propose to forge for you. This huge dark creature with the black triangular wings is a Claremontine wind-rider, also called the *ororo*, a distant analogue to better-known species such as the black banshee of High Kavalaan and the lashtail manta of Hemador. It is a predator of the upper atmosphere, a glider and hunter, born aloft, a creature of the winds that lives and dies in flight, never touching land or sea. Indeed, once having landed, such wind-riders soon perish, as it is impossible for them to go aloft again. On Claremont, the species is small and lightweight, its flesh reported to be tough and leathery. It consumes any birds with the misfortune to venture into the altitudes it hunts, and also several varieties of airborne microorganisms, flying fungi, and windborne slime-molds that I also propose to introduce into your upper atmosphere. I have produced a genetically tailored wind-rider for S'uthlam, with a wing-span of some twenty meters, the ability to descend almost to treetop level, and nearly six times the body mass of the original. A small hydrogen sac behind the sensory organs will enable the beast to maintain flight despite this greater body weight. With your aircars and fliers, you will have no difficulty hunting and killing the wind-riders, and you will find them an excellent source of protein.

"In the interests of full and complete honesty, I must

add that this ecological modification will not be without cost. The microorganisms, fungus, and slime-molds will reproduce very quickly in your skies, having no natural enemies. The upper stories of your taller residential towers will be covered with mold and fungus, and more frequent cleaning will be required. Most of the native S'uthlamese birds and those species you brought to this world from Tara and Old Earth will die out, displaced by this new aerial ecosystem. Ultimately, the skies themselves will darken, you will receive significantly less sunlight, and your climate will undergo a permanent change. I do not project this happening for some three hundred years, however. Since you face disaster in a far shorter time if nothing is done, I continue to recommend the course of action I have outlined."

The newsfeed reporters leaped to their feet and began shouting questions. Tolly Mune was slumped and scowling. First Councillor Cregor Blaxon was sitting quite still, staring straight ahead with a fixed smile on his sharp, thin face, his eyes glassy.

"A moment, if you will," Haviland Tuf said to the turmoil. "I am about to conclude. You have heard my recommendations and seen the species with which I intend to redesign your ecology. Now, attend. Assuming your High Council does indeed opt to deploy the meatbeast, the jersee-pod, and the ororo in the ways that I have outlined, the *Ark*'s computers project a significant improvement in your food crisis. Observe."

All eyes went to the telescreen. Even Tolly Mune craned her head around, and First Councillor Cregor Blaxon, smile still firmly in place, rose from his seat and faced the screen boldly, his thumbs hooked into his pockets. A grid flashed into place, a red line chased a green line across the display, and dates lined up along one axis, population figures along the other.

The noise died.

The silence lingered.

Even way to the back, they heard Cregor Blaxon when he cleared his throat. "Ah, Tuf," he said, "this must be wrong."

"Sir," said Haviland Tuf, "I assure you, it is not."

"It's, ah, the before, isn't it? Not the after." He pointed. "I mean, look, all that eco-engineering, growing nothing but these pods, our seas covered with neptune's shawl, the skies growing darker with flying food, meat-mountains in every cellar."

"Meatbeasts," Tuf corrected, "although I concede that 'meat mountains' has a certain flair. You have a gift for colorful language and memorable terminology, First Councillor."

"All this," Blaxon said doggedly, "is pretty radical, Tuf. We have a right to expect radical improvement, I'd say."

A few loyalists began cheering him on.

"But this," the First Councillor concluded, "this projection says, ah, maybe I'm reading it wrong."

"First Councillor," said Haviland Tuf, "and people of S'uthlam, you are reading it correctly. If you adopt every one of my suggestions, you will indeed postpone your day of catastrophic reckoning. Postpone, sir, not forestall. You will have mass famine in eighteen years, as per your current projection, or in one hundred nine, as this projection indicates, but you will most certainly have mass famine." He raised a finger. "The only true and permanent solution is to be found not aboard my *Ark*, but in the minds and loins of each individual S'uthlamese citizen. You must practice restraint and implement immediate birth control. You must stop your indiscriminate procreation at once!"

"Oh, no," groaned Tolly Mune. But she had seen it coming, and she was on her feet, moving toward him and shouting for a security cordon, well before all hell broke loose.

"Rescuing you is getting to be a puling habit," Tolly Mune said, much later, when they had returned to the safety of Tuf's shuttle *Phoenix*, in its berth way out along spur six. Two whole squads of security, armed with nerveguns and tanglers, stood outside the ship, keeping the growing and unruly crowd at bay. "You have any beer?" she asked. "I could use one. Puling hell." It had been a harrowing run back to the ship, even with guards flanking them to either side. Tuf ran with a strange awkward lope, but he had surprising speed, she had to admit. "How are you doing, anyway?" she asked him.

"A thorough scrubbing has removed most of the spittle from my person," Haviland Tuf said, folding himself into his seat with dignity. "You will find beer in the refrigerated compartment under the gaming board. Make free with it, if you will." Dax began to scale Tuf's leg, digging tiny claws into the fabric of the pale blue jumpsuit into which he had changed. Tuf reached down with a large hand and helped him up. "In the future," he said to the cat, "you shall accompany me at all times, so that I will have ample warning of the onset of such demonstrations."

"You'd have had ample goddamned warning this time," said Tolly Mune, pulling out a beer, "if you'd told me that you intended to condemn our beliefs, our church, and our whole puling way of life. Did you expect they'd give you a medal?"

"A rousing hand of applause would have been sufficient."

"I warned you a long time ago, Tuf. On S'uthlam, it's not popular to be anti-life."

"I decline to be thus labeled," said Tuf. "I stand squarely in favor of life. Indeed, daily I create life in my cloning vats. I have a decided personal aversion to death, I find entropy distasteful, and if invited to the heat death of the universe, I would most certainly make other plans." He raised a finger. "Nonetheless, Portmaster Mune, I said what had to be said. Unlimited procreation as taught by your Church of Life Evolving and practiced by the majority of S'uthlamese, yourself and your fellow zeros excluded, is irresponsible and foolish, producing as it does a geometric population increase that will most assuredly pull down your proud civilization."

"Haviland Tuf, prophet of doom," the Portmaster said with a sigh. "They liked you better as a rogue ecologist and a lover."

"Everywhere I visit, I find heroes to be an endangered species. Perhaps I am more aesthetically pleasing when mouthing reassuring falsehoods through a filter of facial hair in melodramatic vidshows reeking of false optimism and post-coital complacency. This is a symptom of a great S'uthlamese affliction, your blind preference for things as you would have them rather than as they are. It is time that your world looked upon naked truth, be it my hairless face or the near certainty of famine in your future."

Tolly Mune swallowed some beer and stared at him. "Tuf," she said, "you remember what I said five years ago?"

"As I recall, you said a great many things."

"At the end," she said impatiently, "when I decided to help you escape with the *Ark* instead of helping Josen Rael take it from you. You asked me why, and I explained my reasons."

"You said," Tuf stated, "that power corrupts, that absolute power corrupts absolutely, that the *Ark* had already corrupted First Councillor Josen Rael and his associates, and that I was better fitted to retain possession of the seedship because I was an incorruptible man."

She gave him a wan smile. "Not quite, Tuf. I said I didn't think there was such a thing as an incorruptible man, but if there was, you were the item."

"Indeed," said Tuf, stroking Dax. "I stand corrected."

"Now you're making me wonder," she said. "You know what you just did, back there? For starters, you toppled another government. Creg can't survive this. You told the whole world he's a liar. Maybe that's fair enough; you made him, now you unmade him. First Councillors don't seem to last long when you come calling, do they? But never mind that. You also told, oh, some thirty-odd billion members of the Church of Life Evolving that their most deeply held religious beliefs are so much bladder bloat. You as much as said that the entire basis of the technocratic philosophy that has dominated council policy for centuries is mistaken. We'll be lucky if the next damned election doesn't bring the expansionists back in, and if that happens, it means war. Vandeen and Jazbo and the other allies will not tolerate another expansionist government. You probably ruined me, too. Again. Unless I'm even faster on my goddamned feet than I was last time around. Instead of a star-crossed lover, I'm now the sort of gnarly old bureaucrat who likes to lie about her sexual escapades, and I helped Citizen Anti-Life, too." She sighed. "You seem determined to see me in disgrace. But that's nothing, Tuf. I can take care of myself. The main thing is, you took it upon yourself to dictate policy to forty-plus billion people, with only the vaguest conception of the consequences. By what authority? Who gave you the right?"

"I would maintain that any human has the right to speak the truth."

"And the right to demand a worldwide all-net newsfeed to speak it on? Where did that puling right come from?" she said. "There are several million people on S'uthlam who belong to the zero faction, me included. You didn't say much that we haven't said for years. You just said it louder."

"I am aware of this. It is my hope that the words spoken this evening, no matter how bitterly they were received, will ultimately have a beneficial effect upon S'uthlamese politics and society. Perhaps Cregor Blaxon and his technocrats will grasp the truth that no true salvation can be found in what he calls Tuf's Flowering and what you once referred to as the miracle of loaves and fishes. Perhaps from this point on, policies and opinions will be changed. Perhaps your zero faction may even triumph in the next election."

Tolly Mune scowled. "That's damned unlikely, and you should know it. And even if the zero faction won, the question arises as to what the hell we could do." She leaned forward. "Would we have the right to *enforce* population control? I wonder. Never mind about that, though. My point is that you don't have any damned monopoly on truth. Any zero could have given your damned speech. Hell, half the damned technocrats know what the ledger looks like. Creg's no fool. Neither was poor Josen. What allowed you to do that was *power*,

Tuf. The power of the *Ark*. The help you can give us, or withhold, as you choose."

"Indeed," said Tuf. He blinked. "I cannot take issue with you. The sad truth of history has always been that the unreasoning masses follow the powerful, and not the wise."

"And which are you, Tuf?"

"I am but a humble—"

"Yes, yes," she snapped, "I know, a goddamned humble ecological engineer. A humble ecological engineer who has taken it on himself to play prophet. A humble ecological engineer who has visited S'uthlam exactly twice in his life, for a total of maybe a hundred days, and yet feels competent to topple our government, discredit our religion, and lecture forty-odd billion strangers about how many puling children they ought to have. My people may be stupid, they may be short-sighted, and they may be blind, but they are still my people, Tuf. I don't think I entirely approve of you arriving here and trying to remake us according to your own enlightened values."

"I deny this charge, madam. Whatever my personal standards might be, I do not seek to impose them upon S'uthlam. I merely took it upon myself to elucidate certain truths, and to make your population aware of certain cold, hard equations, the sum of which is assuredly disaster, and cannot be changed by beliefs, prayers, or melodramatic romances on your vidnets."

"You're being paid—" Tolly Mune started.

"Insufficiently," Tuf interrupted.

She smiled despite herself. "You're being paid for ecological engineering, Tuf, not for religious or political instruction, thank you."

"You are most welcome, Portmaster Mune." He made a steeple of his hands. "Ecology," he said. "Consider the word, if you will. Meditate upon its meaning. An ecosystem might be likened to a great biological machine, perhaps. If this analogy is pursued, humanity must be seen as part of the machine. No doubt an important part—an engine, a key circuit—but in no case apart from the mechanism, as is often fallaciously assumed. Ergo, when one such as myself re-engineers an ecology, he must by necessity refit as well the humans who inhabit it."

"Now you're giving me a chill, Tuf. You've been alone in this ship for too long."

"This is an opinion I do not share," said Tuf.

"People aren't old pulse-rings, or blast-tubes to be recalibrated, you know."

"People are more complex and recalcitrant than any simple mechanical, electronic, or biochemical component," Tuf agreed.

"That's not what I meant."

"The S'uthlamese are especially difficult," Tuf said.

Tolly Mune shook her head. "Remember what I said, Tuf. Power corrupts."

"Indeed," he said. In this context, she hadn't a clue as to what it meant.

Haviland Tuf rose from his seat. "My stay here shortly will be at an end," he said. "At this very instant, the *Ark*'s chronowarp is accelerating the growth of the organisms in my cloning tanks. The *Basilisk* and *Manticore* are being prepared to effect delivery, on the assumption that Cregor Blaxon or his successor will ultimately decide to accept my recommendations. I would estimate that within ten days S'uthlam will have its meatbeasts, jersee-pods, ororos, et cetera. At that point I shall take my leave, Portmaster Mune."

"Abandoned by my star-bound lover once again," Tolly Mune said crossly. "Maybe I can make something out of that."

Tuf looked at Dax. "Levity," he said, "flavored with bitterness." He looked up again, and blinked. "I believe I have rendered great service to S'uthlam," he said. "I regret any personal distress that my methods have caused you. Such was not my intent. Permit me to make some small redress."

She cocked her head and looked at him hard. "How are you going to do that, Tuf?"

"A trifling gift," said Tuf. "Aboard the *Ark*, I could not help but notice the affection with which you treated the kittens. Nor did it go entirely unreciprocated. I would like to give you two of my cats, as a token of my esteem."

Tolly Mune snorted. "Hoping that stark terror will keep the security men away when they come to arrest me? No, Tuf. I appreciate the offer and I'm tempted, really, but vermin are illegal in the web, remember? I couldn't keep them."

"As Portmaster of S'uthlam, you have the authority to change the applicable regulations."

"Oh, right, and wouldn't that look great? Anti-life and corrupt, too. I'd be real puling popular."

"Sarcasm," Tuf informed Dax.

"And what happens when they replace me as Portmaster?" she said.

"I have every faith in your ability to survive this political tempest, even as you weathered the last," said Tuf.

Tolly Mune laughed raucously. "Good for you, but no, really, it just won't work."

Haviland Tuf was silent, his face blank of all expression. Finally he raised a finger. "I have devised a solution," he said. "In addition to two of my kittens, I will give you a starship. As you know, I have a surfeit of them. You may keep the kittens there, aboard ship, technically outside the jurisdiction of the Port of S'uthlam. I will even leave you with sufficient food for five years, so that it cannot be said that you are giving so-called vermin calories needed by hungry human beings. To further bolster your flagging public image, you may tell the newsfeeds that these two felines are hostages against my promised return to S'uthlam five years hence."

Tolly Mune let a crooked smile creep across her homely features. "That might work, damn it. You're making this hard to resist. A starship, too, you say?"

"Indeed."

She grinned. "You're too convincing. All right. Which two cats, now?"

"Doubt," said Haviland Tuf, "and Ingratitude."

"There's a pointed comment in that, I'm sure," Tolly Mune said. "I won't pursue it. And five years' worth of food?"

"Sufficient until the day, five years hence, when I return again to repay the remainder of my note."

Tolly Mune looked at him—the long, still, white face, the pale hands folded neatly atop his bulging stomach, the duck-billed cap resting on his bald head, the small black cat in his lap. She looked at him long and hard and then, for no particular reason she could name, her hand trembled just a little, and beer spilled from her open glass onto her sleeve. She felt the cold wetness soak into her shirt and trickle down her wrist. "Oh, joy," she said. "Tuf and Tuf again. I can hardly wait."

5
A BEAST FOR NORN

Haviland Tuf was drinking alone in the darkest corner of an alehouse on Tamber when the thin man found him. His elbows rested on the table and the top of his bald head almost brushed the low wooden beam above. Four empty mugs sat before him, their insides streaked by rings of foam, while a fifth, half-full, was cradled in his huge white hands.

If Tuf was aware of the curious glances the other patrons gave him from time to time, he showed no sign of it; he quaffed his ale methodically, his face without expression. He made a singular solitary figure drinking alone in his booth.

He was not *quite* alone though; Dax lay asleep on the table before him, a ball of dark fur. Occasionally, Tuf would set down his mug of ale and idly stroke his quiet companion. Dax would not stir from his comfortable position among the empty mugs. The cat was fully as large, compared to other cats, as Haviland Tuf was compared to other men.

When the thin man came walking up to Tuf's booth, Tuf said nothing at all. He merely looked up, blinked, and waited for the other to begin.

"You are Haviland Tuf, the animal-seller," the thin man said. He was indeed painfully thin. His garments, all black leather and grey fur, hung loose on him, bagging here and there. Yet he was plainly a man of

257

some means, since he wore a slim brass coronet around his brow, under a mop of black hair, and his fingers were adorned with a plenitude of rings.

Tuf scratched Dax behind one black ear. "It is not enough that our solitude must be intruded upon," he said to the cat, his voice a deep bass with only a hint of inflection. "It is insufficient that our grief be violated. We must also bear calumnies and insults, it seems." He looked up at the thin man. "Sir," he said. "I am indeed Haviland Tuf, and perhaps it might be said that I do in some sense trade in animals. Yet perhaps I do not consider myself an animal-seller. Perhaps I consider myself an ecological engineer."

The thin man waved his hand in an irritated gesture, and slid uninvited into the booth opposite Tuf. "I understand that you own an ancient EEC seedship. That does not make you an ecological engineer, Tuf. They are all dead, and have been for centuries. But if you would prefer to be called an ecological engineer, then well and good. I require your services. I want to buy a monster from you, a great fierce beast."

"Ah," said Tuf, speaking to the cat again. "He wishes to buy a monster, this stranger who seats himself at my table uninvited." Tuf blinked. "I regret to inform you that your quest has been in vain. Monsters are entirely mythological, sir, like spirits, werebeasts, and competent bureaucrats. Moreover, I am not at this moment engaged in the selling of animals, nor in any other aspect of my profession. I am at this moment consuming this excellent Tamberkin ale, and mourning."

"Mourning?" the thin man said. "Mourning what?" He seemed most unwilling to take his leave.

"A cat," said Haviland Tuf. "Her name was Havoc, and she had been my companion for long years, sir. She has recently died, on a world called Alyssar that I had the misfortune to call upon, at the hands of a remarkably unpleasant barbarian princeling." He looked at the thin man's brass coronet. "You are not by chance a barbarian princeling yourself, sir?"

"Of course not."

"That is your good fortune," said Tuf.

"Well, pity about your cat, Tuf. I know your feeling, yesyes, I've been through it a thousand times myself."

"A thousand times," Tuf repeated flatly. "You might consider a strenuous effort to take better care of your pets."

The thin man shrugged. "Animals do die, you know. Can't be helped. Fang and claw and all that, yesyes, that's their destiny. I've had to grow accustomed to watching my best get slaughtered right in front of my eyes. But that's what I've come to talk to you about, Tuf."

"Indeed," said Haviland Tuf.

"My name is Herold Norn. I am the Senior Beast-Master of my House, one of the Twelve Great Houses of Lyronica."

"Lyronica," Tuf stated. "The name is not entirely unfamiliar to me. A small, sparsely settled planet, I seem to recall, of a somewhat savage bent. Perhaps this explains your transgressions of civilized manners."

"Savage?" Norn said. "That's Tamberkin rubbish, Tuf. Damned farmers. Lyronica is the jewel of this sector. You've heard of our gaming pits, haven't you?"

Haviland Tuf scratched Dax behind the ear once more, a peculiar rhythmic scratch, and the tomcat slowly uncurled, yawning, and glanced up at the thin man with large, bright, golden eyes. He purred softly.

"Some small nuggets of information have fallen in my ears during my voyagings," Tuf said. "Perhaps you would care to elaborate, Herold Norn, so Dax and I might consider your proposition."

Herold Norn rubbed thin hands together, nodding. "Dax?" he said. "Of course. A handsome animal, although personally I have never been fond of beasts who cannot fight. Real beauty lies in killing-strength, I always say."

"An idiosyncratic attitude," Tuf commented.

"No, no," said Norn, "not at all. I hope that your work here has not infected you with Tamberkin squeamishness."

Tuf drained his mug in silence, then signaled for two more. The barkeep brought them promptly.

"Thank you," Norn said, when the mug was set golden and foaming in front of him.

"Proceed, sir."

"Yes. Well, the Twelve Great Houses of Lyronica compete in the gaming pits. It began—oh, centuries ago. Before that, the houses warred. This way is much better. Family honor is upheld, fortunes are made, and no one is injured. You see, each house controls great tracts, scattered widely over the planet, and since the land is very thinly settled, animal life teems. The Lords of the Great Houses, many years ago during a time of peace, started to have animal fights. It was a pleasant diversion, rooted deep in history. You are aware, maybe, of the ancient custom of cock-fighting and the Old Earth folk called Romans who would set all manner of strange beasts against each other in their great arena?"

Norn paused and drank some ale, waiting for an answer, but Tuf merely stroked Dax and said nothing.

"No matter," the thin Lyronican finally said, wiping foam from his mouth with the back of his hand. "That was the beginning of the sport, you see. Each house has its own particular land, its own particular animals. The House of Varcour, for example, sprawls in the hot, swampy south, and they are fond of sending huge lizard-lions to the gaming pits. Feridian, a mountainous realm, has bred and championed its fortunes with a species of rock-ape which we call, naturally, *feridians*. My own house, Norn, stands on the grassy plains of the large northern continent. We have sent a hundred different beasts into combat in the pits, but we are most famed for our ironfangs."

"Ironfangs," Tuf said. "The name is evocative."

Norn gave a sly smile. "Yes," he said proudly. "As Senior Beast-Master, I have trained thousands. Oh, but they are lovely animals! Tall as you are, with fur of the most marvelous blue-black color, fierce and relentless."

"Might I assume your ironfangs to be of canine descent?"

"But *such* canines," Norn said.

"Yet you require from me a monster."

Norn drank more of his ale. "True, true. Folks from a

dozen near worlds voyage to Lyronica, to watch the beasts fight in the gaming pits and gamble on the outcome. Particularly they flock to the Bronze Arena that has stood for six hundred years in the City of All Houses. That's where the greatest fights are fought. The wealth of our Houses and our world has come to depend on this. Without it, rich Lyronica would be as poor as the farmers of Tamber."

"Yes," said Tuf.

"But you understand, this wealth, it goes to the houses according to their honor, according to their victories. The House of Arneth has grown greatest and most powerful because of the many deadly beasts in their varied lands; the others rank according to their scores in the Bronze Arena."

Tuf blinked. "The House of Norn ranks last and least among the Twelve Great Houses of Lyronica," he said, and Dax purred more loudly.

"You know?"

"Sir. It was obvious. Yet an objection occurs to me. Under the rules of your Bronze Arena, might it not be considered unethical to purchase and introduce a species not native to your own fabled world?"

"There are precedents. Some seventy-odd years ago, a gambler came from Old Earth itself, with a creature called a timber wolf that he had trained. The House of Colin backed him, in a fit of madness. His poor beast was matched against a Norn ironfang, and proved far from equal to its task. There are other cases as well.

"In recent years, unfortunately, our ironfangs have not bred well. The wild species has all but died out on the plains, and the few who remain become swift and elusive, difficult for our housemen to capture. In the breeding kennels, the strain seems to have softened, despite my efforts and those of the Beast-Masters before me. Norn has won few victories of late, and I will not remain Senior for long unless something is done. We grow poor. When I heard that your *Ark* had come to Tamber, then, I determined to seek you out. I will begin a new era of glory for Norn, with your help."

Haviland Tuf sat very still. "I comprehend the dilemma you face. Yet I must inform you that I am not commonly in the habit of selling monsters. The *Ark* is an ancient seedship, designed by the Earth Imperials thousands of years ago, to decimate the Hrangans through biowar. I can unleash a veritable cornucopia of disease and pestilence, and in my cell library is stored cloning material for untold numbers of species from more than a thousand worlds, but true monsters of the sort that I have inferred you require are in somewhat shorter supply."

Herold Norn looked crestfallen. "You have nothing, then?"

"These are not my words," said Haviland Tuf. "The men and women of the vanished Ecological Engineering Corps did in truth make use, from time to time, of species that the uninformed or superstitious might label monstrous, for reasons as much psychological as ecological. Thus I do indeed have a few such animals in stock—a trifling number, a few thousand perhaps, certainly no more than ten thousand. To quote a more accurate figure, I must need consult my computers."

"A few thousand monsters!" Norn was excited again. "That is more than enough selection! Surely, among all those, we can find a beast for Norn!"

"Perhaps," Tuf said. "Or perhaps not. Both possibilities exist." He considered Norn, his long face cool and dispassionate. "This matter of Lyronica does pique my interest in a trifling way, and as I am at the moment without professional engagement, having given the Tamberkin a bird to check their rootworm infestation, I am moved to investigate your world and plight more closely. Return to Norn, sir. I will take the *Ark* to Lyronica and see your gaming pits, and we will decide what is to be done with them."

Norn smiled. "Excellent," he said. "Then I will buy this round of ale."

Dax purred as loud as a descending shuttle.

The Bronze Arena stood square in the center of the City of All Houses, at the point where sectors dominated by the Twelve Great Houses met like slices in a vast pie. Each enclave of the rambling stone city was walled off, each flew a flag with its distinctive colors, each had its own ambience and style; but all met in the Bronze Arena.

The Arena was not bronze after all, but mostly black stone and polished wood. It bulked upwards, taller than all but a few of the city's scattered towers and minarets, topped by a shining bronze dome that gleamed with the orange rays of the sunset. Gargoyles peered from the various narrow windows, carved of stone and hammered from bronze and wrought iron. The great doors in the black stone walls were fashioned of metal as well, and there were twelve of them, each facing a different sector of the City of All Houses. The colors and the etching on each gateway were distinctive to its house.

Lyronica's sun was a fist of red flame smearing the western horizon when Herold Norn led Haviland Tuf to the games. The housemen had just fired gas torches, metal obelisks that stood like dart teeth in a ring about the Bronze Arena, and the hulking ancient building was surrounded by flickering pillars of blue-and-orange flame. In a crowd of gamblers and gamesters, Tuf followed Herold Norn from the half-deserted streets of the Nornic slums down a path of crushed rock, passing between twelve bronze ironfangs who snarled and spit in timeless poses on either side of the street, and then through the wide Norn Gate. The doors were intricate ebony and brass. The uniformed guards, clad in the same black leather and grey fur as Herold Norn himself, recognized the Beast-Master and admitted them; others stopped to pay with coins of gold and iron.

The Arena was the greatest gaming pit of all. It *was* a pit, the sandy combat-floor sunk deep below ground level, with stone walls four meters high surrounding it. Then the seats began, just atop the walls, circling the arena in ascending tiers until they reached the doors. Enough seating for thirty thousand, Norn boasted, although Tuf observed that those in the back had a poor view at best, and other seats were blocked off by iron pillars. Betting stalls were scattered throughout the building.

Herold Norn took Tuf to the best seats in the arena, in the front of the Norn section, with only a stone parapet separating them from the four-meter drop to the combat sands. The seats here were not rickety wood and iron, like those in the rear, but thrones of leather, huge enough to accommodate even Tuf's vast bulk without difficulty, and opulently comfortable. "Every seat is bound in the skin of a beast that has died nobly below," Herold Norn told Tuf as they seated themselves.

Beneath them, a work crew of men in one-piece blue coveralls was dragging the carcass of some gaunt feathered animal toward one of the entryways. "A fighting bird of the House of Wrai Hill," Norn explained. "The Wrai Beast-Master sent it up against a Varcour lizard-lion. Not the most felicitous choice."

Haviland Tuf said nothing. He sat stiff and erect, dressed in a grey vinyl greatcoat that fell to his ankles, with flaring shoulder-boards and a visored green cap emblazoned with the golden theta of the Ecological Engineers. His large pale hands interlocked atop his bulging stomach while Herold Norn kept up a steady stream of conversation.

When the arena announcer spoke, the thunder of his magnified voice boomed all around them. "Fifth match," he said. "From the House of Norn, a male ironfang, aged two years, weight 2.6 quintals, trained by Junior Beast-Master Kers Norn. New to the Bronze Arena." Immediately below them, metal grated harshly on metal, and a nightmare creature came bounding into the pit. The ironfang was a shaggy giant, with sunken red eyes and a double row of curving teeth that dripped slaver—a wolf grown all out of proportion and crossed with a saber-toothed tiger, its legs as thick as young trees, its speed and killing grace only partially disguised by the blue-black fur that hid the play of muscles. The ironfang snarled and the arena echoed to the noise; scattered cheering began all around them.

Herold Norn smiled. "Kers is a cousin, and one of our most promising juniors. He tells me this beast will do us proud. Yesyes, I like its looks, don't you?"

"Being new to Lyronica and your Bronze Arena, I have no standard of comparison," Tuf said in a flat voice.

The announcer began again. "From the House of Arneth-in-the-Gilded-Wood, a strangling-ape, aged six years, weight 3.1 quintals, trained by Senior Beast-Master Danel Leigh Arneth. Three times a veteran of the Bronze Arena, three times surviving."

Across the combat pit, another of the entryways—the one wrought in gold and crimson—slid open, and the second beast lumbered out on two squat legs and looked around. The ape was short but immensely broad, with a triangular torso and a bullet-shaped head, eyes sunk deep under a heavy ridge of bone. Its arms, double-jointed and muscular, dragged in the arena sand. From head to toe the beast was hairless, but for patches of dark red fur under its arms; its skin was a dirty white. And it smelled. Across the arena, Haviland Tuf still caught the musky odor.

"It sweats," Norn explained. "Danel Leigh has driven it to killing frenzy before sending it forth. His beast has the edge in experience, you understand, and the strangling-ape is a savage creature. Unlike its cousin, the mountain feridian, it is naturally a carnivore and needs little training. But Kers's ironfang is younger. The match should be of interest." The Norn Beast-Master leaned forward while Tuf sat calm and still.

The ape turned, growling deep in its throat, and already the ironfang was streaking towards it, snarling, a blue-black blur that scattered arena sand as it ran. The strangling-ape waited for it, spreading its huge gangling arms, and Tuf had a blurred impression of the great Norn killer leaving the ground in one tremendous bound. Then the two animals were locked together, rolling over and over in a tangle of ferocity, and the arena became a symphony of screams. "The throat," Norn was shouting. "Tear out its throat! Tear out its throat!"

The two beasts parted as suddenly as they had met. The ironfang spun away and began to move in slow circles, and Tuf saw that one of its forelegs was bent and broken. It limped on its three remaining limbs, yet still it circled. The strangling-ape gave it no opening, but turned constantly to face it. Long gashes had been opened across the ape's broad chest, where the ironfang's sabers had slashed, but the beast seemed little weakened. Herold Norn had begun to mutter softly.

Impatient with the lull, the watchers in the Bronze Arena began a rhythmic chant, a low wordless noise that swelled louder and louder as new voices joined the chorus. Tuf saw at once that the sound affected the animals below. They began to snarl and hiss, calling battlecries in savage voices, and the strangling-ape moved from one leg to the other, back and forth in a macabre little jig, while bloody slaver ran from the gaping jaws of the ironfang.

The killing chant rose and fell, swelling ever louder until the dome above thrummed with the noise. The beasts below went into frenzy. Suddenly the ironfang was charging again, and the ape's long arms reached to meet it in its wild lunge. The impact of the leap threw the strangler backwards, but Tuf saw that the ironfang's teeth had closed on air while the ape wrapped its hands around the blue-black throat. The canine thrashed wildly as they rolled in the sand. Then came a sharp, horribly loud snap, and the wolf-creature was nothing but a rag of fur, its head lolling grotesquely to one side.

The watchers ceased their moaning chant, and began to applaud and whistle. Afterwards, the gold and crimson door slid open once again and the strangling-ape returned to whence it had come. Four men in Norn black and grey came out to carry off the corpse of the ironfang.

Herold Norn was sullen. "Another loss. I will speak to Kers. His beast did not find the throat."

"What will become of the carcass?" inquired Tuf.

"Skinned and butchered," Herold Norn muttered. "House Arneth will use the pelt to upholster a seat in their section of the arena. The meat will be distributed to the beggars who clamor outside their gold and crimson door. The Great Houses are all of a charitable mien."

"Indeed," said Haviland Tuf. He rose from his seat, unfolding with slow dignity. "I have seen your Bronze Arena."

"Are you going?" Norn asked anxiously. "Surely not so soon! There are five more matches. In the next, a giant feridian fights a water-scorpion from Amar Island!"

"I wished only to determine if all that I had heard of Lyronica's far-famed Bronze Arena was so. I see that it is. Therefore there is no need for me to remain any longer. One need not consume the whole of a flask of mushroom wine to ascertain whether the vintage has a pleasant taste."

Herold Norn got to his feet. "Well," he said, "come with me out to Norn House, then. I can show you the kennels, the training pits. We will feast you as you have never been feasted!"

"This will not be necessary," said Haviland Tuf. "Having seen your Bronze Arena, I will trust my imagination and powers of deduction to visualize your kennels and training pits. I shall return to the *Ark* forthwith."

Norn reached out an anxious hand toward Tuf's arm to restrain him. "Will you sell us a monster, then? You've seen our plight."

Tuf sidestepped the Beast-Master's grip with a deftness belying his size and weight. "Sir. Restrain yourself. I am not fond of being rudely seized and grasped." When Norn's hand had fallen, Tuf looked down into his eyes. "I have no doubt that a problem exists upon Lyronica. Perhaps a more practical man than myself would judge it none of his concern, but being at heart an altruist, I cannot find it in myself to leave you as I have found you. I will ponder your situation and address myself to devising the proper corrective measures. You may call upon me in the *Ark* on the third day hence. Perhaps by that time I will have a thought or two to share."

Then, without further ado, Haviland Tuf turned and walked from the Bronze Arena, back to the spaceport of the City of All Houses, where his shuttle *Basilisk* sat waiting.

*   *   *

Herold Norn had obviously not been prepared for the *Ark*. He emerged from his tiny, battered, black and gray shuttle into the immensity of the landing deck and stood with his mouth open, craning his head this way and that, peering at the echoing darkness above, at the looming alien ships, at the thing that looked like a metal dragon nesting amid the distant shadows. When Haviland Tuf came rolling up to meet him, driving an open three-wheeled cart, the Beast-Master made no effort to disguise his reaction. "I should have known," he kept repeating. "The size of this ship, the *size*. But of course I should have known."

Haviland Tuf sat unmoved, cradling Dax in one arm and stroking the cat slowly. "Some might find the *Ark* excessively large, and perhaps even daunting in its spaciousness, but I am comfortable," he said impassively. "The ancient EEC seedships once had two hundred crewmen, and I can only assume that they, like myself, abhorred cramped quarters."

Herold Norn seated himself beside Tuf. "How many men do you have in your crew?" he asked casually as Tuf set them in motion.

"One, or five, depending on whether one counts feline crew members or only humanoids."

"You are the *only* crewman?" Norn said.

Dax stood up in Tuf's lap; his long black fur stirred and bristled. "The *Ark*'s inhabitants consist of myself, Dax, and three other cats, named Chaos, Hostility, and Suspicion. Please do not take alarm at their names, Beast-Master Norn. They are gentle and harmless creatures."

"One man and four cats," Herold Norn said speculatively. "A small crew for a big ship, yesyes."

Dax hissed. Tuf, steering the cart with one large pale hand, used the other to stroke and soothe his pet. "I might also make mention of the sleepers, since you seem to have developed such an acute interest in the various living inhabitants of the *Ark*."

"The sleepers?" said Herold Norn. "What are they?"

"Certain living organisms, ranging in size from the microscopic to the monstrous, fully cloned but comatose, held in a perpetual stasis in the *Ark*'s cloning vats. Though I have a certain fondness for animals of all sorts, in the case of these sleepers I have wisely allowed my intellect to rule my emotions and have therefore taken no steps to disturb their long dreamless slumber. Having investigated the nature of these particular species, I long ago decided that they would be decidedly less pleasant traveling companions than my cats. I must admit that at times I find the sleepers a decided nuisance. At regular intervals I must enter a bothersome secret command into the *Ark*'s computers so that their long sleep may continue. I have a great abiding dread that one day I shall forget to do this, for whatever reasons, and then my ship will be filled with all manner of strange plagues and slavering carnivores, requiring a time-consuming and vexing clean-up and perhaps even wreaking harm to my person or my cats."

Herold Norn stared at Tuf's expressionless face and regarded his large, hostile cat. "Ah," he said. "Yesyes. Sounds dangerous, Tuf. Perhaps you ought to, ah, abort all these sleepers. Then you'd be, ah, safe."

Dax hissed at him again.

"An interesting concept," Tuf said. "Doubtless the vicissitudes of war were responsible for inculcating such paranoid attitudes into the men and women of the Ecological Engineering Corps that they felt obliged to program in these fearsome biological defenses. Being myself of a more trusting and honest nature, I have often contemplated doing away with the sleepers, but the truth is, I cannot find it in myself to unilaterally abolish a historic practice that has endured for over a millennium. Therefore, I allow the sleepers to sleep, and do my utmost to remember the secret countermands."

Herold Norn scowled. "Yesyes," he said.

Dax sat down in Tuf's lap again, and purred.

"Have you come up with anything?" Norn asked.

"My efforts have not entirely been for naught," said Tuf flatly, as they rolled out of the wide corridor into the *Ark*'s huge central shaft. Herold Norn's mouth dropped open again. Around them on all sides, lost in dimness, was an unending panorama of vats of all sizes and shapes. In some of the medium-sized tanks, dark shapes hung in translucent bags, and stirred fitfully. "Sleepers," Norn muttered.

"Indeed," said Haviland Tuf. He stared straight ahead as he drove, with Dax curled in his lap, while Norn looked wonderingly from side to side.

They departed the dim, echoing shaft at last, drove through a narrow corridor, climbed out of the cart, and entered a large white room. Four wide, padded chairs dominated the four corners of the chamber, with control panels on their thick, flaring arms; a circular plate of blue metal was built into the floor amidst them. Haviland Tuf dropped Dax into one of the chairs before seating himself in a second. Norn looked around, then took the chair diagonally opposite Tuf.

"I must inform you of several things," Tuf began.

"Yesyes," said Norn.

"Monsters are expensive." Tuf said. "I will require one hundred thousand standards."

"*What!* That's an outrage! I told you, Norn is a poor house."

"So. Perhaps then a richer House would meet the required price. The Ecological Engineering Corps has been defunct for centuries, sir. No ship of theirs remains in working order, save the *Ark* alone. Their science is largely forgotten. Techniques of cloning and genetic engineering such as they practiced exist now only on distant Prometheus and perhaps on Old Earth itself, yet Earth is closed and the Prometheans guard their biological secrets with jealous fervor." Tuf looked across to Dax. "And yet Herold Norn feels my price to be excessive."

"Fifty thousand standards," Norn said. "We can barely meet that price."

Haviland Tuf said nothing.

"Eighty thousand standards, then! I can go no higher. The House of Norn will be bankrupt! They will tear down our bronze ironfangs and seal the Norn Gate!"

Haviland Tuf said nothing.

"Curse you! A hundred thousand, yesyes. But only if your monster meets our requirements."

"You will pay the full sum on delivery."

"Impossible!"

Tuf was silent again.

Herold Norn tried to wait him out. He looked around with studied nonchalance. Tuf stared straight ahead. He ran his fingers through his hair. Tuf stared straight ahead. He squirmed around in his chair. Tuf stared straight ahead.

"Oh, very well," Norn said in frustration.

"As to the monster itself," said Tuf, "I have studied your requirements closely, and have consulted my computers. Within the cell library of the *Ark* are samples of thousands upon thousands of predators from uncounted worlds, including fossilized tissue samples, locked within which can be found the genetic patterns of creatures of legend long extinct upon their original homeworlds, thus allowing me to replicate such species. Therefore, the choices are many. To simplify matters, I have taken into account several additional criteria beyond the mere ferocity of the animals under consideration. For example, I have limited myself to oxygen-breathing species, and furthermore to those who might be comfortable in a climate such as prevails upon House Norn's windswept prairies."

"An excellent point," Herold Norn said. "We have, from time to time, attempted to raise lizard-lions and feridians and other beasts of the Twelve Houses, with ill success. The climate, the vegetation . . ." He made a disgusted gesture.

"Precisely," said Haviland Tuf. "I see you comprehend the various and sundry difficulties incumbent in my search."

"Yesyes, but get to the point. What have you found? What is this hundred-thousand-standard monster?"

"I offer you a selection," Tuf said. "From among some thirty species. Attend!"

He touched a glowing button on the arm of his chair, and suddenly a beast was squatting on the blue-metal plate between them. Two meters tall, with rubbery pink-grey skin and thin white hair, the creature had a low forehead and a swinish snout, plus a set of nasty curving horns and daggerlike claws on its hands.

"I will not trouble you with the formal nomenclature, since I have observed that informality is the rule of the Bronze Arena," Haviland Tuf said. "This is the so-called stalking-swine of Heydey, native to both forests and plains. It is chiefly an eater of carrion, but has been known to relish fresh meat, and it fights viciously when attacked. Furthermore, it is reliably reported to be quite intelligent, yet impossible to domesticate. The stalking-swine is an excellent breeder. The colonists from Gulliver eventually abandoned their Heydey settlement because of this animal. That was some twelve hundred years past."

Herold Norn scratched his scalp between dark hair and brass coronet. "No. It is too thin, too light. Look at the neck! Think what a feridian would do to it." He shook his head violently. "Besides, it is *ugly*. And I resent the offer of a scavenger, no matter how ill-tempered. The House of Norn breeds proud fighters, beasts who kill their own game!"

"Indeed," said Tuf. He touched the button, and the stalking-swine vanished. In its place, bulking large enough to touch the plates and fade into them, was a massive ball of armored grey flesh as featureless as battle plate.

"This creature's barren homeworld has neither been named nor settled, yet an exploratory party from Old Poseidon once charted and claimed it, and cell samples were taken. Zoo specimens existed briefly but did not thrive. The beast was nicknamed the rolleram. Adults weigh approximately six metric tons. On the plains of their homeworld, the rollerams achieve speed in excess of fifty kilometers per hour, crushing prey beneath them. The beast is, in a sense, all mouth. Thusly, as any portion of its skin can be made to exude digestive enzymes, it simply rests atop its meal until the meat has been absorbed. I can vouch for the mindless hostility of this species. Once, through an unusual set of circumstances that we need not go into, a rolleram was loosed to run free on one of my decks, where it did a truly astonishing amount of damage to bulkheads and instrumentation before finally battering itself to an early and futile death. Moreover, it was quite implacable in its aggression, and attempted to crush me beneath its bulk whenever I descended into its domain to bring it sustenance."

Herold Norn, himself half-immersed in the looming holograph, sounded impressed. "Ah, yes. Better, much better. An awesome creature. Perhaps . . . but no." His tone changed suddenly. "No, no, this will never do. A creature weighing six tons and rolling that fast might smash its way out of the Bronze Arena and kill hundreds of our patrons. Besides, who would pay hard coin to watch this *thing* crush a lizard-lion or a strangler? No. No sport. Your rolleram is *too* monstrous, Tuf."

Tuf, unmoved, hit the button once again. The vast grey bulk gave way to a sleek, snarling cat, fully as large as an ironfang, with slitted yellow eyes and powerful muscles bunched beneath a coat of dark-blue fur. The fur was striped; long thick lines of smoky silver ran lengthwise down the creature's gleaming flanks.

"Ahhhhhhhh," Norn said. "A beauty, in truth, in truth."

"The cobalt panther of Celia's World," Tuf said, "often called the cobalcat. One of the largest and deadliest of the great cats, or their analogues. The beast is a truly superlative hunter, its senses miracles of biological engineering. It can see into the infrared for night prowling, and the ears—note the size and the spread, Beast-Master—the ears are extremely sensitive. Being of felinoid stock, the cobalcat has psionic ability, but in its case this ability is far more developed than the usual. Fear, hunger, and bloodlust all act as triggers; then the cobalcat becomes a mindreader."

Norn looked up, startled. "What?"

"Psionics, sir. Surely you are aware of the concept. The cobalcat is quite deadly, simply because it knows what moves an antagonist will make before those moves are made. Do you comprehend?"

"Yes." Norn's voice was excited. Haviland Tuf looked over at Dax, and the big tomcat—who'd been not the least disturbed by the parade of scentless phantoms flashing on and off—blinked and stretched lazily. "Perfect, perfect! Why, I'll venture to say that we can even train these beasts as we'd train ironfangs, eh? And *mindreaders*! Perfect. Even the colors are right—dark blue, you know, and our ironfangs were blue-black—so the cats will be most Nornic, yesyes!"

Tuf touched his chair arm, and the cobalcat vanished. "Indeed. I would assume, therefore, that we have no need to proceed further. I shall commence the cloning process immediately upon your departure. Delivery will be in three weeks standard, if that pleases you. For the agreed-upon sum, I will provide three pair—two set of younglings who should be released in your wildlands as breeding stock, and one mated set full-grown, who might be immediately sent into the Bronze Arena."

"So soon," Norn began. "Fine, but . . ."

"I employ a chronowarp, Beast-Master. It requires vast energies, true, but has the power to accelerate the very tread of time itself, producing within the tank a chronic distortion that enables me to hurry the clone to maturity. It would perhaps be prudent to add that, although I provide Norn with six animals, only three actual individuals are represented. The *Ark* carries a triple cobalcat cell. I will clone each specimen twice, male and female, and hope for a viable genetic mix when they crossbreed on Lyronica."

"Fine, whatever you say," Norn said. "I will send the ships for the animals promptly. Then we will pay you."

Dax uttered a tiny little yowl.

"Sir," said Tuf. "A better thought has occurred to me. You may pay the full fee before any beasts are handed over."

"But you said on delivery!"

"Admitted. Yet I am given to impulsive whims, and impulse now tells me to collect first, rather than simultaneously."

"Oh, very well," Norn said. "Though your demands

are arbitrary and excessive. With these cobalcats, we shall soon recoup our fee." He started to rise.

Haviland Tuf raised a single finger. "One moment. You have not seen fit to inform me overmuch of the ecology of Lyronica, nor the particular realms of Norn House. Perhaps prey exists. I must caution you, however, that your cobalcats are hunters, and therefore require suitable game species."

"Yesyes, of course."

"Fortunately, I am equipped to be of help to you. For an additional five thousand standards, I might clone you a breeding stock of Celian hoppers, delightful furred herbivores celebrated on a dozen worlds for their succulent flesh, among diners of a carnivorous inclination."

Herold Norn frowned. "Bah. You ought to give them to us without charge. You have extorted enough money, Tuf."

Tuf rose and gave a ponderous shrug. "The man berates me, Dax," he said to his cat. "What am I to do? I seek only an honest living, and everywhere I am taken advantage of." He looked at Norn. "Another of my impulses comes to me. I feel, somehow, that you will not relent, not even were I to offer you an excellent discount. Therefore I shall yield. The hoppers are yours without charge."

"Good. Excellent." Norn turned toward the door. "We shall take them at the same time as the cobalcats, and release them about the estates."

Haviland Tuf and Dax followed him from the chamber, and they rode in silence back to Norn's ship.

The fee was sent up by the House of Norn the day before delivery was due. The following afternoon, a dozen men in black and gray ascended to the *Ark*, and carried six tranquilized cobalcats from Haviland Tuf's holding tanks to the waiting cages in their shuttlecraft. Tuf bid them a passive farewell, and heard no more from Herold Norn. But he kept the *Ark* in orbit about Lyronica.

Less than three of Lyronica's shortened days passed

before Tuf observed that his clients had slated a cobalcat for a bout in the Bronze Arena.

On the appointed evening, Tuf donned a disguise, consisting of a false beard and shoulder-length wig of red hair, plus a gaudy puff-sleeved suit of canary yellow complete with a furred turban, and shuttled down to the City of All Houses with the hope of escaping attention. When the match was called, he was seated in the back of the Arena, a rough stone wall against his shoulders and a narrow wooden seat attempting to support his weight. He had paid a few irons for admission, but had scrupulously bypassed the betting booths.

"Third match," the announcer cried, even as workers pulled off the scattered meaty chunks of the loser in the second match. "From the House of Varcour, a female lizard-lion, aged nine months, weight 1.4 quintals, trained by Junior Beast-Master Ammari y Varcour Otheni. Once a veteran of the Bronze Arena, once surviving." Those customers close to Tuf began to cheer and wave their hands wildly, as might be anticipated; he had chosen to enter by the Varcour Gate this time, walking down a green concrete road and through the gaping maw of a monstrous golden lizard, and thus was surrounded by Varcour partisans. Away and below, a great door enameled in green and gold slid up. Tuf lifted his rented binoculars to his eyes, and saw the lizard-lion scrabble forward—two meters of scaled green reptile with a whiplike tail thrice its own length and the long snout of an Old Earth alligator. Its jaws opened and closed soundlessly, displaying an array of impressive teeth.

"From the House of Norn, imported from offworld for your amusement, a female cobalcat. Aged—" The announcer paused. "Aged three, ah, years," he said at last, "weight 2.3 quintals, trained by Senior Beast-Master Herold Norn. New to the Bronze Arena." The metallic dome overhead rang to the cacophonous cheering of the Norn sector. Herold Norn had packed the Bronze Arena with his housemen, dressed in Norn colors and betting the grey and black standard.

The cobalcat came from the darkness slowly, with cautious fluid grace, and its great golden eyes swept the

arena. It was every bit the beast that Tuf had promised—
a bundle of deadly muscle and frozen motion, dark-blue
fur marbled with silvery streaks. Its growl could scarcely
be heard, so far was Tuf from the action, but he saw its
mouth gape through his glasses.

The lizard-lion saw it, too, and came waddling forward, its short scaled legs kicking in the sand while the
long impossible tail arched above it like the stinger of
some reptilian scorpion. When the cobalcat turned its
liquid eyes on the enemy, the lizard-lion brought the
tail down hard. With a bone-breaking crack the whip
made contact, but the cobalcat had smoothly slipped to
one side, and nothing shattered but air and sand.

The cat circled, growling. The lizard-lion, implacable, turned and raised its tail again, opened its jaws,
lunged forward. The cobalcat avoided both teeth and
whip. Again the tail cracked, and yet again; the cat was
too quick. Someone in the audience began to moan the
killing chant, others picked it up; Tuf turned his binoculars, and saw swaying in the Norn seats. The lizard-
lion gnashed its long jaws in frenzy, smashed its whip
across the nearest entry door, and began to thrash.

The cobalcat, sensing an opening, moved behind its
enemy with a graceful leap, pinned the struggling lizard
with one great blue paw, and clawed the soft greenish
flanks and belly to ribbons. After a time and a few futile
snaps of its whip that only distracted the cat, the lizard-
lion lay still.

The Norns were cheering very loudly. Haviland Tuf,
his pale features concealed behind his beard, rose from
his cramped seat and took his leave.

Weeks passed; the *Ark* remained in orbit around
Lyronica. Haviland Tuf carefully monitored results from
the Bronze Arena and noted that the Norn cobalcats
were winning match after match. Herold Norn still lost
a contest or two, when using an ironfang to fill up his
Arena obligations, but those defeats were easily out-
weighed by his long string of victories.

Tuf sat communing with Dax, played with his other
cats, entertained himself with recently acquired holo

dramas, ran numerous detailed ecological projections upon his computers, drank many tankards of brown Tamberkin ale and aged mushroom wine, and waited.

Some three standard weeks after the debut of the cobalcats, he had the callers he had anticipated.

Their slim, needle-prowed shuttlecraft was done in green and gold, and the men themselves dressed in scaled armor of gilded plate and green enamel. Three stood stiffly at attention when Tuf rolled up to meet them. The fourth, a florid and corpulent man who wore a golden helmet with a bright green plume to conceal a mottled pate as bald as Tuf's, stepped forward and offered a meaty hand.

"Your intent is appreciated," Tuf told him, keeping both of his own hands firmly on Dax, "and I have noted the fact that you are not clutching a weapon. Might I inquire as to your name and business, sir?"

"Morho y Varcour Otheni," the leader began.

Tuf raised one palm. "So. And you are the Senior Beast-Master of the House of Varcour, come to buy a monster. This turn of events is not entirely unanticipated, I must confess."

The fat Beast-Master's mouth puckered in an "o."

"Your housemen should remain here," Tuf said. "You may seat youself beside me, and we will proceed."

Haviland Tuf let Morho y Varcour Otheni utter scarcely a word until they were alone in the same chamber to which he had taken Herold Norn, sitting diagonally opposite. "You heard of me from the Norns," Tuf said then, "obviously."

Morho smiled toothily. "Indeed we did. A Norn houseman was persuaded to reveal the source of their cobalcats. To our delight, your *Ark* was still in orbit. You seem to have found Lyronica diverting?"

"Diversion is not the crux of the matter," Tuf said. "When problems exist, my professional pride requires me to be of whatever small service I can. Lyronica is rife with problems, alas. Your own individual difficulty, for example. Varcour is, in all probability, now the last and least of the Twelve Great Houses. A man of a more critical turn of mind than myself might remark that your lizard-lions are deplorably marginal monsters at best, and since I understand your realms are chiefly swampland, your choice of arena combatants must therefore be somewhat limited. Have I divined the essence of your complaint?"

"Hmpf. Yes, indeed. You do anticipate me, sir. But you do it well. We were holding our own well enough until you interfered. Since then, well, we have not taken a match from Norn once, and they were previously our chief victims. A few paltry wins over Wrai Hill and Amar Island, a lucky score against Feridian, a pair of death-draws with Arneth and Sin Doon—that has been our lot this past month. Pfui. We cannot survive. They will make me a Brood-Tender and ship me back to the estates unless I act."

Tuf stroked Dax, and quieted Morho with an upraised hand. "No need to belabor these matters further. Your distress is noted. Since my dealings with Herold Norn, I have been fortunate enough to be gifted with a great deal of leisure. Accordingly, as an exercise of the mind, I have been able to devote myself to the problems of the Great Houses, each in its turn. We need not waste precious time. I can solve your present difficulties. There will be some cost, however."

Morho grinned. "I come prepared. I heard about your price. It's high, there is no arguing, but we are prepared to pay, if you can . . ."

"Sir," Tuf said. "I am a man of charity. Norn was a poor House, its Beast-Master all but a beggar. In mercy, I gave him a low price. The domains of Varcour are richer, its standards brighter, its victories more wildly sung. For you, I must charge two hundred seventy-five thousand standards, to make up for the losses I incurred in dealing so generously with Norn."

Morho made a shocked blubbering sound, and his scales gave metallic clinks as he shifted in his seat. "Too much, too much," he protested. "I implore you. Truly, we are more glorious than Norn, but not so great as you suppose. To pay this price of yours, we must need starve. Lizard-lions would run over our battlements.

Our towns would sink on their stilts, until the swamp mud covered them over and the children drowned."

Dax shifted in Tuf's lap and made a small meow. "Quite so," Tuf said. "I am abashed to think that I might cause such suffering. Perhaps two hundred thousand standards would be more equitable."

Morho y Varcour Otheni began to protest and implore again, but this time Tuf merely sat silently, arms on their armrests, until the Beast-Master, red-faced and sweating, finally ran down and agreed to pay his price.

Tuf touched a button on the arm of his chair. The image of a great muscular saurian materialized between him and Morho; it stood two meters high, covered in grey-green plate scales and standing on four squat clawed legs as thick as tree stumps. Its head was a massive thing, armored by a thick yellowish plate of bone that jutted forward like the ramming prow of an ancient warship, with two curving horns at its upper corners. The creature had a short, thick neck; dim yellow eyes peered from under the jut of its brow ridge. Between them, square in the center of the head, a large, dark, round hole pierced the thick skull plate.

Morho swallowed. "Oh," he said. "Yes. Very, ah, large. But it looks—was there originally a third horn in the center, there? It looks as though it has been, ah, removed. Our specimens must be intact, Tuf."

"The *tris neryei* of Cable's Landing," Tuf said, "or so it was named by the Fyndii, whose colonists preceded humanity on that world by several millennia. The term translates, literally, as 'living knife.' There is no missing horn, sir." A long finger made a small, precise motion, pressed down upon a control. The *tris neryei* turned its massive head toward the Varcouri Beast-Master, who hiked his bulk forward awkwardly to inspect its image.

As he reached out toward the phantom, tendons bulged in the creature's thick neck, and a sharpened bone stake, as thick around as Tuf's forearm and more than a meter long, came thrusting out of the beast's head in a blur of motion. Morho y Varcour Otheni uttered a high thin squeak and turned gray as the bone spear skewered him and pinned him to his seat. An unfortunate odor filled the chamber.

Tuf said nothing. Morho, blubbering, looked down at where the horn entered his swollen stomach as if he were about to be sick, and it took him a long horrid minute before he realized there was no blood and no pain and the monster was only a hologram. His mouth made an "o." No sound came out. He swallowed. "Very, ah, dramatic," he said to Tuf.

The end of the long, discolored bone spear was held tightly within rings and ropes of pulsing blue-black muscle. Slowly the shaft began to pull back into the monster's head. "The bayonet, if we may be so bold as to call it that, is concealed within a mucous-lined sheath along the creature's upper neck and back, and the surrounding rings of musculature can deliver it at a speed approximating seventy kilometers per standard hour, with commensurate force. This species' native habitat is not entirely dissimilar to the areas of Lyronica under the control of the House of Varcour."

Morho moved forward so his seat creaked beneath his weight. Dax purred loudly. "Excellent!" the Beast-Master said, "though the name is a bit, oh, alien. We shall call them, let me think, ah, spear-carriers! Yes!"

"Call them what you will," said Tuf. "That is of small concern to me. These saurians have many obvious advantages for the House of Varcour, and should you choose to take them, I will also give you, without any additional charge, a breeding stock of Cathadayn tree-slugs. You will find that . . ."

Tuf followed the news from the Bronze Arena with diligence, although he never again ventured forth to the soil of Lyronica. The cobalcats continued to sweep all before them; in the latest featured encounter, one of the Norn beasts had destroyed a prime Arneth strangling-ape and an Amar Island fleshfrog during a special triple match.

But Varcour fortunes were also on the upswing; the newly introduced spear-carriers had proved a Bronze Arena sensation, with their booming cries and their

heavy tread and the swift and relentless death dealt out
in sudden thrusts of their massive bone bayonets. In
three matches so far, a huge feridian, a water-scorpion,
and a Gnethin spidercat had all proved impossibly un-
equal to the Varcour saurians. Morho y Varcour Otheni
was ecstatic. Next week, cobalcat would face spear-
carrier in a struggle for supremacy, and a packed arena
was being predicted.

Herold Norn called up once, shortly after the spear-
carriers had scored their first victory. "Tuf!" he said
sternly, "you have sold a monster to Varcour. We do
not approve."

"I was not aware that your approval was required,"
Tuf said. "I labored under the impression that I was a
free agent, as were the lords and Beast-Masters of all
the Great Houses of Lyronica."

"Yesyes," Herold Norn snapped, "but we won't be
cheated, you hear?"

Haviland Tuf sat calmly, regarding Norn's twisted
frown while petting Dax. "I take great care to be fair in
all my dealings," he said. "Had you insisted upon an
exclusive monster franchise for Lyronica, perhaps we
might have discussed that possibility, but to the best of
my recollection no such matter was ever broached or
suggested. Of course, I could hardly afford to grant the
House of Norn such exclusive privileges without an
appropriate charge, since my doing so would undoubtedly have deprived me of considerable much-needed
revenue. At any rate, I fear this discussion is moot,
since my transaction with the House of Varcour is now
complete and it would be highly unethical, to say nothing of impossible, for me to negate it now."

"I don't like this, Tuf," Norn said.

"I fail to see that you have a legitimate cause for
complaint. Your own monsters perform as expected,
and it is hardly generous of you to take umbrage simply
because another house shares Norn's good fortune."

"Yes. No. That is—well, never mind. I suppose I
can't stop you. If the other houses get animals that can
beat our cats, however, you will be expected to provide

us with something that can beat whatever you sell *them*. You understand?"

"This principle is easily grasped." He looked down at Dax. "I have given the House of Norn unprecedented victories, yet Herold Norn casts aspersions on my honesty and my comprehension. We are unappreciated, I fear."

Herold Norn scowled. "Yesyes. Well, by the time we need more monsters, our victories should have mounted high enough to afford whatever outlandish price you intend to charge."

"I trust that all goes well otherwise?" Tuf said.

"Well, yes and no. In the Arena, yesyes, definitely. But otherwise, well, that was what I called about. The four young cats don't seem interested in breeding, for some reason. And our Brood-Tender keeps complaining that they are getting thin. He doesn't think they're healthy. Now, I can't say personally, as I'm here in the City and the animals are back on the plains around Norn House. But some worry does exist. The cats run free, of course, but we have tracers on them, so we can . . ."

Tuf made a steeple of his hands. "Undoubtedly their mating season has yet to arrive. I would counsel patience. All living creatures engage in reproduction, some even to excess, and you have my assurances that once the female cobalcat enters estrus, matters will proceed with alacrity."

"Ah. That makes sense. Just a question of time then, I suppose. The other question I wanted to go over concerned these hoppers of yours. We set them loose, you know, and they have demonstrated no difficulty whatever in breeding. The ancestral Norn grasslands have been chewed bare. It is very annoying. They hop about everywhere. What are we to do?"

"This matter will also resolve itself when the cobalcats begin to breed," Tuf said. "The cobalt panthers are voracious and efficient predators, splendidly equipped to check your hopper plague."

Herold Norn looked puzzled, and mildly distressed. "Yes, yes," he said, "but . . ."

Tuf rose. "I fear I must end our conversation," he said. "A shuttlecraft has entered into docking orbit with the *Ark*. Perhaps you would recognize it. It is blue-steel, with large triangular grey wings.

"The House of Wrai Hill!" Norn said.

"Fascinating," said Tuf. "Good day."

Beast-Master Denis Lon Wrai paid two hundred thirty thousand standards for his monster, a powerful red-furred ursoid from the hills of Vagabond. Haviland Tuf sealed the transaction with a brace of scampersloth eggs.

The week following, four men in orange silk and flame red capes visited the *Ark*. They returned to the House of Feridian two hundred fifty thousand standards poorer, with a contract for the delivery of six great armored poison-elk, plus a gift herd of Hrangan grass pigs.

The Beast-Master of Sin Doon received a giant serpent; the emissary from Amar Island was pleased by his godzilla. A committee of a dozen Dant seniors in milk-white robes and silver buckles delighted in the slavering garghoul that Haviland Tuf offered them, with a trifling gift. And so, one by one, each of the Twelve Great Houses of Lyronica sought him out, each received its monster, each paid the ever-increasing price.

By that time, both of Norn's fighting cobalcats were dead, the first skewered on the bayonet of a Varcour spear-carrier, the second crushed between the massive clawed paws of a Wrai Hill ursoid (though in the latter case, the ursoid, too, had died). Undoubtedly the great cats had esped their fate, but in the closed and deadly confines of the Bronze Arena, they had nonetheless proved unable to avoid it. Herold Norn had been calling the *Ark* daily, but Tuf had instructed his computer to refuse the calls.

Finally, when eleven Houses had come and made their buys and taken their gifts and their leave, Haviland Tuf sat down across from Danel Leigh Arneth, Senior Beast-Master of Arneth-in-the-Gilded-Wood, once the greatest and proudest of the Twelve Great Houses of

Lyronica, now the last and least. Arneth was an immensely tall man, standing eye-to-eye with Tuf himself, but he had none of Tuf's fat. His skin was hard ebony, all muscle, his face a hawk-nosed axe, his hair short and iron grey. The Beast-Master came to the conference in cloth-of-gold, with crimson belt and boots and a tiny crimson beret aslant upon his head. He carried a trainer's pain-prod like a walking stick.

Dax bristled as Danel Leigh Arneth emerged from his ship, and hissed when the man climbed in the cart next to Tuf. Accordingly, Haviland Tuf at once commenced his lengthy rambling discourse about the sleepers. Arneth stared and listened; finally Dax grew calm again.

"The strength of Arneth-in-the-Gilded-Wood has always been in variety," Danel Leigh Arneth said early on. "When the other Houses of Lyronica threw all their fortunes on the backs of a single beast, our fathers and grandfathers worked with dozens. Against any animal of theirs, we had an optimal choice, a strategy. That has been our greatness and our pride. But we can have no strategy against these demon-beasts of yours, trader. No matter which of our hundred fighters we send onto the sand, it comes back dead. You have forced us to deal with you."

"I must take exception," said Tuf. "How could a mere seller of animals force the greatest Beast-Master of Lyronica to do anything he did not desire? If you truly have no desire to engage my services, please accept my word that I will take no offense. We may share a meal and some conversation together, and put all thought of business aside."

"Don't play word games, trader," Arneth snapped. "Business is the only reason I'm here. I have no great desire for your odious company."

Haviland Tuf blinked. "I am cut to the quick," he said in a flat voice. "Still, far be it from me to turn away any patron, whatever his personal opinion of me. Feel free to look over my stock, a few poor species that might pique your interest in some small way. Perhaps fortune will see fit to give you back your strategic options." He played upon the controls on the arm of his chair, and conducted a symphony in light and illusory flesh. A parade of monsters came and went before the eyes of the Arneth Beast-Master, creatures furred and scaled and feathered and covered by armor plate, beasts of hill and forest and lake and plain, predators and scavengers and deadly herbivores of sizes great and small.

Danel Leigh Arneth, his lips pressed tightly together, finally ordered four each of the dozen largest and deadliest species, at a cost of one million standards.

The conclusion of the transaction—complete, as with all the other Houses, with a gift of some small harmless animal—did nothing to soothe Arneth's foul temper. "Tuf," he said when the dealing was over, "you are a clever and devious man, but you do not fool me."

Haviland Tuf said nothing.

"You have made yourself immensely wealthy, and you have cheated all who bought from you and thought to profit. The Norns, for example. Their cats are worthless. They were a poor House; your price brought them to the edge of bankruptcy, just as you have done to all of us. They thought to recoup through victories. Bah! There will be no Norn victories now! Each house that came to you gained the advantage over those who purchased previously. Thus Arneth, the last to purchase, remains the greatest House of all. Our monsters will wreak devastation. The sands of the Bronze Arena will darken with the blood of the lesser beasts."

Tuf's hands locked on the bulge of his stomach. His face was placid.

"You have changed nothing! The Great Houses remain—Arneth the greatest and Norn the least. All you have done is bleed us, like the profiteer you are, until every Lyronican lord must struggle and scrape to get by. Our rivals now wait for victory, pray for victory, depend on victory, but all the victories will be Arneth's. We alone have not been cheated, because I thought to buy last and thus best."

"The foresight and acumen are remarkable," said Haviland Tuf. "Obviously, I am out of my depth with a man as wise and sagacious as yourself, and it would do me scant good to dissemble, deny, or try to outwit you. One as canny as you would easily see through my poor ploys. Perhaps it might be best were I to say nothing."

"You can do even better than that, Tuf," Arneth said. "You won't say anything, and you won't do anything either. This is your last sale on Lyronica."

"Perhaps," said Tuf, "and yet again, perhaps not. Circumstances may arise that will cause the Beast-Masters of the other Great Houses to bring me their custom once again, and then I fear I could hardly turn them away."

"You can and you will," Danel Leigh Arneth said coldly. "Arneth has made the last purchase, and we will not be trumped. Clone us up our animals and leave immediately upon making delivery. Henceforth you will deal no longer with the Great Houses. I doubt that fool Herold Norn could meet your price a second time, but even if he found the standards somewhere, you will not sell to him. *Do you understand?* We will not go round and round forever, playing this futile game of yours, paupering ourselves by buying monsters, losing them, buying more, and accomplishing nothing. I'm sure you would sell to us until there wasn't a standard left on Lyronica, but the House of Arneth forbids it. Ignore this warning and it could be worth your life, trader. I am not a forgiving man."

"Your point is well-taken," Tuf said, scratching Dax behind the ear, "although I have no great affection for the manner in which you have expressed it. Still, while the arrangement you suggest so forcefully will undoubtedly be of benefit to the House of Arneth-in-the-Gilded-Wood, the other Great Houses of Lyronica will be the losers for it, and I myself will have to sacrifice the potential for further profit. Perhaps I do not understand the whole of your proposal. I am easily distracted and I may have failed to hear the part wherein you explained the incentive you will offer me for acceding to your request to deal no more with the Great Houses of Lyronica."

"I'm prepared to offer you another million standards," Arneth said, glaring. "I'd like to cram it down your gullet, to tell the truth, but it's cheaper in the long run than playing another round in this damnable game of yours."

"I see," said Tuf. "Ergo, the choice is mine. I may take a million standards and depart, or remain in the face of your wrath and dire threats. I have pondered more difficult decisions, it must be admitted. In any case, I am scarcely the sort of man to remain on a world where his presence is no longer desired, and I confess that lately I have felt an urge to resume my wanderings. Very well. I bow to your demand."

Danel Leigh Arneth grinned a savage grin, while Dax began to purr.

The last of the fleet of twelve glittering gold-flecked shuttles had just departed, carrying the purchases of Danel Leigh Arneth down to Lyronica and the Bronze Arena, when Haviland Tuf finally condescended to take the call from Herold Norn.

The thin Beast-Master looked positively skeletal. "Tuf!" he exclaimed. "Everything is going wrong."

"Indeed," said Tuf impassively.

Norn pressed his features together in a grimace. "No, listen. The cobalcats are all dead, all sick. Four of them died in the Bronze Arena—we knew the second pair were too young, you understand, but when the first couple lost, there was nothing else to do. It was that or go back to ironfangs. Now we have only two left. They don't eat much—catch a few hoppers, but nothing else. And we can't train them, either. A trainer comes into the pen with a pain-prod, and the damn cats know what he intends. They're always a move ahead, you understand? In the arena, they won't respond to the killing chant at all. It's *terrible*. The worst thing is that they won't even breed. We need *more* of them. What are we supposed to enter in the gaming pits?"

"It is not cobalcat mating season," Tuf said. "We have discussed this point before, you may recall."

"Yesyes. When *is* their breeding season?"

"A fascinating question," said Tuf. "A pity you did not ask sooner. As I understand the matter, the female cobalt panther goes into heat each spring, when the snowtufts blossom on Celia's World. It is my understanding that some type of biological trigger is involved."

Herold Norn scratched at his scalp under the thin brass coronet. "But," he said, "but Lyronica has no snowthings, whatever it was you called them. Now I suppose you intend to charge us a fortune for these flowers."

"Sir, you do me a disservice. I would scarcely dream of taking advantage of your plight. Were the option mine, I would gladly donate the necessary Celian snowtufts to the House of Norn gratis. However, as it happens, I have struck a bargain with Danel Leigh Arneth to deal no more with the Great Houses of Lyronica." He gave a ponderous shrug.

"We won victories with your cats," Norn said, with an edge of desperation in his voice. "Our treasury has been growing—we have something like forty thousand standards now. It is yours. Sell us these flowers. Or better, a new animal. Bigger. Fiercer. I saw the Dant garghouls. Sell us something like that. We have nothing to enter in the Bronze Arena!"

"Nothing? What of your ironfangs? The pride of Norn, I was told."

Herold Norn waved impatiently. "Problems, you understand, we have been having problems. These hoppers of yours, they eat anything, everything. They've gotten out of control. Thousands of them, maybe millions of them, all over, eating all the grass, and all the crops. The things they've done to farmland—the cobalcats love them, yes, but we don't have enough cobalcats. And the wild ironfangs won't touch the hoppers. They don't like the taste, I suppose. I don't know, not really. But, you understand, all the other game is gone, driven out by these hoppers of yours, and the ironfangs went with them. Where, I don't know. Gone, though. Into the unclaimed lands, beyond the realms of Norn. There are some villages out there, a few farmers, but they hate the Great Houses. Tamberkin don't even have dog fights. They'll probably try to *tame* the ironfangs, if you can believe it! That's the sort they are."

"Shocking," said Tuf dispassionately. "Nonetheless, you have your kennels, do you not?"

"Not any more," Norn said. He sounded harried. "I ordered them shut. The ironfangs were losing every match, especially after you began to sell to the other houses. It seemed a foolish waste to maintain dead weight. Besides, the expense—we needed every standard. You bled us dry. We had Arena fees to pay, and of course we had to wager, and lately we've had to buy some food from Tamber just to feed all our housemen and trainers. I mean, you would never *believe* the things the hoppers have done to our crops."

"Sir," said Tuf. "Kindly give me a certain amount of credit. I am an ecologist. I know a great deal about hoppers and their ways. Am I to understand that you no longer have your ironfangs, then?"

"Yesyes. We turned the useless things loose, and now they're gone with the rest. What are we going to do? The hoppers are overrunning the plains, the cats won't mate, and our money will run out soon if we must continue to import food and pay Arena fees without any hope of victory."

Tuf folded his hands together. "You do indeed face a series of delicate problems. And I am the very man to help you to their solution. Unfortunately, I have pledged my bond to Danel Leigh Arneth, and accepted his money in good faith."

"Is it hopeless, then? Tuf, I am a man begging—I, a Senior Beast-Master of Norn. Soon we will drop from the games entirely. We will have no funds for Arena fees or betting, no animals to enter. We are cursed by ill fortune. No Great House has ever failed to provide its allotment of fighters—not even Feridian during its Twelve-Year Drought. We will be shamed. The House of Norn will sully its proud history by sending snufflers and barnyard animals onto the sand, to be shredded ignominiously by the huge monsters that you have sold the other houses."

"Sir," Tuf said. "If you will indulge me in a bit of prognostication, it occurs to me that perhaps Norn will not be alone in its quandaries. I have a hunch—*hunch*, yes, that is the proper word, and a curious word it is, too—a hunch, as I was saying, that the monsters you fear may be in short supply in the weeks and months to come. For example, the adolescent ursoids of Vagabond may very shortly go into hibernation. They are less than a year old, you understand. I hope the lords of Wrai Hill are not unduly disconcerted by this, yet I fear that they may be. Vagabond, as I'm sure you are aware, has an extremely irregular orbit about its primary, so that its Long Winters last approximately twenty standard years. The ursoids are attuned to this cycle. Soon their body processes will slow to such an extent that an untrained observer might even assume them to be dead. I fear that they will not be easily awakened. Perhaps, as the trainers of Wrai Hill are men of keen intellect, they might find a way. But I would be strongly inclined to further suspect that most of their energies and their funds will be devoted to feeding their populace, in the light of the voracious appetites of scampersloths.

"In quite a like manner, the men of the House of Varcour will be forced to deal with an explosion of Cathadayn tree-slugs. The tree-slugs are particularly fascinating creatures. At one point in their life cycle, they become veritable sponges, and double in size. A large enough grouping is fully capable of drying up even an extensive swampland." Tuf paused, and his thick fingers beat in drumming rhythms across his stomach. "I ramble unconscionably, I am afraid, and perhaps I am boring you. Do you grasp my point? My thrust?"

Herold Norn looked like a dead man. "You are mad. You have destroyed us. Our economy, our ecology . . . in five years, we will all be dead of starvation."

"Unlikely," said Tuf. "My experience in these matters suggests that Lyronica may indeed suffer a certain interlude of ecological instability and hardship, yet it will be of limited duration and ultimately I have no doubt that a new ecosystem will emerge. It appears unlikely that this successor ecology will offer niches for large predators, alas, but I am optimistic that the quality of Lyronican life will be otherwise unimpaired."

"No predators? No . . . but the games, the arena . . . no one will pay to see a hopper fight a slug! How can the games go on? *No one* will send fighters to the Bronze Arena!"

Haviland Tuf blinked. "Indeed," he said. "An intriguing thought. I will have to consider it thoroughly."

He cleared the screen, and began to talk to Dax.

6
CALL HIM MOSES

Rumors were seldom of any concern to Haviland Tuf. For one thing, he seldom heard any. Tuf was not averse to acting the tourist on most of the worlds he visited, but even when he was mingling with others in public places he remained somehow apart and unapproachable. His chalk-white skin and utterly hairless face and body usually made him conspicuous among the peoples of the planets on which he plied his trade, and even on those infrequent occasions when his complexion might have allowed him to pass, his size made him stand out. Thus, though people might stare at Tuf and talk of him everywhere he went, few of them talked *to* him unless they had business to transact.

Given his nature, then, it was hardly remarkable that Haviland Tuf had never heard of the man called Moses until the evening that he and Dax were assaulted by Jaime Kreen in a restaurant on K'theddion.

It was a small shabby place just off the spaceport. Tuf had finished a plate of smokeroots and neograss and was relaxing with his third liter of mushroom wine when abruptly Dax raised his head from the table. Tuf shook a bit, slopping some wine on his sleeve, and ducked his head quickly to one side, barely far enough so that the bottle Kreen was wielding smashed open against the back of Tuf's chair instead of the back of Tuf's skull.

293

Glass exploded, and the liquid within—a smelly local liquor—went everywhere, soaking the chair, the table, the cat, and both men. Jaime Kreen, a thin blond youth with drunken blue eyes, stood blinking stupidly, holding the broken bottle in a bleeding fist.

Haviland Tuf rose ponderously to his feet, his long white face singularly impassive. He glanced at his assailant, blinked, and then reached down to pick up Dax, who was wet and unhappy. "Can you fathom this, Dax?" he said in a deep bass. "We have here a mystery, albeit an inconvenient one. Why does this odd stranger attack us, I wonder? Do you have any ideas?" He stroked Dax slowly as he cradled him in his arms, and only when the cat began to purr did he look at Jaime Kreen again. "Sir," he said. "It might be wise of you to release the fragments of that bottle. It appears to me that your hand is full of glass and blood and that particularly noxious brew, and I have severe doubts that the combination will enhance your health."

The stricken Kreen seemed to come alive. His thin lips drew back in anger, and he flung the bottle away from him. "Are you mocking me, criminal?" he said in a slurred, dangerous voice.

"Sir," said Haviland Tuf. The restaurant had grown very still: the other patrons were quiet and staring, and the proprietor had vanished. Tuf's deep voice could be heard in every corner of the room. "I would venture that the title 'criminal' is more applicable to you than to myself, but perhaps that is not to the point. No, I am not mocking you. You appear to be upset. Under such conditions it would be folly to mock you, and I am not given to folly." He placed Dax back on the table and scratched the tomcat behind the ear.

"You *are* mocking me," Jaime Kreen said. "I'll *hurt* you!"

Haviland Tuf betrayed no emotion. "You will not, sir, although I believe you are thinking of attacking me once again. I do not approve of violence. However, your boorish behavior leaves me with little choice." So saying, he stepped forward quickly, and lifted Jaime

Kreen high off the floor before the younger man could react. Then, carefully, he broke both of his arms.

Kreen emerged pale and blinking from the tomblike dark of Kytheddene Prison into the bright street. His arms were in slings. He looked baffled and tired.

Haviland Tuf stood by the curbside, cradling Dax in one arm and petting him with the other. He looked up when Kreen came forth. "Your mood appears to have quieted somewhat," Tuf commented. "Moreover, you are now sober."

"You!" Kreen looked more baffled than ever; his face was so screwed up that it threatened to collapse in upon itself. "Do I understand that *you* bought my freedom?"

"You raise an interesting point," Haviland Tuf said. "I did indeed pay a certain sum—two hundred standards, actually, if we want to be precise—and upon that payment you were handed over to me. Yet it is incorrect to say that I bought your freedom. The crux of the matter is that you are not free. Under Kytheddene law, you belong to me, a bound servant whom I may work as I see fit until such time as you have discharged your debt."

"Debt?"

"I calculate it as follows," said Haviland Tuf. "Two hundred standards for the sum I paid to the local authorities in order to bask in your presence. One hundred standards for my suit, which was genuine Lambereen cotton, and which you quite ruined. Forty standards for the damage to the eatery, which damages I paid in order to settle the proprietor's claims against you. Seven standards for the delightful mushroom wine that you gave me no opportunity to drink. Mushroom wine is a noted specialty of K'theddion, and that was a particularly choice vintage. These total some three hundred forty-seven standards in actual damages. Furthermore, your unprovoked assault made Dax and myself the center of a highly unpleasant scene, and much disturbed our tranquility. For that I am assessing you an additional fifty-three standards, which is a generously low sum, to bring your total to an even four hundred standards."

Jaime Kreen chuckled maliciously. "You'll have a hard time getting even a tenth of that out of me, animal-seller," he said. "I have no funds, and I won't be good for much in the way of work. My arms are broken, you know."

"Sir," said Haviland Tuf. "If you had any significant funds of your own, you could have paid your own fines, in which case my assistance would not have been necessary. And since I myself broke your arms, I am aware of that condition as well. Kindly do not belabor the obvious with statements that convey no meaningful information. Despite your handicaps, I intend to take you with me back to my ship, and work you until your obligation has been discharged. Come."

Haviland Tuf turned and took two steps down the street. When Kreen made no move to follow, Tuf stopped and turned back to him. Kreen smiled. "If you want me anywhere, you can carry me," he said.

Tuf stroked Dax dispassionately. "I have no intention of carrying you," he said in even tones. "You forced me to touch you once, and that experience was sufficiently unpleasant that I have no intention of repeating it. If you decline to follow me, I will return to the authorities and hire two guards to take you bodily where I wish you to be. Their wages will be tallied to your debt. The choice is yours." Tuf turned again and moved off toward the spaceport.

Jaime Kreen, suddenly docile, followed behind, muttering under his breath.

The ship that waited for them at K'theddion Star Port was impressive enough to Kreen's eyes. An ancient, deadly looking craft of pitted black metal, with small rakish wings, it loomed half again as tall as the modern big-bellied trading ships that surrounded it. Like virtually all of Haviland Tuf's infrequent visitors, Kreen was awed (though he did not admit it) to discover that the *Griffin* was only a shuttle, that the *Ark* itself waited above, in orbit.

The shuttle deck of the *Ark* was twice the size of the landing field at K'theddion Star Port, and full of ships; four other shuttles identical to the *Griffin*, an old cargo ship with the teardrop shape characteristic of Avalon sitting on its three bent landing legs, a wicked-looking military flyer, an absurd golden barge with baroque ornamentation and a primitive harpoon gun mounted atop it, two craft that looked alien and vaguely untrustworthy, another that appeared to be nothing but a large square plate with a pole in its center. "Do you collect spacecraft?" Jaime Kreen asked, after Tuf had docked the *Griffin* and they had emerged onto the deck.

"An interesting concept," Tuf replied. "But no. The five landing shuttles are part of the *Ark* itself, and I retain the old trader for sentimental reasons, since it was my first ship. The others I have acquired along the way. Perhaps I should clean out the deck at some point, but there is the possibility that some of these vessels might have some commercial value, so I have refrained up to now. I will have to give the matter some thought. Now, come along with me."

They moved past a series of reception rooms and down several corridors, to a motor pool where several small three-wheeled vehicles were parked side-by-side. Haviland Tuf ushered Kreen into one, set Dax between them, and drove them down a great echoing tunnel that seemed to go on and on for kilometers. The shaft was lined by glass vats of many different sizes and shapes, each filled with fluids and gels. In some vats, dark shapes moved sluggishly within translucent bags, and seemed to peer out at them as they passed. Kreen found the suggestive motions somehow terrible and frightening. Haviland Tuf never noticed; he looked neither right nor left as he drove.

Tuf stopped the vehicle in a room identical to the one that they had started from, gathered up Dax, and led his prisoner down another corridor into a cramped, dustily comfortable chamber full of overstuffed furniture. He motioned Kreen to a seat and took one himself, setting Dax in a third chair since, when seated, he had no apparent lap. "Now," said Haviland Tuf, "we shall talk."

The vast dimensions of Tuf's ship had left Jaime Kreen somewhat subdued, but now a bit of spirit returned to his face. "We have nothing to talk about," he said.

"You think not?" said Haviland Tuf. "I disagree. It was not simply the generosity of my soul which bid me to rescue you from the ignominy of imprisonment. You pose a mystery to me, as I remarked to Dax when you first assaulted us. Mysteries disturb me. I desire some clarification."

Jaime Kreen's thin face took on a calculating look. "Why would I help you out? Your false charges put me in prison and now you've bought me as a slave. And you broke my arms, too! I don't owe you anything."

"Sir," said Haviland Tuf, locking his large hands together on his immense paunch, "we have already established that you owe me four hundred standards. I am prepared to be reasonable. I will ask you questions. You will give me answers. For each answer, I will deduct one standard from the sum you owe me."

"One standard! Absurd. Whatever you want to know is worth more than that! Ten standards for each answer! Not a tenth less!"

"I assure you," said Haviland Tuf, "that whatever information you possess is probably worth nothing at all. I am merely curious. I am a slave to curiosity. It is a fault of mine, one I am helpless to correct, and one that you are now in a position to take advantage of. Yet you should not attempt to press me too far. I refuse to be cheated. Two standards."

"Nine," said Kreen.

"Three, and I will go no higher. I grow impatient." Tuf's face was completely emotionless.

"Eight," said Kreen. "Don't try to bluff me."

Haviland Tuf was silent. He sat unmoving except for his eyes, which wandered over to Dax. The big black tomcat yawned and stretched himself.

After five minutes of silence, Kreen said, "Six standards, and that's cheap. I know a lot of important things, things that Moses would want to know. Six."

Haviland Tuf said nothing. Minutes passed.

"Five," said Kreen, swearing.

Haviland Tuf said nothing.

"All right," Kreen said at last. "Three standards. You are a cheat and a scoundrel, as well as a criminal. You have no ethics."

"I will ignore your bombast," said Haviland Tuf. "Three standards is the agreed sum, then. A sudden hunch comes to me that you may attempt to give evasive or confusing answers, so that I would have to ask many questions in order to elicit a small particle of information. I warn you that I will brook no such nonsense. Nor will I tolerate any deception. For each lie you attempt to tell me, I will add an additional ten standards on to your debt."

Kreen laughed. "I have no intention of lying, Tuf. But even if I did, how would you ever know? I am not that transparent."

Haviland Tuf permitted himself a smile, a tiny tight-lipped smile that barely touched his face and then was gone again. "Sir," he said, "I assure you that I would know at once. Dax would tell me, in precisely the same manner that he told me how far you would come down from your absurd demand for ten standards, and warned me of your cowardly attack on K'theddion. Dax is a feline, sir, as no doubt even you will perceive. All felines are at least partially psionic, as mankind has known throughout history, and Dax is the end product of generations of breeding and genetic manipulation that have greatly strengthened this trait in him. So you will save all of us a good deal of time and effort if you will give complete, honest answers. While Dax's talents are not sufficiently sophisticated to pluck difficult abstract concepts from your mind, I assure you that he can easily tell if you are lying or holding something back. So, with this in mind, shall we begin?"

Jaime Kreen was glaring at the big tomcat with venom in his eyes. Dax yawned again. "Go ahead," Kreen said sullenly.

"First," said Tuf, "there is the mystery of your assault upon us. I do not know you, sir. You are utterly a stranger to me. I am a simple merchant, and my services benefit all those who employ me. I had in no way given you offense. Yet you attacked me. This raises several questions. Why? What was your motive? Did you know me in some way? Had I given you offense in some action I have since forgotten?"

"Is that one question or four?" Kreen said.

Haviland Tuf folded his hands against his stomach again. "A point, sir. Begin with this: do you know me?"

"No," said Kreen, "but I know *of* you, by reputation. You and your *Ark* are unique and widely famed, Tuf. And you were easy to recognize, when I chanced across you in that slimy Kytheddene restaurant. Gross hairless white giants are not exceptionally common, you know."

"Three standards," Tuf said. "I will take notice of neither your insults nor your flattery. You did not know me, then. Why did you assault me?"

"I was drunk."

"Insufficient. It is true that you were drunk. But there were a number of other patrons in the eatery, any of whom might have obliged you if you were simply looking for a brawl. You were not. You chose me out of all those others. Why?"

"I dislike you. You are a criminal, by my standards."

"Standards vary, of course," Haviland Tuf replied. "On some worlds, my size itself would be a crime. On others, the fact that you wear boots made of cowhide would be punishable by long imprisonment. So in that sense, we are both criminals. Yet it is my feeling that it is unjust to judge a man by any laws save those of the culture in which he lives, or is presently moving. In that sense, I am no criminal, and your answer is still insufficient. Explain your dislike of me. What crimes do you charge against me?"

"I am a Charitan," Kreen said. He coughed. "Or perhaps I should say I was formerly a Charitan. In fact, I was an administrator, although only sixth grade. Moses destroyed my career. I charge you with the crime of assisting Moses. It is well known. Do not bore me with your denials."

Haviland Tuf glanced at Dax. "You appear to be telling the truth, and your answer contains a fair amount of information, although it raises several questions as well, and is far from clear. Nonetheless, I will do you a kindness and count it as an answer. Six standards, then. And my next questions will be simple ones. Who is Moses and what is a Charitan?"

Jaime Kreen looked incredulous. "Do you want to give me six standards? Don't pretend, Tuf. I won't buy it. You know who Moses is."

"Indeed I do, in a sense," Tuf replied. "Moses is a myth-figure associated with the various orthodox Christian religions, a figure alleged to have lived on Old Earth in the vast distant past. I believe he is somehow associated with or related to Noah, whom my *Ark* is named after, in a fashion. Moses and Noah were brothers, perhaps. The details escape me. In any event, both of them were among the earliest practitioners of ecological warfare, a field with which I am quite familiar. So, in a sense, I do know who Moses is. However, that Moses has been dead for a period sufficiently long to make it unlikely that he had destroyed your career, and even more unlikely that he would care a whit about any information you cared to convey to me. So I must judge that you are speaking of some other Moses, one I do not know. And that, sir, was the thrust of my question, the very point."

"All right," Kreen said. "If you insist on feigning ignorance, I'll play your silly game. A Charitan is a citizen of Charity, as you know perfectly well. Moses, as he styles himself, is a religious demagogue who heads the Holy Altruistic Restoration. With your aid he has conducted a devastating campaign of ecological warfare against the City of Hope, our single great arcology, the center of Charitan life."

"Twelve standards," said Tuf. "Explain further."

Kreen sighed and shifted in his chair. "The Holy Altruists were the original settlers of Charity, centuries ago. They left their original planet because their reli-

gious sensibilities were offended by its advanced technology. The Holy Altruistic Church teaches that salvation
is obtained by living a simple life close to nature, by
suffering and by self-sacrifice. So the Altruists came to a
raw planet and suffered and sacrificed and died quite
happily for a hundred years or so. Then, unfortunately
for them, there was a second wave of settlers. The
newcomers built the arcology we call the City of Hope,
farmed the land with advanced robotic machinery,
opened a star port, and generally sinned against God.
Worse, after a few years, children of the Altruists began
to desert to the City in droves, to enjoy life a little. In
two generations, nothing was left of Altruists except a
few old folks. Then Moses appeared, leading this movement they call the Restoration. He marched into the
City of Hope, confronted the council of administrators,
and demanded that we let his people go. The administrators explained that none of his people *wanted* to go.
Moses was unmoved. He said that unless we let his
people go, closed the star port, and dismantled the City
of Hope to live close to God, he would bring down
plagues on us."

"Interesting," said Haviland Tuf. "Continue."

"It's your money," said Jaime Kreen. "Well, the administrators threw Moses out on his hairy ass, and
everybody had a good laugh. But we also did some
checking, just to be safe. We had all heard ancient
horror stories about biological warfare, of course, but
we presumed those secrets were long lost. Our computers confirmed as much. Techniques of cloning and genetic manipulation such as were employed by the Earth
Imperials survived on only a handful of planets, those
much scattered, and the nearest some seven years from
us even by ftl drive."

"I see," said Haviland Tuf. "Yet no doubt you also
learned of the seedships of the Federal Empire's vanished Ecological Engineering Corps."

"We did," said Kreen, smiling sourly. "All gone,
destroyed or lost or crippled centuries ago, of no concern to us. Until we learned otherwise from the captain

of one trading vessel that put down at Port Faith. Rumors travel, Tuf, even from star to star. Your fame precedes you and condemns you. He told us all about you, you and this *Ark* you stumbled on, and used to line your pockets with standards and your gut with layers of fat. Other crews from other worlds confirmed your existence, and that you controlled a still-functioning EEC seedship. But we had no idea that you were in league with Moses until the plagues began."

A single thin furrow appeared on Haviland Tuf's massive bone-white brow, and then was gone again. "I begin to grasp your complaint," he said. He rose, a slow ponderous movement that was almost tidal, and stood towering above Jaime Kreen. "I will credit you with fifteen standards."

Kreen made a rude noise. "Only three standards, for all that. Tuf, you—"

"Twenty standards, then, if only to quiet you and restore some tranquility to the *Ark*. I have a beneficient nature. Your debt is now three hundred eighty standards. I shall ask you one further question, and give you an opportunity to reduce it to three hundred seventy-seven."

"Ask."

"What are the coordinates for your world, Charity?"

Charity was not so terribly far from K'theddion, as interstellar distances go, and the voyage between took but three standard weeks. For Jaime Kreen, they were busy weeks. While the *Ark* silently ate up the light years, Kreen worked. Centuries of dust had accumulated in some of the most desolate corridors. Haviland Tuf gave Kreen a broom and told him to clean it out.

Kreen begged off, citing his broken arms as a more-than-ample excuse. Haviland Tuf then sedated him, and confined him within the *Ark's* chronowarp tank, where the same great energies that warped the fabric of space could be used to do strange things to time. It was the last and greatest secret of the Earth Imperials, Tuf claimed, and had been lost virtually everywhere else. He used it to bring his clones to full maturity in a matter of days, and now he used it to age Jaime Kreen, and incidentally heal his broken arms in hours.

With his newly mended arms, Kreen set to sweeping at the rate of five standards an hour.

He swept kilometers of corridors, more rooms than he could count, all manner of empty cages where more than dust had accumulated. He swept until his arms ached, and when he did not have broom in hand, Haviland Tuf found other things for him to do. At mealtime Kreen played the butler, fetching Tuf pewter mugs of brown ale and platters heaped high with steamed vegetables. Tuf accepted them impassively in the over-stuffed armchair where it was his custom to take his leisure and read. Kreen was forced to feed Dax, too, sometimes three or four times over, since the big tom-cat was a fussy eater and Tuf insisted that his prefer-ences be indulged. Only when Dax was satiated was Jaime Kreen allowed to see to his own meal.

Once Kreen was asked to make a minor repair that the *Ark's* machinery had not attended to, for some reason, but he bungled the job so badly that Haviland Tuf promptly relieved him of all future assignments of that kind. "The blame lies entirely with me, sir," Tuf said when it happened. "I failed to remember that you are by training a bureaucrat, and thus good for virtually nothing."

Despite all his labors, Jaime Kreen's debt dwindled with excruciating slowness, and sometimes it did not dwindle at all. Kreen very quickly discovered that Haviland Tuf gave absolutely nothing away. For mend-ing his broken arms, Tuf tacked a hundred-standard "medical services" charge onto Kreen's obligation. He also charged a standard a day for air, a tenth-standard for each liter of water, a half-standard for a mug of ale. Meals were fairly cheap; only two standards each if Kreen ate basic fare. But basic fare was an unpalatable fortified mash, so as often as not Kreen paid higher prices for the tasty vegetable stews that Tuf himself favored. He would have been willing to pay even more for meat, but Tuf refused to provide it. On the one occasion that he asked Tuf to clone a steak for him, the trader simply stared and said, "We do not eat animal flesh here," then went on his way as unperturbed as ever.

During his first day on the *Ark*, Jaime Kreen asked Haviland Tuf where the toilet could be found. Tuf charged him three standards for the answer, and an additional tenth-standard for the use of the facility.

From time to time, Kreen thought about murder. But even in his most homicidal moments, when he was drunk as a dog, the idea never seemed quite feasible. Dax was always about when Tuf was, prowling down the corridors by the giant's side or riding serenely in his arms, and Kreen was certain that his host had other allies as well. He had glimpsed them on his travels around the ship—dark winged shapes that wheeled above his head in the more cavernous chambers, furtive shadows that scrambled away between the machines when surprised. He never saw them clearly, any of them, but he was somehow certain that he would see them all too well indeed were he to assault Haviland Tuf.

Instead, hoping to reduce his debt a bit faster, he gambled.

That was not perhaps the wisest course of action, but Jaime Kreen had a bit of a weakness for gambling. So each night they consumed hours playing a ridiculous game that Tuf enjoyed, shaking dice and moving counters around an imaginary star cluster, buying and selling and trading planets, building cities and arcologies and charging other star travelers all manner of landing fees and taxes. Unfortunately for Kreen, Tuf was much better at the game than he was, and usually ended up winning back a fair portion of the wages he had paid Kreen during the day.

Away from the gaming table, Haviland Tuf seldom spoke to Kreen at all except to set him tasks and haggle about payments back and forth. Whatever intentions he had toward Charity, he certainly did not volunteer them, and Kreen did not intend to ask, since every question added three standards onto his debt. Nor did Tuf ask any questions that might have tipped his hand. He simply continued in his solitary habits, worked alone in the various cloning rooms and laboratories of the *Ark*, read dusty ancient books in languages that Kreen could not comprehend, and held long conversations with Dax.

Thus life went on, until the day they entered orbit around Charity, and Haviland Tuf summoned Kreen to the communications room.

The communications room was long and narrow, its walls lined with dark telescreens and softly shining consoles. Haviland Tuf was seated before one of the blackened screens when Kreen entered, with Dax on his knee. He swiveled at the sound of the door panel sliding shut. "I have attempted to open channels of communication with the City of Hope," he said. "Observe." He touched a playback button on his console.

As Jaime Kreen slid into an empty seat, light flared on the viewscreen in front of Tuf, and coalesced into the face of Moses, a man in late middle age, with features that were regular and almost handsome, thinning gray-brown hair, and deceptively gentle hazel eyes. "Move off, starship," the recorded voice of the Altruistic leader said. His tones were deep and mellow, even if his words were harsh. "Port Faith is closed, and Charity is under new government. The people of this world wish no traffic with sinners, and have no need of the luxuries you bring. Leave us in peace." He raised his hand in a gesture that might have meant "Blessings" and might have meant "Halt," and then the screen went blank.

"So he has won," Jaime Kreen said in a tired voice.

"This would appear to be the case," said Haviland Tuf. He scratched Dax behind the ear and began to stroke him. "Your debt to me presently stands at two-hundred and eighty-four standards, sir."

"Yes," Kreen said suspiciously. "What of it?"

"I wish you to undertake a mission for me. You will descend to the surface of Charity in secrecy, locate the former leaders of your council of administrators, and bring them here for a consultation. In return, I will credit you with fifty standards toward your outstanding debt."

Jaime Kreen laughed. "Don't be ridiculous, Tuf. The sum is absurdly small for such a perilous mission. And I wouldn't do it even if you were to make me a fair offer, which I'm sure that you would not. Something like canceling out my entire debt, and paying me some two hundred standards besides."

Haviland Tuf stroked Dax. "This man Jaime Kreen takes us for absolute fools," he said to the cat. "Next I suspect he will also ask for the *Ark* itself, and perhaps title to a small planet or two. He has no sense of proportion." Dax gave a small purr that might or might not have meant something. Tuf looked up again at Jaime Kreen. "I am in an uncommonly generous mood, and I may allow you to take advantage of me in this single instance. One hundred standards, sir. It is twice what this small task is worth."

"Bah," Kreen replied. "Dax is telling you what I think of your offer, I'm sure. This scheme of yours is nonsense. I have no idea whether the council members are alive or dead, to be found in the City of Hope or elsewhere, free or imprisoned. I can hardly expect them to cooperate with me, either—not when I come bearing a summons from you, who we know to be an ally of Moses. And if Moses captures me, I will spend the rest of my life grubbing for turnips. Likely as not, I *will* be captured. Where do you intend me to land? Moses may have a recording set up to answer approaching starships, but he will certainly have posted guards around Port Faith to keep it closed. Think of the risks, Tuf! I couldn't possibly attempt this for anything less than the cancellation of my entire debt! All of it! Not a single standard less, you hear!" He crossed his arms stubbornly against his chest. "Tell him, Dax. You know how adamant I am."

Haviland Tuf's bone-white features remained impassive, but a small sigh escaped his lips. "You are truly a cruel man, sir. You make me rue the day when I carelessly told you that Dax was more than an ordinary feline. You deprive an old man of his one useful bargaining tool, and swindle him mercilessly with this inflexible stubborn attitude. Yet I have no choice but to give in. Two hundred eighty-four standards, then. It is established."

Jaime Kreen grinned. "At last you're being sensible. Good. I'll take the *Griffin.*"

"Sir," said Haviland Tuf. "You will not. You will take the trading ship you noticed on the shuttle deck, the *Cornucopia of Excellent Goods at Low Prices*, the ship wherein I began my own career many years ago."

"That! Absolutely not, Tuf. That ship is in obvious disrepair. I am going to have to make a difficult landing in some wilderness area, and I insist on a craft capable of surviving a bit of rough treatment. The *Griffin*, or one of the other shuttles."

"Dax," said Haviland Tuf to the quiet tomcat, "I fear for us. We are shut up in this small place with a congenital idiot, a man with neither ethics nor courtesy nor comprehension. I must explain every obvious ramification of a task that was childishly simple to begin with."

"What?"

"Sir," said Haviland Tuf. "The *Griffin* is a shuttle. It is unique in its design, and it has no stardrive. Should you be caught landing in such a craft, even a person with less intellectual equipment than yourself might deduce that a larger ship such as the *Ark* remained above, since shuttles frequently need something to shuttle from, and seldom materialize from the vacuum of deep space. The *Cornucopia of Excellent Goods at Low Prices*, in contrast, is a common model Avalon-made starship, complete with drive, albeit dysfunctional in this case. Do you understand the point, sir? Do you grasp the essential differences between the two craft?"

"Yes, Tuf. But since I don't intend to be captured, the distinction is academic. Still, I'll humor you. For an additional fifty standards above and beyond my debt, I will consent to use your *Cornucopia.*"

Haviland Tuf said nothing.

Jaime Kreen fidgeted. "Dax is telling you that I'm

going to give in if you wait, isn't he? Well, I'm not. You can't trick me that way any more, do you understand." He crossed his arms more tightly than ever. "I am a rock. I am steel. I am adamantine in my resolve on this matter."

Haviland Tuf stroked Dax, and said nothing.

"Wait all you like, Tuf," said Kreen. "Just this once, I'm going to fool you. I can wait, too. We'll wait together. And I'll never give in. Never. Never. NEVER."

When the *Cornucopia of Excellent Goods at Low Prices* returned from the surface of Charity a week and a half later, Jaime Kreen had three others with him, all former top administrators of the City of Hope. Rej Laithor was an elderly hatchet-faced woman with iron-gray hair who had formerly chaired the council. Since Moses had taken over, she had been undergoing retraining as a spinning-wheel operator. She was accompanied by a younger woman and a large man who looked as if he had once been very fat, although now his skin hung from his face in loose yellow folds.

Haviland Tuf received them in a conference room. He was seated at the head of the table when Kreen ushered the Charitans in, his hands folded neatly in front of him, and Dax curled up lazily on the polished metal.

"I am pleased that you could come," he said as the administrators took seats. "You appear hostile, however, and I regret this. Let me begin by assuring you that I played no role whatsoever in your vicissitudes."

Rej Laithor snorted. "I interrogated Kreen when he found me, Tuf, and he told me of your protestations of innocence. I believe them no more than he did. Our city and our way of life were destroyed by ecological warfare, by the plagues that this Moses let loose on us. Our computers tell us that only you and this ship are capable of waging such warfare."

"Indeed," said Haviland Tuf. "I might suggest that you consider reprogramming your computers, if they frequently make such errors."

"We have no computers now," the formerly fat man

said dolefully. "I was chief of programming, however, and I resent the inference that I was less than capable."

"You *are* less than capable, Rikken, or you never would have let those lice infest the system," Rej Laithor said. "That makes Tuf not one whit less guilty, however. They were his lice."

"I do not have a monopoly on lice," Haviland Tuf said simply. Then he raised a hand. "We should desist from this squabbling. It takes us nowhere. Let us, instead, discuss the sad history and plight of the City of Hope, and of Moses and the plagues. Perhaps you are familiar with the original Moses, the Old Earth Moses whom your own antagonist patterns himself after. This elder Moses had no seedship, no formal tools for biowar. He did, however, have a god, who proved to be equally effective. His people were being held in captivity. To free them, he sent ten plagues against his enemies. Did your Moses follow this selfsame pattern?"

"Don't answer him for free," Jaime Kreen said, from where he lounged against the door.

Rej Laithor glanced at him as if he were insane. "We looked up the original Moses story," she said when she turned back to Tuf. "Once the plagues started coming, we wanted to know what to expect. Moses used the same plagues as the original, but he varied the order a bit. And we only got six of them, at which point the council gave in to the Altruistic demands, closed Port Faith, and evacuated the City of Hope." She held up her hands. "Look at them—look at those blisters, look at that callus. He has us all scattered through these rotting Altruistic villages, living like primitives. Hungry, too. He's mad."

"First Moses turned the waters of the river into blood," said Haviland Tuf.

"It was disgusting," the younger woman said. "All the water in the arcology, the fountains, the swimming pools, the taps. You turned on the faucet or stepped into the shower and suddenly you were covered with blood. Even the toilets were full of blood."

"It wasn't real blood," Jaime Kreen added. "We analyzed it. Some organic poison had been added to the city water supply. But whatever it was made the water thick and red and undrinkable. How did you do it, Tuf?"

Haviland Tuf ignored the question. "The second plague was a plague of frogs."

"In our yeast tanks, and our whole hydroponics section," said Kreen. "I was the supervising administrator. It ruined me. The frogs gummed up all the machinery with their bodies, and they died and rotted and spoiled the food. Laithor gave me a summary discharge when I couldn't contain them—as if it was my fault!" He grimaced at his former superior. "Well, at least I didn't wind up slaving for Moses. I left for K'theddion when it was still possible to leave."

"Third," said Haviland Tuf, "was the plague of lice."

"Everywhere," muttered the former fat man. "Everywhere. They couldn't live inside the system, of course, so they died there, but that was bad enough. The system went down. The lice just moved on. Everybody had them. You couldn't stay clean enough to avoid it."

"Fourth was the plague of flies."

The Charitans all looked glum. No one said anything.

"Fifth," continued Haviland Tuf, "Moses set loose a murrain that killed all the cattle of his enemies."

"He skipped the murrain," said Rej Laithor. "We had our herds out on the prairies, but we put guards around them, and down in the cellars around the meatbeasts, too. We were expecting him. Nothing happened. He skipped the boils, too, thank goodness, and the hail. I would have liked to have seen him make it hail inside the arcology. He went straight to the locusts."

"Indeed," said Haviland Tuf. "The eighth plague. Did these locusts eat your fields clean?"

"The locusts didn't touch our fields. They were inside the city, in the sealed grain storage compartments. Three years' worth of surplus was gone overnight."

"The ninth plague," said Haviland Tuf, "was darkness itself."

"I'm glad I missed that one," volunteered Jaime Kreen.

"Every light in the city died," said Rej Laithor. "Our

repair crews had to fight through piles of dead flies and live locusts, scratching at their lice all the while. It was hopeless, and the people were already leaving by the thousands. I ordered the city abandoned once it became clear that even the secondary power stations were full of bugs. After that, everything went very fast. A week later I was living in an unheated cabin in the Hills of Honest Labor, and learning how to operate a spinning wheel." Her tone was savage.

"Your fate is a sad one," Haviland Tuf agreed in a placid voice. "Yet you should not despair. When I heard of your plight from Jaime Kreen, I resolved at once to help you. And here I am."

Rej Laithor looked suspicious. "Help us?" she said.

"I will win back your City of Hope for you," said Haviland Tuf. "I will smite Moses and his Holy Altruistic Restoration. I will free you from your spinning wheel and give you back your vocoder."

The young woman and the former fat man were beaming. Rej Laithor continued to frown. "Why?"

"Rej Laithor asks me why," Haviland Tuf said to Dax, stroking the cat softly. "My motives are always imputed. People have no trust in this hard modern age, Dax." He looked at the top administrator. "I will help you because the situation on Charity moves me, because your people are obviously in pain. Moses is no true altruist, as we both know, but this does not mean the impulse to self-sacrifice and benevolence is dead in humanity. I deplore Moses and his tactics, his use of innocent insects and animals in an unnatural manner to impose his will on his fellow human beings. Are these motives sufficient for you, Rej Laithor? If not, say as much, and I will take my *Ark* and depart."

"No," she said. "No, don't do that. We accept. I accept, on behalf of the City of Hope. If you succeed, we will build a statue to you, and set it atop the city to be seen for kilometers."

"Passing birds would relieve themselves upon such a statue," said Haviland Tuf. "The wind would abrade and erode it, and it would be placed too high for any to see its features clearly. Such a statue might tickle my vanity—I am a small man, for all my size, easily pleased by such things—but I would want it set in your largest public square, safe from all harm."

"Of course," Laithor said quickly. "Anything."

"Anything," said Haviland Tuf. It was not a question. "In addition to the statue, I will also require fifty thousand standards."

Her face went pale and then red. "You said," she began in a sort of a choked whisper. "You . . . benevolence . . . altruism . . . our need . . . the spinning wheel . . ."

"I must meet my expenses," said Haviland Tuf. "Certainly I am willing to donate my own time to this matter, but the resources of the *Ark* are too valuable to squander. I must eat. Surely the coffers of the City of Hope are sufficient to meet this small sum."

Rej Laithor made a sputtering noise.

"I'll handle this," Jaime Kreen interjected. He turned to Tuf. "Ten thousand standards. No more. Nothing. Ten thousand."

"Impossible," said Haviland Tuf. "My costs will surely exceed forty thousand standards. Perhaps I can diet for a time, take only that sum, and content myself with a small loss. Your people do suffer."

"Fifteen thousand," Kreen said.

Haviland Tuf said nothing.

"Oh, hell," said Jaime Kreen. "Forty thousand then, and I hope that damned cat dies of gout."

It was the habit of the man called Moses to walk each evening along the rugged footpaths of the Hills of Honest Labor, to watch the beauty of the sunset and contemplate in solitude the problems of the day. He would stride along briskly at a pace few younger men could match, his long crooked staff in hand and a peaceful look on his face, his eyes fixed on far horizons. Often he would cover a dozen kilometers before turning back toward home and bed.

The pillar of fire first appeared to him on such a walk. He had just topped a rise and there it was—a twisting, writhing funnel of orange flame, shot through with flickers of blue and yellow, tracing a path through the rocks and the dust straight toward him. It was easily thirty meters high, crowned by a small gray cloud that somehow paced it.

Moses rested on the crest of the hill, leaning on his staff, and watched it come.

The pillar of fire stopped five meters from him, on slightly lower ground. "Moses," it said in a booming thunderous voice from above, "I am the Lord God, and you have sinned against me. *Give my people back!*"

Moses chuckled. "Very good," he said in his rich tones. "Really, very good."

The pillar of fire trembled and spun. "Release the people of the City of Hope from your cruel bondage," it demanded, "lest in my wrath I bring down plagues upon you."

Moses scowled and pointed his staff at the pillar of fire. "I am the one who brings down plagues around here, I would thank you to remember." There was a hint of irony in his voice.

"False plagues from a false prophet, as both you and I know full well," boomed the pillar of fire. "All of your feeble tricks and travesties are known to me, the Lord God whose name you have profaned. Give my people back, or you shall look upon the terrible face of genuine pestilence!"

"Nonsense," said Moses. He began walking downhill, toward the pillar of fire. "Who are you?"

"I am who I am," the pillar of fire said, retreating hastily as Moses advanced. "I am the Lord God."

"You are a holographic projection," Moses said, "emanating from that silly cloud above us. I am a holy man, not a stupid one. Go now."

The pillar of fire stood its ground and rumbled threateningly. Moses walked right through it, and continued smartly down the hill. The pillar remained, writhing and spinning, until long after Moses had vanished. "Indeed," it boomed in its vast thunderous voice to the empty night. Then it shuddered and winked out.

The small grey cloud scuttled across the hills and

caught up to Moses a kilometer down the road. The pillar of fire snaked down again, crackling with ominous energy. Moses walked around it. The pillar of fire began to follow him.

"You city-dwellers begin to try my patience," Moses said as he walked. "You seduce my people with your sinful, slothful ways, and now you interrupt my evening reflections. I have had a hard day of holy toil. Be warned that you are near to provoking me. I have forbidden all this traffic with science. Take your aircar and your hologram and be gone with you, before I bring down a plague of boils upon your people."

"Empty words, sir," said the pillar of fire, trailing close on his heels. "Boils are well beyond your limited abilities. Do you think to deceive one such as I as easily as you deceived that pack of small-visioned bureaucrats?"

Moses hesitated, and cast a thoughtful look over his shoulder. "You doubt the powers of my God? I would think that my demonstrations had been ample enough."

"Indeed," said the pillar of fire. "Yet the things demonstrated were your own limitations, and those of your opponents. It is clear that you planned long ahead, and well, but your only powers were in that."

"No doubt you believe the plagues that swept the City of Hope were coincidence, bad fortune?"

"You mistake me, sir. I know full well what they were, and there was nothing supernatural in any of them. For generations the young and the disaffected among the Altruists had been emigrating to the City. How simple and obvious to plant among their numbers your own spies, saboteurs, and agents. How cunning to wait a year or two or five until each among those had been fully accepted into the City of Hope, and given positions of responsibility. Frogs and insects can be bred, sir, and easily, whether in a cabin in the Hills of Honest Labor or in an apartment complex within the City itself. Release such creatures in the wild, and they will dissipate and die. The elements will slay them, natural enemies will hunt them down, they will perish for want of food; the complex merciless mechanism of the ecology will set them in their natural place. But how different within an arcology, the veritable architectural ecology that is truly no ecology at all, for it has a niche for no animal but humanity alone. The weather within is always fair and gentle, no competing species or predatory enemies exist, and it is an easy enough thing to find a proper source of food. Under such conditions, the result is inevitably a plague. Yet a false plague, looming large only within the confines of the City. Outside, your little plagues of frogs and lice and flies would be as nothing to the wind and the rain and the wild."

"I turned their water into blood," Moses insisted.

"Indeed, your agents placed organic chemicals in the City's water supply."

"I brought down a plague of darkness," Moses said. His tone had grown quite defensive.

"Sir," said the pillar of fire, "you insult my intelligence with the obvious. You turned out a light."

Moses swung about to face the pillar, glaring up at it defiantly, his face red by reflected light. "I deny this. I deny all of it. I am a true prophet."

"The true Moses brought down a grievous murrain upon his enemies," the pillar of fire boomed in an even voice, as much as thunder can be even. "You brought none. The true Moses set upon his enemies a festering sweat of boils, so that none could stand before him. You did not. Your omissions give you away, sir. True pestilence is beyond your powers. The true Moses devastated the lands of his enemies with hail that rained down day and night. That plague too defeated your own limited capacities. Yet your enemies, beset by your tricks, surrendered the City of Hope before the tenth plague, the death of the first-born, and that was to your great good fortune, for by that time you were of a certainty plagued out."

Moses smote the pillar of fire with his staff. There was no apparent effect on either staff or pillar. "Move off," he shouted. "Whoever you are, you are no God of mine. I defy you. Do your worst! You have said it yourself: in nature, plagues are less simple things than inside an arcology. We are secure in the simple life we live in the Hills of Honest Labor, close to our God. We are full of grace. You cannot harm us."

"Indeed," boomed the pillar of fire. "You are wrong, Moses. *Give my people back!*"

Moses was not listening. He walked through the fire again and, furious, began to race back toward the village.

"When will you start?" Jaime Kreen asked eagerly after Haviland Tuf had returned to the *Ark*. He had remained aboard after taking the other Charitans back to the surface, since—as he had pointed out—the City of Hope was uninhabitable and there was no place for him in the villages and work camps of the Altruists. "Why aren't you working? When will—"

"Sir," said Haviland Tuf. He was sitting in his favorite chair, eating a bowl of creamed mushrooms and lemon-peas. A mug of ale sat on the table by his side. "Do not presume to give me orders, unless you chance to prefer the hospitality of Moses to my own." He sipped at his ale. "Such work as needs be done has been done. My hands, unlike your own, were not entirely idle during our voyage from K'theddion."

"But that was before . . ."

"Details," said Haviland Tuf. "Most of the basic cloning is done. The clones too have kept themselves occupied. The breeding tanks are full." He blinked at Kreen. "Leave me to my dinner."

"The plagues," said Kreen. "When will they begin?"

"The first," said Haviland Tuf, "began some hours ago."

Down through the Hills of Honest Labor, past the six villages and the rocky fields of the Holy Altruists and the sprawling barren work camps where the refugees were quartered, ran the wide slow-flowing river that Altruists called God's Grace and other Charitans the River of Sweat. When dawn broke on the distant horizon, those who had gone down to the riverside to fish or fill their jugs or wash their clothing returned to the villages and work camps with cries of horror. "Blood," they shouted. "The river is blood, as the waters of the City were." Moses was sent for, and he went to the river reluctantly, wrinkling his nose at the smell of dead and dying fish, and the stink of blood itself. "A trick of the sinners of the City of Hope," he said, when he looked down on the sluggish scarlet stream. "The Lord God renews the natural world. I will pray, and in a day the river will be clean and fresh again." He stood in the mud, at his feet a bloody shallow pool full of dead fish, stretched out his staff over the diseased waters, and began to pray. He prayed for a day and a night, but the waters did not clear.

When dawn came again, Moses retired to his cabin, and gave orders, and Rej Laithor and five other top administrators were taken from their families and questioned most intensely. The questioners learned nothing. Patrols of armed Altruists went upstream, searching for the conspirators who were dumping chemical pollutants into the river. They found nothing. They traveled for three days and three nights, as far as the great waterfall in the High Country, and even there the tumbling waters were blood, blood, blood.

Moses prayed without surcease, both day and night, until he finally collapsed from exhaustion, and his lieutenants took him back to his simple cabin. The river remained red and murky.

"He is beaten," Jaime Kreen said after a week, when Haviland Tuf had returned from scouting out the situation below in his airbarge. "Why does he wait?"

"He waits for the river to cleanse itself," said Haviland Tuf. "It is one thing to contaminate the water supply of a closed system like your arcology, where only a finite amount of contaminant will be sufficient for the task. A river is an undertaking of a higher magnitude. Inject any amount of chemical you please into its waters, and sooner or later it will all flow past and the river will be clean again. Moses no doubt believes we shall soon run out of chemicals."

"Then how are you doing it?"

"Microorganisms, unlike chemical substances, multiply and renew themselves," said Haviland Tuf. "Even the waters of Old Earth were subject to such red tides, the ancient records of the EEC tell us. There is a world called Scarne where the corresponding lifeform is so virulent that even the oceans themselves are perpetually stained, and all other creatures must adapt or die. Those who built the *Ark* visited Scarne and took cloning material."

That night the pillar of fire appeared outside of Moses' cabin, and frightened away the guards. "*Give my people back!*" it roared.

Moses staggered to the door and threw it wide. "You are a delusion of Satan," he screamed, "but I will not be tricked. Be gone. We will drink no more from the river, trickster. There are deep wells we can take our water from, and we can dig others."

The pillar of fire writhed and crackled. "No doubt," it commented, "yet you only delay the inevitable. Release the people from the City of Hope, or I will set the plagues of frogs upon you."

"I will eat your frogs," Moses yelled. "They will be fine and delicious."

"These frogs will come from the river," said the pillar of fire, "and they shall be more terrible than you can imagine."

"Nothing lives in that poisoned gutter," Moses said. "You have seen to that." Then he slammed the door, and would listen no more to the pillar of fire.

The guards that Moses sent to the river at dawn came back bloody and hysterical with fear.

"There are *things* there," one of them testified, "moving around in the pools of blood. Little crimson wrigglers, 'bout as big as your finger, but their legs was twice as long. Looked like red frogs, except when we got closer we saw that they had teeth, and they was ripping up the dead fish. Hardly any fish was left at all, and them that were had these frog things crawling all over them. Then Danel tried to pick up one of these frogs, and it snapped at him, right into his hand, and he screamed and all of a sudden the air was full of the

damn things, jumping around like they was flying, biting people, tearing at you when they got hold. It was
terrible. How are you going to fight a frog? Stab it?
Shoot it? How?" He was shaking.

Moses sent another party down to the river, armed
with sacks and poison and torches. They came back in
total disarray, carrying two of their number. One man
died that morning, his throat torn out by a frog. Another went a few hours later, from the fever that many
of those bitten had developed.

By dusk, all the fish were gone. The frogs began to
move up from the river, into the villages. The Altruists
dug trenches and filled them with water and flame. The
frogs leaped over the trenches. The Altruists fought
with knives and clubs and fire, some even with the
modern weapons they had taken from the cityfolk. Six
more people were dead by dawn. Moses and his followers retreated behind closed doors.

"Our people are out in the open," Jaime Kreen said
fearfully. "The frogs will come into the camps and kill
them."

"No," said Haviland Tuf. "If your Rej Laithor can
keep her charges calm and quiet, they have nothing to
fear. Scarnish bloodfrogs are carrion eaters chiefly. They
attack living creatures larger than themselves only when
attacked or frightened."

Kreen looked incredulous, then slowly smiled. "And
Moses hides in fear! That's rich, Tuf."

"Rich," said Haviland Tuf. There was nothing in his
tone to indicate either agreement or mockery. But Dax
was in his arms, and Kreen noticed suddenly that the
cat was still and stiff, his fur slowly bristling.

That night the pillar of fire came not to the man
called Moses, but to the refugees from the City of
Hope, huddled in fear in their ramshackle camp, watching the frogs prowl beyond the fences that kept them
apart from the Altruists.

"Rej Laithor," the pillar of fire said, "your enemies
have imprisoned themselves behind barred doors. You

are free. Go. Take your people in hand and lead them back to your arcology. Walk slowly, watch where you set your feet, make no sudden moves. Do these things without fail, and the frogs will leave you unharmed. Clean and repair your City of Hope, and ready my forty thousand standards."

Rej Laithor, surrounded by her junior administrators, stared up at the writhing flames. "Moses will attack us again as soon as you depart, Tuf," she shouted. "Finish him. Unleash your other plagues."

The pillar of fire said nothing. It turned and crackled for long minutes, and then it was gone entirely.

Wearily, the people of the City of Hope began to file out of camp, being very careful where they set their feet.

"The generators are working again," Jaime Kreen reported two weeks later. "The City will soon function as before. But that is only half our bargain, Tuf. Moses and his followers still sulk in their villages. The bloodfrogs are nearly all dead now, for want of any carrion to eat except each other. And the river shows signs of clearing. When are you going to unleash the lice on them? And the flies? They deserve to scratch, Tuf."

"Take the *Griffin*," Haviland Tuf ordered. "Bring Moses to me, willing or no. Do this and one hundred standards of your City's funds will be yours."

Jaime Kreen looked astonished. "Moses? *Why*? Moses is our enemy. If you think you can turn around and make a deal with him now, sell us back into slavery for a better price . . ."

"Contain your suspicions," Tuf replied. He stroked Dax. "Always people think the worst of us, Dax. Perhaps it is our sad fate to be ever suspect." He addressed Kreen again. "I wish only a conference with Moses. Do as I have told you."

"I am not in your debt any more, Tuf," Kreen said sharply. "I assist you only as a patriotic Charitan. Tell me your motives, and I may do your bidding. Otherwise, do it yourself. I refuse." He crossed his arms.

"Sir," said Haviland Tuf, "are you aware of how many

meals and mugs of ale you have taken aboard the *Ark* since our balance was adjudged even? Are you aware of the quantity of my air you have breathed, and how many times you have used my sanitary facilities? I am abundantly aware of all of these things. Are you further aware that the usual charge for a voyage from K'theddion to Charity is some three hundred seventy-nine standards? All of these amounts could easily be added to your account. I have foregone this, to my great financial disadvantage, only because you have afforded me certain minor conveniences. I can see now that my forbearance was an error. I will rectify the mistakes in my bookkeeping."

"Don't bluff me, Tuf," Kreen said stubbornly. "We're even, and we're a long way from Kytheddene Prison, and any claims you have to me under their absurd laws are null and void on Charity."

"The laws of K'theddion and Charity are alike to me, except when they serve my purposes," Haviland Tuf said very quietly. "I am my own law, Jaime Kreen. And if I should determine to make you my slave until the last days of your life, neither Rej Laithor nor Moses nor your own bravado could help you in the least." Tuf delivered the words as always, evenly, calmly, in his bass voice, with hardly a hint of emotion in his flat inflection.

But Jaime Kreen suddenly felt very cold. And he did as he was bid.

Moses was a tall, strong man, but Tuf had told Jaime Kreen of his nightly reflections, and it was an easy enough thing to wait one evening in the hills beyond the village, in the brush with three others, and overcome Moses as he passed. One of Kreen's assistants suggested killing the Altruistic leader then and there, but Kreen forbade it. They carried the unconscious Moses back to the waiting *Griffin*, where Kreen dismissed the others.

Shortly after, Kreen delivered Moses to Haviland Tuf, and turned to take his leave.

"Stay," Tuf said. They were in a room that Kreen had

never seen before, a vast echoing chamber where the walls and ceiling were of the purest white. Tuf was seated in the center of the chamber, at a horseshoe-shaped instrument panel. Dax sat atop the console, looking quite alert.

Moses was still groggy. "Where am I?" he demanded.

"You are aboard the seedship *Ark*, the last functioning biowar ship of the Ecological Engineering Corps. I am Haviland Tuf."

"Your voice," Moses said.

"I am the Lord God," Haviland Tuf said.

"Yes," Moses said. He stood up suddenly. Jaime Kreen, standing behind him, grabbed him by the shoulders and shoved him roughly back into his seat. Moses protested, but did not try to rise again. "You were the one who brought the plagues, the voice from the pillar of fire, the devil who impersonated God."

"Indeed," said Haviland Tuf. "Yet you misunderstand. You are the impersonator in this company, Moses. You sought to impersonate a prophet, to pretend to vast supernatural powers you do not have. You employed tricks, and waged a primitive form of ecological warfare. I, in contrast, am no pretender. I am the Lord God."

Moses spat. "You are a man with a starship, and a host of machines. You played the plague game well. But two plagues do not make a man a god."

"Two," said Haviland Tuf. "Do you doubt the other eight?" His large hands moved over the instruments before him, the room darkened, the dome ran with light, and it seemed they were out in space, looking down on Charity. Then Haviland Tuf did something else to his instruments. The holograms shifted and they were moving, sinking, soaring, until the blurs resolved themselves. They floated above the settlements of the Holy Altruists, in the Hills of Honest Labor. "Watch," commanded Haviland Tuf. "This is a computer simulation. These things were not, yet could have been. I am confident that you will find this enlightening."

In the domed room, all about them, they saw the villages, and shadow-faced people moving among them,

shoveling the carcasses of dead frogs into pits for burning. They saw within the cabins, too, where weaker
people burned with fevers. "It is after the second plague,"
Haviland Tuf announced, "even as now. The bloodfrogs
have spent themselves." His hands moved. "Lice," he
said.

The lice came. The dust itself seemed to burst with
them, and suddenly they were everywhere. All the
shadow-folk were scratching, and Jaime Kreen (who
had scratched a good bit himself before departing for
K'theddion) chuckled. Then he stopped chuckling. The
lice seemed more than lice. The people broke out in a
scarlet rash, and many of them took to bed, screaming
of the itches, the horrible itches. Some scratched themselves so badly that they drew blood, scratched deep
gouges in their skin, and tore their fingernails loose in
their fury.

"Flies," said Haviland Tuf. And the flies swarmed,
flies of all kinds—the swollen stinging flies of Dam
Tullian, the flies of Old Earth with their ancient diseases, the black and grey fleshflies of Gulliver, the
sluggish flies of Nightmare who plant their eggs in
living tissue. They settled on the villages and the Hills
of Honest Labor in immense clouds, and covered them
as if they were but a particularly large dung heap, and
left them black and thick and stinking.

"The murrain," said Haviland Tuf. They watched the
herds die by the thousands. The gross immobile
meatbeasts in the cellar of the City of Hope turned to
rot and corruption. Burning could not check the pestilence. Soon, no meat was left, and those people who
still lived grew gaunt and bitter-looking. Haviland Tuf
said other words—anthrax, Ryerson's Disease, roserot,
calierosy.

"Boils," said Haviland Tuf, and again disease raged,
but this time among the people and not their animals.
They sweated and screamed as the boils covered their
faces and hands and chests, each swelling until it burst,
so the blood and the pus ran free. Then new boils grew
as fast as the old ones vanished. Men and women
staggered through the streets of the simple villages,

blind and pockmarked, bodies crusted and covered with open sores, the perspiration running like oil over their skin. When they fell in the dirt, among the dead flies and lice and cattle, they rotted there, with none to bury them.

"Hail," said Haviland Tuf, and it came, a great thundering pounding hail, the stones fists of ice, for a day and a night and a day and a night and a day and a night, and on and on, and fire mingled with the hail. Those who went outside died, the hailstones smashing them to the ground. And many of those who stayed within died, too. When the hail had stopped at last, there was hardly a cabin left standing.

"Locusts," said Haviland Tuf. They covered the earth and the sky, clouds of them, worse than the flies. They landed everywhere, crawled over the living and the dead both, and ate what little food was left, until there was nothing at all.

"Darkness," said Haviland Tuf. Darkness moved. It was a gas, a thick black gas, drifting with the wind. It was a liquid, flowing, moving like a sensuous stream of jet, gleaming, shining. It was silence. It was night. It was alive. Where it moved, no life remained behind it; the weeds and grasses were dry and dead, and the soil itself looked raw and ravaged and bruised. It was a cloud larger than the villages, or the Hills of Honest Labor, or the locusts. It settled over all of them, and nothing moved for a day or a night, and then the living darkness rolled on, and behind it was only dust, and dry decay.

Haviland Tuf touched his instruments, and the visions were gone from them. The lights came on again. The walls were very white.

"The tenth plague," Moses said slowly, in a voice that no longer seemed rich or large. "The death of the firstborn."

"I admit to my own failures," said Haviland Tuf. "I cannot make such fine distinctions. I would point out, however, that all of the firstborn *are* dead, in these scenes that never were, even as the lastborn. I am a gross and clumsy god in that; in my awkwardness, I must need kill all."

Moses was pale and broken, but within him was still a strong and stubborn man. "You are only human," he whispered.

"Human," said Haviland Tuf, in his voice without emotion. His huge pale hand was stroking Dax. "I was born human, and lived as such for long years, Moses. Yet then I found the *Ark*, and I have ceased to be a man. The powers I may wield are vaster than those of many gods that humans have worshipped. There is not a man I meet but I could take his life. There is not a world I pause on that I could not waste utterly, or remake as I choose. I am the Lord God, or as much of one as either of you is ever likely to encounter.

"It is a great fortune for you that I am kind and benevolent and merciful, and too frequently bored. You are counters to me, nothing more—pieces and players in a game with which I have whiled away a few weeks. It seemed an interesting game, this plague business, and so it was for a time. Yet it quickly grew dull. Even after two plagues, it was clear that I had no meaningful opposition, that you, Moses, were incapable of anything that might surprise me. My objectives were accomplished—I had taken back the people of the City of Hope, and the rest would be meaningless ritual. I have elected instead to end it.

"Go, Moses, and plague no more. I am through with you.

"And you, Jaime Kreen, see that your Charitans take no further vengeance. You shall have victories enough. In a generation, his culture and his religion and his way of life will all be dead.

"Remember who I am, and remember that Dax can look into your thoughts. If the *Ark* should pass this way again, and find that you have disobeyed me, it will be as I have shown you. The plagues will sweep your little world until nothing lives upon it."

Jaime Kreen shuttled Moses back to his people in the *Griffin*, then—on Tuf's instructions—collected forty thousand standards from Rej Laithor and took it back up to the *Ark*. Haviland Tuf met him on the shuttle deck, with Dax in his arms, and took his payment with only a stately blink.

Jaime Kreen was thoughtful. "You are bluffing, Tuf," he said. "You're no god. Those were only simulations you showed us. You could never have actually done all that. But you can program a computer to show anything."

"Indeed," said Haviland Tuf.

"In-*deed*," said Jaime Kreen, warming now. "You frightened Moses out of his head, but you didn't deceive me for a minute with your picture show. The hail gave you away. Bacteria, disease, pests—all that is within the sphere of ecological warfare. Maybe even that darkness creature, although I think you made that up. But *hail* is a meteorological phenomenon, it has nothing to do with biology or ecology. You slipped up, Tuf. But it was a nice try, and it should keep Moses humble."

"Humble," agreed Haviland Tuf. "I should have hesitated and planned more thoroughly before attempting to mislead a man of your perception and insight, no doubt. At every turn you frustrate my small schemes."

Jaime Kreen chuckled. "I have a hundred standards due me," he said, "for bringing Moses up and back."

"Sir," said Haviland Tuf, "I would never forget such a debt. It is not necessary to chivvy me." He opened the box that Kreen had brought up from Charity, and paid out one hundred standards. "You will find a convenient personal airlock in section nine, just beyond the doors marked Climate Control."

Jaime Kreen frowned. "Airlock? What do you mean?"

"Sir," said Haviland Tuf, "I would think it obvious. I mean airlock, a device by which you may depart the *Ark* without my valuable atmosphere departing with you. Since you have no spacecraft, it would be foolish to use the large airlock here. A smaller personal lock, as I said, may be found in section nine."

Kreen looked aghast. "Are you going to jettison me?"

"Not the best choice of words," said Haviland Tuf. "They sound so harsh. Yet I can hardly keep you aboard the *Ark*, and were you to depart in one of my shuttles, there would be no one to bring it back to me. I can hardly afford to sacrifice a valuable piece of equipment simply for your personal convenience."

Kreen frowned. "The solution to your dilemma is simple. We will both board the *Griffin*. You will take me down to Port Faith. Then you will return to your ship."

Haviland Tuf stroked Dax. "Interesting," he said. "Yet I do believe it might work. You must understand, of course, that such a trip would constitute a distinct annoyance for me. Surely I should receive something for my troubles."

Jaime Kreen stared into the still white face of Haviland Tuf for a minute, then sighed, and handed back the hundred standards.

7
MANNA FROM HEAVEN

The S'uthlamese armada was sweeping the outskirts of the solar system, moving through the velvet darkness of space with all the stately silent grace of a tiger on the prowl, on an interception course with the *Ark*.

Haviland Tuf sat before his master console, scanning the banks of telescreens and computer monitors with small, careful turns of his head. The fleet angling to meet him appeared more formidable with every passing moment. His instruments reported some fourteen capital ships and swarms of smaller fighters. Nine bulbous silver-white globes, bristling with unfamiliar weaponry, comprised the wings of the formation. Four long black dreadnaughts served as outriders on the flanks of the wedge, their dark hulls crackling with energy. The flagship in the center was a colossal saucer-shaped fort with a diameter Tuf's sensors measured as six kilometers from rim to rim. It was the largest spaceship that Haviland Tuf had seen since the day, more than ten years past, when he had first sighted the derelict *Ark*. Fighters swarmed around the saucer like angry stinging insects.

Tuf's long, pale, hairless face was still and unreadable, but in his lap, Dax made a small sound of disquiet as Tuf pressed his fingertips together.

A flashing light indicated an incoming communication.

Haviland Tuf blinked, reached out with calm deliberation, and took the call.

329

He had expected a face to materialize on the telescreen in front of him. He was disappointed. The caller's features were hidden by a faceplate of black plasteel, inset into the helmet of a mirror-finish warsuit. A stylized representation of the globe of S'uthlam ornamented the flanged crest upon his forehead. Behind the faceplate, wide-spectra sensors glowed red like two burning eyes. It reminded Haviland Tuf of an unpleasant man he had once known.

"It was unnecessary to dress formally on my account," Tuf said flatly. "Moreover, while the size of the honor guard you have sent to meet me tickles my vanity somewhat, a much smaller and less prepossessing squadron would have been more than sufficient. The present formation is so large and formidable as to give one pause. A man of a less trusting nature than myself might be tempted to misconstrue its purpose and suspect some intent to intimidate."

"This is Wald Ober, commander of the Planetary Defense Flotilla of S'uthlam, Wing Seven," the grim visage on the telescreen announced in a deep, distorted voice.

"Wing Seven," Tuf repeated. "Indeed. This suggests the possibility of at least six other similarly fearsome squadrons. It would seem that S'uthlamese planetary defenses have been augmented somewhat since my last call."

Wald Ober wasn't interested. "Surrender at once, or be destroyed," he said bluntly.

Tuf blinked. "I fear some grievous misunderstanding."

"A state of war exists between the Cybernetic Republic of S'uthlam and the so-called alliance of Vandeen, Jazbo, Henry's World, Skrymir, Roggandor, and the Azure Triune. You have entered a restricted zone. Surrender or be destroyed."

"You misapprehend me, sir," Tuf said. "I am a neutral in this unfortunate confrontation, of which I was unaware until this moment. I am part of no faction, cabal, or alliance, and represent only myself, an ecological engineer with the most benign of motives. Please do not take alarm at the size of my ship. Surely in the small space of five standard years the esteemed spinnerets and cybertechs of the Port of S'uthlam cannot entirely have forgotten my previous visits to your most interesting world. I am Haviland—"

"We know who you are, Tuf," said Wald Ober. "We recognized the *Ark* as soon as you shifted out of drive. The alliance doesn't have any dreadnaughts thirty kilometers long, thank life. I have specific orders from the High Council to watch for your appearance."

"Indeed," said Haviland Tuf.

"Why do you think the wing is closing on you?" Ober said.

"As a gesture of affectionate welcome, I had hoped," Tuf said. "As a friendly escort bearing kudos, salutations, and gift baskets of plump, fresh, spiced mushrooms. I see that this assumption was unfounded."

"This is your third and final warning, Tuf. We'll be in range in less than four standard minutes. Surrender now or be destroyed."

"Sir," said Tuf, "before you make a grievous error, please consult with your superiors. I am certain there has been a lamentable communications error."

"You have been tried in absentia and found guilty of being a criminal, a heretic, and an enemy of the people of S'uthlam."

"I have been grossly misperceived," Tuf protested.

"You escaped the flotilla ten years ago, Tuf. Don't think to do it again. S'uthlamese technology does not stand still. Our new weaponry will shred those obsolete defensive shields of yours, I promise you that. Our top historians have researched that ponderous EEC derelict of yours. I supervised the simulations myself. Your welcome is all prepared."

"I have no wish to seem ungracious, but it was unnecessary to go to such lengths," said Tuf. He glanced at the banks of telescreens that lined the consoles along both sides of the long, narrow room, and studied the phalanx of S'uthlamese warships rapidly closing upon the *Ark*. "If this unprovoked hostility has its root in my outstanding debt to the Port of S'uthlam, rest assured that I am prepared to render payment in full immediately."

"Two minutes," said Wald Ober.

"Furthermore, if S'uthlam is in need of additional ecological engineering, I find myself suddenly inclined to offer you my services at a much reduced price."

"We've had enough of your solutions. One minute."

"It would seem I am left with but a single viable option," said Haviland Tuf.

"Then you surrender?" the commander said suspiciously.

"I think not," said Haviland Tuf. He reached out, brushed long fingers across a series of holographic keys, and raised the *Ark*'s ancient defensive screens.

Wald Ober's face was hidden, but he managed to get a sneer into his voice. "Fourth generation imperial screens, triple redundancy, frequency overlapping, all shield phasing coordinated by your ship's computers. Duralloy plate armor on your hull. I told you we'd done our research."

"Your hunger for knowledge is to be commended," Tuf said.

"The next sarcasm you mouth may be your last, trader, so you had better take care to make it a good one. The point is, we know exactly what you've got, and we know to the fourteenth decimal how much damage an EEC seedship's defenses can absorb. We're prepared to give you more than you can handle." He turned his head. *"Prepare to commence fire,"* he snapped at unseen subordinates. When the dark helmeted face swiveled back toward Tuf, Ober added, "We want the *Ark* and you can't stop us from taking it. Thirty seconds."

"I beg to differ," said Tuf calmly.

"They'll fire at my command," Ober said. "If you insist, I'll count down the final seconds of your life. Twenty. Nineteen. Eighteen . . ."

"Seldom have I heard such vigorous counting," said Tuf. "Please do not lose track on account of my distressing news."

". . . Fourteen. Thirteen. Twelve."

Tuf folded his hands atop his stomach.

"Eleven. Ten. Nine." Ober looked uneasily to one side, then back at the screen.

"Nine," announced Tuf. "A fine number. It is customarily followed by eight, thence seven."

"Six," Ober said. He hesitated. "Five."

Tuf waited silently.

"Four. Three." He stopped. *"What distressing news?"* he roared at the screen.

"Sir," said Tuf, "if you must shout, you will only oblige me to adjust the volume on my communications equipment." He raised a finger. "The distressing news is that the mere act of broaching the *Ark*'s defensive shields, as I have no doubt you can easily accomplish, will trigger a small thermonuclear device that I have previously secreted within the ship's cell library, thereby instantaneously destroying the very cloning materials that make the *Ark* unique, invaluable, and widely coveted."

There was a long silence. The glowing crimson sensors beneath the darkness of Wald Ober's faceplate seemed to smoulder as they stared into the screen at Tuf's blank features. "You're bluffing," the commander said at last.

"Indeed," said Tuf. "You have found me out. How foolish to think I might hoodwink a man of your perspicacity with such a blatant and juvenile deception. And now I fear you will fire upon me, rend my poor obsolete defenses, and demonstrate my lie for good and all. Permit me only a moment to make my farewells to my cats." He folded his hands neatly atop his great paunch, and waited for the commander to reply. The S'uthlamese flotilla, his instruments avowed, was now well within range.

"I'll do just that, you damned abortion!" Wald Ober swore.

"I wait with sullen resignation," said Tuf, unmoving.

"You have twenty seconds," Ober said.

"I fear my news has confused you. The count previously stood at three. Nonetheless, I shall take shameless advantage of your error and savor each instant remaining to me."

They stared at each other, face to face and screen to screen, for the longest time. Snug in Tuf's lap, Dax began to purr. Haviland Tuf reached down to stroke the cat's long black fur. Dax purred even more loudly and began kneading Tuf's knee with his claws.

"Oh, abort it to hell and gone," said Wald Ober. He pointed at the screen. "You may have us checked for the moment, but I warn you, Tuf, don't even *think* about trying to get away. Dead or fled, your cell library would be equally lost to us. And given a choice I'd sooner you be dead."

"I comprehend your position," said Haviland Tuf, "though I, of course, would sooner be fled. Yet I do have a debt to pay to the Port of S'uthlam, and therefore could not honorably depart as you fear, so please accept my assurances that you will have every opportunity to ponder my visage, and I your fearsome mask, while we sit locked in this irksome impasse."

Wald Ober never got the chance to reply. His battle mask vanished abruptly from the screen, and was replaced by a woman's homely features—a broad crooked mouth, a nose that had been broken more than once, hard leathery skin with the deep blue-black cast that comes from lots of exposure to hard radiation and decades of anti-carcinoma pills, pale bright eyes in a nest of squint-folds, all of it surrounded by a lavish halo of coarse gray hair. "So much for getting tough," she said. "You win, Tuf. Ober, you're now an honor guard. Form up and escort him into the web, damn it."

"How thoughtful," said Haviland Tuf. "I am pleased to inform you that I am now prepared to tender the final payment due the Port of S'uthlam for the refitting of the *Ark*."

"I hope you brought some catfood, too," Tolly Mune said drily. "That so-called 'five-year supply' you left me ran out almost two years ago." She sighed. "I don't suppose you'd care to retire and sell us the *Ark*."

"Indeed not," said Tuf.

"I didn't think so. All right, Tuf, break out the beer, I'm coming to talk to you as soon as you reach the web."

"While I mean no disrespect, I must confess that I am not at the moment in the best frame of mind for entertaining such a distinguished guest as yourself. Commander Ober has recently informed me that I have been adjudged a criminal and heretic, a curious conception, as I am neither a citizen of S'uthlam nor an adherent to its dominant religion, but no less disquieting for all that. I am agog with fear and worry."

"Oh, that," she said. "Just an empty formality."

"Indeed," Tuf said.

"Puling hell, Tuf, if we're going to steal your ship we need a good legal excuse, don't we? We're a goddamned government. We're *allowed* to steal the things we want as long as we put a shiny legal gloss over it."

"Seldom in my voyaging have I encountered any political functionary as frank as yourself, it must be admitted. The experience is refreshing. Still, as invigorated as I am, what assurance do I have that you will not continue your efforts to seize the *Ark* once aboard?"

"Who, me?" said Tolly Mune. "Now how could I do a thing like that? Don't worry, I'll come alone." She smiled. "Well, almost alone. You'd have no objections if I brought a cat, would you?"

"Certainly not," said Tuf. "I am pleased to learn that the felines I left in your custody have thrived in my absence. I shall eagerly anticipate your arrival, Portmaster Mune."

"That's First Councillor Mune to you, Tuf," she said, gruffly, before she wiped the screen.

No one had ever alleged that Haviland Tuf was overly rash; he took up a position twelve kilometers beyond the end of one of the great docking spurs of the orbital community known as the Port of S'uthlam, and he kept his shields up continuously as he waited. Tolly Mune rode out to meet him in the small starship Tuf had given her five years before, on the occasion of his previous visit to S'uthlam.

Tuf opened the shields to let her through, and cracked the great dome on the landing deck so she might set down. *Ark*'s instrumentation indicated her ship was full of lifeforms, only one of which was human; the rest displayed feline parameters. Tuf set out to meet her, driving a three-wheeled cart with balloon tires, and wearing a deep-green mock-velvet suit belted about his ample middle. On his head was a battered green duck-billed cap decorated with the golden theta of the Ecological Engineering Corps. Dax rode with him, an indolent sprawl of black fur draped across Tuf's broad knees.

When the airlock opened, Tuf drove with all deliberate speed through the scrapyard of battered spacecraft that he had somehow accumulated over the years, directly to where Tolly Mune, former Portmaster of S'uthlam, was thumping down the ramp of her ship.

A cat walked at her side.

Dax was on his feet in an instant, his dark fur bristling as if his huge, fluffy tail had just been plugged into an electric socket. His customary lethargy was suddenly gone; he leapt from Tuf's lap to the hood of the cart, drew back his ears, and hissed.

"Why, Dax," Tolly Mune said, "is that any way to greet a goddamned relative?" She grinned, and knelt to pet the huge animal by her side.

"I had expected either Ingratitude or Doubt," said Haviland Tuf.

"Oh, they're fine," she said. "And so are all their goddamned offspring. Several generations' worth. I should have figured it when you gave me a pair. A fertile male and female. I've got . . ." she frowned, and counted quickly on her fingers, once through and then again. ". . . let's see, sixteen, I think. Yes. And two pregnant." She jerked a thumb at the starship behind her. "My ship has turned into one big cat-house. Most of them don't care any more for gravity than I do. Born and raised in zero gee. I'll never understand how they can be so graceful one moment and so hilariously clumsy the next."

"The feline heritage is rife with contradiction," said Tuf.

"This is Blackjack." She picked him up in her arms and rose to her feet. "Damn, he's *heavy*. You never realize that in zero gee."

Dax stared at the other feline, and hissed.

Blackjack, cradled against the chest of Tolly Mune's old, smelly skinthins, looked down at the huge black tom with disinterested haughtiness.

Haviland Tuf stood two-and-a-half meters tall, with bulk to match, and Dax was just as large, compared to other cats, as Tuf was, compared to other men.

Blackjack was larger.

His hair was long and silky, smoky gray on top, with a lighter silver undercoat. His eyes were silver-gray as well, vast deep pools, serene and somehow eerie. He was the most incredibly beautiful animal ever to dwell in the expanding universe, and he knew it. His manner was that of a princeling born to the royal purple.

Tolly Mune slid awkwardly into the seat beside Tuf. "He's telepathic, too," she said cheerfully, "just like yours."

"Indeed," said Haviland Tuf. Dax was stiff and angry in his lap. He hissed again.

"Jack here was the way I saved the other cats," Tolly Mune said. Her homely face took on a look of reproach. "You said you were leaving me five years of catfood."

"For two cats, madam," said Tuf. "Obviously, sixteen animals consume more than Doubt and Ingratitude alone." Dax edged closer, bared his teeth, bristled.

"I had problems when the stuff ran out. Given our food shortfalls, I had to justify wasting calories on vermin."

"Perhaps you might have considered steps to limit your feline reproduction," Tuf said. "Such a strategy would undoubtedly have yielded results. Thus your home could have served as an educational and sobering illustration of S'uthlamese problems, in microcosm as it were, and the solutions thereof."

"Sterilization?" Tolly Mune said. "That's anti-life, Tuf. Out. I had a better idea. I described Dax to certain friends—biotechs, cybertechs, you know—and they made me a familiar of my own, worked up from cells taken from Ingratitude."

"How appropriate," said Tuf.

She smiled. "Blackjack's almost two years old. He's been so useful I've been given a food allowance for the others. He's helped my political career no end, too."

"I have no doubt," said Tuf. "I note that he does not appear discomfitted by gravity."

"Not Blackjack. These days they need me downstairs a hell of a lot more than I'd like, and Jack goes with me. Everywhere."

Dax hissed again, and made a low rumbly threatening sound. He darted toward Blackjack, then drew back suddenly and spit disdain at the larger cat.

"You better call him off, Tuf," Tolly Mune said.

"Felines sometimes demonstrate a biological compulsion to battle in order to establish deference rankings," Tuf said. "This is particularly true of tomcats. Dax, undoubtedly aided and abetted by his enhanced psionic capabilities, long ago established his supremacy over Chaos and my other cats. Undoubtedly he now feels his position threatened. It is not a matter for serious concern, First Councillor Mune."

"It is for Dax," she said, as the black tom crept closer. Blackjack, in her lap, looked up at his rival with vast boredom.

"I fail to grasp your point," said Tuf.

"Blackjack has those enhanced psionic capabilities, too," said Tolly Mune. "Plus a few other, ah, advantages. Implanted duralloy claws, sharp as goddamned razors, concealed in special paw sheaths. A subcutaneous net of nonallogenic plasteel mesh that makes him awfully tough to hurt. Reflexes that have been genetically accelerated to make him twice as quick and dextrous as a normal cat. A very high pain threshold. I don't want to be puling crass about it or anything, but if he gets jumped, Blackjack will slice Dax into little bloody hairballs."

Haviland Tuf blinked, and shoved the steering stick over toward Tolly Mune. "Perhaps it might be best if you drove." He reached out, picked up his angry black tomcat by the ruff of the neck, and deposited him, screeching and spitting, in his lap, where he held him very still indeed. "Proceed in that direction," he said, pointing with a long pale finger.

"It appears," said Haviland Tuf, steepling his fingers as he regarded her from the depths of a huge wingback armchair, "that circumstances have altered somewhat since I last came to call upon S'uthlam."

Tolly Mune studied him carefully. His paunch was larger than it had been, and his long face was just as miserly of expression, but without Dax in his lap, Haviland Tuf looked almost naked. Tuf had shut the big black tom up on a lower deck to keep him away from Blackjack. Since the ancient seedship was thirty kilometers long and several of Tuf's other cats roamed the deck in question, Dax would scarcely lack for space or for companionship, but must be baffled and distraught nonetheless. The psionic tomcat had been Tuf's constant and inseparable companion for years, had even ridden in Tuf's ample pockets as a kitten. Tolly Mune felt a little sad about it.

But not *too* sad. Dax had been Tuf's hole card, and she'd trumped him. She smiled and ran her fingers through Blackjack's thick smoke-and-silver fur, eliciting another thunderous purr. "The more things change the more they stay the same," she said in answer to Tuf's comment.

"This is one of those venerable sayings that collapses upon close logical examination," Tuf said, "being obviously self-contradictory on the face of it. If indeed things have changed upon S'uthlam, they obviously cannot have remained the same as well. To myself, coming as I have from a great distance, it is the changes that seem most notable. To wit, this war, and your own elevation to First Councillor, a considerable and unanticipated promotion."

"And a puling awful job," Tolly Mune said with a grimace. "I'd go back to being Portmaster in a blink, if I could."

"Your job satisfaction is not the subject under discussion," Tuf said. He continued. "It must also be noted that my welcome to S'uthlam was distinctly less cordial than on the occasion of my previous visit, much to my chagrin, and notwithstanding the fact that I have twice placed myself squarely between S'uthlam and mass famine, plague, cannibalism, pestilence, social collapse, and other unpleasant and inconvenient events. Moreover,

even the most venomously rude races frequently observe a certain rudimentary etiquette toward those who
are bringing them eleven million standards, which you
recall is the amount of principal remaining on my debt
to the Port of S'uthlam. Ergo, I had every reason to
expect a welcome of a somewhat different nature."

"You were wrong," she said.

"Indeed," Tuf said. "Now that I have learned that
you occupy the highest political office on S'uthlam,
rather than a menial position upon a penal farm, I am
frankly more mystified than ever as to why the Planetary Defense Flotilla felt it necessary to greet me with
fierce bombastic threats, dour warnings, and exclama-
tions of hostility."

Tolly Mune scratched at Blackjack's ear. "My orders,
Tuf."

Tuf folded his hands atop his stomach. "I await your
explanation."

"The more things change—" she began.

"Having already been pummeled with this cliche, I
believe I grasp the small irony involved in it by now, so
there is no need for you to repeat it over and over
endlessly, First Councillor Mune. If you would proceed
to the essence of the matter I would be deeply appreciative."

She sighed. "You know our situation."

"The broad outlines, certainly," Tuf admitted. "S'uthlam suffers from an excess of humanity, and a paucity of
food. Twice I have performed formidable feats of ecological engineering in order to enable the S'uthlamese
to forestall the grim specter of famine. The details of
your food crisis vary from year to year but I trust that
the essence of the situation remains as I have outlined
it."

"The latest projection is the worst yet."

"Indeed," said Tuf. "My recollection is that S'uthlam
stood some one hundred nine standard years from mass
planetary famine and societal collapse, assuming that
my recommendations and suggestions were dutifully
implemented."

"They tried, damn it. They did try. The meatbeasts,

the pods, the ororos, neptune's shawl—everything's in place. But the changeover was only partial. Too many powerful people were unwilling to give up the luxury foodstuffs they preferred, so there are still large tracts of agri-land devoted to raising herds of food animals, entire farms planted with neograss and omni-grain and nanowheat—that sort of thing. Meanwhile, the population curve has continued to rise, faster than ever, and the puling Church of Life Evolving preaches the sanctity of life and the golden role of reproduction in humanity's evolution to transcendence and godhood."

"What is the current estimate?" Tuf asked bluntly.

"Twelve years," said Tolly Mune.

Tuf raised a finger. "To dramatize your plight, perhaps you ought to assign Commander Wald Ober to count down the remaining time over the vidnets. Such a demonstration would have a certain grim urgency that might inspire the S'uthlamese to mend their ways."

Tolly Mune winced. "Spare me your levity, Tuf. I'm First Councillor now, goddamn it, and I'm staring right into the pimpled ugly face of catastrophe. The war and the food shortages are only part of it. You can't imagine the problems I'm facing."

"Perhaps not the fine detail," said Tuf, "yet the broad outlines are readily discerned. I make no claim to omniscience, but any reasonably intelligent person could observe certain facts and from them draw certain inferences. Perhaps these deductions thus arrived at are wrong. Without Dax, I cannot ascertain the truth of that. Yet somehow I think not."

"What puling facts? What inferences?"

"Firstly," said Tuf, "S'uthlam is at war with Vandeen and its allies. Ergo, I can infer that the technocratic faction that once dominated S'uthlamese politics has yielded up power to their rivals, the expansionists."

"Not quite," said Tolly Mune, "but you've got the right puling idea. The expansionists have gained seats in every election since you left, but we've kept them out of power with a series of coalition governments. The allies made it clear years ago that an expansionist government meant war. Hell of it is, we still don't have an expansionist government, but we got the damned war anyway." She shook her head. "In the last five years we've had nine First Councillors. I'm the latest, probably not the last."

"The grimness of your current projections suggests that this war has not yet actually touched your populace," Tuf said.

"Thank life, no," said Tolly Mune. "We were ready when the allied war fleet came calling. New ships, new weapons systems, everything built in secret. When the allies saw what was waiting for them, they backed off without firing a blast. But they'll be back, damn it. It's only a matter of time. We've got reports that they're preparing for a major strike."

"I might also infer," said Tuf, "from your general attitude and sense of desperation, that conditions upon S'uthlam itself are already deteriorating rapidly."

"How the hell do you know that?"

"It is obvious," said Tuf. "Your projection may indeed indicate mass famine and collapse to be some twelve standard years in the future, but this is hardly to say that S'uthlamese life will remain pleasant and tranquil until that moment, whereupon a bell will ring loudly and your world will fall to pieces. Such an idea is ludicrous. As you are now so close to the brink, it is only to be expected that many of the woes symptomatic of a disintegrating culture will already be upon you."

"Things are—puling hell, where do I begin?"

"The beginning is frequently a good place," said Tuf.

"They're my people, Tuf. That's my world turning down there. It's a good world. But lately—if I didn't know better, I'd think insanity was contagious. Crime is up some two hundred percent since your last call. Murder is up five hundred percent, suicide more than two thousand percent. Service breakdowns become more common daily—blackouts, systems failure, random strikes, vandalism. We've had reports of cannibalism deep in the undercities—not isolated instances, but entire puling cannibal *gangs*. Secret societies of all kinds, in fact. One group seized a food factory, held it for two weeks, and fought a pitched battle with world police.

Another bunch of crazies have taken to kidnapping pregnant women and . . ." Tolly Mune scowled; Blackjack hissed. "This is hard to talk about. A woman with child has always been something special to the S'uthlamese, but these . . . I can hardly even call them people, Tuf. These *creatures* have cultivated a taste for—"

Haviland Tuf raised a hand, palm outward. "Say no more," he said. "I have grasped the inference. Continue."

"Lots of solitary maniacs, too," she said. "Someone dumped highly toxic waste into a food factory holding tank eighteen months ago. More than twelve hundred fatalities. Mass culture—S'uthlam has always been tolerant, but lately there's a hell of a lot more to be tolerant *of*, if you catch my float. There's this growing obsession with disfigurement, death, violence. We've had massive resistance to our attempts to re-engineer the ecosystem according to your recommendations. Meatbeasts have been poisoned, blown up, and fields of pods set afire. Organized thrill gangs hunt the goddamned wind-riders with harpoons and high-altitude gliders. It makes no goddamned sense. The religious consensus—all kinds of weird cults have been emerging. And the war! Life only knows how many will die, but it's as popular as—hell, I don't know, it's *more* popular than sex, I think."

"Indeed," said Tuf. "I am unsurprised. I take it the imminence of disaster remains a closely guarded secret of the S'uthlamese High Council, as in years past."

"Unfortunately, no," Tolly Mune said. "One of the minority councillors decided she couldn't hold her bladder, so she called in the puling peeps and pissed the news out all over the vidnets. I think she wanted to win a few million more votes. The hell of it is, it worked. It also kicked off another goddamned scandal and forced yet another First Councillor out of office. By then there was no place to look for a new human sacrifice but upstairs. Guess who got grabbed? Our favorite vidshow heroine, controversial bureaucrat, and Ma Spider, that's who."

"You are obviously referring to yourself," said Tuf.

"By then nobody hated me much any more. I had a certain reputation for efficiency, the remnants of a popular romantic image, and I was minimally acceptable to most of the big council factions. That was three months ago. So far it's been one hell of a term of office." Her smile was grim. "The Vandeeni listen to our newsfeeds, too. Simultaneous with my goddamned promotion, they decided S'uthlam was, I quote, a threat to the peace and stability of the sector, end quote, and got together their goddamned allies to try and decide what to do about us. The bunch of them finally gave us an ultimatum: enforce immediate rationing and compulsory birth control, or the alliance would occupy S'uthlam and enforce it for us."

"A viable solution, but not a tactful one," Tuf commented. "Thus your present war. Yet all this fails to explain your attitude toward me. I have been able to offer your world succor twice before. Surely you did not feel I would be remiss in my professional duties on this third occasion."

"I figured you'd do what you could." She pointed a finger. "But on your own terms, Tuf. Hell, you've helped, yes, but always on your own terms, and all of your solutions have proved unfortunately impermanent."

"I warned you repeatedly that my efforts were mere stopgaps," Tuf replied.

"There are no calories in warnings, Tuf. I'm sorry, but we have no choice. This time we can't allow you to clap a stick-on bandage over our hemorrhage and shunt off. The next time you came back to check on how we were faring, you wouldn't find a puling world to come back to. We need the *Ark*, Tuf, and we need it permanently. We're prepared to use it. Ten years ago you said that biotech and ecology were not our areas of expertise, and you were right. Then. But times change. We're one of the most advanced worlds in human civilization, and for a decade we've been devoting most of our educational efforts to training ecologists and biotechs. My predecessors brought in top theorists from Avalon, Newholme, and a dozen other worlds. Brilliant people, geniuses. We even managed to lure some leading genetic wizards off Prometheus." She stroked her cat and smiled. "They helped with Blackjack here. A lot."

"Indeed," said Tuf.

"We're ready to use the *Ark*. No matter how capable you are, Tuf, you're only one puling man. We want to keep your seedship permanently in S'uthlamese orbit, with a full-time staff of two hundred top scientists and genetic technicians, so we can deal with the food crisis *daily*. This ship and its cell library and all the lost data in its computers represents our last, best hope, you can see that. Believe me, Tuf, I didn't give Ober orders to seize your ship without considering every other god-damned option I could think of. I knew you'd never sell, damn it. What choice did I have? We don't want to cheat you. You would have been paid a fair price. I'd have insisted."

"This assumes I remained alive after the seizure," pointed out Tuf. "A doubtful proposition at best."

"You're alive now, and I'll still buy the damned ship. You could stay aboard, work with our people. I'm prepared to offer you lifetime employment—name your own salary, anything you want. You want to keep that eleven million standards? It's yours. You want us to rename the puling planet in your honor? Say the word, and we'll do it."

"Planet S'uthlam or Planet Tuf by any name would be as overcrowded," Haviland Tuf replied. "Should I agree to this proposed purchase, undoubtedly it is your intent to use the *Ark* only in these efforts to increase your caloric productivity and thus feed your starving people."

"Of course," said Tolly Mune.

Tuf's face was blank and serene. "I am pleased to learn that it has never occurred to you or to any of your associates on the High Council that the *Ark* might be employed in its original capacity as an instrument of biological warfare. Sadly, I have lost this refreshing innocence, and find myself prey to uncharitable and cynical visions of the *Ark* being used to wreak ecological havoc upon Vandeen, Skrymir, Jazbo, and the other allied homeworlds, even to the point of genocide, thereby preparing those planets for mass colonization, which I seem to recall is the population policy advocated by your troublesome expansionist faction."

"That's quite a goddamned implication," snapped Tolly Mune. "Life is sacred to the S'uthlamese, Tuf."

"Indeed. Yet, poisonous cynic that I am, I cannot help but suspect that ultimately the S'uthlamese may decide that some lives are more sacred than others."

"You know me, Tuf," she said, her tone crisp and chilly. "I would never allow anything like that."

"And if any such plan was enacted over your objections, I have no doubt that your letter of resignation would be quite sternly worded," Tuf said flatly. "I find this insufficiently reassuring, and have a hunch, yes, a hunch, that the allies might share my sentiments on this point."

Tolly Mune chucked Blackjack under the chin. The cat began to growl deep in his throat. Both of them stared at Tuf. "Tuf," she said, "millions of lives are at stake, maybe *billions*. There are things I could show you that would curl your hair. If you had any puling hair, that is."

"As I do not, this is obvious hyperbole," said Tuf.

"If you'd consent to shuttle in to Spiderhome, we could take the elevators downstairs to the surface of S'uthlam—"

"I think not. It would seem to me to be conspicuously unwise to leave the *Ark* empty and undefended, as it were, in the light of the climate of belligerence and distrust that presently festers upon S'uthlam. Moreover, though you may think me arbitrary and overfastidious, with the passage of years I find I have lost whatever small degree of tolerance I once had for swarming crowds, cacophony, rude stares, unwelcome hands, watery beer, and minuscule portions of tasteless food. As I recall, these are the principal delights to be found upon the surface of S'uthlam."

"I don't want to threaten you, Tuf—"

"Nonetheless, you are about to."

"You will not be allowed to depart the system, I'm afraid. Don't try to hoodwink me like you did Ober.

That business with the bomb is a goddamned fabrication and we both know it."

"You have found me out," Tuf said expressionlessly.

Blackjack hissed at him.

Tolly Mune looked down at the big cat, startled. "It's not?" she said in horror. "Oh, damn it to hell."

Tuf engaged the silver-gray feline in a silent staring contest. Neither of them blinked.

"It doesn't matter," Tolly Mune said. "You're here to stay, Tuf. Resign yourself to it. Our new ships *can* destroy you, and they will if you try to pull out."

"Indeed," said Tuf. "And for my part, I will destroy the cell library if you attempt to board the *Ark*. It appears we have arrived at a stalemate. Fortunately, it need not be of long duration. S'uthlam has never been far from my thoughts as I voyaged hither and yon across starry space, and during the periods when I was not professionally engaged, I have engaged myself in methodical research in order to devise a true, just, and permanent solution to your difficulties."

Blackjack sat down and began to purr. "You have?" Tolly Mune said dubiously.

"Twice the S'uthlamese have looked to me for a miraculous salvation from the consequences of their own reproductive folly and the rigidity of their religious beliefs," Tuf said. "Twice I have been called upon to multiply the loaves and fishes. Yet it occurred to me recently, while engrossed in a study of that book which is the chief repository of the ancient myths from which that anecdote is drawn, that I was being asked to perform the wrong miracle. Mere multiplication is an inadequate reply to an ongoing geometric progression, and loaves and fishes, however plentiful and tasty, must in the final analysis be found insufficient to your needs."

"What the hell are you talking about?" Tolly Mune demanded.

"This time," Tuf said, "I offer you a lasting answer."

"What?"

"Manna," said Tuf.

"Manna," said Tolly Mune.

"A truly miraculous foodstuff," said Haviland Tuf.

"The details need not concern you. I will reveal all at the proper time."

The First Councillor and her cat looked at him suspiciously. "The proper time? And when will it be the proper puling time?"

"When my conditions have been met," Tuf said.

"What conditions?"

"First," said Tuf, "as the prospect of living out the rest of my life in orbit about S'uthlam is one I find unappealing, it must be agreed that I am free to go after my labors here are completed."

"I can't agree to that," Tolly Mune said, "and if I did, the High Council would vote me out of office in a puling second."

"Secondly," Tuf continued, "this war must be terminated. I fear I will be unable to concentrate properly on my work when there is every likelihood of a major space battle breaking out around me at any moment. I am easily distracted by exploding starships, webs of laser fire, and the screams of dying men. Moreover, I see little point in exerting great efforts to make the S'uthlamese ecology balanced and functional once more when the allied fleets threaten to deposit plasma bombs all over my handiwork, and thereby undo my small achievements."

"I'd end this war if I could," Tolly Mune said. "It isn't that damned easy, Tuf. I'm afraid what you ask is impossible."

"If not a permanent peace, then perhaps at least a small cessation in hostilities," Tuf said. "You might send an embassy to the allied forces and petition for a short armistice."

"That might be possible," Tolly Mune said tentatively. "But why?" Blackjack gave an uneasy meow. "You're plotting something, damn it."

"Your salvation," Tuf admitted. "Pardon me if I deign to interfere with your diligent joint efforts to encourage mutation through radioactivity."

"We're defending ourselves! We didn't want this war!"

"Excellent. In that case, a short delay will not unduly inconvenience you."

"The allies will never buy it. Neither will the High Council."

"Regrettable," said Tuf. "Perhaps we ought to give S'uthlam some time to consider. In twelve years, the surviving S'uthlamese might have more flexible attitudes."

Tolly Mune reached out and scratched Blackjack behind the ears. Blackjack stared at Tuf, and after a minute uttered a small, strange, peeping sound. When the First Councillor stood abruptly, the huge silver-gray cat leapt nimbly from her lap. "You win, Tuf," she said. "Lead me to a comm set and I'll set the damned thing up. You're prepared to wait forever and I'm not. People are dying every moment we delay." Her voice was hard, but inside, for the first time in months, Tolly Mune felt hope mingled with her unease. Maybe he *could* end the war and solve the crisis. Maybe there was really a chance. But she let no hint of that creep into her tone. She pointed. "But don't think you're going to get away with anything funny."

"Alas," said Haviland Tuf, "humor has never been my forte."

"I've got Blackjack, remember. Dax is too freaked out and intimidated to do you any good, and Jack will let me know the instant you start thinking about treachery."

"Always my best intentions are met with suspicion."

"Blackjack and me, we're your puling shadows, Tuf. I'm not leaving this ship until things are settled, and I'm going to look hard at everything you do."

"Indeed," said Tuf.

"Just keep a few damned things in mind," Tolly Mune said. "I'm First Councillor now. Not Josen Rael. Not Cregor Blaxon. Me. Back when I was Portmaster, they liked to call me the Steel Widow. You might pass an hour or two pondering how and why I got that puling name."

"I shall indeed," said Tuf, rising. "Is there anything else you would like me to recall, madam?"

"Just one thing," she said. "A scene from that *Tuf and Mune* vidshow."

"I have striven diligently to put that unfortunate

fiction out of my memory," Tuf said. "Which particular
of it would you force me to recall?"

"The scene where the cat rips the security man to
shreds," Tolly Mune said, with a small, sweet smile.
Blackjack rubbed up against her knee, turned his smoky
gaze up at Tuf, and rumbled deep in his massive body.

It took almost ten days to arrange the armistice, and
another three for the allied ambassadors to make their
way to S'uthlam. Tolly Mune spent the time haunting
the *Ark*, two steps and a hasty thought behind Tuf,
questioning everything he did, peering over his shoulder when he labored at his console, riding by his side
when he made the rounds of his cloning vats, helping
him feed his cats (and keep a hostile Dax away from
Blackjack). He attemped nothing overtly suspicious.

Dozens of calls came through for her daily. She set
up an office in the communications room, so she would
never be far from Tuf, and handled the problems that
could not wait.

Hundreds of calls came through daily for Haviland
Tuf. He instructed his computer to refuse all of them.

When the day came, the envoys emerged from their
long, luxurious diplomatic shuttle and stood gazing about
at the *Ark*'s cavernous landing deck and fleet of derelict
starships. They were a colorful and diverse lot. The
woman from Jazbo had waistlong blue-black hair that
shone with scented iridescent oils; her cheeks were
covered with the intricate scars of rank. Skrymir sent a
stocky man with a square red face and hair the color of
mountain ice. His eyes were a crystalline blue that
matched the color of his scaled metal shirt. The envoy
from the Azure Triune moved within a haze of holographic projections, a dim, fractured, shifting shape
that spoke in an echoey whisper. Roggandor's cyborg
ambassador was as broad as he was tall, made in equal
parts of stainless duralloy, dark plasteel, and mottled
red-black flesh. A slight, delicate-looking woman in transparent pastel silks represented Henry's World; she had
a boyish adolescent body and ageless scarlet eyes. The
allied party was led by a large, plump, opulently dressed

man from Vandeen. His skin, wrinkled by age, was the
color of copper; his long hair fell past his shoulders in
thin, delicate braids.

Haviland Tuf, driving a segmented vehicle that glided
across the deck like a snake on wheels, stopped directly
in front of the ambassadors. The Vandeeni stepped
forward beaming, reached up and pinched his own full
cheek very vigorously, and bowed. "I would offer my
hand, but I recall your opinion of that custom," he said.
"Do you remember me, fly?"

Haviland Tuf blinked. "I have some vague recollection of encountering you upon the train to the surface of
S'uthlam some ten years ago," he said.

"Ratch Norren," the man said. "I'm not what you call
a regular diplomat, but the Board of Coordinators figured they'd send somebody who'd met you, and knew
the Suthies, too."

"That's an offensive term, Norren," Tolly Mune said
bluntly.

"You're an offensive bunch," Ratch Norren replied.

"And dangerous," whispered the envoy from the Azure
Triune, from the center of his holographic fog.

"You're the puling aggressors," Tolly Mune started.

"Defensive aggression," boomed the cyborg from
Roggandor.

"We recall the last war," said the Jazbot. "This time
we decline to wait until your damnable evolutionists
burst forth and try to colonize our worlds again."

"We have no such plans," Tolly Mune said.

"*You* don't, spinneret," Ratch Norren said. "But look
me in the optics here and tell me your expansionists
don't have wet dreams about breeding all over Vandeen."

"And Skrymir."

"Roggandor wants no part of your cast-off human
detritus."

"You will never take the Azure Triune."

"Who the hell would *want* the puling Azure Triune?"
snapped Tolly Mune. Blackjack purred approval.

"This glimpse into the inner working of high interstellar diplomacy has been most elucidating," Haviland
Tuf announced. "Nonetheless, I sense that more press-

ing business awaits. If the envoys would be so cooperative as to board my vehicle, we might proceed onward
to our conference."

Still muttering among themselves, the allied ambassadors did as Tuf bid them. Fully loaded, the vehicle
set out across the landing deck, weaving a path between the myriad abandoned starships. An airlock, round
and dark as the mouth of a tunnel or the jaws of some
insatiable beast, opened at their approach and swallowed them. They entered and stopped; the lock closed
behind them, engulfing the party in darkness. Tuf ignored the whispered complaints. Around them came a
screeching metallic noise; the floor began to descend.
When they had dropped at least two decks, another
door opened in front of them. Tuf turned on his
headlamps and they drove out into a pitch-black corridor.

They drove through a maze of dark, chilly corridors,
past countless closed doors, following a dim indigo trace
that flitted before them, a ghost embedded in the dusty
floor. The only light was the beam from the train's
headlamps, and the faint glow of the instrument panel
in front of Tuf. At first the envoys bantered among
themselves, but the black depths of the *Ark* were op-
pressive and claustrophobic, and one by one the members of the delegation fell silent. Blackjack began to
knead Tolly Mune's knees rhythmically with his claws.

After a long time rolling through dust, darkness, and
silence, the train approached a towering pair of double
doors that hissed open ominously at their approach, and
closed with a loud clang of finality behind them. Within,
the air was moist and hot. Haviland Tuf stopped, and
turned off the headlamps. Total darkness enveloped
them.

"Where *are* we?" Tolly Mune demanded. Her voice
rang off some distant ceiling, although the echo seemed
strangely muffled. Though black as a pit, the room was
obviously cavernous. Blackjack hissed uneasily, sniffed
the air, and made a tiny, uncertain mewing sound.

She heard footsteps, and a small light flicked on two
meters away. Tuf was bent over an instrument console,
watching a monitor panel. He pressed one key in a

luminescent keyboard, and turned. A padded wingback
floater chair came whispering out of the warm darkness.
Tuf climbed into it like a king ascending a throne, and
touched a control on the arm. The chair lit up with a
faint violet phosphorescence. "Kindly follow," Tuf announced. The floater swiveled in the air and began to
drift off.

"Puling hell," Tolly Mune muttered. She climbed
out of her seat hastily, cradling Blackjack, and scrambled after Tuf's retreating throne. The allied ambassadors followed en masse, whining and complaining every
step of the way. She could hear the cyborg's massive
footsteps behind her. Tuf's floater was the only spot of
light in an enveloping sea of darkness. As she rushed
after him, she stepped on something.

The sudden feline yowl made her recoil, bumping
into the cyborg's armored chest. Confused, Tolly Mune
knelt and reached out a tentative hand, holding Blackjack awkwardly in the crook of her arm; her fingers
brushed soft fur. The cat rubbed up against her furiously, purring loudly. She could barely make out its
shape—a small shorthair, hardly more than a kitten. It
rolled over so she could scratch its belly. The Jazbot
almost stumbled over her as she knelt there. And then
suddenly Blackjack had leaped free and was sniffing
around the new cat. It returned the favor briefly, then
whirled, and in a blink it had vanished into the darkness. Blackjack hesitated, then howled and bounded
after it. "Goddamn it," Tolly Mune shouted. "Goddamn
it, Jack, get your puling ass back here!" Her voice
echoed, but her cat did not return. The rest of the
party was growing more distant. Tolly Mune swore
loudly and hurried to catch up.

An island of light appeared ahead of her. When she
arrived, the others were settling into seats arrayed along
one side of a long metal table. Haviland Tuf, in the
thronelike floater, was on the other side of the table,
his face expressionless, his white hands folded atop his
stomach.

Dax was stalking back and forth across his shoulders,
purring.

Tolly Mune stopped, glared, swore. "Damn you to hell," she said to Tuf. She turned around. *"Blackjack!"* she screamed at the top of her lungs. The echoes seemed swaddled in thick cloth, curiously indistinct. *"Jack!"* Nothing.

"I hope we have not come all this way simply to listen to the First Councillor of S'uthlam practice animal calls," the envoy from Skrymir said.

"Indeed not," said Tuf. "First Councillor Mune, if you will kindly take your seat, we may proceed at once."

She scowled, and sank down into the only vacant chair. "Where the hell is Blackjack?"

"I can hardly venture an opinion on that subject," said Tuf flatly. "He is, after all, your cat."

"He ran off after one of yours," Tolly Mune snapped.

"Indeed," said Tuf. "Interesting. At the moment it so happens that I have a young female who has recently gone into heat. Perhaps that explains his actions. I have no doubt that he remains quite safe, First Councillor."

"I want him back for this puling conference!" she said.

"Alas," said Tuf, "the *Ark* is a large ship and they might be sporting in any of a thousand places, and in any case, to interfere with their sexual congress would be unconscionably anti-life by S'uthlamese standards. I would hesitate to do such violence to your cultural mores. Moreover, you have stressed to me repeatedly that time is of the essence, as many human lives are at stake. Ergo, I think it best we proceed with all due haste."

Tuf moved his hand slightly, touched a control. A section of the long table sank out of sight. A moment later, a plant rose from within, directly in front of Tolly Mune. "Behold," said Tuf. "Manna."

It grew from a low bedding pan, a tangle of pale green vines almost a meter high, a living gordian knot, tendrils weaving back and forth on themselves and edging over the lip of the container. All along the vines were thick clusters of leaves, as tiny as fingernails, their waxy green surface shot through with a delicate tracery

of black veins. Tolly Mune reached out and touched the
nearest leaf, and discovered that its underside was covered with a dusting of fine powder that came off on the
tips of her fingers. Between the clusters of leaves, the
branching vines were swollen with clusters of fat white
carbuncles, larger and more pustulent-looking in toward the central tangle of growth. She saw one palp,
half concealed under a canopy of leaves, that had grown
as big as a man's hand.

"Ugly looking weed," opined Ratch Norren.

"I fail to understand why it was necessary to declare
an armistice and travel all this way to behold some
festering hothouse monstrosity," said the man from
Skrymir.

"The Azure Triune grows impatient," whispered their
envoy.

"There's some puling motive in this madness," Tolly
Mune said to Tuf. "Get on with it. Manna, you said. So
what?"

"It will feed the S'uthlamese," said Tuf. Dax was
purring.

"For how many days?" asked the woman from Henry's World, in a sweet voice that dripped sarcasm.

"First Councillor, if you would be so kind as to break
off one of the larger paps, you will find the flesh delec-
tably succulent and quite nutritious," Tuf said.

Tolly Mune leaned forward, grimacing. She wrapped
her fingers around the largest fruit. It felt soft and
pulpy to her touch. She tugged, and it came off the
vine easily. She broke it apart with her fingers. The
flesh tore like fresh bread. Deep within its secret center was a sac of dark, viscous liquid that flowed with
seductive slowness. A marvelous smell filled her nos-
trils, and she began to salivate. She hesitated for an
instant, but it smelled too good. Quickly, she took a
bite. She chewed, swallowed, took another bite, and
another. In four bites it was all gone, and she was
licking the stickiness off her fingers.

"Milkbread," she said, "and honey. Rich, but tasty."

"Nor will the taste pall," Tuf announced. "The secre-
tions in the heart of each palp are mildly narcotic. They

are individual with each specimen of the manna plant, its distinct and subtle flavors a factor of the chemical composition of the soil in which the plant has taken root and the genetic heritage of the plant itself. The range of tastes is quite broad, and can be further expanded through cross-breeding."

"Hold on," Ratch Norren said loudly. He tugged at his cheek and frowned. "So this damned bread-and-honey fruit tastes just swell, sure, sure. So what? So the Suthies have something tasty to snack on after they make some more little Suthies. A nice treat to relieve the tedium of conquering Vandeen and breeding all over it. Pardon, folks, but Ratch don't feel like applauding right now."

Tolly Mune frowned. "He's rude," she said, "but he's right. You've given us miracle plants before, Tuf. Omnigrain, remember? Neptune's shawl. Jersee-pods. How's manna going to be any different?"

"In several respects," said Haviland Tuf. "Firstly, my previous efforts have been directed at making your ecology more efficient, to increasing the caloric output from the finite areas of S'uthlam given over to agriculture, to getting more from less, as it were. Unfortunately, I did not adequately account for the perversity of the human species. As you yourself have reported, the S'uthlamese food chain is still far from maximum efficiency. Though you have meatbeasts to provide protein, you persist in raising and feeding wasteful herd animals, simply because some of your wealthier carnivores prefer the taste of such flesh to a slice of a meatbeast. Similarly, you continue to grow omni-grain and nanowheat for reasons of flavor and culinary variety, where jersee-pods would yield you more calories per square meter. Succinctly put, the S'uthlamese still persist in choosing hedonism over rationality. So be it. Manna's addictive properties and flavors are unique. Once the S'uthlamese have eaten of it, you will enounter no resistance on the grounds of taste."

"Maybe," Tolly Mune said doubtfully, "but still—"

"Secondmost," Tuf continued, "manna grows swiftly. Extreme difficulties demand extreme solutions. Manna represents such a solution. It is an artificial hybrid, a genetic quilt sewn together with DNA strands from a dozen worlds, its natural ancestors including the bread-bush of Hafeer, insinuating nightweed from Noctos, Gulliverian sugarsacs, and a specially enhanced variety of kudzu, from Old Earth itself. You will find it hardy and fast-spreading, in need of scant care, and capable of transforming an ecosystem with astonishing swiftness."

"How astonishing?" Tolly Mune demanded bluntly.

Tuf's finger moved slightly, pressed down on a glowing key set within the arm of his floater. Dax purred.

The lights came on.

Tolly Mune blinked in the sudden glare.

They sat in the center of a huge circular room a good half-kilometer across, its domed ceiling curving a hundred meters above their heads. Behind Tuf a dozen towering plasteel ecospheres emerged from the walls, each open at the top and full of soil. There were a dozen different types of soil, representing a dozen different habitats—powdery white sand, rich black loam, thick red clay, blue crystalline gravel, gray-green swamp mud, tundra frozen hard as ice. From each ecosphere a manna plant grew.

And grew.

And grew.

And grew.

The central plants were five meters high; their quest-ing vines had long since crawled over the tops of their habitats. The tendrils snaked halfway across the floor, to within a half-meter of Tuf, winding together, branch-ing and rebranching. Manna vines covered the walls three-quarters of the way around the room. Manna vines clung precariously to the smooth white plasteel ceiling, half-eclipsing the light panels, so the illumina-tion drifted down to the floor in shadow patterns of incredible intricacy. The filtered light seemed greenish. Everywhere the manna fruit bloomed, white pods the size of a man's head drooping from the vines overhead and pushing through the tangle of growth. As they watched, one pod fell to the floor with a soft liquid *plop*. Now she understood why the echoes had sounded so curiously muted.

"These particular specimens," Haviland Tuf announced in an expressionless voice, "were begun from spores some fourteen days ago, shortly before my first meeting with the estimable First Councillor. A single spore in each habitat was all that was required; I have neither watered nor fertilized in the interim. Had I done so, the plants would not be nearly so small and stunted as these poor examples you see before you."

Tolly Mune got to her feet. She had lived for years in zero gee, so it was a strain to stand under full gravity, but there was a tightness in her chest and a bad taste deep in the back of her mouth, and she felt she had to grasp for every psychological advantage, even one as small and obvious as standing when the rest of them were seated. Tuf had taken her breath away with his manna-from-the-hat trick, she was outnumbered, and Blackjack was life-knows-where while Dax sat by Tuf's ear, purring complacently and regarding her with large golden eyes that saw right through every puling artifice. "Very impressive," she said.

"I am pleased you think so," Tuf said, stroking Dax.

"Exactly what are you proposing?"

"My proposition is thus: we will immediately commence seeding S'uthlam with manna. Delivery may be effected through use of the *Ark*'s shuttlecraft. I have already taken the liberty of stocking the shuttle bays with explosive air-pods, each containing manna spores. Released into the atmosphere in a certain predetermined pattern that I have devised, the spores will ride upon the winds and distribute themselves about S'uthlam. Growth will commence immediately. No further effort will be required from the S'uthlamese but that they pick and eat." His long still face turned away from Tolly Mune, toward the envoys from the allied worlds. "Sirs," he said, "I suspect that you are presently wondering as to your own part in this."

Ratch Norren pinched his cheek and spoke for them all. "Right," he said. He looked around uneasily. "Comes back to what I said before. So this weed feeds all the Suthies. So what, that's nothing to us."

"I would think the consequences obvious," said Tuf.

"S'uthlam is a threat to the allied worlds only because the S'uthlamese population is perpetually threatening to outstrip the S'uthlamese food supply. This renders S'uthlam, an otherwise peaceful and civilized world, inherently unstable. While the technocrats remained in power and kept the equation in an approximate balance, S'uthlam has been the most cooperative of neighbors, but this balancing, however virtuoso, must eventually fail, and with that failure inevitably the expansionists rise to power and the S'uthlamese become dangerous aggressors."

"I'm no puling expansionist!" Tolly Mune said hotly.

"Such was not my implication," said Tuf. "Neither are you First Councillor for life, despite your obvious qualifications. War is already at hand, albeit a defensive war. When you fall, should an expansionist replace you, the struggle will become a war of aggression. In circumstances such as those the S'uthlamese have created for themselves, war is as utterly certain as famine, and no single leader, however well-intentioned and competent, can possibly avoid it."

"Exactly," the boyish young woman from Henry's World said in a precise voice. Her eyes had a shrewdness in them that belied her adolescent body. "And if war is inevitable, we had just as well fight it out now, and solve the problem once and for all."

"The Azure Triune must agree," came a whispered second.

"True," said Tuf, "granting your premise that war must come inevitably."

"You just told us the bloody expansionists would start a war inevitably, Tuffer," Ratch Norren complained.

Tuf soothed the black tomcat with a large white hand. "Incorrect, sir. My statements as to the inevitability of war and famine were predicated upon the collapse of the unstable balance between the S'uthlamese population and S'uthlamese food supplies. Should this tenuous equation be brought back into alignment, S'uthlam is no threat whatsoever to the other worlds in this sector. Under these conditions, war is both unnecessary and morally unconscionable, I would think."

"And you avow this pestilential pop-weed of yours will be the thing to do the job?" the woman from Jazbo said contemptuously.

"Indeed," said Tuf.

The ambassador from Skrymir shook his head. "No. A valid effort, Tuf, and I respect your dedication, but I think not. I speak for all the allies when I say that we cannot put our faith in yet another breakthrough. S'uthlam has had its greenings and flowerings and blossomings and ecological revolutions before. In the end, nothing changes. We must conclude this matter once and for all."

"Far be it from me to interfere with your suicidal folly," said Tuf. He scratched Dax behind an ear.

"Suicidal folly?" Ratch Norren said. "What's that mean?"

Tolly Mune had been listening to it all. She turned to face the allies. "That means you lose, Norren," she said.

The envoys laughed—a polite chuckle from the Henry, a guffaw from the Jazbot, a booming thunder from the cyborg. "The arrogance of the S'uthlamese never ceases to amaze me," said the man from Skrymir. "Don't be misled by this temporary stalemate, First Councillor. We are six worlds united as one. Even with your new flotilla, we outnumber you and outgun you. We defeated you once before, you might recall. We'll do it again."

"You will not," said Haviland Tuf.

As one, the envoys looked at him.

"In recent days I have taken the liberty of doing some small research. Certain facts have become obvious. Firstly, the last local war was fought centuries ago. S'uthlam suffered an undeniable defeat, yet the allies are still recovering from their victory. S'uthlam, however, with its greater population base and more voracious technology, has long since left all effects of that struggle behind. Meanwhile, S'uthlamese science has advanced as swiftly as manna, if I may be permitted a colorful metaphor, while the allied worlds owe what small advances they claim to knowledge and techniques imported from S'uthlam. Undeniably, the combined allied fleets are significantly more numerous than the S'uthlamese Planetary Defense Flotilla, yet most of the allied armada is functionally obsolete in the face of the sophisticated weaponry and technology embodied in the new S'uthlamese ships. Moreover, it is grossly inaccurate to say the allies outnumber S'uthlam in any real sense. You comprise six worlds against one, correct, but the combined population of Vandeen, Henry's World, Jazbo, Roggandor, Skrymir, and the Azure Triune totals scarcely four billion—less than one-tenth the population of S'uthlam alone."

"One-tenth?" the Jazbot croaked. "That's wrong. Isn't it? It must be."

"The Azure Triune has been given to understand that their numbers are barely six times our own."

"Two-thirds of them are women and children," the envoy from Skrymir was quick to point out.

"Our women fight," Tolly Mune snapped.

"When they can find the time between litters," commented Ratch Norren. "Tuf, they can't have *ten times* our population. There are a lot of 'em, agreed, sure, but our best estimates—"

"Sir," said Tuf, "your best estimates are in error. Contain your chagrin. The secret is well kept, and when one is counting such multitudes, one can easily misplace a billion here or a billion there. Nonetheless, the facts are as I have stated them. At the moment, a delicate martial balance holds sway—the allied ships are more numerous, the S'uthlamese flotilla more advanced and better armed. This is obviously impermanent, as the S'uthlamese technology enables them to produce war fleets far more swiftly than any of the allies. I would venture to guess that just such an effort is currently underway." Tuf looked at Tolly Mune.

"No," she said.

But Dax was looking at her, too. "Yes," Tuf announced to the envoys. He raised a single finger. "Therefore, I propose you take advantage of this present rough equality to capitalize on the opportunity I am offering you to solve the problem posed by S'uthlam without resort to nuclear bombardment and similar unpleasantries. Extend this armistice for one standard year, and allow me to seed S'uthlam with manna. At the end of that time, if you feel that S'uthlam still constitutes a threat to your homeworlds, feel free to resume hostilities."

"Neg, trader," the cyborg from Roggandor said heavily. "You are impossibly naive. Give them a year, you say, and let you do your tricks. How many new fleets will they build in a year?"

"We'll agree to a moratorium on new arms-building if your worlds will do the same," Tolly Mune said.

"So you say. I suppose we should trust you?" Ratch Norren sneered. "To hell with that. You Suthies proved how trustworthy you were when you rearmed secretly, in express violation of the treaty. Talk about bad faith!"

"Oh, sure, you'd have preferred it if we were helpless when you came to occupy us. Puling hell, what a damned hyprocrite!" Tolly Mune responded in disgust.

"It's too late for pacts," declared the Jazbot.

"You said it yourself, Tuf," the Skrymirian said. "The longer we delay, the worse our situation becomes. Therefore, we have no choice but an immediate all-out strike at S'uthlam itself. The odds will never get any better."

Dax hissed at him.

Haviland Tuf blinked, and folded his hands neatly on his stomach. "Perhaps you would reconsider if I appealed to your love of peace, your horror of war and destruction, and your common humanity?"

Ratch Norren made a contemptuous noise. One by one, the other members of the delegation looked away, demurring.

"In that case," said Tuf, "you leave me no choice." He stood up.

The Vandeeni frowned. "Hey, where are you going?"

Tuf gave a ponderous shrug. "Most immediately to a sanitary facility," he replied, "and afterwards to my control chamber. Please accept my assurances that no personal animosity of any sort is intended toward any of you. Nonetheless it appears, unfortunately, that I must now go forth and destroy your respective worlds. Perhaps you would like to draw straws, to determine where I might best start."

The woman from Jazbo choked and sputtered.

Deep inside his haze of blurred holograms, the envoy from the Azure Triune cleared his throat, a sound as small and dry as an insect scuttling across a sheet of paper.

"You would not dare," boomed the cyborg from Roggandor.

The Skrymirian folded his arms in a chilly silence.

"Ah," said Ratch Norren. "You. Ah. That is. You won't. Yes, but surely. Ah."

Tolly Mune laughed at them all. "Oh, he means it," she said, though she was no less astonished than the rest of them. "And he can do it, too. Or the *Ark* can, rather. Commander Ober will be sure he gets an armed escort, too."

"There is no need for haste," the woman from Henry's World said in precise, measured tones. "Perhaps we might reconsider."

"Excellent," said Haviland Tuf. He sat back down. "We will proceed with all deliberate haste," he said. "A one year armistice will go into effect, as I have outlined, and I shall seed S'uthlam with manna immediately."

"Not so fast," Tolly Mune interjected. She felt giddy and triumphant. Somehow the war had just ended—Tuf had done it, S'uthlam was safe for at least a year. But relief did not make her entirely lightheaded. "All this sounds fine, but we'll have to run some studies on this manna plant of yours before you start dropping spores all over S'uthlam. Our own biotechs and ecologists will want to examine the damn thing, and the High Council will want to run a few projections. A month ought to do. And of course, Tuf, what I said before still goes— you're not just dumping your manna on us and leaving. You'll stay this time, for the duration of the armistice, and maybe longer, until we have a good idea of how this latest miracle of yours is going to work."

"Alas," said Tuf, "I fear I have pressing engagements

elsewhere in the galaxy. A sojourn of a standard year or more is inconvenient and unacceptable, as is a delay of a month before commencing my seeding program."

"Wait just one puling second!" Tolly Mune began. "You can't just—"

"I can indeed," said Tuf. He looked from her to the envoys, significantly, and then back again. "First Councillor Mune, allow me to point out the obvious. A rough balance of military force now exists between S'uthlam and its adversaries. The *Ark* is a formidable instrument of destruction, capable of wasting worlds. Just as it is possible for me to throw in with your forces and destroy any of the allied planets, so the converse is also within the realm of possibility."

Tolly Mune suddenly felt as though she'd been assaulted. Her mouth gaped open. "Are you . . . Tuf, are you threatening us? I don't believe it. Are you threatening to use the *Ark* against S'uthlam?"

"I am merely bringing certain possibilities to your attention," said Haviland Tuf, his voice as flat as ever.

Dax must have sensed her rage; he hissed. Tolly Mune stood helplessly, bewildered. Her hands balled into fists.

"I will charge no fee for my labors as mediator and ecological engineer," Tuf announced. "Yet I will require certain safeguards and concessions from both parties to our agreement. The allied worlds will furnish me with a bodyguard, so to speak—a small fleet of warships, sufficient in number and weaponry to stave off any attacks upon the *Ark* from the Planetary Defense Flotilla of S'uthlam and to escort me safely out of the system when my task here is done. The S'uthlamese, for their part, will agree to allow this allied fleet into their home system in order that my fears may be laid to rest. Should either side initiate hostilities during the period of the armistice, they will do so in full knowledge that this will surely provoke me to a most awful fit of wrath. I am not overly excitable, but when my anger is indeed aroused, I ofttimes frighten even myself. Once a standard year has passed, I shall be long departed and you may feel yourself free to resume your mutual slaugh-

ter, if you so choose. Yet it is my hope, and my predic-
tion, that this time the steps I am initiating will prove
so efficacious that none of you will feel compelled to
resume hostilities." He stroked Dax's thick black fur,
and the tomcat regarded each of them in turn with his
huge golden eyes, seeing, weighing.

Tolly Mune felt cold all over. "You are imposing
peace on us," she said.

"Albeit temporarily," said Tuf.

"And you are imposing this solution, whether we
want it or not," she said.

Tuf looked at her, but did not reply.

*"Just who the goddamned puling hell do you think
you are?"* she screamed at him, unleashing the fury
that had been swelling inside her.

"I am Haviland Tuf," he said evenly, "and I have run out
of patience with S'uthlam and the S'uthlamese, madam."

After the conference was over, Tuf drove the ambassadors back to their diplomatic shuttle, but Tolly Mune
refused to go along.

For long hours, she roamed the *Ark* alone, cold,
tired, yet relentless. She called out as she went. "Blackjack!" she shouted, from the top of the moving stair-
cases. "Here, Blacky, here," she sang as she strode
through the corridors. "Jack!" she cried when she heard
a noise around a corner, but it was only a door opening
or closing, the whirr of some machine repairing itself,
or perhaps the scurrying of some stranger cat, some
familiar of Tuf's. "Blaaaaackjaaaaaaaaack!" she shouted
at intersections where a dozen corridors crossed, and
her voice boomed and rattled off his distant walls and
echoed back at her.

But she did not find her cat.

Finally her wanderings took her up several decks,
and she emerged in the dimly lit central shaft that
cored the vast seedship—a towering, echoing immensity thirty kilometers long, its ceiling lost in shadows,
its wall lined by cloning vats large and small. She chose
a direction at random and walked, and walked, and
walked, calling out Blackjack's name.

From somewhere ahead she heard a small, uncertain meow.

"Blackjack?" she called. "Where are you?"

Again she heard it. Up there, ahead. She took two hurried steps forward, and began to run.

Haviland Tuf stepped out from beneath the shadow of a plasteel tank twenty meters high; Blackjack was cradled in his arms, purring.

Tolly Mune stopped dead.

"I have located your cat," said Tuf.

"I can see that," she said coldly.

Tuf handed the huge gray tomcat to her gently, his hands brushing against her arms as he made the transfer. "You will find him none the worse for his wanderings," Tuf declared. "I took the liberty of giving him a full medi-probe, to ascertain that he had suffered no misadventures, and determined that he is in the best of health. Imagine my surprise when I also chanced to discover that all the various bionic augmentations of which you informed me have somehow mysteriously and inexplicably vanished. I am at a loss to explain it."

Tolly Mune hugged the cat to her chest. "So I lied," she said. "He's telepathic, like Dax. Maybe not as powerful. But that's all. I couldn't risk him fighting with Dax. Maybe he'd have won, maybe not. I didn't want him cowed." She grimaced. "So you got him laid instead. Where's he been?"

"Having left the manna chamber by a secondary entrance in pursuit of the object of his affections, he subsequently discovered that the doors were programmed to deny him readmittance. Therefore, he has spent the intervening hours roaming through the *Ark* and making the acquaintance of various other feline members of my ship's company."

"How many cats do you have?" she asked.

"Fewer than you," Tuf said, "yet this is not entirely unanticipated. You are S'uthlamese, after all."

Blackjack was warm and reassuring in her arms, and all at once Tolly Mune was struck by the fact that Dax was no longer in evidence. She had the edge again. She scratched Jack behind an ear; he turned his limpid silver-gray eyes upon Tuf. "You don't fool me," she said.

"I thought it unlikely that I could," Tuf admitted.

"The manna," she said. "It's some kind of a trap, isn't it? You fed us a batch of lies, admit it."

"Everything I have told you of the manna is the truth."

Blackjack uttered a peep. "The truth," said Tolly Mune, "oh, the puling truth. That means there are things you haven't told us about the manna."

"The universe abounds in knowledge. Ultimately, there are more facts to be known than humans to know them, an astonishing realization considering that populous S'uthlam is included in humanity's tally. I could scarcely hope to tell you everything concerning any subject, however limited."

She gave a snort. "What are you going to do to us, Tuf?"

"I am going to resolve your food crisis," he said, his voice as flat and cold as still water, and as full of secret depths.

"Blackjack's purring," she said, "so you're telling the truth. But how, Tuf, *how*?"

"The manna is my instrument."

"Bladder bloat," she said. "I don't give a puling wart how tasty and addictive the manna fruit is, or how fast the damned things grow, no plant is going to solve our population crisis. You've tried all that. We've been around those coordinates with omni-grain and the pods and the wind-riders and the mushroom farms. You're holding something back. Come on, piss it out."

Haviland Tuf regarded her in silence for well over a minute. His eyes locked with hers, and it seemed briefly as though he were looking deep inside her, as if Tuf too were a mind reader.

Perhaps it was something else he read; finally, he answered. "Once the plant has been sown, it will never be entirely eradicated, regardless of how diligently you may attempt to do so. It will spread with inexorable rapidity, within certain parameters of climate. Manna will not thrive everywhere; frost kills it, and cold is inimical to its growth, but it shall indeed spread to cover the tropical and subtropical regions of S'uthlam, and that will be enough."

"Enough for *what*?"

"The manna fruit is extremely nutritious. During the first few years, it will do much to relieve the pressures of your present caloric shortfalls and thereby improve conditions upon S'uthlam. Eventually, having exhausted the soil in its vigorous spread, the plants will expire and decay, and you will of necessity be forced to employ crop rotation for a few years before those particular plots are capable of sustaining manna once again. Yet, meanwhile, the manna shall have completed its real work, First Councillor Mune. The dust that collects upon the underside of each leaf is in actuality a symbiotic microorganism, vital to manna pollination, yet with certain other properties. Borne upon the wind, carried by vermin and human alike, it shall touch every cranny and nook upon the surface of your globe."

"The dust," she said. She had gotten it on her fingertips when she touched the manna plant . . .

Blackjack's growl was so low she felt it more than heard it.

Haviland Tuf folded his hands. "One might consider manna dust as an organic prophylactic of sorts," he said. "Your biotechs will discover that it interferes powerfully, and permanently, with libido in the human male and fertility in the human female. The mechanisms need not concern you."

Tolly Mune stared at him, opened her mouth, closed it, blinked to hold back tears. Tears of despair, tears of rage? She could not say. Not tears of joy. She would not let them be tears of joy. "Deferred genocide," she said, forcing out the words. Her voice was hoarse and raw.

"Scarcely," Tuf said. "Some of your S'uthlamese will display a natural immunity to the effects of the dust. My projections indicate that somewhere between point oh-seven and point one-one percent of your base population will be unaffected. They will reproduce, of course, and thus the immunity will be passed on and grow more prevalent in successive generations. Yet a population implosion of considerable magnitude will commence upon S'uthlam this year, as the birth curve ceases its upward thrust and starts a precipitous descent."

"You have no right," said Tolly Mune slowly.

"The nature of the S'uthlamese problem is such so as to admit but one lasting and effectual solution," Tuf said, "as I have told you from the very beginning."

"Maybe," she said. "But so what? What about freedom, Tuf? What about individual choice? My people may be selfish and short-sighted fools, but they're still *people*, just like you. They have the right to decide if they're going to have children, and how many children. Who the hell gave you the authority to make that decision for them? Who the hell told you to go ahead and sterilize our world?" She was growing angrier with every word. "You're no better than we are. You're only human, Tuf. A puling peculiar human, I'll give you that, but only human—no more and no less. What gives you the goddamned *right* to play god with our world and our lives?"

"The *Ark*," Haviland Tuf said, simply.

Blackjack squirmed in her arms, suddenly restless, uneasy. Tolly Mune let him jump to the ground, never taking her eyes off Tuf's blank white face. Suddenly she wanted to strike him, hurt him, wound that mask of indifference and complacency, mark him. "I warned you, Tuf," she said. "Power corrupts and absolute power corrupts absolutely, remember?"

"My memory is unimpaired."

"Too bad I can't say the same thing about your goddamned morality," said Tolly Mune. Her tone was acid. Blackjack growled counterpoint at her feet. "Why the hell did I ever help you keep this goddamned ship? What a damned *fool* I was! You've been alone in a power fantasy too damn long, Tuf. Do you think somebody just appointed you god, is that it?"

"Bureaucrats are appointed," said Tuf. "Gods, insofar as they exist at all, are chosen by other procedures. I make no claims to godhood in the mythological sense. Yet I submit that I do indeed wield the power of a god, a truth that I believe you recognized long ago, when you first turned to me for loaves and fishes." When she began to reply, he raised a hand, palm outward. "No, kindly do not interrupt. I will endeavor to be brief. You and I are not so different, Tolly Mune—"

"We're *nothing* alike, damn you!" she shrieked at him.

"We are not so different," Tuf repeated calmly, firmly. "You once confessed that you were not a religious woman; nor am I one to worship myths. I began as a trader, yet having come upon this ship called *Ark*, I began to find myself dogged at every step by gods, prophets, and demons. Noah and the flood, Moses and his plagues, loaves and fishes, manna, pillars of fire, wives of salt—I must needs have become acquainted with all. You challenge me to declare myself a god. I make no such claim. And yet, it must be said, my first act upon this ship, so many years ago, was to raise the dead." He pointed ponderously at a work station a few meters away. "There is the very spot at which I performed that first miracle, Tolly Mune. Moreover, I do indeed wield godlike powers and traffic in the life and death of worlds. Enjoying as I do these godlike abilities, can I rightfully decline the accompanying responsibility, the equally awesome burden of moral authority? I think not."

She wanted to reply, but the words would not come. *He's insane,* Tolly Mune thought to herself.

"Furthermore," Tuf said, "the nature of the crisis on S'uthlam was such that it admitted to a solution only by godlike intervention. Let us suppose briefly that I consented to sell you the *Ark*, as you desired. Do you truly suppose that any staff of ecologists and biotechs, however expert and dedicated, could have devised a lasting answer? It is my belief that you are too intelligent to entertain such a fallacy. I have no doubt that, with all the resources of this seedship at their beck and call, these men and women—geniuses with intellects and training far superior to my own—could and would undoubtedly have devised numerous ingenious stopgaps to allow the S'uthlamese to continue breeding for another century, perhaps two, perhaps even three or four. Yet ultimately, their answers too would have proven insufficient, as did my own small attempts five years ago, and five years before that, and all the breakthroughs your technocrats engineered in centuries past. Tolly Mune, there is no rational, equitable, scientific, technological, or human answer to the dilemma of a population increasing in an insane geometric progression. It admits to answering only with miracles—loaves and fishes, manna from heaven, and the like. Twice I failed as ecological engineer. Now I propose to succeed as the god that S'uthlam requires. Should I approach the problem as human a third time, I would assuredly fail a third time, and then your difficulties would be resolved by gods crueler than myself, by the four mammal-riders of ancient legend who are known as pestilence, famine, war, and death. Therefore, I must set aside my humanity, and act as god." He paused, looking at her, blinking.

"You set aside your damned humanity a hell of a long time ago," she raged at him. "But you're no god, Tuf. A demon, maybe. A puling megalomaniac, certainly. Maybe a monster—yes, a puling abortion. A *monster*, but no god."

"A monster," said Tuf. "Indeed." He blinked. "I had hoped that one of your undoubted intellectual prowess and competence might display better understanding." He blinked again. Twice, three times. His long white face was as still as ever, but there was something strange in Tuf's voice that she had never heard before, something that frightened her, that bewildered her and disturbed her, something that sounded almost like emotion. "You slander me grievously, Tolly," he protested.

Blackjack made a thin, plaintive meow.

"Your cat displays a keener grasp of the cold equations of the reality confronting us," Tuf said. "Perhaps I ought to explain again from the beginning."

"Monster," she said.

Tuf blinked. "My efforts are eternally unappreciated and met only with undeserved calumny."

"Monster," she repeated.

His right hand briefly curled into a fist, uncurled slowly and deliberately. "It appears some cerebral tic has dramatically reduced your vocabulary, First Councillor."

"No," she said, "but that's the only word that applies to you, damn it."

"Indeed," said Tuf. "In that case, being a monster, it behooves me to act monstrously. Consider that, if you will, as you grapple with your decision, First Councillor."

Blackjack jerked his head up suddenly and stared at Tuf as if something unseen were flitting about that long white face. He began to hiss; his thick silver-gray fur rose up slowly as he backed off. Tolly Mune bent and picked him up. The cat trembled in her arms, and hissed again. "What?" she said in a distracted voice. "What decision? You've made all the damned decisions. What the hell are you talking about?"

"Permit me to point out that, as of this moment, not a single manna spore has been released into the atmosphere of S'uthlam," Haviland Tuf said.

She snorted. "So? You've made your damned deal. I have no way of stopping you."

"Indeed. Regrettable. Perhaps one will occur to you, however. Meanwhile, I suggest that we repair to my quarters. Dax is waiting for his evening meal. I have prepared an excellent cream-of-mushroom bisque for our own repast, and there is chilled great-beer from Moghoun, a beverage sufficiently heady to please either gods or monsters. And, of course, my communications equipment is at your disposal, should you find you have something to say to your government."

Tolly Mune opened her mouth for a cutting reply, then closed it again in astonishment. "Do you mean what I think you mean?" she said.

"This is difficult to say," Tuf replied. "You are the one holding a psionic cat, madam."

It was an endless silent walk and an eternal awkward meal.

They took their dinner in a corner of the long, narrow communications room, surrounded by consoles, telescreens, and cats. Tuf sat with Dax across his lap, and spooned up his dinner with methodical care. On the other side of the table, Tolly Mune ate without tasting the food. She had no appetite. She felt old and dizzy. And afraid.

Blackjack reflected her confusion; his serenity gone, he huddled in her lap, infrequently lifting his head above the table to growl a warning at Dax.

And finally the moment arrived, as she had known it would: a buzz and a flashing blue light signaled an incoming communication. Tolly Mune started at the sound, scraping her chair backwards against the deck and swinging around sharply in her seat. Blackjack leapt off in alarm. She started to rise, and froze in indecision.

"I have programmed in strict instructions that I am on no account to be disturbed while dining," Tuf announced. "Ergo, that call is for you, by the process of elimination."

The blue pinpoint flashed off, and on, and off, and on.

"You're no puling god," Tolly Mune said. "Neither am I, damn it. I don't want this goddamned burden, Tuf."

The light was flashing.

"Perhaps it is Commander Wald Ober," Tuf suggested. "I suggest you take his call before he begins counting backwards."

"No one has the right, Tuf," she said. "Not you, not me."

He gave a ponderous shrug.

The light flashed.

Blackjack yowled.

Tolly Mune took two steps toward the console, stopped, turned back toward Tuf. "Creation is part of godhood," she said with suddenly certainty. "You can destroy, Tuf, but you cannot create. That's what makes you a monster instead of a god."

"The creation of life in the cloning tanks is an everyday and commonplace element of my profession," Tuf said.

The light flashed on, went out, flashed on again.

"No," she said, "you replicate life there, but you don't *create* it. It has to have existed already, somewhere in time and space, and you have to have a cell sample, a fossil record—something—or you're helpless. Puling hell, yes! Oh, you have the power of creation all right. The same goddamned power that I have, and that every man and woman down in the undercity has. Procreation, Tuf. There's your awesome power, there's the only miracle there is—the one thing humans have that makes us like gods, and the very thing *you* propose to take away from ninety-nine-point-nine percent of the people on S'uthlam. The hell! You're no creator, you're no god."

"Indeed," said Haviland Tuf, expressionlessly.

"So you don't have the right to make godlike decisions," she said. "And neither do I, damn it." She moved to the console in three long, confident strides, touched a control. A telescreen ran with colors, resolving into a mirror-finish battle helmet emblazoned wth a stylized globe insignia. Twin sensors burned crimson behind a dark plasteel faceplate. "Commander Ober," she said.

"First Councillor Mune," Wald Ober said. "I was concerned. The allied ambassadors are saying all kinds of wild things to the newsfeeds. A peace treaty, a new flowering. Can you confirm? What's going on? Is there trouble there?"

"Yes," she said. "Listen to me, Ober, and—"

"Tolly Mune," Tuf said.

She whirled on him. *"What?"*

"If procreation is the mark of godhood," Tuf said, "then cats are gods, too, it would seem to follow. They, too, reproduce themselves. Permit me to point out that, in a very short time, we have arrived at a situation whereby you have more cats than I do, though you started with but a single pair."

She scowled. "What are you saying?" She punched off the sound, so Tuf's words would not transmit.

Wald Ober gestured in sudden silence.

Haviland Tuf pressed the tips of his fingers together. "I am merely pointing out that, as much as I relish the properties of the feline, I nonetheless take steps to control their breeding. I reached this decision after careful consideration, and the weighing of all the alternatives. Ultimately, as you yourself will discover, there are but two fundamental options. You must either reconcile yourself to inhibiting the fertility of your cats, entirely without their consent, I might add, or, failing that, some day most assuredly you will find yourself about to cycle a bag full of newborn kittens out your airlock into the cold vacuum of space. Make no choice, and you have chosen. Failure to decide, because you lack the right, is itself a decision, First Councillor. In abstaining, you vote."

"Tuf," she said, her voice agonized, "*don't!* I don't *want* this damned power."

Dax jumped up on the table, and turned his golden eyes upon her. "Godhood is a profession even more demanding than ecology," Tuf said, "though it might be said that I knew the job to be hazardous when I accepted its burdens."

"It's not," she started. "You can't say," she fumbled. "Kittens and babies aren't," she tried. "They're people, they, they have the power of, that is, minds, minds and hearts as well as gonads. They're rational, it's their choice—theirs, not mine. I can't possibly make it for them—the millions, the billions."

"Indeed," said Tuf. "I had forgotten about the good people of S'uthlam and their long history of rational choice. Undoubtedly they will look in the face of war, of famine, and of plague, and then in billions they will change their ways and deftly avert the shadow that threatens to engulf S'uthlam and its proud towers. How strange that I failed to see this."

They stared at each other.

Dax began to purr. Then he looked away, and began to lap up cream-of-mushroom bisque from Tuf's bowl. Blackjack rubbed up against her leg, keeping a wary eye on Dax as he stalked across the room.

Tolly Mune turned back to the console very slowly; it took her a day to make that turn—a week, a year, a lifetime. It took her forty billion lifetimes, but when she had completed that turn, it had only taken an instant, and those lives were gone as if they had never been.

She looked at the cold silent mask confronting her over the comm link, and in that dark shiny plastic she saw reflected all the faceless horror of war, and behind it burned the grim, fevered eyes of starvation and disease. She turned the sound transmission back up.

"What's going on there?" Wald Ober was demanding, over and over. "First Councillor, I can't hear you. What are your orders, do you hear me? What's going on there?"

"Commander Ober," Tolly Mune said. She forced a broad smile.

"What's wrong?"

She swallowed. "Wrong? Nothing. Nothing at all. Puling hell, everything is incredibly right. The war's over and so's the crisis, Commander."

"Are you under coercion?" Wald Ober barked.

"No," she said quickly. "Why do you say that?"

"Tears," he replied. "I see tears, First Councillor."

"Of joy, Commander. Tears of joy. Manna, Ober, that's what he calls it. Manna from heaven." She laughed lightly. "Food from the stars. Tuf's a genius. Sometimes . . ." She bit her lip, hard. "Sometimes I even think he might be . . ."

"What?"

". . . a god," she said. She touched a button: the screen went dark.

Her name was Tolly Mune, but in the histories they call her all sorts of things.